# ON THE BACKS OF DRAGONS

*AN ADVENTURE STORY*

## BY JEREMY MORONG

This book is dedicated to my two girls. To my wife Abby, for putting up with, well, everything, and to my daughter Madelyn Lu, who often wondered why I was "playing on the 'puter again." I love you both!

-Jeremy

# On The Backs Of Dragons

## Areas of Interest

# Table of Contents

# Prologue - The King Is Dying

Corrado, the King's advisor, stepped through the entryway and slowly closed the oaken door behind him. He looked back as he did, and where before he saw his old friend King Renwick lying on his deathbed, his line of sight was now interrupted and he saw only the glossy wood of the door behind him.

It was difficult to close that door, knowing that it was likely the last time he would see his King alive. But the deed was now done, so he looked to his friend and fellow advisor Marelli, who was accompanying him on this desperate attempt to save the King's life. They shared a meaningful glance - if only there were more they could do...

For eight days the King had been lying in bed nearly motionless, moving only to babble gibberish that made sense to neither of them, nor to the King's wife, Queen Vanessa. The babbling merely confirmed their suspicions that the King was reaching his end, and their efforts to save him were failing.

They had called for the best doctors around, all of whom arrived with high hopes and lofty promises, only to leave with slumped shoulders and exasperated expressions. The end was near, even though he hung on for day after wretched day.

With nothing more to do, they kept vigil, waiting for the end. It was hard to watch, and even harder to listen to, as the incoherent chatter only worsened. At times, it would seem he was reliving an experience from childhood. At others, he would talk to his mother as if she were standing there, though she had died some thirty years ago. He would soon tire of that and drift off to a restless sleep, only to wake up hours later seemingly transported to his coronation as King. Later, he was giving instructions to his army before a big battle. He even once asked to go on a dragon ride. That was particularly baffling. Like any other Ambrosian, the King was justifiably terrified of dragons. The three observers could only look at each other and shake their heads.

But that was far from everything. Tonight, when he reached his most feverish, he gibbered incessantly about Akari, one of the more notable soldiers in the King's Army. Despite his valor, Akari had little to do with court matters and thus little contact with the King. It was perplexing to all, and only then did Corrado truly realize how far he was gone. Akari! Corrado knew the name well, as he would know of any important and extraordinary soldier in the Great Army of Ambrosia, but what good could a soldier do in such a situation? It was jarring to see this powerful and noble man reduced to such gibberish.

After listening to the King repeat Akari's name without pause, the Queen suddenly fell from her chair. She had missed the meaning of the King's utterance, but all at once, it made sense.

"Of course! Akari!" she yelled out as if discovering the answer to a particularly vexing riddle. She raised such a racket that she awoke Corrado and Marelli, both of whom had fallen asleep in a pair of padded chairs. The Queen noticed her outburst had stirred them and so she continued.

"Why didn't I think of it earlier? Fool that I am, it never crossed my mind when they told me the Great Army arrived today! Corrado and Marelli, you must bring this man to me."

Corrado and Marelli were confused by this request, but went off to fulfill it. It was late, but Corrado agreed to visit the soldier, desiring to speak to the man.

The Queen's request is what took them outside of the King's door. They were awake, but their tired bodies cried for sleep and their minds were uneasy at leaving their King in such a dire state. Corrado knew it would not be long before his King took his rest. So, after a lingering look at the door, through tear-filled eyes, Corrado shifted his gaze. He stared down a narrow, stone-lined hall that led to a spiral staircase. He sighed at the thought of carrying his aching, ancient legs down that hallway and staircase to the front of the castle. But it had to be done.

The elderly courtier looked at Marelli to ensure he was ready to go. He appeared confused and lost, but that was Marelli's normal state. So

Corrado tugged at his companion's shirt to pull him forward, and together they moved down the hall.

Marelli had seen better days. Corrado was elderly, but Marelli was downright decrepit. Marelli's hearing was poor, especially in his right ear, in which he could barely hear at all. His eyesight was declining, and as he shuffled along the stone floor, he struggled to lift his feet from the ground.

The long hallway was similar to the rest of the ancient castle, dank and dreary. The only light in the space was cast by lanterns, hung intermittently on the wall. Making it down the staircase would prove challenging. It would be wiser to conserve their energy, but Marelli decided to make conversation anyway.

"What's that he said about being sorry? Wanted to make a deathbed confession, did he? Not sure why we had to get up and leave when things were going to get interesting," Marelli said, the disappointment registering in his voice. After all, he was a gossipy sort and would have enjoyed hearing the King spill his guts.

Corrado, a foot taller than his friend, leaned down and spoke into Marelli's bad ear, again forgetting which one was still good. "He didn't say anything about being sorry - he said Akari!"

"Scarring? What's he worried about his scar for? They'll fix that up just fine for the funeral if that's what bothers him, though he won't look quite the same without it." Marelli was referring to a diagonal scar that ran from just below the King's left eye down to his chin, a souvenir from the Last Dragon Battle. "I don't much care for the way they make people up when they're dead, looking like they were someone else at their funeral. Couldn't even recognize my own mother after they fixed her all up! Thought I had shown up for someone else's funeral."

Corrado again stopped and yelled in his friend's deaf ear, failing to realize his mistake. "Not scarring! He said Akari, you dog! Akari!"

"Dog barking? I didn't hear any dog barking." He gasped. "Oh, you don't say - the *King* heard a dog barking. That's bad, real bad. Too late for him now. He must be moving on from this world - let's go back in there and be with him. It's always bad when you start hearing your old pets call you to the afterlife—"

Corrado grabbed Marelli by the elbow, cutting off his steps and words with one move. This time he looked his friend directly in the face and enunciated very clearly, so that Marelli could both hear him better and read his lips.

"He said Akari! The soldier! The Queen wants us to bring Akari! She wouldn't say why. The King couldn't, seeing as he fell back asleep and there was nothing I could do to wake him. Anyway, he's been babbling that name off and on if you would bother to listen."

"Oh, Akari!" Marelli's eyes bugged slightly, disbelieving. "What does he want with him? He's just a soldier! A good one, but a soldier nonetheless. Besides, Akari is a lunatic. They all say it. Are you sure that's what he said?"

"Yes, I'm sure. Like I said he's been mumbling it for days, but I guess now that Akari has returned from a skirmish for the Dragon Festival, she wants to see why the King's jabbering about him."

Marelli paused to ponder this, wearing the confused expression that had become a trademark in his old age. His once sharp mind was now like a dull, worn knife.

Corrado grew impatient and pulled Marelli's collar to get him moving again. While purely by accident, he managed to move to Marelli's left side and in the range of his good ear. "Didn't you hear me? She ordered us to bring him back without delay."

Marelli contemplated this and whistled. "That Queen sure is smart. She always knows what everybody else should be doing."

"Oh sure, she's a smart one," Corrado said with no lack of sarcasm. "Never could figure out what the King saw in her, but what do I know? He never did much listen to me. Well, let's go get this Akari. If that's what they want, far be it for little old me to stand in their way. Especially *her* way."

Marelli again whistled through his teeth. "I suppose it didn't occur to her to send a messenger after Akari?"

"Never mind that, it's better for us to go. These are delicate matters and as few as people as possible need to know that the King is ill. Besides, she was probably sick of listening to your nonsense and when she saw an opportunity to get rid of us, she took it."

"So where do we find him? You seem to know what's going on, oh Wise One." Marelli's chest puffed up, believing he had scored a good shot against his friend.

"Certainly I do," Corrado said. "Don't you pay attention to things that go on around here? I bet someone could sneak a herd of dragons in here and you'd never see a thing. I know you wouldn't *hear* a thing, that's for sure.

"Now listen. The Great Army is here for the Dragon Festival. Well, of course he'll be with them, bivouacked with the rest of the forces. We'll be there in no time, if you could shut your mouth for just a second."

"Well, let's get a move on then, Corrado. Now what could he want with that nut Akari? He's a heck of a soldier - how many dragons do they say he killed? Was it fifteen? But what good does that do? We're looking to save the King, not kill him, you know?"

"I am aware, Marelli. It seems obvious to me what the King wants, and anyone with any sense would've seen it too, which of course rules you out." Now Corrado puffed up his chest and continued. "*I've* seen the way the Princess looks at Akari. Clearly, he wants to give his permission to allow him to marry her before he passes. Awfully noble, our King."

"His daughter? She's nearly 40 years old - and besides, she's already married!" Marelli's voice took on a high pitch and a little vein popped out from his forehead in exasperation.

"Not her, you dolt! I'm talking about his *granddaughter* - there's more than one princess around here, you know."

"I don't think that's it. He would never let anyone marry his granddaughter. It's a miracle he let anyone marry his *daughter* - remember the convincing that took? Prince Jacob had to slay a mess of barbarians to prove his worth before he was even allowed in the same room as her!"

As always with these two, a short journey was made long as they ambled at a snail's pace to the end of the hall, when Marelli spoke up again.

"I've got it. Of course! Akari must be his illegitimate child. Making a clean breast of things before he passes on - good for him."

"Oh, come on. The King doesn't have any illegitimate children!" Corrado was stunned at the levels of stupidity his friend was sinking to. Once again they stopped walking to argue over trivialities.

"Don't be naïve," Marelli said. "Course he does! They all do. Did you think the dungeons were just for criminals and prisoners? Oh, no. There are heaps of illegitimate kids down there. Twas a regular nursery back in the days of King Dublin from what I hear. Just as soon as you'd get one out of diapers, there'd be two or three more along to take its place. What a racket!"

"That's ridiculous, Marelli, even for you."

Marelli took no notice of the insult. "Well, maybe he wants to thank him for ending the dragon threat? We've all heard about the things he did during the Last Dragon War. Saved the Kingdom from what I hear, even if he is a lunatic. Akari Dragonslayer they called him after that."

"Maybe, but what about this?" Corrado's voice rose with the belief that he had puzzled it out. "Come to think, I've heard of other things he did on the battlefield beyond killing dragons. Juniper, the King's Chief Guard, told me Akari cured 15 or 20 men, right there on the field. Saved their lives, he said. Just went up to 'em, looked over 'em a little bit, uttered a few incantations, and presto, they were good as new. They were up and walking around later that same day when earlier they were lying in the grass, bleeding out all over the place, blubbering like a bunch of babies and making a big mess of things."

Marelli considered this and scratched at his gray beard. "Hmm, very odd. Don't suppose he could help the King, do you? Awfully suspicious though - cured 'em, you say?"

"I didn't say it - Juniper did! He was there. I wasn't. As I recall, I was huddled in the basement of the castle during the Last Dragon War, trying to talk you out of running away and heading for the hills."

"Yeah, and you shouldn't have done it," Marelli replied. "I would've liked it in the hills, where it's nice and quiet, away from this clamor.

"But I still don't know how this Akari done what he done during the war - how many dragons did he kill? Don't you know? Was it twenty? And now you say he was healing folks as a side line? Sounds like *magic* doings to me. And likely charged 'em a small fortune!" He shook his head. "Don't hold with magic myself. Didn't know the King to hold with it either, but I suppose he's getting desperate. Dying will do that to a man."

The two men finally came to the top of the spiral staircase. They stopped talking long enough to make their way down and through a door that led to the courtyard. The fresh air felt good, causing them to realize how long they'd been cooped up in the moldy castle.

"He should be easy enough to find," Corrado said as they passed through the castle gate. "He's young but he's one of the Generals, so look for a tent bedecked with flags and standards."

"Yes, I know that, fool," Marelli spat back, while catching his breath after their long walk. "You act like I was born yesterday."

"Trust me, nobody would make that mistake with *you*, Marelli," Corrado shot back, glaring at his friend, who simply waved him off, too out of breath to respond.

They made it to the outskirts of the camp alongside the horse stables and came upon a young soldier standing guard. Making a quick, sharp salute in acknowledgment, the two men sought directions before making their way to the rear of the campsite, where the golden tents of the Generals stood. They passed many splendid tents, including that of the Chief Knight Eston Strongheart, before arriving at their target.

The tent was made of a golden material like the others, simple in its design yet regal. There was a large flag flapping wildly in the breeze, decorated with a painting of a man standing in glory abreast a dragon lying on its back. Corrado stared at the design and nodded at Marelli. There was no doubting that this tent belonged to Akari Dragonslayer.

All of the other tents in the encampment were dark at this late hour, with their occupants fast asleep. So they were more than a little surprised to find a faint light glowing from inside the tent.

The walls were made from canvas, so they hemmed and hawed devising a way to get Akari's attention without seeming rude. After all, one could not simply knock on canvas.

Failing to find a solution, Corrado shrugged his shoulders before pulling back a flap to peek at what was going on inside. He wished to investigate a little before making his presence known. It did seem odd that Akari Dragonslayer would be awake at this late hour.

Corrado glanced in and saw what must be Akari, kneeling with his back to them. He was in front of a small bench on which a collection of colorful bottles were in a disorderly row, steam pouring from some while others appeared nearly frozen.

Akari moved from bottle to bottle, stopping to write down what he saw as he held the bottles to candlelight. He shook his head as he made his notations. It seemed clear he was doing some kind of experiment, but Corrado and Marelli knew little about such things. Corrado released the flap of the tent as he had seen all that he needed to see. He had planned on coughing and stamping his feet to alert Akari to their presence, but before he could, a voice called out from the tent.

"Do I sense the presence of the honorable Corrado and Marelli behind me?" said the voice. "Good to see my efforts to stay awake to receive you both properly were not in vain."

Corrado stared at the tent, wondering both how Akari had known they were there and what would possess him to speak in such a playful manner to two distinguished men, such as themselves. This will be interesting, Corrado thought, before replying to Akari.

"May we come in?" he asked.

"Certainly," Akari replied. "But if you've come to ask me to heal the King, I'm afraid my powers have been greatly exaggerated in that regard. I won't be able to help him."

Both men entered the tent to find Akari facing them. He was wearing a plain white shirt splattered with the stains of various chemicals and potions, a simple costume that stood in marked contrast to the royal robes worn by the courtiers. His beard was well kept and his dark eyes were piercing. He had light brown skin and his long dark hair was tied neatly behind him, presumably to keep it from interfering with his work.

"How did you know we were coming, Akari?" asked Corrado.

"Now what kind of General would I be if I allowed just anybody to sneak up to my tent and catch me unaware?" He grinned knowingly. "The King is not the only one with spies. Even in this friendly encampment I daresay there are many that would like to slash my throat.

"As to why you are here - as I said, there is nothing I can do. From what I understand the King will be dead by the morning, which will begin the requisite seven days of planning for what will surely be an expensive, over-the-top royal funeral. So I will be there to fulfill my stately duties as a General and will thus see you at such a time. It has been a pleasure, but now I must say good night, gentleman."

8

Corrado looked at his friend to make sure he had heard correctly. The look of shock on Marelli's face told Corrado that he did. Strange, this Akari.

Never before had they heard someone speak with anything but awed reverence in regards to either themselves or the King. Corrado could not help but be impressed despite himself - with brazen courage like that, it was no wonder he was able to drive the dragons from Ambrosia during the Last Dragon War and rout the Barbarians who had attacked from the Green Sea in the North just last year. But as impressed as he was, Corrado was not going back to the castle without him.

"Good night, nothing," Corrado barked. "The King has requested you and it's your duty to come along. Besides, I think you greatly understate your abilities - we know all about what you've done on many a battlefield after the fighting was over. There's no use pretending around us."

Akari stared back at Corrado as his eyes began to water, and fill with tears. Corrado flinched, not expecting such a reaction.

"Don't tell me about myself," Akari snapped. "I couldn't even save my own sister a few months ago. I sat there and watched her die as she gave birth to her son Jonas. I couldn't do a thing to save her! Tried everything I know, *everything*, and to no avail." He drew in a deep breath and regained his composure. "So, as I say, my abilities have been greatly exaggerated."

Corrado considered this. Seldom did he feel compassion, but he felt himself draw back at the depth of the man's grief, the wound clearly still raw. He decided to soften his tactics slightly.

"I am sorry for your loss. Nonetheless, your presence has been requested, and the Queen has already sent for everyone else.

"If you can't save him, at least you can try. All others have failed. Every arrogant doctor that arrived with high boasts left shaking their heads. We sent for a few wizards and they all wanted to feed him salamanders and other such nonsense, none of which worked. We even sent for an old woman who was plying her trade as a fortune teller and healer. She quickly proved to have little ability in either, so we threw her in the dungeon. You're our last resort, and there's no point in discussing it further."

Marelli stood by Corrado's side, taking it all in, when he decided to chime in. "Say, how many dragons did you kill? I heard it was fifteen - is that right?"

Corrado rolled his eyes and nudged his friend in the ribs, disgusted by his cluelessness.

Akari either didn't hear Marelli, or ignored him, as he was lost in thought. With his empathy already waning, Corrado walked over to Akari and grabbed him lightly by the elbow, a forceful gesture. "Come on, Akari."

Akari looked at Corrado and smirked as a sudden thought came to mind. "Are you really certain the King wants to be saved? As long as he's been married to the Queen, he might be ready to move on."

Marelli cackled. He liked this young warrior, very much, although he knew Corrado would not share his opinion.

"You have a good point, young man. Why, I thought the same!" Marelli laughed heartily again. "But yes, he wants to be saved. Many things are worse than dying, but I guess living with the Queen isn't one of them."

Akari finally relented, though there was never any doubt he would. He had reasons for wishing to meet with the King but was playing coy, trying not to appear too eager.

"Well, I'll come along, but it's a waste of time. I have nothing at my disposal to help him," he declared, but when the two older men looked elsewhere he discretely snatched a few potions from the bench and stuffed them into a small bag worn on his hip. He then wrapped a cloak around his shoulders and walked out of the tent with the courtiers.

They travelled the same way Corrado and Marelli had just journeyed. Their steps were the only sound in the cool night air. Corrado looked over at Akari walking alongside them and decided it would be a good time to impart some wisdom on this impetuous soldier.

"Now listen here, Akari. I'll admit I like your style - for far too long have I tempered my words and said what I thought others wanted to hear, rather than saying what they perhaps *needed* to hear - and lived to regret it later. But there are good reasons for holding one's tongue - the King is one thing, and he's a decent and honorable man. Words do not need to be dipped in honey with him. But it would serve you well to watch what you say around the Queen. She's a bit... sensitive."

"Plain nuts, you mean!" Marelli nearly shouted, though he was quickly shushed by Corrado. "The things she's whispering in the King's ear, dividing the kingdom and such..."

"Enough!" Corrado cut him off.

Akari listened to all this, noting what was not said as much as what was. He nodded slightly, not wishing to join the argument. But with Corrado in a talkative frame of mind Akari reasoned it was a good time to get the lay of the land as well as change the subject.

"Where are his children? Why haven't they been around with their father dying?"

But Corrado ignored the query as they had arrived at the castle gate. He reached out and pulled on a rope, which triggered the sharp ringing of a bell, signaling the guardhouse there were people at the gate. The three of them waited for an answer from inside while Corrado responded to Akari's question.

"The King's children are quite busy, Akari. His eldest son Wilhelm is off paying the annual tribute to the dragons as part of our treaty - a treaty that was reached in large part thanks to you, from what I understand." The old man clapped Akari's back in a gesture of respect. "And his youngest son Maldazor is up north, supervising the building of the castle and fortress to protect the island. You should know all about that, of course. Never know when those Barbarians or pirates will be back, and from now on, we will be well fortified."

Corrado impatiently rang the bell again and continued. "As far as his daughter, you should be well aware that Vanessa is tending to matters in Birdsong, supervising the construction of a new castle to protect us from the South. The ancient tales warn us of invaders that have come from the south and Renwick won't stand for that happening again."

A young guard rubbing the sleep from his eyes finally emerged from the guardhouse and raised the gate. Upon noticing Akari, he snapped to attention. Akari saluted in return, as they began their short walk through the courtyard to the castle. Soon, they were back at the old oaken door. Corrado knocked and waited for the Queen to answer.

"Now, listen Akari - the King is in awful bad shape and blabbering nonsense. But I have a suspicion you haven't been fully honest with us. It is your duty to—"

Just then the door swung open with the Queen behind it, staring wild-eyed with her hair going in fifty directions, her face taut with worry. She saw Akari and yanked him in by the wrist, with Corrado and Marelli closely following.

"Please, Akari. Save my husband. Use all of your powers! I know your secret, and I don't care." She grabbed a piece of parchment with sloppy writing all over it and held it up to the warrior. "See this? The King just signed it into law this past week. He has rescinded the law against the use of magic. There are no more secrets to keep - everything is ready - now save him!"

Akari looked at the piece of paper fleetingly and considered his options. He was not surprised she knew of his talents, as he had once saved the Queen's own brother on the battlefield. At the time he knew that could bring trouble, but he would not let a man die to protect his own secrets. It wasn't *that* man who had outlawed the use of magic in the kingdom of Ambrosia many generations ago, so why should he die for such a law? But because of the law, few knew the lore or practiced its arts - which made Akari a very valuable man right now.

For his part, the King cared little that Akari used the art of magic. If it would bring more of his soldiers back to him, or save his wife's kin, then so be it. And now it had paid off, or so his wife hoped, as magic would extend the King's life.

Akari crouched down, lowering himself to the Queen's level by the side of the bed. He looked her in the eyes as he spoke. "I'm not sure what you've heard about me, but it's not true. I don't know anything about magic, and I don't know how to save the King."

Corrado heard this and went apoplectic. He had seen enough. He was old and tired, but he was once a great warrior himself and his arms still rippled with strength, unlike his old friend and the ailing King. He quickly and stealthily pulled free a small dagger stashed amongst his clothing, holding it carefully so that it was hard to see. With Akari's back turned, it was easy to slink behind him and put the dagger across the warrior's neck. He wrapped his arm around Akari's stomach and held tight, the dagger pressing against his throat.

"That's enough, Akari. Not sure why you are playing these games, and frankly, I don't care. But you have a duty - heal him now or you're going to have to heal yourself!"

Corrado then reached into the pouch on Akari's side, removing a handful of various potions that Akari had placed there earlier. The glass bottles clinked together as he handed them to the Queen. They were all different colors - green, yellow, blue, red, and one a dark black. "Didn't think I saw, did you? You're not the only cunning one around here."

Akari felt the pressure of the dagger on his throat but remained calm. He chuckled lightly at the old man's power move, then started to laugh louder, and before they knew it, he was cackling away. All eyes were on him, staring as if he was a lunatic.

Corrado was disturbed, distracted just enough to where he took a little pressure from his hold. It was just the slip-up Akari was looking for. Without any hesitation he grabbed Corrado's forearm and pulled back the old man's arm from his throat, then swung around and knocked the dagger from Corrado's grip.

The dagger went flying toward Marelli, but before the old man could stoop over to pick it up, Akari was there to jump on it, his weight holding the blade to the floor. Akari then kicked the dagger out of reach, drew his sword, and backed up toward the wall, keeping everyone in front of him. The Queen and the two courtiers held their hands in the air, surrendering to the warrior.

"There'll be no more of that! Queen, put the potions down right there, on the bed." While long unaccustomed to taking orders, she reacted as anyone lacking the fortitude of a trained soldier would when confronted with a man holding a sword. "Thank you," Akari said, and rather politely, all things considered.

He then waved his sword in their direction and spoke loudly. "Now listen here! I'll do my best to help the King, but I want it understood that if anything should go astray, I shan't be held liable. These are delicate matters, especially when someone is as far gone as the King is. And it won't do to have people sticking a knife on my throat, or in my back, or any other place."

The three of them nodded in assent, their faces showing their shock. This man truly was a lunatic - nobody had ever dared to treat people of their stature this way before.

With a cooperative audience Akari made one last demand, pointing his sword at Marelli and Corrado in a sweeping motion. "Now, you two. Go stand in the hall and make sure I'm not interrupted." He then bowed slightly to the Queen. "And your Majesty, I'm going to need your help."

The Queen nodded, indicating her cooperation. She walked to the door, her heels clinking on the stone floor, and held it open so that Marelli and Corrado would do as they were asked. "Go on you two - if I need you, I'll call."

With the door shut, Akari took action. First, he walked up to the King and felt his forehead, nodding as if it confirmed something of great import. He then felt the King's wrist to measure his pulse before doing something especially odd - he opened his mouth and pulled out his tongue.

"There's so much you can tell about a person by giving their tongue a once over," he explained, then looked at the tongue and shuddered. "It's bad. And bad is putting it lightly."

He grabbed the potions and looked them over carefully. "Do you have some kind of cup I could use?"

The Queen nodded and went to the nightstand, finding a half full cup of water. With nowhere to empty its contents, she simply splashed it on to the floor and handed the now empty cup to the soldier.

"Good. Now let me see here." He laid the five potion bottles out in a row, popped the corks from each and tossed them aside, then poured various amounts of each into the cup.

He mumbled to himself, just loud enough so that the Queen could hear. "OK, one part red, a splash of blue, some of this black, a dash of yellow, and, let's see, half of this green."

The Queen watched transfixed. "Will this save him?" she asked in a hopeful voice.

"On its own, no," Akari replied. "But it should wake him up from this coma he has slipped into, which will qualify as a minor miracle in and of itself. He's pretty far gone. In order to bring him all the way back to the realm of the living we've got to wake him up first. But don't worry. I once saw a Sasquatch in similar condition, and I was able to bring him back."

"Bring him back? Do you mean..." The Queen stammered before Akari interrupted.

"Exactly. He's already moving on to the next world. His next adventure awaits him, *if* we don't do anything, which we will certainly not do - we will do *something*, though we don't have much time. Won't do to dawdle."

With that said, he used his finger to stir the contents of the cup. The concoction, a rather unappetizing shade of brown, bubbled in the vessel as steam wafted over the rim. Akari instructed the Queen to pinch the King's nose while prying his mouth open. The Queen grimaced but did as asked, and Akari poured the drink down his gullet in one fluid motion.

The King choked it down, coughing and sputtering as he did. He looked as bad as ever but soon his eyes began to blink and some color returned to his face as he slowly awoke. He rubbed his eyes and stretched his legs. The Queen's face lit up and she almost danced into the wall with excitement. Akari watched her, somewhat surprised by her reaction. The rumor was that she had only married him to become Queen; he vowed to take such stories at face value from then on. The Queen embraced her husband and they held on to each other gratefully.

As the King became more aware of his surroundings, Akari spoke. "Good! You're awake," he said cheerfully, then transitioned quickly to a sterner tone. "Well, Your Majesty, let's get down to business. No sense beating around the bush or wasting any time. You wish to live, and I wish to save you – if certain of my demands are met."

The Queen heard this and spoke up. "Demands? Insolence! Who are you to demand anything of the King? You are his servant, and if he says save him then you do it, and you don't ask any questions while you do it, let alone make demands!"

The King held up his hand. "Peace, my Queen. I'm willing to hear him out. In fact, I'm willing to try just about anything right now."

The Queen rolled her eyes and held her hands up as if to wash them of the situation. Akari chuckled quietly, stunned by her sudden turnaround in attitude.

"Now Akari, I daresay that I owe you more than my life after the feats you have achieved over the years. You've always exhibited extraordinary bravery, and I know all about your, shall we say, *other* exploits. I'm likely to acquiesce to your request, so long as it is reasonable - you do have me over the proverbial barrel here. So let's hear it."

Akari's face was grim. "Well, Your Majesty, my request, in my opinion, is quite small, but it's never been granted before though many have asked."

"Get to the point," the Queen screeched. The King again held out his hand, more weakly this time.

Akari continued. "It is in regards to your Chief Knight. You may or may not know this, but he's my brother-in-law."

The King interrupted. "Yes, I am aware. Lost his wife a few months back as I understand, during the birth of their second child - your sister, no?"

Akari was a bit surprised, being of the opinion that the King knew little about the men that fought for his life and kingdom.

"Yes, that is true," he confirmed. "Which brings me to my request. There's a section of Cemetery Hill just north of Ambrosia City devoted to the Chief Knights of the Ambrosian Army. Well, as you know, each and every one of those tombs is filled with men who died in their job. Not a single one allowed to walk away on their own terms."

"I am well aware," the King replied. "I've had to bury a few during my lifetime." He coughed, a harsh barking cough that caused great anxiety in the Queen.

Akari ignored the cough and continued. "Yes, it's true. Always has been and still is. Take my brother-in-law - Eston Strongheart, we call him. How many years has he loyally served? How many times has he saved Ambrosia? Yet what does he receive for his loyal service?

"Nothing. Worse than nothing. And what does he ask for? Does he ask for gold? For riches? Of course not. He asks for nothing more but to be allowed to raise his family.

"Your Highness, for the last five weeks he has submitted his resignation each day, desiring to go home and raise his family since his wife passed. And every single time it has been refused. Who could refuse such a reasonable request? So I ask, in exchange for my services - release him from his oath. That is all that I ask, Your Highness." He bowed low and awaited response.

The King lay in bed and briefly mulled this over. "Well, that's easy enough - I've never been slavishly devoted to all of our traditions, my young General, which you will soon learn if you can carry out your end of the bargain. So, I'll grant you your boon, but only if you grant me mine - I want *you* to take his place. It wouldn't do to not have a Chief Knight." He leaned back on the pillows, weakened further by the effort it took to speak.

The Queen gasped; even Akari betrayed his emotions by blinking hard. He had not foreseen this as there were many able candidates to fill such a position. In the heat of the moment, it seemed to be a good idea - if the King was in earnest.

"Are you certain of this?"

The King nodded that indeed he was. Akari tilted his head, stretching his neck as he did, before nodding in assent. "I'm agreeable, but there are plenty of other Generals who are more ready to assume—"

The King cut him off. "Nonsense. I didn't hear any stories about them killing fifteen dragons, even if you and I both know it was only *two*. No, you're the right choice. Chief Knight Akari Dragonslayer, General of the Ambrosian Army. Sounds right to me. As far as Eston, I will allow him to retire to domestic life if that is what he desires, though I expect him to fulfill his obligation to his king through his labors in the family armory."

"Then so be it," Akari replied. "I'll fulfill my end, and you take care of yours." With that, they shook hands to finalize the deal.

Through a long and difficult night, Akari mixed and matched potions, while putting the King through some difficult spells. When the morning sun rose the Kingdom of Ambrosia had their King alive and well for another three years. King Renwick thus had the time needed to make arrangements for the Kingdom's future to his satisfaction, and Eston Strongheart was free to raise his children - his daughter Caroline and son Jonas - while Akari went on to serve as Chief Knight of the Ambrosian Army.

And from that fateful night, the Kingdom of Ambrosia would never be the same again.

# Chapter One - Thirteen Years Later

I s that all you ever do, Caroline - read?" Jonas was once again pestering his older sister in that unique way little brothers seem to take so much pleasure in. Jonas was thirteen and acted it, while Caroline was sixteen and acted anything but. So she ignored the question and continued to lose herself in her book, sprawled out on the deck near the river, enjoying the day. Of course, that didn't deter Jonas, it only encouraged him to continue.

"So, what'cha reading?" He bent his knees and leaned down to look at the book's title. "*Akari the Dragonslayer.*" That again? You know our uncle's not going to rise from the dead just because you keep reading that book, right? Akari is long dead."

He then held his arms out straight and walked stiff-legged, as if his legs were sticks -- imitating the way he imagined a dead person would act upon returning from beyond the grave.

Caroline rolled her eyes. "Yes, I am aware, thank you, Jonas. Don't you have anything better to do? Why don't you go finish up your chores before Dad returns?"

"Don't have to. I made a bet with Mouse and he lost, like usual." Jonas walked onto the dock and plopped down in a sagging chair beside Caroline. He gestured with his thumb toward a wooden building with a thatched roof - their father's workplace. "He's sweeping up the foundry now."

He took a handful of small stones from his pocket and started flinging them one by one into the nearby Great River, acting as if he did not have a care in the world. Caroline found this obnoxious.

"Jonas, why don't you go help him? He's always doing your chores. It's not fair," Caroline complained.

Jonas threw another stone into the river before responding. "Well, he needs to learn how to fight better if he's going to be this *great warrior* like that old wizard Wallary told him, don't you think? Even if we were using broom handles instead of swords."

Caroline blanched at the mention of the old wizard. During her 14th birthday reading, an Ambrosian custom where one's Fate was determined, the ancient Wallary told her that she was going to be *married* to a great warrior - not a great warrior herself, but simply the wife of one. The very idea made her sick.

Caroline shuddered but forced herself to move her thoughts back to Mouse, a nickname he had earned the day that he came into their lives. His real name, Alexander, didn't fit as well; "Mouse" described her adopted brother perfectly and there was no getting around it.

She looked at Jonas and sighed in resignation. "I guess that's true, but that doesn't mean you can't go easy on him once in a while - maybe let him win a contest once or twice? Give him a little confidence? He hasn't had the easiest life, you know."

Those words caused them both to look back at Mouse, the small boy scarcely taller than the broom he was using to sweep out the foundry where their father made his living as a weapons maker. Caroline liked to think of him as her brother by circumstance, no less of a brother than Jonas was, and no less of a son to her father. She could not fathom how he would ever become a great warrior, but her place was not to question the Fate that had been chosen for him.

Or at least that was what she had been telling herself. It would not do to let it be known that the more she thought about the preposterousness of a system that told you what the rest of your life would be at age fourteen, the more it made her furious. But what could she do? There was no changing her Fate. She had been tattooed with the mark stating her lot in life, and that was that.

Jonas felt a pang of remorse as he watched Mouse hard at work. "Well, maybe you're right, Caroline." But Jonas being Jonas, his sympathy quickly passed. "If that wizard told *Mouse* he would become a great warrior, I can only imagine what they're going to tell me next week. Why, I could be

*Chief Knight*, like father!" He took another rock and threw it as hard as he could - it landed halfway across the wide river with a small "plunk."

"It's very possible, Jonas. I only hope you get a better reading than I did. But you know they don't tell anyone they will be Chief Knight on their birthday - that's up to the King when the time comes. No, they'll just say you're going to be a great warrior or something. While you're off on great adventures, I'll be waiting at home, hoping that I won't hear bad news about you, or Mouse, or my husband, helpless to do a single thing about it even though I'm as good as anyone with a sword or a bow. What a life!"

Caroline shot up from her chair and kicked at a pile of debris lying on the dock, then tried to compose herself as she watched the rubbish fall into the water with frogs diving deep to avoid her tantrum. While looking into the water, she saw her expression and almost had to laugh at her pouting face. She knew she was acting childish, and seeing herself caused her to quickly regain her composure and act the leader that she was. With that, she looked back at Jonas.

"Father should be back any minute. Why don't you help Mouse finish up real quick? As soon as you're done, come back down so we can all meet him together."

As a pleasant surprise, without a word Jonas went up the hill to join his brother. In between his frequent obnoxious spells, Caroline thought, she really liked her brother. But he sure did not make it easy at times.

Caroline shifted her gaze from Jonas to down river, where she was eagerly looking to see her father standing on his canoe as it came around the bend, using a pole to push off the bottom of the river to propel upstream. It was tough work - she had tried it herself - but somehow her father made it look easy. Though he was getting older, he remained surprisingly strong.

Seeing no sign of her father, she returned to her book. It was her seventh time reading it, yet she still found herself enthralled. Good books were often that way, always happy to be cracked open and read again, revealing something new each time.

It was a perfect, late spring afternoon for reading - the air was warm and pleasant, and the sun was shining down from a clear blue sky after seemingly being lost forever during the cold, dark winter. There wasn't even a hint of chill in the light breeze that blew over the Great River and into her face.

As she sat at the edge of a dock, with her feet dangling over the swells of the river, with her chores over and her mind fixed on *Akari the Dragonslayer* -- she couldn't ask for a better day. All was right in the world.

That sense of wellbeing almost always seemed to be the case in their pleasant little town of Frogpond, named after an endless supply of sleepy little pools of water that gave home to turtles, otters, and of course, frogs.

Caroline sipped from her iced tea and stretched her legs out. As perfect as it was, she had a hard time focusing on the printed words because of what awaited - her father had promised to bring back an especially interesting book when he returned. Caroline could not recall him having made such a promise before, so naturally she could not wait to see what was in store. She especially hoped that it was the second book about Akari, one which would cover his later adventures as Chief Knight of the Ambrosian Army. But Caroline tried to put those thoughts away and turn her attention back to the book she held in her hands, awaiting her father's gift.

After she had read a chapter or so, Jonas and Mouse arrived and sat beside her on the deck. She closed the book and greeted them. "Hi Mouse. See Jonas, that didn't take long, assuming you really are all done with your chores?"

"Yep, everything is clean," Mouse answered for the two of them. He craned his neck to peer down the river, hoping for a sign and found nothing. "Don't you think Dad should be back by now?"

Caroline noted the sun's placement. It was a little later than normal for her father's return, although not unheard of. Nothing to get worked up over.

"Oh, he's probably just running a little late today. He'll be back soon. So, everything look good up there? You know how father can be about keeping the shop clean."

"It's spotless!" Mouse replied. "Say, are you reading that book again, Caroline?" Mouse winked at Jonas, who had put him up to asking her about it.

Caroline put down the book and threw up her hands in exasperation. "Geez, yes, I am! What's the big deal? I like it! So what?" She stopped as

Jonas and Mouse both laughed, realizing they were just teasing her. Caroline sighed. "Ugh, you guys!"

"Sorry, Caroline," replied Mouse, smiling. "But it does seem like you're always reading that book. Anyway, I hope dad is back soon - hey, there he is now!"

Mouse pointed to a figure coming around the bend, standing on a canoe and making his way very slowly against the current of the river. He was using a large pole, dipping it in and out of the water to push forward.

They watched the figure intently as it drew nearer.

Excitement filled Caroline, giving her a light, giddy feeling. Yes, she was excited to see her dad as he had been gone all day, but she'd be lying if she was not even a bit more excited to see what he had brought for her.

As the figure drew nearer, her mind began to race as she realized there was something unusual about it. She rubbed her eyes as the image she expected to see did not match with the one she was seeing - there was no familiar cloud of smoke and no beard. Soon, the figure was close enough for there to be no doubt - the man using a pole to push her father's canoe was *not* her father.

Dread instantly filled her heart. Her desire for a simple book was cast aside, as a terrible feeling pulsed through her body. Her legs felt so weak she could barely stand. Worse, there was nothing to do but wait for the canoe to draw close enough to find out what was going on.

The suspense was dreadful.

"Jonas! Mouse! What's happening? Where's Dad?" she called out.

She took a deep breath and tried to stay calm. She was the oldest and her father had impressed upon her numerous times that it was her job to set an example for her younger brothers. It was not always easy to do, but now was the time to prove that she could lead the way.

As the canoe neared the dock, Caroline watched it in disbelief. An old man was slumped over as he dipped the pole in and out of the water, panting heavily and perspiring profusely. An old man, but not her father.

Caroline was distraught. It was their father's canoe, yes, but how was it that he wasn't there. What could have happened?

# Chapter Two - Out of the Blue

As their father's canoe drew within thirty feet of the dock, they recognized the old man. It was Matthias, a shopkeeper from the nearby town of Enduro. He had been a mentor to their father when he was but a young tenderfoot in the Great Army, and he was as close a family friend as they had. With the effort proving too great, Matthias could do no more; his arms gave out and the large pole fell to the side of the canoe, disappearing into the river.

Caroline feared that Matthias was dying, the strain too much for his elderly body, so she took action. Taking off what clothing was acceptable, she dived into the water and swam. Unlike both of her brothers, she was a capable swimmer and made her way to the canoe, cutting quickly through the choppy water.

Once she arrived, she found herself in a precarious position. She could not simply pull herself into the canoe without capsizing it, nor could she pull the canoe to the dock. She stretched out to grab a side of the canoe, looking for a way to bring it to shore.

While Caroline clung to the canoe, Mouse and Jonas scrambled near the dock, trying to find a way to help. With no clear ideas of how to assist, Mouse froze. Jonas, however, sprang into action. He flew into the boathouse and grabbed a rope. Gripping it in his hands, he ran toward the canoe.

"Caroline! Use this! Tie it around the canoe. We'll pull it in," Jonas yelled. He grabbed one end with his right hand while holding on to the other with his left and threw it as far as he could. It fell woefully short.

Jonas furrowed his brow as he pulled the rope back. A solution came to him as he surveyed the river bank and spied a thick stick. Reacting quickly, he tied the rope around it, hoping the added weight would allow him to make the throw. Taking care not to hit Caroline in the head, he again tossed the rope. This time, the throw was true.

Caroline untied the stick, took the rope in hand, and swam underneath the canoe. She looped the rope around the canoe and closed it off with a tight knot, then resurfaced. "It's ready!" she declared.

Jonas and Mouse grabbed the rope, hand over hand, and together pulled the canoe in with Caroline hanging on, kicking her legs behind.

As the canoe neared the dock, the old man seemed to be regaining his faculties. Mouse put his foot on the edge of the canoe to steady it, and Jonas held Matthias by the wrist and pulled him to safety. As soon as Matthias' feet hit the boards, Mouse led him to Caroline's chair, allowing him to take a seat and gather himself.

"I'm sorry about that, children - I came as fast as I could and I guess it was just too much for me," Matthias said, a note of depression evident in his voice. After all, it had not been long ago when he could race up and down the river with ease, yet here he was, exhausted after a short trip.

Matthias held his forehead in his hands, a distressed look on his wrinkled, weathered face. He wasn't sure where to begin his story. Sweat dripped from his brow, drenching his shirt.

Caroline emerged from the river, water from her soaked clothing splattering on the deck. When she saw that Matthias was feeling better, she began asking him questions.

"Matthias, where is my father? And why are you in his canoe? Is everything all right?"

Tears formed in his eyes as he struggled to reply. His lower lip quivered. He looked down at the dock. After what seemed an interminable wait, he spoke.

"Well, last time I saw him he was alive, Caroline. Alive, but in a bad way. Oh, I am so sorry to tell you this. He was kidnapped!"

"Kidnapped? Matthias, what are you talking about? How could he be kidnapped?" Caroline asked.

Matthias frowned. He struggled to keep his composure. "I saw it with my own eyes. As you know, he came to town for supplies, same as he always does, nothing out of the ordinary. We talked for a while and caught up on news until it was time for him to leave.

"As usual, I helped load up the canoe when all of the sudden this large raft heading upstream pulled up to the dock. They were big, surly looking fellows, five of them, but you know, I don't judge people by the way they look. So long as they want to spend money, they're all right by me.

"So I welcomed them and introduced myself. And would you believe, the biggest one of the bunch -- an ugly fellow with a beard hanging past his chest -- strode over and threw me to the ground without a word?! I never even had a chance to brace myself!

"Well, I tried to get up, but darned if I could. It's no fun getting old, youngsters, don't let it happen to you, if you can." He coughed a few times, then continued.

"So there I am, lying on the ground and feeling just as worthless as you can. I tried to holler for your father, as he was back in the store loading a few items. But before I could get the words out, your father came flying at them with an oar. It's about all he had - when was the last time we had need to carry a sword? He knocked one of them upside the head and sent him clean off the raft into the river. That was a poor job for him, because he floated away, to where I don't know.

"Once your father walloped that guy, he went after another and caught him pretty good across his backside. Sent him flying into the river, too. That was good, but it wasn't enough, being as it was still three against one and he no longer had surprise on his side. Those dastards roughed him up a little bit and knocked Eston out - bopped him on the head with something, they did. Next thing I knew, one of them tied his arms and another bound his legs, and they threw him on the raft like it was nothing. I've never seen Eston Strongheart treated like that, I can tell you. Then the louts went into my store and helped themselves to half the place as far as I could tell."

He stopped to wipe the sweat from his brow and took a deep breath. "I can't tell you how thankful I am that my wife wasn't around, because I don't know what they would've done to her." He shuddered, finally overcome by emotion.

Caroline ran her fingers through her hair, stress radiating from her face. Her brothers were beside themselves, pacing back and forth on the dock, unsure of what to do.

"Why would they do this? Who are these people?" Jonas asked.

"Sounds like the Barbarians that come from the Green Sea, from the way Matthias describes them," Caroline stated.

"Most likely, although I don't know how they made it this far. But I saw them sneak up the Corkscrew River, where it drains into the Great River – up *that* river if you can believe it. But those brutes can do it, strong as they are.

"Before they fled, I heard them say something about going through the caves. If I had to guess, the Burmian Caves. Those are the only ones I know hereabouts, but they're crazy if they're going through there! I wouldn't expect even big brutes like that to make it through those caverns with their lives." He shook his head without bothering to elaborate.

Mouse took this all in and thought back to a series of unusual events that had taken place over the last couple of weeks. They had bothered him at the time, but after talking with his father, he promised not to say anything. In light of the circumstances, he decided to speak up, thinking that those events might shed light on why their father was taken hostage, as it seemed there was a good chance the events were related.

"Well," he cleared his throat, the word sticking. Mouse took a deep breath, swallowed, and began again. "Dad asked me not to tell you about this, as you were away each time it happened. But we had a few visits lately from some man. Said his name was Cyril. Kind of a strange fellow, wore a cloak pulled down low over his face so I couldn't see much of him. Only thing I could really make out was a hint of a beard on his chin. He smelled kind of funny, too. He would just show up out of nowhere, arriving on foot - no horse, no boat, nothing. He didn't say much, just asked if Eston Strongheart was around and waited quietly for me to get him.

"He met with dad a few times, but the only thing Dad told me was that the man had made him a job offer, that he wasn't interested, and the man seemed to have a hard time taking no for an answer. I could tell Dad was annoyed by this Cyril, but he hid it pretty well.

"That is, until last week, which was the last time I saw him. The man was very forceful this time, and Dad no longer hid his displeasure. He threw him out and told him to never return. The man didn't seem too put out, just kind of shrugged his shoulders and walked away. Dad wouldn't tell me who he was or who he wanted him to work for, just said not to mention it so you wouldn't worry. I'm sorry. I probably should've told you." The worried expression on Mouse's face told the rest of the tale.

Caroline stopped him. "No, you did right, if that's what Dad wanted. But I don't get it - why would someone want dad for a job?"

"Strange, very strange," replied Matthias, rubbing his chin thoughtfully. "Cyril, huh? Doesn't sound familiar. But your Dad is the best at what he does. You don't know how well regarded his swords are - perfect balance, sharp as can be, and light. You won't find another sword even close. His chain mail, same thing, light but sturdy, hardly know it's on when you wear it, and that's saying something as I've been tempted to go into battle without wearing any at times rather than weigh myself down. And his arrows always sail true! I wouldn't trust my life with any others if I had to make a shot *just so*, with no room for error, and I've had to make a few, believe me.

"I know many years ago that Maldazor wanted to have Eston make some weapons for him, and he might have done it, I don't recall. I guess his reputation has really spread if strange men are offering him jobs. It should - he's the best there is."

The three of them stood speechless while Matthias shivered under a blanket. Surprisingly, the shy Mouse was the one to break the silence.

"We've got to do something. If I'm going to be this 'great warrior' then now is the time to prove it. I'll go after him, and I'll save him. I promise."

He gripped his sword tightly and turned grim. It was off-putting seeing the small boy with such a fierce expression on his face, but even Jonas had to admit that maybe there was more to his brother than he had figured.

"Well, Mouse let's talk things over," Caroline said. "Seems to me that we are under attack and someone needs to warn the King. But we don't want to get the country in an uproar either, seeing as we don't *exactly* know what's going on. How about this? I will go after Father. I know I'm going to be some housewife, but I'm not married yet."

She clenched her teeth, grimacing at the thought. "There's plenty of time for me to sit at home and pop out babies, but not now." Jonas started to speak, but she held up her hand, stopping him. "I can handle myself, Jonas, and you know it. I'll go after these kidnappers, follow them to the caves, and save Dad."

Jonas threw his arms up in the air. "No, Caroline. I'll go after him," he said, only to be talked over by Mouse.

"I'll do it," Mouse yelled. "They'll never hear me. I can sneak right behind them—"

Hearing this, Matthias tossed the blanket aside and slowly stood up, holding his aching back. "Now, kids, you are in over your head. If they make it to the Burmian Caves then it's too late, and they've got a head start. Nobody goes in those caves and comes out alive, unless the In-Betweeners let you."

"The In-Betweeners? They live in the caves? I thought those were the people stuck between this world and the next world after dying?" Jonas asked.

"No, you're thinking of the Nether-worlders, those poor, miserable souls," Matthias responded. "The In-Betweeners are something altogether different though you are not the only one to confuse the two, at least among the few that have even heard of In-Betweeners. *Tweeners*, I call them. A foul breed.

"The story I heard was that they once lived near the earth's core but were driven closer to the surface by an even fouler breed. But being closer to the surface hasn't taken to the Tweeners, and they're as miserable and as cruel as can be."

"You don't suppose the Barbarians have formed an alliance with these Tweeners, do you? Or conquered them?" said Jonas.

"That I don't know, but either way I wouldn't go through those caves. You're either dealing with Tweeners, or dealing with Barbarians that *conquered* the Tweeners, or a united force of Barbarians and Tweeners. Whew, that's tough. So no matter what, you're heading to doom.

"I know you love your father, but he wouldn't want you to go, of this I am certain. And if they wanted to kill him, they would've done so - no, they need him alive for something. Leave it to him and he'll surely escape."

"I can't take that chance," Caroline replied grimly. "I appreciate your wisdom Matthias, but I am going to bring my father back. If they make it past those caves, I don't believe we'll ever see Dad again. I can cut them off by taking the pass through the Kin Kara Mountains. There's no telling where they're taking him, and I will not let it happen.

"Jonas and Mouse, gather up your weapons and pack necessities — food, water, blankets - you know what to bring. Then take the canoe to Ambrosia City, the city on the hill, and warn the King. Tell them who you are and more importantly who our dad is, and I'm certain you will be granted an audience. I will go after Dad - ALONE - and I will save him. We're already short on time - let's go!"

Before they could do anything further, Matthias put his hand on Caroline's shoulder and held her in place. He was shaky, but still strong.

"Caroline, stop right there. You're going on a suicide mission, and I cannot and will not let that happen. Knock off this foolishness! Your father is one of the toughest men I've ever seen. Those Barbarians might have gotten the jump on him at the dock, but he'll find a way to escape, I promise you. Going after him, especially alone, can only end badly."

Matthias spoke with a stern tone they had never heard from him before and it surprised them. They stared at the ground sheepishly, not sure of what to do next, feeling almost embarrassed by their big talk.

But Caroline steeled herself. She would not be easily dissuaded. She raised her gaze from the ground and looked Matthias in the eyes.

"Matthias, I'll follow behind and those Barbarians will never suspect a thing. They won't even know I'm there! You know it's a lot easier for one person to sneak around than it would be for more.

"It's three or four days to the caves. I can catch up, keep my eyes open, and when father makes his move, I'll be there to help. It's not suicide. And I can cut them off before they reach the caves. If I can't, I promise I will not enter the caves."

The displeasure on the face of their old family friend told her Matthias was far from convinced, so she continued.

"Matthias, what happens if Father makes an escape attempt and the Barbarians try to cut him down? I have to be there, in case he needs me."

"Blame it Caroline, that's enough! Your father should have put an end to this years ago, instead of training and encouraging you."

He paused momentarily to make sure of what he wanted to say. Before he even spoke, the pain was etched in his face, knowing it would hurt Caroline. But he felt there was no avoiding it.

"There's no other way to say this. Caroline, you're a *girl*. I'm sorry to say it like that, but this is not your place. If you insist on someone following your father, send one of your brothers. Send Jonas. He's young, sure, but a warrior's blood runs through his veins—"

"And warrior blood does not run through mine? I am the daughter of Eston Strongheart, niece of Akari the Dragonslayer. I am going and I will—"

"ENOUGH!" Matthias' shouted. His voice rose to a level they never thought they would hear. He pounded his fist against his other hand for emphasis. "Caroline, I love you, almost as much as if you were one of my own - but this must end. You can go off with Mouse to alert the King. That's important, too."

Tears of anger formed in Caroline's eyes - not from sadness, but from pure anger. She hated that she would tear up when she was mad, because to anyone who did not know her they would say she was *just a typical girl, unable to control her emotions*, and that just made her even angrier, which caused the tears to flow even more. It was awful. But she wiped them away and narrowed her eyes, for she would not be deterred.

Jonas had been strangely silent as conflicting emotions ran through him. He wanted to save his father as much as Caroline did, and thought he could do it, too. But the odds were better with Caroline - she was older, smarter, and a better fighter. Caroline was right. She gave them the best chance to succeed, and he would go with Mouse to see the King.

He couldn't quite explain it, but there was something special in his sister, and there always had been - his father used to say she had *sand*, and while that never quite made sense to Jonas, it seemed to fit. His sister did have sand. She would save their father, and Jonas had to speak up and say as much. So he strode forward, stepping between his sister and Matthias.

"Matthias, Caroline is right. You can say she is just a girl if you want, but I've never seen anyone like her - girl or boy. So you can either send your blessing, or stand aside. This is our father, and this is our quest. I appreciate what you're trying to say, but you're wrong."

Jonas held his head high in the air, his nostrils flaring. Mouse walked over and moved to his brother's side in a gesture of solidarity.

Caroline never expected this. Clearly, Jonas was between obnoxious spells as now she *really* liked this brother of hers. Not knowing what else to do, Caroline gave Jonas a big hug and did the same to Mouse, who seemed equally as stunned and inspired by Jonas' behavior.

Matthias threw his arms up and sat down in the chair. "Fine," he said. "I wipe my hands of the matter."

With that, Caroline ran up the hill to their home with her brothers close behind. They gathered weapons and supplies. In a matter of minutes, everything they might need was packed and ready. With nothing else to do, they stopped in their tracks, and without saying a word, each seemed to recognize that this could be the last time they saw one another.

Caroline removed her sword from its sheath and raised it. She had the odd sensation that a strange surge of power transmitted itself through the sword into her arm, which filled her body with a pulsing energy, almost as if it had a life of its own. Her brothers did the same with their swords, all crafted by the man they hoped to save.

With swords held high, Caroline lifted her head proudly. "This is what father has trained us to do, and now is the time we put that training to good use. We each have our part to play. Jonas, Alexander," she winked. "Jonas and *Mouse*, I love you both. To our father!" The three swords clanged as they touched each other.

They hugged quickly. Then, without hesitation, Caroline fled up the hill that ran behind her house and toward the pass that led through the Kin Kara Mountains. Her brothers ran the opposite way, to the dock, where Matthias still sat in front of the Great River. They prepared to deliver grave tidings to the King of Ambrosia.

That message was simple. War was at hand. The Barbarians were here, and King Wilhelm must be warned. It would be a grave quest for all – a duty that sprang up, out of the blue on an ordinary spring morning – and that would forever change their lives.

## Chapter Three - Their Adventure Begins

Eight years ago, at the age of five, Mouse was adopted into Eston's family. From the start, he was treated the same as his other children, because Eston thought of him as such. It was as simple as that; Eston would have it no other way.

It all began with what Eston thought was a rodent issue. He had taken every step imaginable to stop mice from getting in and eating their food, yet he would still awaken to find holes ripped in grain sacks and apples missing from barrels. Each time he would shake his head and curse his little gray cat, Hank, for not doing his job. What was the use of a cat if the thing couldn't prevent mice from eating him out of house and home?

But after five futile days, Eston rose early one morning determined to catch the culprit. He crept to the shed where their food was stored, then came to the door and stopped, listening to what sounded like quiet breathing from inside. He waited a few moments before pulling open the door, and stood back to peer in.

Expecting a rodent, he instead found a small boy. He was curled up on the floor fast asleep, with his arm wrapped around Hank. The youngster was covered in crumbs and apple cores were scattered at his feet. He looked peaceful. His chest rose and fell as he slumbered in a deep, comfortable sleep.

Eston stared at the child and took pity.

The boy's face was dirty, his nose crusted, and clothes ragged. There was not one spare ounce of meat on his bones. The little guy clearly lacked proper care. Eston quickly determined that the boy came from a family known as the Ranks, from up the river just outside of Frogpond. He seethed with anger. That family!

The Ranks were not well regarded by the villagers in town, and for good reason. The father was a lazy sort, rarely working, and when he did, he would knock off halfway through the job. He seemed to subsist by selling a small catch of fish every now and then. The bulk of those meager funds were squandered. A small portion was spent on food and the rest went for whiskey. As for the mother, she would drag herself into town to beg from the villagers, bringing underfed and malnourished children in tow to play upon their hearts.

The villagers tried repeatedly to have the children removed for their safety and well-being, but the town judge was a naive sort. He was hesitant to take the children from their natural family, saying he wanted to do all he could to keep fathers and mothers with their kids. Despite the best efforts of the townspeople, the judge could not be brought to see it any other way, leaving the villagers no real options.

Eston was contemplating what to do when he heard the pitter-patter of his daughter's feet behind him. Seeing that her father was interested in something, eight-year old Caroline was naturally curious and peeked around her father's tree-trunk legs, where she saw the boy lying asleep. She watched him for a moment before tugging on her father's robe.

"Can we keep him?" she asked, her voice pleading.

Eston scratched his head and bunched his lips. "Well, Caroline, he's not like a stray cat - I reckon the boy has a family already, and we will have to get him home. I imagine they have been searching everywhere for him."

"Oh, Father, he's from that nasty Rank family. You *know* he is," Caroline said. Her face was fierce, her lip curled in disgust. Eston could not help but smirk as Caroline continued. "We have to do something! They don't care if he comes home or not, and you know it!"

"Well, I suppose you're right," Eston said, laughing at Caroline's expression. "All right, I know you are. Curse those Ranks! I'll see what I can do. There is a new judge after all these years. Maybe this one will be sensible."

With that, Eston entered the shed and walked over to the boy, gently shaking him. Hank woke up quickly and went scrambling, a cross look on his face. He turned toward Eston and hissed.

"Oh, go on with you, creep," Eston said in a light-hearted away. Caroline knew that her father loved Hank, even though he pretended not to. The boy finally awoke and his eyes grew large as he stared at Eston, who towered over him. He was frozen with fear, but Eston held out his hand in a pleasant manner and smiled.

"You're pretty small for a boy, but awfully big for a mouse. Come on, up with you."

He pulled him up, then grabbed the loop of his pants as the boy tried to run off. The boy kept spinning his legs but went nowhere as Eston hung on tightly with an iron grip.

"I don't take kindly to people stealing food, but I reckon you don't know much better." Eston tousled the boy's hair. "Don't worry about it, son. If I get a chance, we'll bring you out of the wild. I don't suppose you're a lost cause *just* yet - we've still got time."

Soon enough, with the help of the new judge, Eston was able to bring the young boy into the family. They took to calling him *Mouse* and soon his given name, Alexander, was all but forgotten. After all, as Eston said, it seemed "an awfully big name for an awfully small boy." Mouse did not mind, and even had to be reminded from time to time that Alexander was indeed his real name.

From the start, Caroline had made him part of the family, and at times she seemed to be more of a mother than a sister. She was always there when he needed her, encouraging, supporting, and teaching him.

Today, Mouse had stood there and watched her walk away for possibly the last time, in search of the man who had given him the gift of such a family. Mouse watched as her outline approached the crescent of the hill. Soon, she would soon rise over and disappear from sight. He waved as she took one last look behind her before going over the crest.

The thought of losing both father and sister was beyond his comprehension. He sniffed back tears, trying to stay strong when he felt so weak and helpless. Mouse thought to himself that if he was to be a great warrior, it would not do to be seen in such a way. But he gave in and the tears flowed. After all, why should he be ashamed to have such feelings? Two of the people he loved most in the world might never return -- it would be wrong *not* to cry.

After composing himself, he wiped the tears away on his sleeve. He looked over to Jonas, who was freely allowing the tears to roll down his face. Mouse was stunned, unable to recollect ever seeing his brother cry. It was a strange sight. The only thing that Mouse could think to do was to pat him on the back while they looked at the empty space where Caroline had disappeared moments before. They looked on momentarily, but realized there was nothing more to do, except focus on their mission.

It was crucial that they warn King Wilhelm of the attack made on his kingdom. They were the only ones who could bring the message, so they walked to the dock where Matthias sat waiting to finalize their plans.

Matthias wore an uneven expression as he awaited their return. He did not approve one bit of what was happening, but he had said his piece and decided to leave it at that. Matthias was a good man, but a man that had the tendency to predict the worst and then take a perverse satisfaction when things unrolled the way he foretold.

So with nothing more to say, he decided it was a good time for a smoke. He pulled out his pipe, stuffed and lit it while Mouse and Jonas both quickly stepped back, recoiling from the smoke. They hated it when their dad smoked, so he made a point to do it away from them, but Matthias did not take such considerations and freely let the smoke fly.

With a cloud forming around his head, Matthias decided to impart some wisdom. "Well, boys, your sister's gone and that's that. I hope you made your good-byes meaningful, as I don't like the odds of you ever saying 'hello' to her again, as much as I hate to say it. But I said my piece, you didn't listen, and that's fine.

"So what are your plans? You really figuring on heading to Ambrosia City?"

"Yes, sir, and it won't do to waste any time," Jonas said. "But we can't just abandon our home while we're gone, especially the horses. Father will be back, and so will Caroline. I'd hate to see the place a shambles when they arrive."

"Don't worry about it boys, I'll find someone. I'd do it myself, but don't know that my wife would be too crazy about me not being around, and I do have the store to run. But I'll find someone, course I will."

He sighed. "What a mess I have to clean up at home! Curse those Barbarians!" Matthias chewed on the end of his pipe, caught in the middle of a thought. It occurred to him that complaining about some groceries strewn about seemed pretty minor compared to what happened to his friend Eston and he decided to soften his tact a bit.

"Well, how about this, fellows? You boys pack up for your journey, and if you'd help me get home, I'd appreciate it. Still have that old raft in the boathouse, do you?"

"Yes, we do. We'll go get it," Mouse said. They went off to the boathouse where they began moving tools and supplies to pack for their trek.

The boys quickly gathered necessities for their journey and pulled the old raft out, dusting it off with their hands to make it somewhat presentable. Each brother grabbed one of the ropes tied to the raft and moved it down to the river. They were ready to leave – all that was left was to say good-bye.

This was the only home Jonas had ever known as they had moved here shortly after his birth. Memories flooded through his mind. This was where he learned how to sword fight with his father and Caroline; where he trained to become a blacksmith to run the forge, and where he often sat around the fire talking and laughing. Simple times, but happy. Things had seemed so much easier just this very morning; now here they were, stuck in the middle of a burgeoning war.

Jonas took one last glance and pushed on. It was hard to turn away from the place, knowing that things would likely never be the same, and for reasons he could not understand. Why would Barbarians kidnap an old man? What use could he be to them? In fact, why would they kidnap anyone? They were known for taking no prisoners, hacking and slashing their way through the world, leaving bodies in their wake.

Jonas kicked at the dock, looking for someone to blame. How did those Barbarians get through the northern defenses anyway? Since the division of the Kingdom many years ago between Renwick's three heirs, Maldazor had ruled Azoria fiercely, repelling all invading armies and keeping the island safe. Maldazor had fortified the north to such a degree that the last attack by Barbarians actually came from the southern end of the island, known as Birdsong and ruled by Queen Vanessa. There, a bitter struggle was fought and their uncle Akari had been killed. But that was seven or eight years ago, and they had not been seen since.

Jonas shook his head to clear these thoughts. With Mouse on the other side, they pulled on ropes to drag it to the Great River. It was an easy journey of an hour or so to the village to drop off Mathias, and from there they would leave the raft and use the canoe, which would be swifter and easier to handle.

The journey from there on would be arduous. The Great River ran all the way to Ambrosia City, where it spilled over the edge of the Parrish Cliffs, ending in a spectacular waterfall that fell into the Dragon Sea. From what Jonas knew of the river it would take about three days to navigate its waters to the castle, where they would find Wilhelm, the obese and somewhat clueless, but well-meaning King of Ambrosia.

One point in their favor was that the Ambrosian River would be fairly calm and the trip leisurely until they reached Enduro. At that point, the canal would narrow, the river would gain speed, and the rapids would grow ever more dangerous. It would prove difficult to make it to Ambrosia City but Jonas cared little, as it was his fondest wish to someday become a great warrior, and in order to do so, these sorts of risks would have to become routine.

They stowed the canoe on board with the rest of their gear and climbed on, with Matthias holding his sore back and shuffling his feet. As soon as Matthias pronounced himself ready, Mouse untied the ropes that held the raft to the dock and set them free. The river was flowing fast, but the brothers helped things along by paddling in turn. Matthias hunched down in the middle to get as far away from the sides as possible, leery of falling in.

They quickly entered the current of the river, and made good time to Enduro - they had not known the river to flow this fast before and it was their first lucky break of the day. It felt strange not to have their father on board, even though he usually sat back and let his children take control. Still, they always knew that if things went awry he was there to protect them, and now that feeling of well-being was gone. Their father was kidnapped and heading toward the Burmian Caves.

After a half-hour or so on the river, Jonas decided that it was a good time to find out more from Matthias.

"Matthias, are you sure that those were Barbarians? Seems hard to believe they would've made it through the northern defenses," Jonas said.

"I think I would know a Barbarian when I saw one, young Jonas," Matthias replied. "Though I agree that it is hard to believe – I was in denial myself. But now I am certain. I may be old, but even I could fend for myself with your average person, at least for a little while. These brutes were something else - Barbarians. Certainly were! Shoved me down hard, they did, just raw brute strength."

"But why would they take our father, Matthias? When have Barbarians ever done anything but kill?" Mouse asked.

"You've got me. It's all a riddle, and my hunch is there are deeper forces at work. Could be a smarter breed of Barbarians than we're used to, holding him for a ransom or something. The King might pay a princely sum to get back his primary weapons maker."

Matthias puffed from his pipe and continued. "Like I said, if you want a sword, you go to Eston. I've had swords that I wouldn't use to cut through a loaf of bread, but I've never had a problem with one if his blades. Saved my life a few times, they have. Run through a few Barbarians as well, which I hope our friends aren't aware of. You boys consider yourselves lucky for being able to carry a couple of his finest on your mission, though I daresay you won't use them for much more than cleaning fish!"

"It doesn't add up," Jonas replied as he paddled, his brow furrowing as thoughts raced through him.

The frustration built as questions with no ready answers piled up. All he could do to take out his anger was paddle harder, leaving poor Mouse struggling to keep up. But during this fury, an idea came to Jonas.

"Say Mouse, do you think this Cyril fellow that met with Dad could've been a Barbarian?"

Mouse dipped his oar into the water and considered the question. "I don't know. Didn't seem big enough from the descriptions I've heard of that type, but he was kind of a swarthy looking guy. And real mysterious-like. Gave me a creepy feeling right from the start."

"I see," Jonas replied, shaking his head, the mystery no closer to being solved.

He looked up and saw they were nearing Enduro. The river was running very swift indeed, as none of them could recall making the trip this quick before. "Matthias, is there anything you can tell us about Ambrosia City?" Mouse asked.

"Well, as soon as you arrive, announce your presence and demand audience with the King. It won't sit well with him that a former Chief

Knight has been taken from his kingdom let alone his weapons maker, and he's certain to send an army out after him."

His face lit up as an idea came to mind. "While you're there, ask for a man named Amaru. Good man. I've run into him a few times down there on visits. Seemed to know who your father was as he always asked about you kids, although your father said his name didn't ring a bell. Anyway, he's one of the King's guards, and he'll look out for you."

The boys led the raft to the same dock where their father had been beaten and captured earlier in the day. Both of them felt sick being there, wishing they had been there to help.

"Whew, I am beat," Matthias gasped. "What a day! Boys, I thank you for the ride, and I wish you good luck on your journey. I'll make sure everything is OK back at home, and I'll get this raft back as well."

"And boys, please be careful. The rapids are going to be very swift this time of year, with the spring thaw and all. It will be worse downstream. Besides that, there's no telling what's going on with these Barbarians. I wish I wasn't so darn old, or I'd be right there with you. What'd I say earlier? Oh yeah. *Don't let getting old happen to you, if you can.* Now, don't forget to stop here on your way back and let me know how things went."

With that, he slowly hobbled off the raft and walked off to his store, waving as his sagging shoulders rounded the corner and disappeared from sight. The boys were growing tired of seeing the backsides of people they cared for as they walked away.

"Well, we're on our own now, Mouse." Jonas slapped Mouse on the back. "But I'm in the company of a future strong warrior, so we should be just fine!"

Mouse could not tell if Jonas was joking, so his response was to ignore the remark and silently clench his fist as they sat down in the canoe and pushed it back into the current. He did not know how, but he would show Jonas that he could live up to the Fate chosen for him.

The current caught them quickly and flung them into the main stream of the river. They would soon enter dangerous rapids, and already the current was increasing in ferocity, with the roar of the river growing ever louder as they entered the canyon ahead.

And so their adventure began.

# Chapter Four - Far From Home

On day two it had become all too clear that going on an adventure was nothing at all like *reading* about going on an adventure.

Caroline had felt differently on day one, although she knew the situation was quite dire. Her journey had begun with a lightness in her step as she tread easily along the grassy pathway that led to the mountain pass. The sky had been a brilliant shade of blue, the sun warmed her back, and most of all she felt lifted by the faith and confidence her brothers had placed in her. But that euphoria soon faded as the cold reality of her situation set in. And things were certain to get tougher - if she was already struggling to stay positive, how would she react when she came face-to-face with the Barbarians that had kidnapped her father?

From the books Caroline had read, it seemed that adventures were typically filled with one excitement-filled trial after another, battling monsters and evil creatures one second, running from wolves and bears the next, then paddling canoes over waterfalls, falling headfirst into the swirling waters below with nary a chance of survival, and yet through Fate or just plain old-fashioned luck, always making it through with little more than a scratch or bruise to show for it. The heroes barely had time to breathe along the way, let alone stop to pick the mud and rocks out of their shoes, and yet, that was exactly what she was doing right now, pausing momentarily after two days spent navigating the rocky terrain of the Kin Kara Mountains, feeling a strange mix of utter boredom and nervous energy. It had all sounded fun, but now it seemed all too clear that the kind of task she had embarked on would not prove pleasurable.

Despairing, she wished that her brothers were at her side, or a great warrior like Akari, or anyone for that matter. Going it alone made a certain amount of sense, but now that she was by herself, tired and sore, it did not seem so appealing.

As her feet ached more with every step, she thought of her horses back home. Caroline had hated to leave behind Riley, Copper, and Cocoa, the three horses she had groomed and rode for as long as she could remember. But she knew they would not be able to navigate the rocky pass. Still, she missed them, and worse, she barely had a chance to say good-bye. There were few things in life that brought her as much pleasure as going for a ride on horseback, galloping through the countryside that surrounds the family home. During those jaunts she often pictured herself as a knight heading off to do battle.

It was impractical to bring them along, but it felt wrong to leave them behind. She hoped that Jonas and Mouse had enough sense to get someone to take care of them. In her haste to depart, it hadn't crossed her mind to remind them to be sure someone took care of the horses. Still, they wouldn't forget that, would they? They are smarter than most boys she knows, but still...

With her mind wandering, she lost track of what she was doing and stumbled on a tree root -- and that snapped her back to reality. The task at hand was daunting. Her hope was to cut the Barbarians off. Failing that, she would follow the winding path of the Corkscrew River upstream until it became shallow and was no longer navigable by raft. The Barbarians would then abandon their raft to travel by foot or other means, giving her a chance to catch up.

The plan seemed preposterous, now - what if Matthias hadn't even heard them correctly? But then again, what other option did she have? Certainly Matthias could be trusted enough to correctly determine that the Barbarians went up the Corkscrew River after capturing her father.

But the river was still far away. All things considered, the journey had begun well, with Caroline sticking to well-worn trails familiar to her from family trips. She made good time before the sun started to go down, and then she began dreading the night fall. She was not looking forward to camping out in the middle of the mountains again, all alone, nobody else within miles.

But the sun moved from sight. It disappeared behind the mountains, leaving behind nothing but a cold, black sky in its place. Even the moon and the stars were hidden behind clouds, rendering it nearly impossible to see. Caroline had no choice but to pitch her tent and call it a night.

She threw off the straps of her pack, poured out the canvas tent and rolled it onto the ground. She fumbled with the strings, struggling to set it up in the dark, but soon the tent was up. She thought of the misery of last night spent in the cold mountain air, shivering and afraid, clutching her sword and raising it in fear any time the wind flapped the tent around. It was the first night she had ever spent on her own, and every sound stirred her imagination, as she conjured wild animals trying to get at her, a spirit from the beyond, or even worse, Barbarians.

Caroline would quickly realize there was nothing to worry about; it was only the wind whipping the canvas or the rustling of an overhead pine branch, so she would chide herself for being scared. Still, the next unusual sound would prompt alarming thoughts, and, again she would admonish herself for being childish. She knew she had it easy compared to her father, who was in the clutches of Barbarians.

But that was *last* night. Those fears had been abandoned once the sun rose and lit up the world around her. She had laughed at herself - it all seemed so silly in the daylight. She felt confident that tonight would surely go better than last night. Right?

She crawled in, laid out a bedroll, and closed her eyes. But her mind would not stop racing. Soon, she began fearing every unusual noise.

But as scared as Caroline felt, she could only fight sleep for so long, and just like the night before, she eventually drifted off to a tossing-and-turning sleep – but her fingers remained wrapped around the hilt of her sword.

She awoke the next morning, cold and stiff, but seeing the sun rejuvenated her spirits and warmed her. She packed her things and resumed her journey up the mountain pass. No matter what else happened, today would be an improvement. She would soon reach the crest of the pass and interior of the Kin Kara mountain range, which was horseshoe-shaped and circled a great valley below. She also would soon be traveling downhill. The young adventurer felt a small amount of pride as she had never traveled this far with her family. In fact, Caroline had never been this far from home.

After a bit, Caroline stopped for a simple breakfast of cold jerky and apples. It was her sixth straight meal of the same, and she was rather tired of it. But it was all she had and she supposed it beat starving.

She finished her lonely meal and found she greatly desired a hot bath. Of course, knowing she could not have one meant she wanted it all the more. Caroline seldom gave much thought to her appearance, but, she had never been this filthy before. In fact, she used to laugh at her classmates who obsessed over every tiny detail, down to the last eyelash. Caroline never quite fit in, stronger and taller than even most of the boys, and happier swinging a sword than preening in front of a mirror. Being naught but the wife of a great warrior would be perfectly fine for most of her classmates, but not Caroline.

At this point, she was past the stage of obsessing over appearance. But her hair felt greasy after camping in the woods and long days spent walking. It was awful, yet she did not feel quite dirty enough to plunge into a cold mountain spring. So, she used a cloth to take what she called a "standing bath," dipping the cloth in the spring to wash up. It was better than nothing.

Throughout the day she made steady progress on the pathway, which was surprisingly well-worn, considering that few travelers that came this way. Soon, she would be near the top, but it was becoming an increasing struggle. The thin air in the upper altitude made it hard to breathe and exhausted her. Her pack, heavy with supplies, had seemed relatively light yesterday. Today, it ground painfully into her shoulders, rubbing them raw. Her feet were taking the greatest punishment. Every step caused her blisters to sting and the arches of her feet to ache. Her thoughts turned once again to her horses - if only she could ride them for a little while to take some of this load off. She sighed and shook her head. Adventures, it seemed, were awfully tough on the feet.

Feeling down and overwhelmed, lost in her thoughts, Caroline casually glanced behind her and felt a wave of optimism. She had been so focused on what was ahead that she failed to notice what was behind her. She had come a long, long way, so far, in fact, that a narrow blue ribbon in the distance was all she could see of the Great River.

The thin blue ribbon sparkled in the sun and she could picture, in her mind's eye, her brothers floating down it on their way to warn the King. They were there somewhere and she suddenly felt even lonelier. The vastness of the mountains around her made that feeling worse.

Still, the raw beauty of the landscape gave her a sense of hope, making her feel part of something much bigger than herself. A view like this put things into perspective, making her keenly aware of her relative insignificance in the world. Even large problems appeared small when compared to the majesty of the sparkling river, lush foothills, green forests and ponds of blue. After admiring the scene for a few moments, she got back to her feet. Just like that, the determination was back in her step.

That said, it would be nice to have a little company. It was exceedingly rare for anyone to journey along this mountain pass and Caroline had no reason to expect differently now. She usually did not care much for people, her family excepted, until she found herself without them, and the slim chance she would run across anyone made it even harder.

It was not that Caroline hated people, but some times it seemed to Caroline that they hated *her*. Take her classmates. They were always teasing her about something: she was too tall, or not skinny enough; her skin was too dark brown, or she did too well in school. Caroline ignored the insults and buried herself deeper in her schoolwork, but she would be lying if she said it didn't bother her at all.

Caroline wondered if she was alone after all. She had a strange sensation that she was being watched. Stopping, she scanned the forest around her, finding nothing. She tried to shake the eerie feeling; perhaps her imagination was running wild.

To distract from such worries, she thought back to cheerful visits from the rare travelers who had come this way. Father enjoyed the company, eager to hear stories from the lands their guests had come from, while swapping his own tales in return. It was then his children heard about his adventures as Chief Knight. Everyone looked forward to such times.

The memories continued as she walked, to times when the family would gather around a roaring fire while hearty mountain climbers guzzled beer and munched on turkey legs roasted over the hearth. The visitors brought tidings from Ambrosia City, Birdsong, and other spots on the map. Then they would wash dinner down with tankards of honey mead, eagerly listening as the great Eston Strongheart would tell of wars with the invading Barbarians, or of clashes with the wild men of Mulvaria. But eyes would open widest as he regaled them with tales of the Last Dragon War, when he fought alongside his Akari Dragonslayer and together killed the mighty Gorg, foulest of all the dragons. In each telling, though, Eston humbly gave all of the credit to Akari.

The death of Gorg had so shaken the dragons that they fled the island and abandoned war with man, leaving behind only an emissary to negotiate with Ambrosia. Eston himself built the weapon that was crucial to their newfound success, and it seemed silly to call it anything but what it was: *the Dragonkiller.* With that leverage, King Wilhelm negotiated a favorable peace settlement, one that banished dragons from the main island forever, and in return the Ambrosians only had to pay a small tribute to the dragons each year, a sign of their promise to abide by the agreement. It was a major victory for Ambrosia and before long they began to celebrate the Dragon Festival each year at this time.

For Caroline and her brothers, hearing these tales was even more thrilling than reading about them. But no matter how much they begged, her father only told them after a few glasses of honey mead, as he had little use for bragging otherwise. And since he only indulged in the presence of company, they had to make do.

Enough! Caroline forced herself to stop thinking of such things. The thoughts of home and better times were not helping now when things were difficult. If she wanted more of those happy times with her father and brothers, than she had to push on and somehow save her father. That meant she had to overcome thin air, sore feet, shoulders rubbed raw, and anything else that would stand in her way. Again she gritted her teeth with purpose and determination.

Then she saw it. Or did she? From the corner of her eye, just off in the thick pine trees, she thought there was a massive brown shape walking alongside her, but when she stopped for a clearer view, whatever it was, if it was anything to begin with, was gone. Caroline turned grim - she hoped she was not losing her mind in the woods.

Her pace quickened as she wished to leave anything in the woods behind her. A few hours later, she came to a large boulder lying on the pathway. It had been obscuring her view for some time. She went around its mossy surface and was stunned to see she was only a few feet from the top. In her excitement, she ran up the rest of the way.

Arriving at the top, panting, she set her hands on her hips and stared out at the majestic view. It was absolutely stunning. She wondered why they had never come this far before. It was sad that it took something as awful as having her father stolen away to find something so beautiful.

The view stretched for miles and miles, almost beyond measure. She gazed at the road ahead where the mountain dropped, a steep slope covered in more thick pine trees. It was going to be a tough climb down, but before she tackled it she gave herself a few moments to drink in the glorious view.

All around her, the peaks of the Kin Kara rose into the sky from the faces of the mountains, faces painted nearly black from the pines that covered their surface. The peaks circled a flat valley floor, with gentle hills rising here and there, gradually increasing in height and slope. Those led to still higher hills that formed the base of the mountains, which stood imposing in front of Caroline.

The valley itself was sliced into parcels by creeks and streams, green grass divided by blue water, and in between all of that, the Corkscrew River split the valley nearly in half. She strained her eyes, trying to catch a glimpse of a raft or someone camped beside the water, but she was still too far away and could see nothing, if anything was even there to begin with.

Caroline sighed. It seemed as good a time as any for a light lunch, which meant more jerky. Their stores weren't exactly stocked with much food that was good for traveling, just a lot of jerky and apples. It was now the seventh straight meal of such, long since rendered flavorless and dull.

Chewing on the jerky, bored with it all and wishing she had something else to eat - just about anything would do - she estimated the distance left to travel and figured the end of tomorrow she would be to the river. Then again, she noticed things seemed to be closer in the mountains than they really were, so that brought her brief rest to an end. I can chew while I walk, she thought. With one more glance back at the world she was leaving, she began the trek down the heavily forested slope.

After a long day admiring the breathless vistas she walked among, she pitched her tent and was ready to fall asleep as soon as her head hit the ground - no distracting thoughts, just a blanket spread out on the hard ground and another one pulled tight over her. The wind was as bitterly cold as the night before, swooping down from the peaks above to rattle her tent, but she was much too tired to care.

Caroline didn't think anything could wake her up and was concerned she'd oversleep, so she thought back to one of her father's old woodsman tricks, relayed from one of his stories. So before she laid down for the night, she drank as much water as her body could hold, knowing that her bladder would be certain to wake her up nice and early. With that done, she was soon asleep

*

Her father's trick worked wonderfully and very early that next morning – the sun had not even thought about showing itself from behind the mountains – she was wide awake, bursting to empty the water from the night before. Her plan had worked, but almost too well, as it felt like she was going to explode. She rushed from the tent, wrapping herself with a blanket to shield against the cold night air. She went out into the woods and found a log to sit on.

"They sure don't talk about going to the bathroom in the woods in the adventure books I've read," Caroline said to herself ruefully, her body shaking in the chill air. Her voice sounded strange in the darkness. When she finished, her fingers ran through her hair, stopping as they were quickly tangled. She felt even dirtier than yesterday, as if the filth had soaked through clean to her bones.

Caroline yawned, fighting the temptation to lie back down for a few more minutes of sleep, but she knew better - if she did, she was liable to sleep for hours, hours she could not afford to lose. She had to get moving, so with the light from the moon and stars shining through the trees, she folded her tent and packed her belongings.

It was a quiet, peaceful morning, the only sound the gentle stirring of the breeze through pine trees, which added to her sleepy mood.

Then, from somewhere in the woods, a small rock whizzed toward her, skipping by her feet and bouncing down the slope. Caroline jumped back and scanned the trees. Surely, that was thrown. But by whom, and from where? She searched for a sign of the culprit, but failed to find anything.

She feared that she really was going crazy, and so she rationalized the event. "Just a rock falling from high above. Nothing to worry about, Caroline. Snap out of it!"

But then a slight breeze blew her direction and she almost fell over at what she smelled. It was disgusting, *it* being a Sasquatch, also known as a Skunk Ape. Judging by the smell, it was a name well-deserved. There was not a doubt in her mind, she was being tailed by a Sasquatch, or worse, Sasquatches.

Caroline had heard about the rotten smell of garbage mixed with months-old spoiled milk that belonged to a Skunk Ape, but truthfully, she thought it had to be an exaggeration. *Wrong.* In fact, the description may have been an understatement, as the odor was simply staggering. Caroline was frightened – not only was there a Sasquatch nearby, it was throwing stones at her.

All sorts of thoughts ran through Caroline's mind, but the overwhelming one was shock. Sure, everyone *claimed* that Sasquatches lived in these mountains, even her father, but Caroline had wondered at the truth. Jonas, for his part, doubted it strongly. "Nonsense," he would say. "Those critters don't even *exist*, let alone live in the mountains around us. Simply preposterous."

But Caroline had to change her opinion as a small hail of rocks flew in her direction. Caroline grabbed her pack and used it to shield herself, as sheer terror pulsed through her. She watched as the stones sailed toward her, landing on all sides, hoping that somehow they would continue to miss their mark.

Strangely, they all landed quite close but none hit, and she wondered if the thrower was not missing on purpose. Perhaps they were hitting their mark after all? But it was small comfort as she gripped her pack tightly and did the only thing that felt right - she ran. She ran down the slope as fast as her feet would carry her, with all kinds of thoughts racing through her head, and in the heat of the moment she remembered hearing that bears had trouble running downhill - maybe the same was true of Skunk Apes? Why not?

So she sprinted downhill in the early morning hours, but running down a steep hill is not easy for anyone - bears, Skunk Apes, or sixteen-year old girls, even one as agile as Caroline. She was all but sprinting when she tripped over something - a rock, a tree root, something, it did not matter what. She was twisted around and struggled to regain her balance, but she fell backwards, cracking the back of her head on the ground. Light flashed across her eyes and she lay back on the ground. She tried to raise her head but couldn't. Before she was able to draw another breath she was unconscious.

It was some time before Caroline awoke, and as she did she rubbed her eyes before a shooting pain in her skull caused her to feel her head, where her fingers ran across a large knot underneath her hair. She struggled to remember what had caused such a lump, and it all came pouring back. She panicked as she finally opened her eyes to find herself looking into at the hairiest, toothiest, scariest creature she had ever seen.

It was a Skunk Ape, a Sasquatch. As she looked at it, it looked back at her, its large fangs bared. The Skunk Age was real and terrifying and there was no way out for Caroline.

## Chapter Five - Blind-sided

Mouse could not believe how thoroughly soaked he was. He was drenched from head to toe with cold water from the raging rapids that splashed over the sides of the canoe. The Great River was freezing, brought to a chill from the snow melt that drained into mountain springs feeding the river. There was no point in attempting to dry off, because as soon as he did another splash would come his way, soaking him anew. All he could do was fight through and keep paddling until the river calmed down.

*If* it ever calmed down, as Mouse could only see choppy waters ahead, with narrow pathways to navigate. No, things were not going to turn for the better any time soon.

At least the canoe was intact and holding up well to the battering, although Mouse could not help but wonder how much more it could take. They were being dashed to and fro among the rocks lining the river that jutted out like the jagged teeth of a dragon. Each hit jarred his body and sent shock waves down his spine. He gritted his teeth and braced for the drowning yet to come, as he was certain the canoe would shatter to splinters.

Worst of all, Mouse could no longer see. His eyes gave up after being blinded again and again by the steady stream of water, so each battering came as a surprise with no opportunity to brace for it. He could only hold on as best he could and lean against his brother, who was packed tightly in the seat in front of him. It was a miserable time, with two days of travel still ahead. Mouse could only hope that somehow the worst was nearly behind them.

Just when they did not think they could take anymore, the river calmed. They shot free from one last swarm of rapids to find the river widening. The canyon was at an end, with the larger pathway instantly calming the water's wrath. It was not unlike being in the middle of a driving rainstorm, thunder and lightning crashing all around, with the wind nearly knocking you down – when suddenly the sun emerges and birds chirp happily in the trees. It was an amazing feeling. Mouse rubbed his eyes, looking behind him as if he needed to prove to himself that he had not imagined the whole thing.

Soon, the deafening roar of the river vanished. If not for their wet clothes, coupled with debris in the canoe, it would be impossible to know they had been hanging on for their lives just seconds earlier. Relief washed over them and filled their souls while the sun warmed their skin.

Jonas and Mouse paddled for the shore, desperate for a respite, despite their mission's grave urgency. It would do no good to die from exhaustion halfway to the castle. They needed to rest, and there was no sense in feeling bad about it.

The canoe bumped against the shore and came to a stop. They unfolded their bodies and without a word, they spilled out on the river bank. Going down this river was exhausting, brutal labor and they lay huffing and puffing on their backs.

"Wow, that was fun," Jonas said, between breaths.

Mouse stared at him with his eyes ready to pop from his skull. "Are you serious?" he replied. "That was crazy! The worst I've ever seen the river. I thought we were goners." He held out one of his hands, which trembled. "Look! I'm still shaking!"

"Yeah, but it was still fun," Jonas said. "It was an adventure! A *real* adventure. If we're going to be great warriors, we better get used to it."

"Yeah, I suppose so," Mouse replied, not persuaded by his brother's logic.

After a bit of rest, the two found their strength somewhat restored and sat up to take in their surroundings. The river was flowing peacefully in front of them and to their rear stood tall Cottonwoods with their leaves waving in the breeze. All in all, it was a pleasant spring day.

But it would not last, as further inspection by Mouse revealed an empty canoe lying downstream. "Jonas, do you see that? There's another canoe. Where do you think it came from?"

"*Who* it came from is more important than where it came from, I think," Jonas replied. "Let's go take a look."

They peered inside and found the canoe empty, but Jonas leaned for a closer look.

As he did, a gruff, snarling voice yelled out from behind them. "Hey! What are you doing in there?"

Mouse and Jonas turned to see two large men emerging from the woods. In fact, they were massive, thickly built and tall, with beards down to their chests. The rest of their hair was a tangled rat's nest.

They were about the same height with similar builds, virtually indistinguishable from each other but for the color of their coarse hair - dark black for one, a light brown shade for the other. Their pale white skin stood in contrast to the bronzed tone of the boys. They were also nearly as soaked as Jonas and Mouse were, and Jonas quickly surmised that they had recently been down the river the same way the boys had.

Jonas stepped back and brushed his hand along the hilt of his sword. There was no doubt about it - they were Barbarians, and likely the same two their father had sent into the river. So they hadn't drowned after all, Jonas thought. Great. After an awkward silence, Jonas decided he better answer the Barbarian's question, and thought up a story as they drew closer with each step.

"We're not doing anything, sir," Jonas replied. "Just looking at this canoe. It, umm, looked like one that belongs to a friend of ours, so I was checking it out."

"Well, I ain't no friend of yours, and that's my canoe, so keep your head outta there," the fair-haired one said. "You got no business here."

"Yes, sir," Jonas replied, looking over at Mouse, who was wisely easing back to their canoe in preparation for escape. Jonas followed his lead and without wasting a second, darted to the shore, right on Mouse's heels. They shoved the canoe into the river and hopped in, wasting nary a breath.

They paddled furiously, knowing that they had to escape or they'd never be able to warn the King. Unfortunately, the Barbarians wasted no time climbing into their canoe, and they took mighty strokes with their paddles that pulled them quickly through the water. They were rapidly closing the distance between themselves and the boys - Jonas had to think of something, and fast.

"Mouse, I'm going to try to take these guys by surprise. It's our only chance, I think."

Jonas dropped the paddle in the canoe basin and wrapped his fist around the hilt of his sword. The sword felt comfortable in his hand, as it should, as it was the sword he had been learning to use for seemingly his entire life. And Matthias was certainly right about the quality of the weapon, as it felt light in his hand. Still, he knew there was no way to match raw strength with their foes. His only chance was to outsmart them - seeing as these were Barbarians, that might not be such a tall order.

Jonas tersely spat out an order to his brother. "Mouse, let them catch up. When they're almost next to us, swing the canoe completely around. I've got an idea!"

His voice strained under the tension, but Mouse admired the way that he took control of the situation. "If I'm destined to be a great warrior," Mouse thought, "what Fate awaits Jonas? He'll be Chief Knight, easy."

But Chief Knight could wait. Right now, they had Barbarians to deal with. Mouse dipped the paddle in and out of the water, putting on a show of trying to escape, and watched from the corner of his eye as the Barbarians closed in. When he could hear the heavy sounds of their breathing, he judged they were close enough, so he did as instructed and whirled the canoe around. It took a strong effort to spin it, with Mouse nearly dropping the paddle from the force. But he had just enough strength to finish the job and the canoe faced the Barbarians head on, ready for their showdown.

As soon as the canoe completed its rotation, Jonas stood up, wobbling as he struggled to keep his legs underneath him. He held his arms out to gather his balance, with the sword extending from his right arm. As soon as he felt steady and sure of himself, Jonas shifted his footing and grasped the sword with both hands.

Jonas grit his teeth and took a mighty swing. It landed perfectly, chopping through the front of the Barbarians' canoe, sending splinters and chunks of wood flying into the air and leaving behind a large gash. Cold river water poured in and quickly filled the ship, causing the canoe to start sinking. The front nose-dived into the river and the back rose from the surface like the light side of a teeter-totter.

The Barbarians panicked, and with good reason. The dark-haired one in front was stuck between the canoe walls, crammed in and unable to get loose under duress. The fair-haired one in back managed to stand up, but he was off-balance and flailing his arms about like a madman.

Mouse swung the canoe around to point it downstream. He dipped the oar in the water and paddled for all he was worth. But before they went far, his hands, weak and shaking from terror and strain both, dropped the paddle. He stretched out desperately to save it from sinking, but it exceeded his grasp and disappeared from sight.

"Jonas! I dropped the oar! Help!" Mouse yelled, but Jonas had other things on his mind, as the light-haired Barbarian leaped from his sinking ship and crashed down on their canoe. It dipped down due to the weight of the Barbarian and nearly went under, barely bobbing back to the surface.

The situation was dire, but they wouldn't go down without a fight. Mouse shoved the Barbarian, trying to catch him off-balance, but the Barbarian kicked him away with little effort. Jonas saw what was happening and just like that, another plan came to mind. He rocked his weight back and forth while grasping the sides of the canoe, first pushing down on the right side with all of his weight, then the left, back to the right, and so on, each movement shaking the canoe more than the last. The rocking knocked their attacker off his feet, causing him to splash into the water.

"Great job! Now paddle Jonas, paddle!" Mouse yelled. But from the corner of his eye, he saw that the other Barbarian was finally free of the sinking canoe.

Jonas heard the call and sunk his oar into the water, pushing with all of his might, alternating strokes on each side to propel the canoe forward.

But it was too late. Like his cohort, the dark-haired Barbarian leaped from his sinking canoe - but he fell short and landed in the river. He disappeared underwater and the boys cheered!

Just as they thought they were free, the Barbarian emerged. He grasped the side of the canoe, pulled himself up, and ripped the oar from Jonas' grip, using his raw strength to wrench it free.

Together, Jonas and Mouse tried to pull the oar back, but the Barbarian was simply too strong. He took it and threw it toward the shore, then followed it to swim to the river bank.

The boys were completely and totally stuck, literally up the river without a paddle, as they say. They were at the mercy of the current to carry them downstream. Desperate, Mouse dipped his hands into the water and tried to propel the canoe forward, but it was futile. They were sitting ducks, and could only watch as the Barbarians swam to shore.

"What are they doing now, Jonas?"

Jonas frowned and pointed to a raft on the river banks. The invaders had found another means of attack.

"Of course! There just happens to be a raft waiting for them!" Jonas shouted. "I sure wish something would fall from the sky to help us - like another paddle, for instance."

"Jonas," Mouse shouted back. "Why don't we use our shields as paddles? It's worth a shot."

Jonas wrinkled his brow. It wasn't a bad idea. "Nice thinking, Mouse. We're going to need them anyway, so might as well get them out now."

They needed two hands to control the large shields but found they did a decent job as makeshift paddles. But it wasn't enough, as the Barbarians were already catching up, with the raft swiftly pulling them through the water.

"Jonas, I guess we better prepare to fight to the death..." Mouse's voice trembled with fear. He felt a long way from being a great warrior at the moment.

"To the death," Jonas agreed. They raised their swords with their right hands, their dripping shields with their left, and held their chins proudly aloft.

There was no choice but to take the fight to the Barbarians, knowing full well the long odds of success. So when the raft caught up, they jumped from their stranded canoe, ready for battle.

They landed roughly. Mouse scrambled to his feet, but slipped and clumsily fell to his knees. Desperate, he chopped at the ankles of the lighter-haired Barbarian, deciding that was as good a place as any to attack. It was his only chance, but it was easily thwarted, the attempted blow so weak that the Barbarian simply stepped backwards to avoid the strike, then stepped on Mouse's sword, rendering it useless.

"Pitiful," the Barbarian growled. "Completely pathetic." He lifted Mouse from the raft surface, holding him in a headlock while the boy kicked and screamed, uselessly struggling against the strong grip of the Barbarian.

Meanwhile, Jonas managed to land cleanly on his feet after leaping from the canoe. From there, he quickly moved to strike, his sword clanging against that of the dark-haired savage. In fact, Jonas fared a lot better than his brother, standing strong against his foe, with the bull-headed tactics of the large man countered deftly by Jonas' superior technique and speed. Again and again Jonas parried his blows, and soon the Barbarian was gasping for air, his chest heaving while sweat poured down his face.

Jonas' confidence grew as he had a stunning revelation: so long as he didn't do anything stupid, he could win this fight. He dodged his blows and ran him ragged, and when the Barbarian was completely gassed, Jonas prepared to finish his opponent.

But just then, the other Barbarian, with Mouse in his arms, sneaked behind Jonas and kicked him sharply in the back, which sent him sprawling. From there, the brothers were restrained, tied up, and placed back to back. Just like that, they were prisoners, and Jonas cursed their luck. They were supposed to have the *easy* job while Caroline took the more dangerous path. He could only hope that she was having more success than they were.

They brought the raft into shore. The dark-haired Barbarian looked at his two prisoners and spat. "Time for you to learn some respect!" He kicked Jonas in the ribs, frustrated and embarrassed by being nearly waylaid by what looked like a ten-year old to his eyes - not that it would have made it easier to take if he had known that Jonas was nearly fourteen. "Who are you little rats, anyway? Who taught you to fight like that?"

Jonas said nothing, his face grim, seething in anger. But Mouse could not help himself.

"I can tell you exactly who taught us. The same guy that sent you into the river for a bath - Eston Strongheart!" Mouse said, his voice filled with pride. "Sorry to say the bath didn't help - you still reek of garbage."

"That so? Well, we owe someone a bit of payback for that, and seeing as he's long gone you'll do as well as anybody."

He raised his fist and considered where he would strike the young, defenseless boy. The Barbarian mulled over his options, thinking the ribs would suffice, but then again the face was always good. So many routes he could take, but he settled on breaking Mouse's nose.

He clenched his fist and prepared to strike his captive, who braced for the blow. But behind the fist, Mouse saw a massive green figure high over the Barbarian's shoulder that was far worse than a punch in the nose. Far, far worse.

A dragon. In fact, three of them, and heading right toward them - three huge, loathsome dragons, their outlines so large they blotted out the sun. Mouse's jaw opened but he could say nothing, frozen in fear and unable to move his lips. But his face told the tale to the Barbarians, who grew worried from his terrified expression.

Jonas, with his back to Mouse, could see nothing, but soon his spine shivered with terror as a deafening roar went up so loud it rattled his teeth. His senses were overcome as he heard the terrifying screech of what could only be a dragon. He had never heard a dragon roar before, had never even seen one, yet there was no doubt in his mind.

No, Jonas thought, they didn't get the easy job at all, and it seemed that their short-lived adventure would soon be over.

The last thing Jonas had ever hoped to hear was the roar of a dragon. Now it seemed it would be the last thing he ever heard, as the three dragons swooped down and flew straight toward them.

## Chapter Six - Unmasked

Akari regretted many things he had done in his life. But faking his death had not been one of them. That was, until now.

Sure, there were aspects he regretted, the most obvious being that he was no longer able to see his niece Caroline or nephew Jonas. Missing out on seeing his sister's children grow up was a difficult decision and one he had not taken lightly, but it was ultimately not enough to stop him. When your options are either faking your own death or facing a real one, the decision is clear.

And he was glad he did it, for faking his death had made it possible to escape the lifelong commitment of serving as Chief Knight of the Great Army of Ambrosia. Once escaping that Fate, he was able to live at Dragon Mountain, where he completed his studies of the art of magic under the tutelage of the wisest dragons. Much of his work had been completed during that time and Akari was quite satisfied.

But a man could live amongst dragons for only so long before desiring to return to his own kind, and as rewarding as the experience had been, eventually he grew weary of life at Dragon Mountain and knew that it was time to go home.

After pleading his case to the Council of Dragons, Akari was allowed to return home - so long as he agreed to become a spy on their behalf. With few other options at hand, coupled with a desire to make his friends happy, Akari agreed, and soon he was living the boring life of a King's guard in Ambrosia Castle, using his skills in magic to take on a new identity.

It went well for a time, content as he was to be among other people again, living under his assumed name of Amaru. He was also able to stay apprised of his family through tidings brought by Matthias, and thus he knew that all was well with them. All in all, he had no regrets.

Until now.

Now, he was ready for a change, as every day in the life of a King's guard was exactly the same, one after another, tedious and boring. Torturous did not even begin to describe what it was like listening to that blithering idiot King Wilhelm, the eldest son of Renwick, who possessed none of what had made his father a great ruler. Akari would watch the King's feeble efforts to lead and Akari would shake his head, doing little to hide his disgust.

In a way, it was his fault. It was he that had saved Renwick with high hopes that the King had reached the same conclusion he had - that the age of Kings was at an end. It was all too obvious. One only had to look at the heirs Renwick would leave behind: the incompetent Wilhelm, the power-mad and bloodthirsty Maldazor, and his youngest daughter Chloe, who proved Akari's point - as both a female and youngest born, she had no possibility of serving as monarch despite clearly being the most able.

Instead of doing something noble and brave, Renwick squandered the opportunity and used the extra time afforded him to divide his kingdom into thirds, leaving territory to each heir.

If Akari had a second chance, he would think long and hard before choosing to extend Renwick's life, knowing he would oversee such brainless ideas, as his solution would prove ineffective at best. After all, Wilhelm was still incompetent, Maldazor remained bloodthirsty, and Chloe could only lead Birdsong to prosperity while the other two nations meandered aimlessly.

But that was all in the past. As for now, that figured to be as boring as ever. So Akari walked slowly up the old stone stairs, dreading the workday. He stared at the ground, watching his feet as he trudged upwards. As they always did on this daily trek, his thoughts turned to the first time he had ever climbed these stairs, the night when he was brought here to save King Renwick.

He shuddered as he thought back to his decision to take his brother-in-law's place as Chief Knight. It had seemed like the right decision at the time, but it shaped so much of his life to where the only way out that he could see was death. Compared to the drudgery of serving as Chief Knight, death almost seemed welcome - almost.

Akari may not have enjoyed being Chief Knight but he was quite good at it and their enemies had given up on bringing battle to Ambrosia. Even the mighty Barbarians from the North moved on as a peace won through strength ruled the land -- and throughout the kingdom Akari was hailed as a hero. There were even songs and books written about him, though Akari despised all of it.

With such success, Akari begged the King to free him from his oath. He was making progress along that line until King Renwick up and died.

Distraught, Akari decided his only option was to die in battle – a hero's death. But with the whole kingdom lamenting Renwick's death - not even Akari could save him this time - and plans being made for both a funeral and three coronation ceremonies, well, there wasn't much interest in starting a war. If Akari wanted to move on he would have to find another way.

And then Akari had an idea. The more he thought about it, dying was a bad idea, as it had one major drawback – it didn't leave much of a future. With all of the progress he had made with his experiments and discoveries, it would be a disservice to the world if he was not there to see them through. Right?

So what to do? Well, if he didn't want to die, it seemed the next best thing was to fake his death. After all, what difference would it make to the King if Akari was actually dead or only believed to be? Either way they would appoint a new Chief Knight and Akari could start a new life elsewhere.

But how could he pull it off? It was a head-scratcher, but quickly solved. In fact, it was simple! Plant rumors about a dragon in the south, journey to verify said rumors, and then disappear for some time, only to have a reasonable facsimile of your mangled body eventually wash up. After all, he was known across the land as Akari Dragonslayer, acquiring a reputation for killing dragons without actually killing any. Therefore, it made sense for him to die at the hands of a dragon without actually dying.

Not only would Akari allegedly die at the hands of a dragon (or claws, rather), but the ultimate irony was that he would go on to again live with the creatures, as many years ago he had studied their magic and lived on

Dragon Island. He even sat in on Dragon Councils, including the famous day when dragons decided they no longer wished to battle with humans. From there, they devised a plan where Akari would chase them off after slaying their evil ruler Gorg, enemy of man and dragon alike, in the name of freeing the kingdom of Ambrosia from the beasts.

But that is another story.

These thoughts seemed to flash through his head nearly every morning. Somehow recounting the steps of his life as he lifted his feet one by one up the stairs seemed to put him in the right frame of mind to be utterly and completely bored for the rest of the day, guarding a King that he should rightly remove for the betterment of all, the same way the dragons once dealt with Gorg.

But working with the King was what the Dragon Council wanted, and strange were their ways. Little did they trust Ambrosia and greatly did they desire a spy deep inside the throne room, so here Akari was, ready to start the day as he looked down the hall that led to the King's living quarters. He sighed. It was time to go to work.

\*

The man once known as Akari watched as King Wilhelm stuffed himself silly at the dinner table while seated in his throne, a massive thing covered in various gemstones, gaudy and ridiculous. It wasn't practical, but he would throw a fit until one of his servants shoved it to the table.

It was all Akari could do to not gag at the revolting sight. Watching the King eat was more disgusting than a pack of buzzards picking away at carrion that had rotted in the sun for a week. After all, the buzzard was only doing what a buzzard was supposed to do. But was a man, especially a King, supposed to get sauce all over his face and chunks of meat stuck in the ragged beard that sprouted from all three of his chins, the last of which hung over his neck clear down to the opening of his shirt?

The red padding that made up the cushioned throne was worn, and the legs were bending inwards - one could almost hear them groan each time the King placed his massive frame upon it.

He was on his twelfth course today - one of Akari's few amusements was to count the various dinner courses served to the King during a given day. The record was seventeen, not counting apple pie for dessert, of which Akari noted the King took seconds.

Akari had seen enough, turning his head to spare his eyes further pain, although he could still hear the relentless smacking of the King's mouth. It was a shame that the King's mother had never bothered to instruct her son to close his mouth while chewing.

Watching this scene play out for what felt like the thousandth time, Akari could not grasp why Wilhelm's father, Renwick, had not simply cut him out of the monarchy all together. Akari cared little for Maldazor, Wilhelm's younger brother, but at least Maldazor was intelligent and had something on his mind besides looking for the finest pastry chef in the kingdom.

The smacking finally stopped, and Akari let out a sigh of relief. Unfortunately, the moment of peace was fleeting, as smacking was replaced by slurping. The King had moved from the main course to a large bowl of soup. Rather than bother with a spoon, he held the bowl to his lips and drank it down noisily. Even the Princess looked disgusted.

The King only paused to wipe what he spilled from his chin. Akari gagged, struggling to make it sound like a cough, to avoid attracting attention.

His precaution wasn't needed. The King continued slurping, drinking a second bowl and finishing it just in time to wave in a consort. She walked into the hall carrying two serving trays heavily laden with more food. The consort struggled under the weight of the platters, grunting as she walked down the aisle.

Akari shuddered again as the King dug into the new platters. Akari was forced to look away, and so doing, observed two younger guards of the King, who were also watching King Wilhelm. They were every bit as disgusted with the King as Akari was, perhaps more so. Frankly, they were getting carried away, laughing and pointing, and at great risk of being caught in the act. Wilhelm was not especially bright but even he would eventually catch on if the guards continued, so Akari got their attention and gave them a quick wink, a signal to knock it off. The guards smiled back mischievously, but Akari noted that they heeded his warning and moved on to something else.

Akari shifted his weight back and forth, chewing absent-mindedly on a fingernail. The same question that always lingered in his mind pushed to the forefront of his thoughts once again. Was this why he faked his death -

to serve as a mere guard to the King? It was the most boring position in the entire King's army, one that could be ably filled by an idiot.

The consort again walked past, which happily broke Akari's concentration. He looked past the empty dishes piled high on the serving trays and lingered on the consort, watching her long brown hair trailing behind her as she left the hall.

She was fairly new to the castle and not well known to Akari, but he'd be lying if he said he did not want to get to know her better. All he knew was her name - Abigail. He was too scared to introduce himself - leading an army into battle was one thing, but meeting a woman produced an entirely different level of fear.

*

After some time, Akari settled into a trance-like state, leaning against a wall and using his sword as a sort of cane to keep his body upright. It was part of his normal routine to survive the day. But as he stared into the distance, he was stunned - King Wilhelm actually *pushed* away a plate of food, proclaiming that he did not feel well. Akari's guard instantly went up.

Clearly, the King was about to have a heart attack - Akari had been anticipating it for some time. Wilhelm was gasping, coughing violently, and leaving spittle all over the table. Akari had to steady himself, but sprung into action as he couldn't very well stand there and let him die - could he?

Princess Natalia, the only daughter of King Wilhelm, loosed a desperate call. "Someone help my father! He's dying! Oh, please help!" Tears burst from her eyes, a horrible expression of despair on her face as she leaned over the King's helpless body.

Akari ran toward the King and considered his options, wondering if he really wanted to save another King's life - especially *this* King. After all, things had not gone well the last time he did so. And he could safely say that this time, it would go even worse.

He could have stood back and watched King Wilhelm die, and he rather disliked the man, loathsome as he could be, but still, he was a man. Akari had to do something. The problem was doing something meant revealing his secret and risking the penalties that would come with it, as he would be unable to stay disguised as Amaru while using spells to try to save the King. So as he made his way to the monarch, he noted the escape routes he would soon require.

The dragons would not be pleased, but his mind was made up, and the escape plan he was formulating would leave them even angrier. Akari did not relish upsetting the Council of Dragons, but it would not be the first time he had done so - although if he was unable to escape, it would certainly be the last.

Akari removed a few of his ever-present potions he kept stowed in a small satchel. But he needed water. He found a pitcher at the end of the long table and sprinted full speed ahead, the leather soles on his shoes squeaking across the floor. He inadvertently crashed into the consort Abigail, who had served the King only moments earlier. Her lithe body went flying while a vial filled with black liquid flew from her hand and across the hall, alarming the warrior. What was in that vial?

"Someone grab that!" Akari yelled. "Might be poison!" The consort rose to her feet and tried to escape, but Akari held her tight.

"It's medicine," she yelled from underneath Akari's arm, which was pinning her to the ground. "The Princess gave it to me!"

"A likely story," Akari responded, then called to the guards who had been laughing at the King moments earlier. "Come here! Don't let her go," he ordered. "Something is not right here!"

He would have to figure it all out later, but his suspicion was aroused - could the Princess be framing Abigail? It sounded preposterous. But right now, there were more pressing concerns.

He made it to the King's side and thought about which mixture he would use, although the odds were strongly against him. Poisoning was not an easy thing to deal with and chances were he was too late.

He dropped to his knees and nodded at the Princess in an attempt to calm her. "Princess, I may be able to help. I once saved your grandfather." He showed her the potions, bright and colorful, and bent down by the King's side. "But it is going to take a miracle."

The Princess said nothing, only nodded back and nervously pulled at her hair. Something was very strange about her behavior, and Akari was struck with the sense she was not hoping for Akari to find success. But he pushed that aside and eyed the potions scattered on the floor.

"What to use, what to use?" Akari muttered. Many possible combinations ran through his mind.

He cast aside a green bottle he had been testing on some of his fellow guards. No, *that* wouldn't do any good here, though Akari felt pangs of disappointment, as that bottle represented failure. He was certain that he had discovered a way for bald men to grow a full head of hair. He was close, but not quite there. The potion did grow hair, and very well, but only on your feet, back, and hands, not exactly where most people want or need hair. Akari didn't think this was all bad - one could save a fortune on socks as the hair was thick and quite warm - but so far none of his test subjects had seen it the same way. If only guard duty did not stand in the way- he would have solved the problem months ago.

Akari took the potions he did need and went to work, mixing a few flasks together. He swirled them around while the King lay beside him, panting heavily, looking worse by the moment.

Still, Akari had to try. After all, as one of his guards he had taken an oath to protect the King, although truth be told it was not an oath he had taken seriously. Akari had taken many oaths, almost all of them at times when it was convenient for him. And he had broken those same oaths, when convenient, or more exactly, when necessary - or at least necessary in his mind.

This is not unusual. Many people promise to do one thing based on a certain set of information available to them, and when more information becomes available they realize the error in their promise and adjust accordingly. In this, Akari was no different. But he had sworn to the Council of Dragons that he would spy as long as he could, and this was one oath that he would not forgo, despite the complications it had caused him.

Akari finally had the mixture he wanted, a gold-colored liquid that sparkled in the sun. Before he delivered the dose, Akari paused, regretting that his vow to the dragons was likely at an end. He sighed. Life can become awfully complicated when you make promises you intend to keep.

And things were about to get awfully complicated.

Akari pried open the King's jaw and poured the potion down, mumbling a little spell under his breath to help the formula do its work. A little spell, but one with big consequences - disastrous ones.

The King managed to choke some of the liquid down, but he coughed violently while doing so, thus most of it spilled to the floor. The color sank further from his face. Akari knew it was too late when his eyes opened wide, empty and hallow, staring vacantly into space. He was simply too late, assuming he even had a chance at all.

The King drew one last breath and exhaled, the death rattle moving the King's lips for the last time and his eyes sealed shut. Akari lifted an eyelid and examined his pupils, confirming that he was indeed gone. He grew grim as he prepared to inform the Princess.

Akari rose to his feet and bowed to the King's daughter. "Princess, I am so sorry. I did what I could, but the poison was too strong - I've never seen anything like it."

The Princess buried her face in her hands and shook violently. After some time passed, she rubbed the tears from her eyes and managed to raise her head. Her eyes grew big when she did so, as she was gazing into the eyes of Akari. Not Amaru the guard, but Akari Dragonslayer. Her frown suddenly changed into a demented smile.

"It worked! I don't believe it, but it worked! Akari, it's you!" The Princess jumped in the air and danced in a circle, filled with joy.

To Akari, it was quite clear that she had gone mad from the trauma, although she was hardly normal before this tragedy. And what did she mean by "it worked"?

Then Akari's heart skipped as he realized she had called him *Akari*. He knew the transformation would be swift, but not *that* swift. He touched his face and felt his beard growing back in as the disguise of Amaru was wiped away. Just as he figured, the concealment spell wore off while attempting to save the King, and there was no turning back now.

Akari's temper rose and he fought off the urge to kick something. Of all the times for his spell of disguise to wear off, why now? And what was the Princess talking about? What worked? Nothing worked. Her father was dead!

At that, he cringed. Exactly. Her father was dead. Poisoned. It *had* worked. Worked indeed. He shook his head as he put the pieces together. The Princess had killed her own father and then framed the consort Abigail. But how did she come across a poison so powerful it could kill a man of Wilhelm's size before anything could reverse it?

He smirked. Of course! Maldazor. But how was he able to acquire the assistance of the King's own daughter?

Before he could think it through, Princess Natalia threw her arms around him and kissed him. Akari pulled her away and shoved her aside, with no thought to proper decorum around a Princess. Then again, what was the point of propriety around one who would murder their own father? In his cluelessness, Akari had never realized that the Princess had been in love with him, completely obsessed. He knew much about magic, and of science, but little of matters of the heart.

The Princess would not give up easy and ran right back, again throwing her arms around him and whispering in his ear while he tried to break free. "Akari, I love you! I brought you back, Akari. It worked! I did it for you! I brought you back to life. It worked even better than my uncle said it would!"

"Umm," was all that Akari could manage to reply in his flustered state. He picked up a silver platter from the table and looked at his reflection, seeing the familiar though long hidden visage once again. He was back. There was only one thing to do - run.

As he contemplated his next move, searching for the least-guarded route, he suddenly dropped the plate and recoiled in pain. "Now what?" he thought.

It was his head. There was a dull, aching pain that was increasing in intensity, causing the warrior to nearly fall over.

He stood up straight, shaking his head as if a gnat was buzzing in his ear. But no matter what he tried, he couldn't escape the feeling that his nephew was in danger, and he must go to his aid.

It seemed that an old promise was coming back to haunt him - an oath made thirteen years ago during his sister's dying moments, when he had sworn to always protect her son and his nephew.

Somehow, someway, his long departed sister had made certain that he would fulfill his duty. The rules of magic could be fickle, but Akari quickly pieced it all together - his sister must have placed a spell on him to ensure he lived up to his promise. The throbbing in his skull was unrelenting. If his nephew needed saving, then he would do it, or the consequences could be dire as the spell appeared to be quite powerful.

Unfortunately, he had to save himself first. Talk about bad timing.

Very bad timing. The King's guards had witnessed the transformation and closed in with swords raised high in the air. The guards were uncertain as to *why* their old Chief Knight had suddenly materialized in front of them, but coupled with the apparent murder of their King, the best course was to capture him and sort it out later.

Akari would have to fight his way free.

## Chapter Seven - Chupwah

Caroline, wake up. Wake up, Caroline!"

Caroline mumbled something indecipherable in response and rolled over. At the same time, she brushed aside the hand that had been shaking her in an effort to roust her. But as soon as her hand felt the one shaking her, she pulled back, as her fingers ran unexpectedly across thick fur. This was unlike any other hand she had felt before.

Startled, Caroline opened her eyes to find the hairiest, toothiest, scariest creature she had ever seen looking down at her. She gasped. How did this creature know her name and what did it want with her? And worse, she realized it was not just one hideous face looking at her, but three.

Caroline dug her heels into the earth and pushed herself backwards across the rough ground. The morning sun outlined the creatures' features, giving their fur a golden, bronzed look, and somewhat softened her initial impression. But she was still terrified, even if they weren't monsters.

She had never seen these animals before and had doubted their very existence, even though her father had said they indeed were real. Obviously he was right. Her father also described them as peaceful creatures unless provoked, and Caroline reasoned, quite rightly, that she was not provoking them. Still, she was desperate to escape. But when she tried to get up and take off, a furry paw pressed down on her shoulder and held her in place, which sent a clear message: "you're not going *anywhere*."

Her hand went for her throbbing forehead. A nasty headache was the souvenir from her fall, a product of the large, painful bump she found on the back of her head.

Caroline looked around, finding that she was now at the bottom of the slope, right on the banks of the Corkscrew River. She had come a long way, but did not know how. Had they carried her? She was resting in a pile of leaves, a crude bed apparently fashioned for her by the Sasquatches. Her father was probably right. They apparently bore her no ill will, so she stopped trying to escape. Instead, she listened as the creatures talked amongst themselves. Much to her surprise, she understood every word - then again, one of them had spoken her name and told her to wake up, quite clearly, though it did not seem natural they should speak the same language.

"Be careful. You're going to scare the poor thing!" one of them said in a distinct rough, growling voice that nevertheless Caroline was certain belonged to a female, though she knew not why.

"She's fine," another voice growled back, this one undoubtedly male in her estimation.

"Let her up. She had quite a tumble and I'm sure seeing the likes of us standing around her isn't helping her constitution one bit," the female voice said.

Caroline decided to speak up, but her mouth failed to work as well as hoped. "I'm...I'm...I'm fine," she stammered. "Can you understand me?"

"Of course we can young one. Why couldn't we? Worsi, would you let her up already?" The facial expression on the female softened as she looked down at Caroline and continued.

"What's strange is that you seem to understand *us*. Of course, you humans are usually running away from us before we can get more than three words out." The female Sasquatch looked thoughtful for a moment. "Guess I never thought of it that way. Anyway, you are Caroline, daughter of Eston Strongheart, no?"

"Yes, that's right. How do you know him?" Caroline asked, her brow furrowing.

A look of surprise appeared on the Sasquatch's face before she answered. "Not know Eston Strongheart? Who doesn't know of Eston Strongheart, Caroline? We all know of the Chief Knight that gave it all up to raise his family!" While she said this, Worsi helped Caroline to her feet. She brushed off the dirt and stray bits of leaves that clung to her clothing and hair while the female Sasquatch continued.

"Caroline, my name is Sheena." She pointed. "This is Worsi, as you doubtless heard, and here is our son, Chupwah. I think he has something he'd like to say."

Chupwah was smaller than his parents, and clearly younger, but still massive and of stout build. He stood alongside his mother while staring at the ground and looking generally ashamed.

"I'm sorry for throwing rocks at you and scaring you," he said, his face titled downward. "I guess I misunderstood when my parents said we needed to keep you away from the Burmian Caves. I'm not used to *talking* to humans to keep them away. I'm awfully sorry you were hurt."

"It's, umm, OK," Caroline responded. She was not quite sure how to take these creatures, though they seemed friendly enough. From force of habit, she held out her hand. Chupwah grasped it and gave it a shake, with a shaggy, massive hand. Caroline marveled at his gigantic hand; his fingers and palm were lined with thick padding while his nails were hard and strong. She felt sympathy for anything that tried to pick a fight with a Sasquatch.

Sheena watched them shake. "Good! Now that that's settled, there are more important matters to address. We heard about what happened to your father, and it's a shame we weren't around when it occurred. But as soon as we heard the news, we left with all haste. But we were high in the mountains and a good distance away - it's too warm this low in the valley during the spring. Anyway, we had a feeling about who you were and what you were up to last night. We've quietly been following you to make sure, until Chupwah was apparently confused on how we planned to keep you from the caves. Chupwah, you worry me sometimes!" The younger Skunk Ape bowed his head bashfully.

Caroline looked at the Sasquatches, unsure of what she should reveal about her mission and journey. They did *appear* to be trustworthy, but she wondered if it would not be better to start asking some questions of her own first. "How did you know what I was up to?"

Worsi spoke up, his voice deep and gravelly. "We know you are going after your father. It's a mistake. It wouldn't be safe for a *Sasquatch* in the Burmian caves, let alone a human girl! Your father wouldn't hear of it!"

His wife smacked him on the back of the head. "Who are you to tell her what she can or can't do? Her father is out there somewhere, carted off by Barbarians, and you want her to stay home? Is that what you would expect from Chupwah? Give your advice but never *tell* her to do anything, you dimwit!"

Worsi growled back softly, but gritted his teeth and stayed calm. "We're not getting into this right now, dear. But yes, I am going to say my piece, and that will be enough for me. So let me lay the facts out and she can do what she will with them."

He turned to Caroline and assumed a fatherly tone. "Caroline, I hate to tell you this, but from what our sources tell us, the Barbarians are nearly to the caves. We are too late. Far too late. Surely you do not insist upon following him into *those* caves?"

Caroline's eyes grew big and her face frantic as she pondered these tidings. "How do you know this?"

"We have our ways," Sheena replied, then pointed skyward where a hawk was circling above. "They see nearly everything up there. Of course, trying to actually get anything out of them is another thing. Stubborn! But they can be bought. We've been bribing that one with chunks of our fur - there's nothing a hawk loves more than Sasquatch hair to build their nests. I've been giving that fellow a fistful, now and then, for information." She held out her arm and revealed a small bald patch on her forearm as proof.

"Amazing!" Caroline said, awestruck. "But are you sure it's too late? Can we trust a hawk?"

"Hawks aren't given to lies, Caroline. I would regret to say it is safe to believe him," Sheena offered with sorrow in her voice. "And Worsi is right to worry. I don't advise entering those caves and hope you are not considering it. Dear, have you never heard of the In-Betweeners that dwell there?"

"I'm afraid I have no choice. I have to rescue my father!"

Worsi saw his chance to interject again. "Caroline, under no circumstances should you enter the caves. I know your father well and he would agree. Please, listen to me! The caves are bad enough on their own, but you are dealing with Tweeners that worked with Barbarians to carry off this hideous act. That makes things far worse."

He stared hard at Caroline, who stared back with steely eyes, clenched jaw, and her hand resting on the hilt of her sword. There would clearly be no backing down by her.

Worsi relented. "Very well. I can see you are determined to keep your own counsel and won't heed my advice, but at least listen to this - your only chance to survive is to go alone. I've heard stories, and they are few, of lone travelers that have lived to tell the tale of sojourning the Burmian Caves. Some say the Tweeners are unusually impressed by someone with the audacity to travel their lands alone, and have allowed some to pass through in weak moments - when they don't torture and kill them, that is."

Caroline shuddered but her mind was made up. Not only did her father need her, but her brothers were also depending on her. What choice did she have?

"Worsi and Sheena, I appreciate your honesty, but my father needs me, and my brothers and I need him. I have to try. I'm going through the caves as there is no other way."

Sheena nodded and put her arm across Worsi, who was preparing to object one more time. "Worsi, you've said your bit, and you're right, but this is her decision. If you don't allow her to make her own decisions now, then when will she? So that's enough. Chupwah, come here my son."

The still sheepish Sasquatch stood in front of his mother. "Son, I want you to walk with Caroline until you get to the entrance to the caves. You can carry her pack for her until you arrive. It'll gain back a little of the time your actions cost her.

"But understand, Chupwah, you cannot follow. Those In-Betweeners despise Sasquatches, though I don't know why. If you go in with her, she won't have any chance at all. Alone, well, you never know. Understand?"

"Yes, mother," the youngster nodded, his head still hanging low. He held out his arm to Caroline, who reluctantly handed her supplies over, not wanting assistance but wishing to avoid the argument that would likely ensue if she refused.

"I want to thank you both for your advice, and for bringing me down the hill and looking after me," she said.

"Of course," Sheena replied. "Oh, I don't like this, not one bit! You will be careful?"

Caroline nodded that she would be.

Sheena continued. "Keep your sword out in front of you at all times. Maybe one of them will come along and skewer themselves on it, the nasty things. Ugh." She shook her head in disgust.

"I will," Caroline said. To Caroline's surprise, Sheena embraced her with a powerful hug, nearly squeezing the air from her lungs. She was surprised by the pleasant woodsy smell of the creature, a hint of fresh pine needles, nothing at all like one would expect from a *Skunk* Ape.

"It has been an honor to finally meet Sasquatches, and I hope to meet you two again," Caroline said. Worsi gave her a pat on the back and Sheena smiled. With that, Caroline walked off with Chupwah beside her.

They journeyed for some time in silence. Caroline struggled to keep pace with the longer legs of the young Sasquatch, and they made good time. They kept the Corkscrew River to their right, following its meandering path to the Burmian Caves. Despite the frantic nature of the journey, Caroline found the sounds from the river peaceful, reminding her of the Great River back home.

Around the noon hour, with her legs aching and head throbbing, Caroline decided it would be a good time to rest. Chupwah, who was still going strong, and clearly had no need for a respite, simply shrugged and sat beside her. He had said little since they had left and Caroline hoped the break would give him opportunity to open up a bit.

But first she needed to eat, as she felt nauseous, likely an after effect from striking her head the night before. Once again, she munched quietly on an apple, and offered one to Chupwah, who eagerly accepted. He took the apple from her, polished it with the fur on his belly, and held it out, admiring the fruit.

"Amazing! Where do you find apples this time of year? Seems too early for them," he asked.

"They bring them up to Frogpond from down south, from Birdsong. They can grow things like that year-round down there," she replied.

"Is that so? We mainly stick to pine nuts and such this time of year. This is incredible." He turned the apple over and over in his hands, mesmerized, before taking the entire thing and stuffing it into his mouth, stem and all. CRUNCH! Just like that, the apple was gone. They sat silently while overlooking the river, resting with their arms on their knees.

Caroline watched him in amazement, still having difficulty coming to terms with the existence of these beings. "How come I've never seen any of you before? People used to say Skunk Apes were nothing but a myth - 'a figment of someone's imagination' is how they put it, I believe. Yet here you are."

"Yet here I am," Chupwah replied, taking another apple offered to him. "My father explained that it was better for us not to exist in man's world, as men would fear us and eventually try to destroy us, hunting us down and hanging our pelts on the wall as a trophy to their bravery. After all, few things are as brave as shooting at something from a quarter a mile away.

"We're mostly a peaceful people with no desire for warfare, yet men would fear our strength and desire to get rid of us, the same way they did to the dragons. So we have always kept our distance, with a few exceptions, like your father. Won't find any men around here, though. It's unlikely anyway, or father wouldn't let me be seen like this."

"I see," Caroline replied. "My father always said Sasquatches existed, but he never told me how he knew."

Chupwah nodded. "My people know Eston well. In fact, Father belongs to a group with yours - the *Watchtower*, they call it. They keep tabs on the Kings and such of the world - especially Maldazor. That's why we came so fast to help, as any member of the Watchtower would," he explained.

Caroline shook her head. There was so much she did not know about her father. She wished she knew more, but there were more pressing matters at hand. "What do you know about these Tweeners - do you really believe I'm better off going alone into the caves?"

"I don't know much, really. Never met any before nor anybody that has. All I really know is that they can see very little, relying primarily on their keen sense of smell and hearing. Not much point in being able to see when you live in a cave, I guess. As far as going alone, I have heard that before, but I'm not so sure. People say all kinds of crazy things that aren't true."

"I see. Well, I appreciate you coming along. It helps to have a little company right now." She looked up at the sky and noted the movement of the sun. As time was always moving, so should they. "We better get going. I want to make it there while the sun is still shining." She lifted herself from the ground and started walking again with Chupwah back at her side. Caroline was growing more comfortable with her new friend and wanted to know all about him and his mysterious race.

"Chupwah, about last night – when I saw you in the woods I smelled something awful. Like a skunk, only worse. What was that? Some people call you Skunk Apes, yet you seem to smell fine to me. So what was that?"

Chupwah chuckled. "Yeah, it was me. We can control that just like a skunk. Sorry about that. I don't know what I was thinking! When father said that we needed to keep you from the caves I thought he wanted me to frighten you. That is normally the way we keep people away, by scaring them. You know, you're the first human I've ever talked to!"

"Is that so? Well, I hope I live up to your expectations!"

*

It was late that afternoon when they neared the end of the navigable portion of the river. The river was beginning to shallow and would not have been able to carry a raft much longer, so Caroline quickened her step and looked for a sign of her father's conquerors.

It was not long before she found what she was looking. A raft heading down the river toward them, drifting aimlessly, caught in the river's current, with all manner of leaves and sticks stuck in its side, floating along at the will of the river.

"Chupwah, over there!" Caroline yelled breathlessly. "That has to be the Barbarian's raft. Has to be! We need to corral it and take a look."

Without hesitating, Chupwah surprised her by dropping the pack and supplies he'd been carrying. He backed up to make room, then sprinted as fast as he could and jumped; he seemed to grow wings from his back while soaring through the air. He must have flown 25 feet before crashing on to the raft. It nearly capsized from the creature's girth, with half of it dipping into the water - even a small Sasquatch is a massive animal. Chupwah found an oar on deck and steered the raft to shore, where Caroline eagerly awaited its arrival.

"That was some jump!" she shouted. "Incredible."

"Well, these long legs are good for something," he replied modestly. He gave one last pull of the oar through the water and let the ship coast to the banks.

Caroline scrambled aboard and looked the raft over, hoping for some sign of her father. It was an eerie feeling to stand where she was certain he had just been that same day. She scoured the raft, unsure of what she was looking for but hoping for anything that could provide a clue.

And then she saw it - exactly the sign she had been searching for. It was a book, with *Akari the Dragon Lover* written on its face, the book her father was bringing back to her, as promised. It was all she could do to choke back the tears threatening to roll down her cheeks.

"Wait," she mumbled to herself. "Dragon Lover? What does that mean? I thought he was Akari the Dragonslayer." She flipped through the pages, most of which were torn and tattered, likely by the Barbarians. She skipped to the end and read the final page out loud.

*"And so the warrior known as Akari the Dragonslayer, the Chief Knight of the Ambrosian Army, who had been bewitched by the dragon Gorg, was now killed by a dragon. The great warrior had mistakenly believed that man and dragon could co-exist, a mistake he regretted when such a dragon blew a horrible fire and sent Akari up in flames."*

Caroline slammed the book shut with the page only half read, not wishing to continue. She had never heard this version of her uncle's death - she was told he had died in a war with Barbarians who had invaded from the South. Strange. She took the book and stuffed it into her pack.

"My father *was* on this raft, Chupwah. He told me he was going to bring back that book about my uncle Akari." Again she held back tears and kept her composure, although she could not shake the sick feeling that had resided in her stomach since her father was taken by such monsters.

"Is everything OK?" Chupwah asked.

"Yeah, I'm fine." Caroline bit her lower lip and focused again on the mission. She reminded herself that it was a good thing she discovered the book. They were on the right track, just as Matthias had told them.

"How far away from the caves are we now?" she asked Chupwah.

"About an hour or so, I think. We're close," he responded.

They searched the rest of the raft, but found no clues of value. On the bright side, there was no blood or any other sign that her father had been harmed.

After a brief rest, they began moving again. Caroline relished the waning moments of their journey, fearful they could be her last above the surface. She felt the sun shining down on her face and drank in the breeze that carried all the earthy smells of the forest. If she truly was heading to her death, then it would be a noble way to die. She believed it was better to die a warrior's death then live as a warrior's wife, which could hardly be called living at all.

In what felt like no time at all, they were at the entrance to the Burmian Caves. It was hard to miss with it's large, wide opening at the base of the mountain. Caroline could feel the cool air blowing out from the cave along with a queer smell that she figured was from either the Tweeners, hordes of bats, or both.

She stopped in front of the entrance, knowing that it was now time to say good-bye to her new friend. She felt as if she barely knew him, and she wanted to know him so much better, but there was no chance now for that to happen.

"Chupwah, I appreciate you coming along with me. It's time for me go on my own." Much to Caroline's surprise a small tear fell from the Sasquatch's right eye, leaving her touched, yet slightly amused. She stood on her tippy-toes and stretched to wipe the tear from his face.

"It's OK, Chupwah. I will survive, one way or another," she said with a confidence she did not feel inside. Chupwah sniffled and nodded back, too overcome with emotion to speak. With words failing, he reached out and gave Caroline a big hug, similar to the one his mother gave her earlier.

"I'll be all right, buddy." She tousled his hair and gave him one last squeeze. "Thanks again for coming along. Maybe we'll meet another time?"

"I hope so. Are you sure you need to leave tonight? Maybe it can wait until morning?"

"No, I need to keep moving." She shook his giant paw, took her pack, and removed a candle. She bent down to light a fire using two twigs and a rock, but before she could finish, Chupwah bent down and quickly rubbed the sticks together with his brute strength. He had a nice flame going in no time, which was easily transferred to the candle.

Caroline chuckled. "You are something else. Thanks, Chupwah. Until we meet again!" She turned, raised her hand in the air with a wave, her candle flickering in the other, and followed the path that led to the Burmian Caves.

Chupwah watched silently, fighting the urge to follow. It didn't feel right to stay back and let a young human girl head to her doom - especially a young girl like *that*, with so much courage and fearlessness. Chupwah felt helpless, knowing that he was ordered to stay behind. Yet he did not feel comfortable walking back to his family already. No harm in waiting back in the trees by the entrance, he thought.

For her part, Caroline fought the urge to turn and run, belying the courage that Chupwah saw in her. But the sign of true courage is facing down such fear. After all, if she was not afraid, what bravery would be needed?

This was her mission. Was it her Fate? She was unsure of what Fate meant anymore. It seemed to Caroline that Fate was simply what some old wizard, who did not know a thing about her, told her she would be. But in her heart, she knew that she could be the master of her own Fate. After all, it was Caroline's choice to go rescue her father, and it was Caroline that would suffer the consequences if she failed. Not some wizard.

Caroline embraced her freedom, her choice, and entered the Burmian Caves with the candle's flicker barely lighting the way. Fate or not, she was determined to try to rescue her father, or face the consequences of failure, whatever they may be.

Chupwah watched as she disappeared into the blackness, mulling over what his next move would be. But there was nothing he could do, so he turned to begin the walk back, leaving Caroline on her own, though it troubled him to do so. His head hung low as he kicked at stray rocks. Everything about this felt wrong.

But did he have any other choice?

# Chapter Eight - Into the Horizon

Akari never imagined that one day he would have to oppose the Army of Ambrosia. Yet here he was, with royal guards closing in on him, brandishing swords, ready to take him dead or alive.

The first to reach him were two he did not know well. With no time to think, he acted instinctively. He unsheathed his sword and raised it in defense. The first guard, a fresh Army recruit, came at him with his sword swinging. Akari parried the strikes, knocking the sword away. Shoving the guard aside, he ran to meet his next combatant, an older guard named Victor. He was just as easily dealt with – their blades crossed, and Akari, with the raw strength that had never abandoned him, knocked Victor's sword free and sent it flying. The force sent Victor sprawling head over heels onto the King's table.

From there, Akari considered his next move, but was distracted by the screaming Princess. Her shrill voice hammered into his brain; it was all he could do to ignore her.

The path was clear to the door, but he had to move fast as 10 guards prepared to respond. Not even Akari could handle that many foes - at least, not without having to kill someone, which he didn't want to do.

He wasted no time and sprinted by them, running as fast as he could. He raced through the throne room and out the door, taking him into a long corridor, which ended with a curving stairwell that would lead out of the castle and into the courtyard.

From there Akari could run to the stables and then, well, then he would have some quick explaining to do if he was going to make it out alive, let alone go to the aid of his kin. If all went well, he would not be the only one shedding a disguise, and once *those* disguises were removed, it would shake the Kingdom far worse than even the death of their King.

Chaos broke out in the throne room after Akari's hasty exit. Some guards ran to offer the King assistance while others simply stood frozen in place. Only a few brave warriors dared to chase after Akari. Although they snapped at his heels, Akari eluded them and was pleased to find after all his time wasted as a guard, he could still move like few others. Unable to catch the superior runner, the guards let their voices do the chasing.

"Stop him! Stop Akari! Murderer! Traitor! The King is dead!" they yelled, a cascade of voices. The speech was garbled together, yet the message was clear to all who heard - *Akari* had murdered the King. It was unthinkable. Staggering. But they must do their duty and capture him.

Meanwhile, the Princess had fallen to the floor, raving like a madwoman. "Why is he leaving me? Akari, come back! Come back!" she yelled as he ran away.

Throughout the castle, other voices rang out and guards sprang to action. From all directions, they made their way toward the throne-room.

Akari dashed through the corridor without incident and arrived at the door to freedom. He opened the large wooden door and was greeted by the sounds of heavy footsteps rising up the stairs. Someone was preparing to block his path - but Akari was not going to let them.

A young soldier's head bobbed up over the winding stairwell as Akari climbed down. Akari knew the face but was unsure of his name. It mattered not. What mattered was that he was in his way. He had no desire for blood on his hands, but they were sure making it tough.

The wiry soldier was tall, standing a few inches over Akari. He was clad in chain mail but wore no helmet - it was a time of peace and such costume was not required.

The young man, named Jaret, knew Akari's reputation well, aware of his history as one of the greatest warriors of Ambrosia. The conqueror of the dragons, the savior of King Renwick, a Chief Knight - it was all Jaret could do to stop his knees from knocking together as he moved to oppose him. Jaret fought the urge to run -- but not wanting to be labeled a coward, he was prepared to give it his all.

"Sir, please, um, please drop your weapon and surrender peacefully," Jaret stammered.

Akari's response was fierce and grim. "Move," he snarled. "I don't want to hurt you, but I will."

Jaret's clumsy response was to draw his sword from a metal scabbard, the metal on metal sound tingling in Akari's ears. Akari seldom thought during such situations - it was all reaction. In a situation like this, thinking too much could get you killed.

Jaret saw that Akari was coming fast and they would soon engage in combat. Sweat beaded heavily on his forehead even though a single blow had yet to take place.

The guards above stood atop the staircase and yelled at Akari below, who ignored it as he came upon the young soldier. Jaret slashed at Akari's feet to undercut the older warrior, but Akari avoided the strike. Gritting his teeth, he used the butt of his sword's hilt to strike Jaret in the jaw, jacking him hard and knocking him unconscious. Jaret fell back, but before he could tumble down the stairs, Akari caught him in his arms and gently laid him down. The fallen soldier would likely have a nasty headache when he awoke, and maybe some loosened teeth, but he'd be alive.

Akari looked back at those who pursued him and grimaced; he had no desire to become a fugitive, resorting to the life of an outlaw to survive. But he saw no other future, as the guards were yelling things like "He has killed Wilhelm! Capture him!"

The frustration boiled over and his head throbbed. He didn't kill the King, but it was obvious why they thought he had. After all, he was fleeing the scene of the crime. But there was nothing he could do; he'd worry about that later. What mattered now was that he had to rescue Jonas.

He charged downstairs and found yet another young soldier positioned at the bottom. Why were all of these youngsters on duty today, Akari wondered? But it was a lucky break for Akari on a day in short supply of those.

The guard drew his sword and set his jaw as he prepared for combat. Akari sighed. He didn't have time for this, so he moved fast yet again, swinging his sword at the guard, knowing full well he would easily parry the strike. As expected the young soldier did so, but Akari was ready, and as soon as their swords were joined, he kicked him in the shin. It was a cheap shot, but he was little concerned with chivalry at this time. The kick stunned the young man, distracting him enough for Akari to swing his sword around, turn, and this time use his weapon's handle to strike the young man on the back of his head. Another knockout. He fell in a heap, and Akari carefully leaped over his crumpled body, racing down a small corridor toward the door that would take him out of the castle.

Akari shot out into a vast courtyard into a bright sunny day.

He ran across the courtyard, finding it filled with horses and carriages as people shopped at the farmer's market. Booths were filled with fruits and vegetables. Vendors hocked their wares. Kindly old women sold flowers. The traffic would serve Akari well in evading his pursuers. The crowd would slow them down, giving him a better chance to get away.

He finally broke free from the mass of people and ran as fast as he could to the stables. He burst through an open gate, kicking up loose hay as he ran by, waking a young boy who took care of the horses, but had fallen asleep on a bale of hay. Akari darted to the back of the stable to a large stall that housed his three horses, unlatched the door, and sprang inside.

He was surprised to find the horses sleeping soundly. The tan one he called Tod was laying on its side, so deep in sleep that it almost appeared to be dead, a rather unnerving sight. Its flowing golden mane covered its eyes and its legs were sprawled out awkwardly. The other horses, Grayson and Drake, were asleep on their feet.

Akari whistled sharply. Tod jumped to his feet while the others shook the sleep from their eyes.

"Boys, I'm afraid our situation has changed and I won't be of further use as a spy. My cover is blown, as you can see." He held his arms out wide with his hands pointed upwards, shrugging his shoulders with a smirk, allowing the horses to take in his visage as Akari rather than Amaru.

"There's a lot to tell so I'll make it quick. The King is dead - poisoned. I did what I could to save him, but it was powerful stuff. There's more. Much more. Seems to be all kinds of trouble today, as my nephew is in some kind of danger."

The horses stood impassively, as Akari continued. "How do I know, you may wonder? It seems my sister intended that I live up to my oath." He pointed to his head, which still throbbed in pain, as if that explained everything. "I should have figured as much. In short, we must rescue him."

The horses looked at each other as if they understood. Akari was pleased.

"Yes, that's right! Time to reveal your true selves to the people of Ambrosia. I know the consequences, and the Council won't be happy - but they never are, are they? My nephew is in dire need. This I am sure of, and we won't make it in time on horseback, will we?" The horses nodded their heads up and down, seemingly agreeing.

Akari bent over and reached for a bag stored under a bench, slipping it over his back. Dust fell from the bag as it had been stashed away for some time, but he knew the contents well. In fact, he knew them all too well, for it was his getaway bag.

The horses stamped their feet and lined up, ready to leave the stable. "It is time, nags," Akari teased. The horses' eyes bulged, perhaps taken aback by the insult, but again nodded their understanding. Tod galloped toward Akari, who pulled a saddle from the stable wall and flung it over the horse's back. But Tod promptly shook it off and neighed with an annoyed tone.

Akari could not resist laughing at himself. "That's right! Forgive me, Tod. I suppose a saddle won't be of much use shortly, will it?" So saying, he climbed aboard bareback, pulling himself up with grace. Once seated, he briefly paused to look them all in the eyes.

"Boys, I'm taking you home as I know the Council will want, but first, we must rescue my kin. They need me. The day we feared is now here." Akari mumbled a few words, and the horses kind of shuddered in the way that one does when they taste something bitter when they expected sweet. With that done, Akari dug his heels into Tod's ribs and the horses emerged from their stall.

But escape would not be easy. Even though it was a straight route from the stable to the exit, the exit was blocked by two soldiers clad in armor from head to toe. The silver finish on their Knight's costume sparkled in the sunlight that shone through the doors, contrasting brightly to the relative darkness of the stables. Akari desperately tried to think of a way out of the jam. Again, he did not want to kill them, but they were sure making it tough to let them live. He sighed deeply, looking for anything of use - and found exactly what he needed. Perfect! Next to the stable, some construction work had been under way and there just so happened to be a long wooden pole leaning against the wall. Tod trotted over to allow Akari to grab it, and so doing he gave a slight kick to the horse's ribs. He was ready.

"All right, CHARGE!" he yelled, to which they snorted their assent.

The horses thundered away and came to a sprint, with Akari maneuvering the pole to a jousting position in front of Tod. They bore down on the two Knights, who Akari noted were Knights Sanwell and Zarken. He didn't particularly care for either of them, as they were arrogant and vain, which made what was coming for them a bit easier to do. In fact, it was a lot easier. He grasped the horse's mane with one hand and held the pole with the other as the horses charged at full speed.

The makeshift joust hit Sanwell full on in the chest with the clang of wood on steel echoing throughout the stables. The force threw Sanwell from the stable and out the door. Before Knight Zarken could react, Akari swung the pole around and hit the Knight from behind, knocking him down face first. The stable boy woke up to watch was happening in wonder. What a story he would have for his friends tonight.

"Should've brought your lances, boys! Woo!" Akari yelled as he exited the stable. He was enjoying himself a bit too much, but those Knights really did rub him the wrong way and it had been so long since he had felt this kind of adrenaline.

They came through the gate with the sun shining on them, which lent them a triumphant aura. The horses galloped determinedly through town as they prepared for their next move.

Onlookers would swear in retelling the experience that the horses had a distinctly reptilian appearance about them, and some would go so far as to claim they actually had scales. And they were right, as little did they know that moments earlier Akari had undone a spell, a powerful one that had kept hidden in plain sight something that would stun the King in the same way he had concealed himself as Amaru.

Though they escaped the stable, more guards could be heard coming from another corner of the courtyard. These guards, arriving on horseback, were eager to make a name for themselves by battling one such as Akari. It was time for Akari to make his final move

The horses narrowly dashed through the castle gate before it shut. Unfortunately, they were now headed into a group of forces from the surrounding village. It appeared a great many more were eager to make their name fighting against the legendary warrior Akari. In no time at all, Akari and the horses were surrounded on every side except the one that led to the Great Falls. Falling from such a cliff would mean likely death.

Nonetheless, that was the path they took. The horses' hoofs kicked up clouds of dirt as they thundered down the path, heading closer to the edge. The villagers watched in amazement - the horses weren't slowing down; in fact, they were moving faster. They raced to the end of the path and kept going, disappearing over the edge, horses and rider together, a mass of legs and hair and tails, with the thunderous noise of their hooves turning to silence as their legs left earth and flew into the air.

Many onlookers gasped while others screamed. Some cried, sickened to see a man act in such a way. What would drive Akari to fight so hard for his life only to go plunging over the edge with the horses? All around people looked at each other, slack-jawed, mouths moving but no words passing through their lips. Finally, an older man who had watched it all said what many were thinking.

"Bewitched, he was," said the onlooker.

"Cracked, more like it," added another.

One by one, the villagers began to walk slowly toward the ledge, afraid of what they would discover below. Many resisted the impulse to look. But most did, unable to resist their curiosity regardless of what they might see.

The boldest of the group, an old retired soldier named Lucroy, was the first to the edge. He cautiously leaned over, as if afraid that the madness that had overtaken Akari would pull him over as well. As he peered below, Lucroy jumped back, and immediately turned to run as fast as his ancient legs would carry him. Others who had followed him had the same reaction, taking flight as soon as they looked over the edge. Before anyone had time to question why they were running, Lucroy yelled out: "DRAGONS! RUN! RUN FOR YOUR LIFE!"

It was inconceivable. If it had not been for the terror in his voice, no one would have believed him. Dragons had not been seen on the mainland for a generation. Sure, there had been rumors and unconfirmed sightings, but the reports typically came from someone thought to be a lunatic who lived miles and miles away with no one able to corroborate the story. Dragons simply no longer existed in Ambrosia. They were made extinct during the Last Dragon War by Akari Dragonslayer.

The idea was so preposterous that some of those running stopped, deciding that they would take a look for themselves, figuring they could make a laughingstock of the others. But as they turned to head back to the cliff, the doubters were stunned to see three shapes rising above the edge, confirming the panic that had befallen the others. Indeed, they were dragons. Horrific, terrifying, awful fire-breathing dragons! Their reptilian wings flapped in the air, whipping up breezes that tossed the branches of trees. Steam poured from their nostrils, and their terrifying teeth protruded from their green bodies. It was a hideous sight to behold and the crowd reacted in terror, screaming and lamenting. Some were so consumed by hysteria that they had convulsions; others fainted and dropped to the ground. A few raised the blades of their swords, as if such a weapon could do the slightest harm to a dragon. A few brave souls notched arrows on bows and fired, but the arrows bounced harmlessly off the armored scales.

The more observant people in the crowd noticed Akari riding on the back of one of the dragons. But most in the crowd were so scared they focused only on the winged creatures, not on who was riding one. Of course, later, everyone who was there claimed they saw Akari. Some even claimed they saw Akari breathing fire. In fact, they insisted that they did, and refused to change a word of their story.

Before much else could be gleaned from the dragons, their wings flapped loudly, kicking up waves of dust, and they shot high into the sky. Against a background of puffy white clouds, their dark green outlines were visible to all as they scattered and flew off into the west, three terrible masses that melted into the horizon.

## Chapter Nine - Blinded By the Light

The light from the candle in Caroline's hand reflected on the low-hanging ceilings and walls of the cave, creating shadows that unleashed a thousand terrors in her mind. With every step, she imagined In-Betweeners lurking just out of sight in the shadows, made worse by the knowledge that she really had no idea what a Tweener looked like. Her head was full of awful thoughts. For all she knew, they could be standing all around her, as the narrow light cast by the candle did not create a sense of security.

Again and again she desperately fought the urge to turn back and run. Only the thought of her father out there with those Barbarians drove her forward. She had made the mistake of looking behind her, as she was still able to faintly make out the soft glow of sunlight from the cave entrance. And now, she was filled with a foreboding feeling that she might never see sunlight again.

But she pushed on, going at a slow pace, taking great care to watch each step to avoid falling in a pit. The floor of the cave was difficult to navigate. It was uneven and filled with holes of undetermined depth. Her arms were also getting tired, as she shifted her sword from arm to arm to keep it ready as the Sasquatches had advised.

Once again, she rued that adventures were in no way as easy as they appeared in books.

Gradually, the path began to decline. It was quite steep, which made it difficult to move along at a slow pace. The slope was so steep her knees ached from her effort to maintain control.

An eerie quiet surrounded her, the only sounds being her footsteps and her breathing, which was hampered by the stifling air. Every noise she made brought new fears that the In-Betweeners would hear her and would rush to attack.

She came to the end of the pathway and could feel the flow of the air change around her. It was less stale and stifling. The candlelight revealed that the narrow tunnel had widened into a large cavern. It was difficult to tell exactly how large it was in the low light. But it felt enormous and it gave her an odd sensation to look up. She did, but could see no ceiling -- just complete and total blackness.

Caroline stood in the entryway and contemplated her next move. The best route seemed to be to use the wall as a guide until it branched off into another tunnel. So she inched along by playing her knuckles along the wall and decided to follow the edge wherever it led. She was basically traveling blindly, and the chance of succeeding in her mission never seemed less likely. But she carried on.

Caroline thought about the creatures that lived in these parts and began preparing for an inevitable encounter with them. Chupwah had warned her that the creatures relied almost solely on their keen senses of hearing and smell, but especially smell. This was no good, as it had been days since her last proper washing and she felt filthy. She could only imagine how she smelled! If Tweeners really could smell that well, then they probably knew she was on her way before even taking her first steps inside. Again she longed for a hot shower, but would even settle for a brisk cold bath.

She removed another candle from her pocket as the other was reaching its end. Her hand was coated in wax, adding to her dirty feeling. She lit the new with the flame of the old and cast the dying remains of the old one aside. It landed with a dull thud, as if it hit something fleshy and not rocky. She whirled around, shining the light against the wall - but nothing was there, or if there had been, it was long gone.

Caroline panted as if she had just finished a long run and scolded herself for letting her imagination run wild, although it never occurred to her that the piece of candle thrown aside was nowhere to be found either.

So she regained her composure and could not help but think of the adventures of Akari she had read about. He too had once been trapped in a cave with minimal light, only it had been a cave inhabited by dragons. If Akari could make it through *that*, she could certainly deal with a few

Tweeners. That was the motivation she needed and she picked her pace up.

But she still stepped gingerly, which proved a wise course as the candlelight revealed a sizable hole in her path. She held the candle down the chasm, searching for the bottom but not finding it. What a fall that would be. She exhaled, thankful she had played things safe. But there remained the little matter of getting around it.

Her options were limited. To get by, she had to either shuffle along a narrow ledge beside the pit or risk venturing out into the cavern without the wall to guide her. Caroline chose the ledge.

She leaned with her back against the wall and shimmied, shuffling bit by bit. With her head hanging over the hole, she took one last peek, curious to see if now she could find a bottom. So again the light reached into the chasm as Caroline leaned ever so slightly for a closer look - and screamed!

The light revealed a vile face, one of the ugliest things she had ever laid eyes on, and worse, it belonged to a body that was lunging for her! It was a Tweener - had to be.

The creature had bulbous eyes that housed large black pupils, so large that none could ever claim to have seen the whites of a Tweener's eyes. Its nose was all nostril with teeth jagged and sharp, skin as pale as a fish belly, and a plain costume of dark cloth covering its body. Strangest of all, a thin appendage grew from its forehead, from which a small bit of light shined. It was a Tweener, no doubt.

Caroline ran, narrowly eluding the creature's grasp. She threw caution aside, tripping over loose rocks and holes in the uneven ground with no thought to where she was going, so long as she was going. The candle fell from her hands and flickered out, but even in the pitch black she pushed forward, desperate to avoid the cold, clammy grip that sought her.

Then Caroline barreled into something hard - something living. A Tweener. Unluckily, her sword just missed running it through. Their arms and feet tangled together as they collided and fell to the ground.

They struggled to their feet, trying to get an edge over the other. Caroline twisted and got behind the creature, wrapped an elbow around its neck and held it tight. With her free arm, she took the sword and held it to the Tweener's throat. The Tweener spat and tried to bite its way free, but

Caroline held strong, and lifted the surprisingly light creature off the ground while pressing the sword firmly against its throat.

"Listen to me!" she shouted. "I have no quarrel with you. Show me the way out and no harm will fall on you!" But the creature's only response was to continue to bite and scratch.

Unfortunately, the noise brought company, and from all around Caroline, whispery voices talked amongst themselves in an eerie language she did not understand. The effect was chilling. She gulped, well aware she was completely surrounded - front, back, on all sides. Still, she would not surrender easily.

"Do you hear me? What say you?" She yelled at the snarling creature, choking as she caught a whiff of its hot, stinky breath. She wondered if their sense of smell was as honed as rumors indicated, and if so, how was it they were able to stand each other?

The creature finally answered in a high-pitched, slimy voice, though thankfully in words she could understand and not the language used by the others.

"It won't do any good to kill me, and if you do, you'll be dead before my body hits the floor. Let me go, and maybe we'll do the same for you."

"That's a likely story," she said.

Caroline moved in a circle, holding the captive while searching the darkness for a way out, but it was no good. It was simply too dark. But maybe she could use the Tweener's lights to her own advantage?

She cleared her throat and shouted. "I don't believe that I'm surrounded. It's likely a trick played on my ears by the echoes of this cavern. I'd bet there are only three or four of you Tweeners, and a hundred echoes."

As soon as Caroline used the word Tweener a symphony of voices responded back in voices equally as high-pitched and slimy as the one Caroline held captive. "Tweeners?!? Tweeners?!?" The sound echoed back and forth from wall to wall, traveling throughout the large cavern

The symphony of voices ceased when one voice carrying an authoritative tone spoke loudest of all, in a deeper tone than what seemed to pass as normal among them.

"We are not Tweeners, Earth dweller. We are the people of the core, driven so close to the wretched surface through the evil of others. The word Tweener is a grave insult and I warn you not to use it again."

"I don't mean to offend." Caroline responded. "Nonetheless, I am convinced there are no more than a handful of you. You are capable of revealing yourself and cutting through this darkness, so prove me wrong!"

Again the voices rang out and surrounded her in the tongue she could not decipher until the deep-voiced one quieted them. A few voices responded back, sounding upset, but again they were shouted down. This went on for some time while Caroline waited anxiously for the argument to end.

Finally the voices ceased. "So be it, earth dweller!" the deep voice exclaimed. "Behold the Core-People!"

Instantly a chain of lights began to form, one by one, traveling in a row. It began on Caroline's left and moved through the cavern, heading to her right, moving up and down depending on where the Tweener was positioned. In no time, the entire cavern was filled with small lights that dangled in front of the Tweener's foreheads.

Caroline was awed. It was truly mesmerizing. But there was no time to admire it, and she used the light to gather her bearings, trying to find an escape route. And there it was, just ahead, with only one of the creatures in her way.

As quickly as they appeared, one by one the lights went out, and whether they were deliberately putting them out or if they could only stay on for a short time, Caroline did not know.

The creature in her grasp had stopped struggling by this time, utterly exhausted by its efforts. The Tweener was surprisingly light and easy for Caroline to out-muscle and grapple with, despite some legends that said they stood ten-feet tall. Not even close. She knew she could handle them physically - that was the least of her worries. One on one, with light to guide her, there was nothing to fear, as their advantage lie in their ability to navigate the caves, and in their great numbers, not in their individual abilities.

But just before she made her escape, the Tweener in her arms started sniffing, inhaling deeply before speaking.

"Well," it said, drawing the word out slowly. "You don't stink like those three Barbarians that came through here a while ago. Nasty, nasty things. Awful!"

Caroline's heart rate rose, hoping more would be revealed. As the cavern darkened Caroline was torn. Should she between make a dash for it, or hear what else this *thing* had to say?

There was no choice. She had to confirm her father was with the Barbarians, and to her great relief the creature quickly answered her unsaid question.

"Hmm, you smell..." It paused, thinking. "Yes, that's it! You smell like that other one! He smelled nothing like those Barbarians, no. Smelled rather nice, not like those other stinkers!"

"That other one - the, err, non-stinker. Was he safe? Was he harmed?" Her tone was desperate and she was so caught up in conversation that she failed to notice the cavern had gone dark. The Tweener answered back, speaking slowly to stall her.

"Harmed? No, not harmed, not harmed. Just tied up and led on a rope, that is all. Not harmed at all. Long gone now, left the caves a few hours ago, yes."

"Which way did they go, thing, or I will cut your throat!" Caroline threatened, panicking.

"So heartless," the Tweener responded. "But you will do nothing! Grab her!"

In a snap, Caroline felt the grip of many hands on her, taking her sword and prying free her captive. They pulled on her, grabbed at her, and ripped at her clothes and hair. Caroline broke free, heading to the general area of where she thought the exit was, holding her hands out in front of her to avoid crashing headfirst into a wall. It was slow going, to say the least, and terrifying.

Caroline crashed into Tweeners with every step, shoving them down to clear the way. They went down remarkably easy, but their numbers were too great and they soon overwhelmed her. Her hands were quickly bound behind her back. She was a captive of the dreaded Tweeners, terror filling her heart at the thought of what they might do to her. They would have no mercy on her now. She had completely and totally blown it.

The Tweeners surrounded her and took turns at sniffing her, an odd and disturbing feeling. It reminded her of going to a neighbor's home and being greeted by an aggressive dog, only multiplied by a hundred. These Tweeners relied on their keen sense of smell much more than Caroline had imagined. Yuck, Caroline thought, squirming with utter repulsion.

She struggled at her coarse bonds but only managed to rub her wrists raw. The same terrible thought kept going through her head – that Matthias was right. Following after her father was a terrible idea, after all. She should have been with her brothers seeking aid from Ambrosia City, not off on a fool's mission that had failed miserably. It was all she could do not to cry.

The deep voice spoke sternly in the language she did not understand and Caroline could no longer hold back the tears, which flowed freely as she lost all hope for escape.

# Chapter Ten - A Promise Fulfilled

*T**he shadow of the three dragons passed over the Kingdom of Ambrosia, leaving panic and terror in their wake. Villagers across the land fled home to bring down dust-covered shields and swords from walls on which they had been ceremoniously hung years, even decades before.*

*In the country, shepherds tending sheep and cattle saw the serpentine shadows and ran into the woods, hoping that if the monstrous creatures were craving a snack, they'd go for the easy pickings of livestock and avoid the animals' keepers. Farmers in the field hurried to hide behind bales of hay or tried to conceal themselves among cornstalks not yet tall enough to conceal a rabbit.*

*In the span of an hour, fear consumed the people and the entire world had gone cataclysmic. The King was dead, the country was under attack, and that scoundrel Akari Dragon Lover had not only returned from the dead, but returned to forsake his own people for the love of fell beasts.*

*Dragons were known for wanton destruction, but these three seemed to have something far more sinister planned than mindless terror. They passed over their usual targets. They left the livestock untouched. They flew over the villages. They even ignored the goldmine, leaving its treasure intact. They flew straight and true over the Great River, seemingly focused on a specific destination. Were they out for revenge against a certain enemy? Did they seek a specific town to destroy? What thoughts could be passing through these monsters' minds? Even the wizards of the hills were baffled - for once, the Fate of the land was a complete and total mystery. And the question that arose from most Ambrosians was simple.*

*Who would save the kingdom?*

If they weren't terrified beyond understanding, Mouse and Jonas would have been awestruck by the dragons that were flying toward them. Their wings stretched out nearly as wide as the river they soared over, and the breeze they created was so powerful that waves formed and crashed violently on the banks, spilling over the sides. Their sharp teeth glistened in the sunlight, drawing even more attention to their ferocity. Worst of all were their eyes, black and dead, promising nothing but evil and ill times.

Jonas and Mouse strained against their bonds, rubbing their wrists raw with the effort to no avail. The Barbarians had done their work well. Worse, the dragons were nearly upon them.

With no ropes to hold them, the Barbarians fled, racing off as fast as they could. They would have had a better chance if they had jumped into the river and let it carry them off, as it is often said that dragons fear large bodies of water, but Barbarians were ignorant of such matters.

As fast as they ran, it was of no use. The two riderless dragons swept down with claws extended and stole the Barbarians from the ground, like an eagle plucking a fish from a pond. They roared viciously, while the other dragon, which held a rider, hovered above. It looked on while the swarthy Barbarians let out high-pitched screams, a surprising sound from such gruff characters. The dragons landed on the ground with their hind legs, each holding a Barbarian in their grasp.

Mouse and Jonas watched with fearful eyes, hoping somehow to be spared the fate that befell their captors. But they too soon felt the shadow of the other dragon upon them, growing larger and larger as it hovered lower and lower, before it dropped from the sky and landed directly in front of them, the shadow replaced by the dragon itself. Mouse clamped his eyes shut, too stricken with panic to even look at the beast and rider.

For a moment, the dragon and rider simply stared upon them with their cold eyes. Jonas matched their gaze, and though terrified, refused to back down.

"Whoever you are, loosen these bonds and meet me in one on one combat, if you dare to leave your perch! You'll find me a tougher match than either of those Barbarians, I assure you!"

In response to this bold threat, the rider dismounted, swinging down from a height of ten feet or so. He landed smoothly in a crouch, stood up, and walked toward the boys, his dark face barely visible from underneath the cloak pulled low over his head. Curiously, he wore the armor of the Ambrosian Army. Mouse finally opened his eyes and peeked. Seeing the dragon directly in front of them, he fainted, nearly pulling Jonas down with him.

The man watched Mouse fall before responding. "I imagine you would be much tougher of a match, as you say, than a Barbarian, young Jonas."

Jonas started at the sound of his name, wondering how the man could know.

"And I admire your gallantry in the face of such terror, although there is something to be said for your friend's response. Playing dead in front of a large predator such as a dragon can often be a successful tactic, though I haven't tried it myself." The man stopped and turned toward the dragon. "Would that work on you, Tod?"

The dragon shook its head, indicating that no, it would not work. "Kind of what I figured. Still, there's *logic* behind it. I saw a man do it with a bear, once. Or maybe a bear did it with a man - I disremember."

Mouse quickly came to and chanced a look at the dragons that had captured the Barbarians. He shuddered. It appeared they were toying with their prisoners in the same manner a cat might bat at a piece of string. Mouse cringed, vowing to make a break for the river if he had chance to do so. He would rather take a chance of drowning than become a dragon's snack.

Mouse watched as the strange man walked over with his sword drawn. He cursed himself for even bothering to open his eyes, so he closed them anew and winced, bracing for the final blow. What an awful way to die, Mouse thought. Then again, he supposed it was better than being eaten alive, although he realized he did not exactly relish being a cold lunch any more than being a warm one.

He could somehow feel the man raise his sword in the sky and prepared for the death blow - but it never arrived. Instead, Mouse was stunned to feel the ropes that bound him being loosened and his arms freed as the bonds were cut away from his wrists. The rope fell to the ground in a harmless heap while his head remained firmly attached.

Mouse scrambled to his feet and without thinking, dashed to the river. He jumped in – SPLASH! – while the strange man simply stood and watched before chuckling lightly.

"Well, I've always said that Barbarians are no good in a situation that calls for brains, and there you have it. That boy has brains," he said.

"Tried to throw a dragon off by playing dead, and once that failed he didn't panic, oh no, he took the route that anyone with sense would take when fleeing a dragon, which is to head for water. Impressive boy, and you know, you'd almost think he was terrified out of his mind if you didn't know better."

It was unclear if he was speaking to the dragon, Jonas, or both, but he carried on as he approached Jonas and sliced through his bonds. "Now as for the Barbarians, I have no time for them. Imagine running away from a river when you have a fire-breathing dragon heading toward you. Shameful. Pure idiocy, but not surprising."

Jonas rubbed his arms, happy to be free, but chose not to follow his brother just yet, wishing to determine who this strange man was. For one, the man was dressed as a Knight of the Ambrosian Army. For another, he was not threatening them. Just because Mouse had gone into a complete panic and failed to think rationally did not mean he had to join him. And lastly, the man knew his name.

Jonas struggled to solve the riddle standing before him. There was something very, very strange, yet familiar, about him. Come to think of it, the strange man looked an awfully lot like paintings he had seen of Akari, especially one on the cover of Caroline's book. Of course, that was impossible - his uncle had been dead for years - but this certainly looked like the man in the paintings. A cousin, perhaps?

Better to cut to the chase, Jonas thought. "Who are you, and what do you want?"

The Knight held his sword up, indicating he had no intention of fighting. "I'm not here to hurt you. Relax."

Suddenly, Mouse could be heard shouting from afar and then took serious the idea of his brother drowning. "I don't know who you are, but if you're not here to kill us, then please help me - my brother can't swim well!" Jonas exclaimed. If the man helped, this would also verify his intentions.

The man looked at him with a puzzled expression on his face. "Here to kill you? Of course not. No, I'm here to save you."

"We don't need saving," Jonas replied.

"Yes, I can see that," he said, then used his sword to point to the ropes that had been cut away from Jonas' wrists, then the Barbarians who were still occupying the dragons, and lastly toward the river. "Yes, everything seems to be under control. As far as the little guy - maybe you should go get him. I'd hate to jump in, truth be told. Wet clothes are the worst - takes all day to dry out."

At this, the dragon sent a little bit of flame from his throat, demonstrating that a dragon could have its uses, such as drying clothes. But the effect was terrifying, and Jonas's jaw dropped.

"Wow," he said sheepishly. "Please, help him, whoever you are. I can't swim."

"No problem. Neither could your father. Never made much sense to me, a man as strong as that, but what can you do? Well, all right, I'll go get him."

"How do you know my father?"

"In due time. Right now, we better take care of your brother. He could've gone down the Great Falls by now, or drowned, if he hasn't learned how to put his feet down anyway."

"What do you mean?"

"Go see."

They went to the river bank and found that Mouse had not made it far. In fact, he was peering over the bank, standing in knee deep water and shivering.

The man chuckled. "Well, you didn't make it far! Did you decide dragons weren't so scary after all?" The man held out his hand, wishing to help the bewildered and silent Mouse from the water. Mouse extended his hand, reasoning that the man was not there to kill them after all, although he remained leery of his motivations.

With Mouse safely on shore and the Barbarians occupied, Jonas decided it was time for answers. "So who are you? And why are you helping us?"

"Well, one answer should suffice for both. I am your uncle, Akari," he said. "And it all comes clear now! You must be Mouse. It's nice to finally meet you, as I've heard so much about you."

He then stuck out his hand to Jonas, who ignored it and continued with his line of questioning. "My uncle? Are you crazy? He's been dead for years!"

"Ah, you're wrong there, through no fault of your own, Jonas. I shall explain, but let's tackle one question at a time. Am I crazy? Yes, most likely, but it helps me quite a bit with my work, and it's wonderfully freeing to be looked at as crazy - you can do just about anything so long as you don't actually hurt anyone and people will just say 'well, he's crazy, what did you expect?' So I rather value that reputation.

"Now to the other question. Do I look dead?" He held out his hands as if showing his flesh would set the matter to rest. "See? I do not look dead because I am not!"

Jonas and Mouse simply looked confused, so he continued. "Being dead and pretending to be dead are two different things, would you not agree?"

"Pretending to be dead? You are crazy! Why would anyone do that?" Jonas made no attempt to present himself as anything but annoyed.

"Perhaps it was a little out there. But when your enemies want you dead, it's remarkably effective. They're happy you're dead while I'm quite pleased to still be alive and only thought dead. It all works out rather nicely."

"Who would want you dead in Ambrosia?" Mouse asked. "You were a great hero - the Chief Knight of the Great Army!"

"Well, that was true, I suppose, but you try palling around with dragons and see what the King thinks about you. No, Wilhelm and Maldazor did not like that at all, seeing as dragons were our sworn enemies. But they could never fully prove that the stories of me associating with dragons were true either. As you say, I was a great hero, and it wouldn't do to imprison me - or worse - without any evidence.

"So they took another tact to be rid of me, which meant I was sent on a slew of suicide missions. Oh, it was terrible, but being me - a great hero, as you say - I made the mistake each time of coming back alive. I got to be rather tired of the whole thing. Going off to fight pirates or Barbarians with meager supplies and forces was a bother, let me tell you, and the way things were heading, they would be burying me on Cemetery Hill soon enough. Now you'd think they would have let me resign, but oh no, they couldn't have that!

"So I had my reasons, and I have my regrets to go along with them - deceiving my family was never easy - but I did what I had to do. On the whole I'm rather pleased it's all out in the open now."

"So why now? Why reveal yourself after all of this time?" Jonas asked.

"Well, when it comes to that, it was as much a shock to me as it probably was to you, but then again magic never ceases to amaze me so I suppose I should have expected it. I've studied it off and on my entire life and it seems I still don't know a thing about it. It's awfully frustrating!

"But your mother - my sister - she knew an awful lot about it. So let me put it simply, which is really the only way you should put anything if you want people to understand you. On the night your mother died, my sweet sister made me vow to always protect you - a sacred oath. And I did, as any brother would do for their sister, and lived up to it too, or so I thought. I won't get into the details now, but there's a reason that your father was able to retire as Chief Knight while every other one was carried away and dumped in a cold grave when their time was up.

"But as far as my vow, it turns out that I had little choice in the matter- I would carry it out the way Lizabell wanted me to, not the way I wanted. Well, that was her way. Stubborn, and always had to get the last word.

"Which is why I'm here. This very morning I was struck by a rather strange, painful feeling in my head, something that told me you were in serious trouble, Jonas, and I needed to rescue you. So once I rounded up the dragons, we decided to fly up river to your home and it just so happened we ran into you on our way. Very strange thing, magic. Soon as I made up my mind to come along, the pain was gone."

He felt his head as if confirming this. "Awful timing, though. Now everyone seems to think I killed the King!"

"Killed the King! Who killed the King?" Mouse exclaimed. "That's who we were on our way to see!"

"Well, you can still see him, but he won't be much for conversation. From what I know of royal custom, his funeral will take place in a week and anyone who wants can come along and say their good-byes. But what were you going to him for? And why are you out here by yourself anyway? Where's your father?"

"That's what we were coming to tell the King," Jonas replied. "Our father has been captured, Akari! We were going to warn the King that Barbarians were invading."

"So I noticed. But not these two anymore!" Akari thumbed at the two still in the grasp of the dragons. He chuckled softly before growing serious. "You say he was kidnapped? How? When? And where's your sister, for that matter?"

Jonas and Mouse both took turns explaining the situation while Akari listened in amazement. "This is incredible. And what a girl Caroline has turned out to be!

"But after all of these years old Maldazor has finally made his move. Has to be coming from him, there's no doubt. It's not nearly as clever as I would've expected from him - a Tweener blinded by the sun in broad daylight could see through this plan."

"Maldazor? What would he have to do with this?" Mouse asked.

"Well, nothing at all - besides everything! Many of us have expected it for years. Never did figure he'd be happy with just the Northern part of the kingdom no matter what his father had hoped, and I told him as much the night I saved his life. But you know how Kings can be. Once they decide to do a thing there's nothing to stop them. He thought his plan would keep his children happy. It was worth a try, I suppose, but skewering Maldazor would've been worth a try as well." He blinked, and then cracked his knuckles as he seemed to think a thousand thoughts at once.

"So you did save King Renwick's life! I thought that was just made up for your book!" Mouse said.

"Those dratted things. They're filled with the worst kinds of lies and rubbish. You were wise to doubt anything in them. Don't get me started on those things. They left out so much of import, and added in all this nonsense about me being hypnotized by dragons and this and that.

"But if they said I saved King Renwick, that's true, sure enough. I gave him another three years or so of life, which was enough time to divide up his kingdom, build a couple of castles and swap it all out between the children - for all the good it did. A waste of good potion. But enough of that. There will be plenty of time to talk. I'd like to see what's going on with these Barbarians. I suppose the dragons are rather tired of them."

Akari moved to do so before Jonas stopped him. "Not just yet. There's something I'd like to get straight," Jonas declared. "So you claim you took a vow to protect us - a vow to your own sister - yet your solution was to fake your death and hope never to be seen again? Some vow. We don't need your help. Come on, Mouse." He tugged on Mouse's sleeve but Mouse stood firm, wishing to hear more from their uncle.

"You've mentioned that, and yet if it wasn't for me there's no telling what the Barbarians would be doing to you right now. You seemed to have things right under control, no question. Well done," Akari responded eying the now helpless Barbarians, gone limp from fear in the arms of the great creatures. Jonas fumed while Akari continued.

"As far as my vow, nephew, I tried to avoid this, but here goes - on the night I saved King Renwick, I made a deal to relieve your father from his lifetime commitment as Chief Knight. Never done before in Ambrosian history. So when I made that deal I considered my vow fulfilled, and now that your father was home, he could protect you.

"As I said, the only way out of that job is through death. I feel no shame in admitting that I wanted out in the worst way - but there was no convincing Renwick or his idiot son Wilhelm. No, Wilhelm would rather I died in combat so that they could prop me up as some hero. This kingdom thrives on propping up heroes, whether they deserve it or not - and most don't.

"So I faked my death and gained my freedom. You say we've got Caroline off on a suicide mission and your father kidnapped by Barbarians. I would think you could use someone with my talents - and I say that with all humility."

"It makes sense to me, Jonas," offered Mouse. "But what do we do now? Should we warn the Princess?"

"Why bother when she already knows?" said Akari.

"How could she know?" Jonas shot back, growing ever more agitated.

"She's in on it with her uncle Maldazor," Akari replied, his expression grim. He viewed the skeptical expression worn by Jonas and continued. "Hear me out. The strangest thing happened after her father died - turns out the Princess was in love with me, and what's more, she believes she resurrected me, or played a part in it anyhow. All I can figure is she made some kind of deal with Maldazor, although don't ask me to offer any details.

"Now I was aware of her infatuation years ago as she certainly didn't hide it, but I don't hold much with Princesses - especially insane Princesses, though when I think about it I know of no other kind."

"You are crazy, Akari. She's beautiful," Jonas replied. "I saw her once when Father took us to Ambrosia City."

"She's an awful human being. Doesn't take much to see that, blinded by her beauty or not. She takes after her uncle and always has - thought she was a gift to the world and the rest of us should forever be grateful to simply bask in her presence. I never had any feelings for her and made it clear, but we need to move on, as the hour is late. Suffice to say I don't anticipate anyone will bother to come looking for dragons right now, especially not any of the so-called heroes who will find their swords rusted and boots rotted away. But I'd still feel better if we moved from the river before we bed down for the night."

He stopped, as his face made clear that he had forgotten something and had just remembered it. "First, there remains the little matter of these Barbarians. I noticed a raft down by the river when we flew over. Nice craft, and not in use. Why don't we tie them up and float them down the river - let the current determine their Fate."

He looked to the dragon, who nodded in agreement to Akari's plan.

Mouse, on the other hand, looked confused. "You mean the dragons aren't going to eat them?"

The dragon laughed, a rough sort of laugh that made their skin crawl. "Goodness no," the dragon Tod said, speaking for the first time in a powerful voice that seemed to vibrate through the earth. "Man flesh is no good, and besides, few have enough meat to take and bother with even if it was. It's all bone and sinew, bad for the digestion. I might take a nip of that King Wilhelm if it came down to a pinch - he was plenty fat! Might be worth bothering with if one had to, I suppose, but even that would be a last resort." The dragon laughed before continuing.

"By the way, since you don't seem keen on introducing yourself - guess you were raised without manners - my name is Todmadelynnatterat. I realize that's an awful lot to say, so most humans call me Tod. Well, the few that don't mind talking to a dragon, anyway. The darker one over there you can call Grayson, and the other one is Drake- I won't bother with *their* real names, for you'd never be able to pronounce them."

Mouse and Jonas simply stared. They had virtually forgotten the dragon was still present and were left with their mouths wide open.

"Awfully rude of you boys to stare, but I think we can forgive you this one time," Akari said, who then whistled in the direction of the other two dragons. "OK fellows, bring those miscreants here. You've had your fun with the rogues."

The dragons walked over and dropped both Barbarians as softly as they could at Akari's feet, though they still landed with a thud. They woke up from the hard landing and instantly pleaded with their captors in much different tones now that roles had been reversed.

"Please sir," one of them begged. "Don't let those things eat us. Please, I beg of you! But if they must eat, don't eat me! I'm a family man, see. My companion has nobody that cares for him, but I have a wife and kids back home."

"You do not, you lying piece of garbage," the other Barbarian replied, kicking his cohort in the ribs. They started fighting while lying on the ground, kicking and biting until Akari separated them.

"Hold them for a second while I tie these gentlemen up," Akari ordered the dragons, then bound them with some rope he kept in his bag.

"Awfully far south to come across some Barbarians. Who sent you?" The Barbarians said nothing, but Akari continued. "If you tell me, I might consider letting you go."

That was all they needed to hear. They both shouted over the other before Akari even finished speaking, with the dark-haired one making his booming voice heard clearest of all. Akari walked over to the fair-haired Barbarian and covered his mouth with his bare hand to silence him, allowing the dark-haired one to speak more freely.

"We don't know sir, but heard tell it came all the way from Maldazor! We walked straight through Azoria with no one to stop us, then through the caves where those nasty Tweeners gave us safe passage, lighting every step of the way, and then found our way to the town of Frogpond."

Akari made eye contact with Mouse and Jonas, raising his eyebrows in a gesture that seemed to say 'I told you so'. "And were you sent specifically to kidnap Eston?"

"Yes we were, and we knew exactly where to find him. That's all I know, sir! We're victims of circumstance, we are - they held our families and said if we didn't do it they'd slash all of their throats! They did, yes!" With that the Barbarian let loose tears the likes of which none present had ever seen, and all of them buried their faces in their chest and stifled laughter at the pathetic sight.

After some time, Akari gained his composure. "I see. Quite a few stories you told there, and I suppose maybe somewhere in there was a grain of truth, although I may have missed it with all of your boo-hooing. I doubt it, but it's possible. Maldazor chose poorly if he thought Barbarians wouldn't blabber his secret. May it be the first of many mistakes he makes!"

He leaned down and spoke softly to the Barbarians. "I'll tell you what. The dragons won't eat you."

"Oh thank you, thank you," they stammered, but Akari shushed them, holding his finger to his lips. "As for the rest, I leave it to Fate. Good luck to you!"

The fair-haired Barbarian escaped Akari's grasp and ran toward his fellow Barbarian with intention to do harm, despite having his hands tied. But before he could get there, the dragons seized them both and dropped them into the canoe the way a cat lifts its kittens. Tod then used his tail to shove them into the water and push them downstream.

Akari watched from afar and yelled out to them. "Great Falls is a day away, boys! I've never known anyone to have survived a fall down there, but I'd love to hear you were the first. Be a real shame if someone catches you beforehand and robs you of your shot at eternal fame and glory!" He waved good-bye, smirking, then turned back to his nephews.

"That'll be the end for them as far as we are concerned. Now let's go off and find somewhere to camp for the night so you two can rest up. If you thought today was busy, tomorrow will be something else entirely!"

Jonas raised his eyebrows, his curiosity piqued, while Mouse couldn't help but shiver, more than a bit overwhelmed after the long day they had just narrowly survived.

"I can't wait," he said.

# Chapter Eleven - Cave In

Caroline was completely surrounded by Tweeners. They numbered in the hundreds, with each one apparently taking a turn to take a whiff of her. Caroline was terrified.

But the sniffing stopped, at the command of a deep voice, speaking in their language.

The creatures pulled away. Soon the little lights on their heads began to spark and they formed a line out the exit she'd been trying to reach.

The lights allowed her to make out her surroundings, but before she could commit them to memory, a Tweener pulled on the rope she was tied to and she lurched forward.

Caroline did not particularly care to be led like a dog but she was in no position to object, as she quickly learned when she yanked at the rope and dug her heels in the ground. A Tweener ran up and cuffed her roughly across the face, then leaned into her. The creature's hot breath was rancid, smelling of sulfur and dead fish, and in the faint light she could see his jagged teeth arranged haphazardly in uneven rows.

"Get up. If you don't want to walk, we'll kill you where you stand and carry you from here," the creature hissed. It reached down and struck her again, splitting her lip. Caroline tasted the blood on her tongue and felt her lip swell. Her heart pumped with adrenaline, but there was nothing to do but get up and walk, knowing that the Tweener was serious. She could only play along until a chance to escape presented itself.

Suddenly, the opportunity arrived. The caves began shaking and Tweeners ran wildly around, with high-pitched squeals and shouts cascading throughout the cave. Caroline watched them crash into each other and fall into pits, squealing horribly as they fell. They were as terrified as she was, and she pitied them, despite their foul treatment. But this was what she had been waiting for - the cave creatures clearly had bigger things on their minds than her. What could scare the Tweeners so?

The remnants of the awful breath still lingered when another smell drifted her way. It was only a whiff, tickling her nose, but it quickly picked up strength and soon overwhelmed her. The narrow tunnel was consumed by an unspeakably bad odor, one that was far, far worse than the Tweener's breath. It smelled so bad it nearly knocked Caroline out, leaving her light-headed. She almost wished for the Tweener's breath rather than this new, far more powerful scent.

The rope binding Caroline went taut as her captor fled. Caroline was forced to follow, but she stumbled, her feet coming out from under her. She landed on her back, scraping her arms against the rocky surface of the cave. It was a hard fall, but it jerked the rope from the Tweeners' fingers. Her elbows were skinned and her knee was twisted – but she was free!

But her arms were still bound, which made it seem impossible to get up. She lay helplessly on the ground, struggling, trying to recall that horrible odor – it seemed that she had smelled it before, although it was far more powerful when trapped in the cavern, with no fresh air to dilute it. It was a simply horrid smell; in this, the Tweeners clearly agreed.

The panic among those foul creatures was increasing. Throughout the cavern she saw them falling, their little lights going out as they toppled. Their stupendous sense of smell was becoming their undoing. The scent was so powerful it was driving them insane.

Caroline rolled over onto her stomach, and by bringing one knee up to her chest, she pulled her body up and rose to her knees, and from there she could stand. She ran awkwardly from the cavern and found the exit. She noticed that the length of the tunnel was dotted with little piles of unconscious Tweeners. Some were alone. Others were in clumps of three or four. And then, the last of their lights went out.

She was alone in the dark. It was eerily silent – the screaming, the squealing, the panic was over. The only thing left was Caroline, and a vast emptiness.

She felt her way around, stumbling over the sleeping Tweeners, holding her nose against the smell. How ever could she hope to escape? She was blind and lost.

She ran her fingers along the tunnel wall, slowly advancing. She thought she might burst, so desperate was she to escape these caves. It felt as if the walls were going to press down on her.

But Caroline looked back and saw a light heading toward her, brighter and stronger than those of the Tweeners. Perhaps it was a collection of the creatures massed together, made up of those that did not succumb to the odor? Then the light flickered, bouncing off of the cave walls. It was no Tweener - the light was from a flame, so bright it hurt Caroline's eyes, which had grown used to the darkness. She strained to look past it to make out what was holding it. Whatever it was, it was massive, and had to crouch to enter the tunnel where Caroline was waiting. What could it be?

The form drew nearer and as Caroline's eyes finally adjusted to the light she was both stunned and relieved. It was Chupwah! He crashed down the tunnel while stepping over the lifeless Tweeners, torch in hand, and came running as soon as he saw Caroline.

Of course! That smell! It was the same as the night Chupwah had been chasing her, the one he was able to spray like a skunk. Chupwah had connected the dots, realizing that if anything could topple the Tweeners it was a smell so powerful that their sensitive noses would overload. Before Caroline could even form the questions going through her mind into words, Chupwah was ready with answers.

"I had to, Caroline, I had to. I couldn't let you go it alone, no matter what my parents said, not with these Tweeners in here. I kept thinking over and over of what they said about their sensitive noses and I knew that I had to try. It's a good thing I did! Evil things, just like everyone said."

He then ripped the ropes still tied around Caroline in half. Caroline felt instant relief, grateful to stretch her arms out once again.

Chupwah noted the piles of unconscious bodies. "It really worked, didn't it? Now I see why these things hate us so much!"

Caroline gave the Sasquatch a big hug, which was returned shyly. "Chupwah, I don't know how to thank you."

She stepped back, wiped away a few tears of joy, and turned her thoughts back to their mission - there was no time to celebrate. "We have to hurry. The Tweeners confirmed my father came this way." She pointed at the piles of bodies. "How long are these things going to stay like this?"

Chupwah shrugged his shoulders. "I have no clue, Caroline. But it won't do to wait and find out. I'm coming with you, so let's go!"

Caroline was ecstatic to again have Chupwah by her side and found she had no words with which to reply. So she simply smiled, and with that the two of them ran down the tunnel, hopeful they could soon find their way from the claustrophobic caverns.

The torch was much more effective than the candle, allowing them to run without fear, and Caroline was grateful not to worry about Tweeners nipping at her heels.

Soon, Caroline's heart nearly leaped from her chest as her eyes found the welcome sight of sunlight pouring through a crack in the ceiling. She could hardly believe it. They were so close to an escape.

She examined the crack but it was too narrow. No matter - she would keep searching. Before long, they found another fissure with light bleeding through, and wide enough, although a tight squeeze for Chupwah. But he wriggled free after helping Caroline first.

Caroline burst to the surface, blinking in the sun, which shone large and bright. She wished she could kiss the sky she was so grateful to see it. If it had been night they likely would have passed right on by the exit, trapped in an endless maze of caverns and tunnels, taking them deeper and deeper into the bowels of the earth.

She shook her head, stunned that entire night had elapsed. Had it really taken that long? All sense of time was lost in these deep, dark places.

Together, they took in the scenery and drank in the fresh air. They were in the middle of a tree-lined slope high up the mountainside. Ambrosia was a memory, as now they were on the Azorian side of the Kin Kara Mountains.

"Chupwah, I owe you my life!" said Caroline. "I can't believe you came back for me!"

"Of course," Chupwah said. "And I found this, too." He handed Caroline her sword, which had been taken from her moments ago.

"Wow, thank you!"

"Does this mean you forgive me for my idiocy the other night?"

"Of course, my friend! I had long ago forgiven you for that!" She placed her hand on the taller Chupwah's shoulder in a token of appreciation, standing on her tippy toes to do so. She took another deep breath of mountain air, grateful to be free of Chupwah's scent as well as the dank aroma of the caves. But she was all too aware that while one obstacle was cleared, many yet remained.

"Are you certain you don't want to go back?" Caroline asked reluctantly, hoping he would not.

"No. I've made my decision and I hope someday my parents can forgive me. But I'm going with you, and together we will rescue your father." The creature stuck out his fur-covered hand to Caroline, who shook it. "It would be my honor."

"The honor will be mine, Chupwah. Now let's move. No offense, but I don't think I can take that smell anymore and I'd hate for it to catch up! That is some gift you have."

"Just imagine if I hadn't used it the other night! It takes some time for it to recover its full power. That wasn't even close to full strength. Thankfully, it worked as well as it did."

"Indeed! Forgive my insult, Chupwah. It was the smell of freedom and nothing less. A sweet smell I will recall many times over the course of my life. Now let's find a way down this mountain."

With considerable effort, they journeyed down the slope, finding a small clearing where the trees thinned out and allowed them to look below. A cool stream ran through the middle of the clearing and Caroline gratefully drank before filling her canteen with fresh water.

Chupwah did the same, surveying the valley as he did. He slurped the water sloppily, rather like a dog, and stopped mid-drink. The water dribbled down his furry chin as his eyes bugged out, for off in the distance he could see four figures walking down below. His heart rate rose - was he looking at Eston and his captors?

"Caroline, come here. Look! Way over there." He pointed while his huge paw dripped with water from the stream. "Do you see that?"

She held her hands over her eyes and squinted. Her eyes were not quite as good as her friends but she could just make out four little dots moving across the landscape.

"That must be them! Oh Chupwah, we're so close. Can we catch them?"

"Some how, some way, we will. But the terrain is rocky and hilly. We need to find a better way to travel. Agreed?"

Caroline nodded and felt her fat lip, a gift from the Tweeners. "Yes. But how?"

Without another word, Chupwah scooped Caroline up and swiveled her to his back, taking her by complete surprise. With her legs dangling awkwardly, she hung on while he carried her piggy-back style, running as fast as he could. His long legs strode effortlessly and covered large swaths of ground with each step.

After an hour or so, they came upon another open area with another clean, clear stream. Chupwah drank his fill while Caroline looked out into the valley. She could make out their quarry much better and was almost certain it was her father, a distant figure walking behind the others. Her body trembled nervously. If it was not her father, Fate was playing a cruel joke.

Caroline watched from her perch for a few moments and was stunned as a large battalion of soldiers appeared, stopping in front of the Barbarians and her father.

"Chupwah, it is my father! I am certain of it. But look at this." The giant beast came running and lent his powerful eyes to the situation.

"It's the Great Army of Azoria," Chupwah said. "But why would the Barbarians head right to them? I would think they'd run away as fast as they could in the face of such odds. This is very strange."

The conversation appeared to be peaceful, although at one point Eston began to argue and act as if agitated. A Barbarian reached out, cuffed him in the ears, and shoved him to the ground.

"Father!" Caroline screamed, unable to control herself. Her voice seemed to echo across the mountains, but it went unheard down below; fortunately, they were out of range. "Chupwah, we have to get down there!" she said, preparing to run toward them.

But Chupwah held her back with his powerful forearm. "Wait. Let's see what happens first. Besides, it would take some time to get there. We don't want to lose sight of them and make it harder to follow. The Barbarians are cagey and may leave many false trails."

They watched the conversation from afar, which seemed amiable enough. But suddenly, the battalion struck. Arrows rained down from the bows of the soldiers and soon the three Barbarians fell to the ground, mortally wounded.

One of the soldiers moved to Eston, who had remained on the ground. The soldier helped him to his feet, and with the help of another, tossed him on to the back of a rider-less horse with his arms still bound.

The leader of the band held his arm high and motioned for the soldiers to ride. Soon the horses galloped away, leaving nothing but a cloud of dust while the Barbarians lay dying.

Caroline's face drained of all color. Her lower lip quivered as her father disappeared from sight.

"I don't understand, Chupwah - why did they carry him off like a prisoner? Why didn't they cut his bonds? And the Barbarians didn't seem scared at all, and then they were cut down? It makes no sense that sworn enemies of Azoria would stride through without any fear and then be slayed. What will Maldazor do when he hears of this?"

"I'd bet it was Maldazor's plan, Caroline. You know how we feel about that man. Your father, too. That's why the Watchtower was formed. I have never been to a meeting, but from what my father tells me, there are representatives from all over the map. There's even a dragon!"

"A dragon!" Caroline exclaimed. "Weren't they cast aside from the island by Akari years and years ago?"

"Officially, yes," Chupwah replied. "Unofficially, no. Father does not much care for them but says there are many still around, and disguised as all kinds of things - horses, birds, bats. There's one right outside of Maldazor's castle from what I understand."

Caroline held her head in her hands and tried to make sense of it all. She had not grown up with the idea that Kings needed to be watched and wondered why her father had shielded her from such matters. "Maldazor would never work with Barbarians. Would he?"

"I would put little past him. But we will find out for ourselves. Maybe we can get to the Barbarians before it's too late and find out what they know, though I doubt they'll be much help."

They were off, with Caroline riding on Chupwah's back as great speed was required. From their view, the Barbarians visibly still clung to life. They seemed to be in agonizing pain, evident by the way they rolled around and kicked out their legs.

They made the distance in an hour, quicker than Chupwah had even figured, but it appeared they were too late, as none of their targets were moving. Caroline hopped down and felt the pulse of the first savage, whose eyes were wide open, a haunting expression on his face. Despite everything, her stomach turned at the sight. She confirmed he was gone and closed his eyes, and Chupwah did the same to the second, also gone. Caroline turned to the last one, who was separated from the others, lying on his side with his back toward them.

He was younger than the others – in fact, he was just a boy. And he was alive, barely, his chest heaving from the painful effort of breathing. Arrows stuck out from his ribs and there was a large gash on his neck. It was clear that he did not have much time left, but he still responded at the sound of their approaching feet.

"My...my...father. Is he?" He coughed from the effort. Caroline put her hand under his head, lifting it slightly, disgusted by the empathy she felt. He was naught but an evil Barbarian, one that had captured her father for no reason, and undeserving of compassion. Still, she tore a piece of cloth from his shirt and held it against the gaping wound to staunch the bleeding.

"Was one of those men your father?" She gestured toward the general direction of where the two men lay.

"Yes, and my uncle. Are they gone?"

Caroline frowned, before nodding quietly to confirm their deaths. The young Barbarian said nothing. He only returned the nod slightly, showing no other reaction. Death was just part of the life one leads as a Barbarian.

The cold reaction did not sit well with Caroline. "Who are you? And why did you take my father, Eston? What did he ever do to you?" Her voice betrayed the anger she felt, and Chupwah put his hand on her shoulder to help her maintain her composure.

"He was your father?" The young savage coughed with what little strength he had. "I am sorry, now. I was always told you were all savages, though now that I look upon you—" He coughed again before continuing.

"Why did we take him? We were paid, of course. Why else does anyone do anything? Maldazor promised us riches. My father worked it all out with him, or one of his emissaries, but we knew Maldazor was in charge. They said this Eston was an enemy of his kingdom and we were to bring him back to be dealt with." He stopped yet again to cough. "Have you been following us?"

"Yes, because I was following my father!" Her blood boiled. She paused before saying something she would regret, holding back the desire to scream at the Barbarian that had helped bring so much pain to her life. But she held back and continued probing for information. "What do you mean Maldazor paid you?"

The Barbarian coughed again, each breath growing more troubled, and finally his voice grew so weak that Caroline had to lean in to hear the whispers he uttered. "Hadn't paid us yet, but was going to. That's what my father said."

Chupwah finally spoke up, having somehow gone unnoticed by the Barbarian in his delirium. "Your father dealt directly with Maldazor? That seems unlikely."

"Told you...an emissary," he spat out before drawing another deep, ragged breath. "It was one of his knights. Cyril was his name. He's the one that just ordered the attack! They betrayed us, just as grandfather said they would. 'Back stabbers, all of them', he said, 'don't trust them, whatever you do.' But we didn't listen, and now they've gone and got us all killed! Curse Maldazor, and curse Cyril!"

With that the young Barbarian rolled over, coughing violently before giving one last gasp. His neck had been bleeding out for some time and soon he was gone. Caroline watched him take his last breath and again felt pity.

"Do you believe it, Chupwah?" Caroline's face was filled with worry, her eyes almost pleading for Chupwah to say that the Barbarian was lying.

"I do. As I said earlier, we have never trusted Maldazor. He has searched for us relentlessly and we've greatly feared what would happen if he ever found the Sasquatch. It seems obvious that your father is at the mercy of an evil plot by King Maldazor, although we know not why."

Caroline looked at the hoof prints left behind by the Army of Azoria. There was much she did not understand, and so many questions left unanswered. It appeared that her journey had ended in failure. Her father was long gone on the back of a horse, being carried away some place where they would likely never find him. She followed the hoof prints until they trailed off into the horizon, past the foothills of Azoria and toward the High Plains.

With nothing else to do and nowhere else to go, she touched the hilt of her sword and walked, with Chupwah trailing behind. No, she had not failed. Not yet. Her father was still alive, so they would follow the prints to roads unknown and a destination uncertain. Caroline did not know how, but she was going to rescue her father, even if she had to fight Maldazor's Army by herself.

# Chapter Twelve - Akari

It had been a long day, to say the least, yet Jonas could not sleep. It was not the camping, or sleeping on the ground, or anything like that keeping him awake - in fact, he rather enjoyed all that. The hard ground never bothered him, or the cooler temperatures at night, nor even having to cram into a tent smaller than his own room with his entire family. No problem. When it came to camping, he was fine with everything - well, almost everything. The mosquitoes, which seemed to go hand-in-hand with camping, *those* he hated.

And on this night they were especially brutal. It didn't matter how he turned, how many he killed or even if he pulled the blankets over his head for cover, they were relentless. As tired as he was, he could not sleep through it - unlike Mouse, who was snoring away loudly with his head under his blanket. Jonas wished he knew what Mouse was doing to keep them at bay, because nothing was working for him. Jonas felt like he had a bug bite on every inch of his body, and worse, when the mosquitoes were not stinging him they were hovering near his ears, driving him insane with their buzzing.

After being stung in three places at once, Jonas threw off his blankets. He walked over to the roaring campfire that Akari had built, which he had insisted he needed in order to have light for his work. So the boys had gathered firewood before going to bed, leaving him a nice pile from the surrounding forest. Meanwhile, the dragons tended to their scales and claws, saying they had fallen into disrepair during their long transformation. Of course, after the firewood was gathered Tod did what dragons do best, and set the fire ablaze.

Jonas arrived at the fire and was surprised to find the hazy outline of Akari behind the flame, still awake and hard at work - at this late hour Jonas had assumed he would have fallen asleep in the middle of working, the same way he would often find Caroline snoring at the table with her nose buried in a book.

And just like Caroline, Akari had a book open, except he was not asleep. He was dipping a pen in ink to write on its pages, doing various calculations, so engrossed in his work he failed to notice his nephew's approach.

"Still awake, Akari?" Jonas asked.

Akari looked up, surprised. "I see I'm not the only one," he replied.

"It's the mosquitoes. They're driving me crazy! Won't leave me alone." Just mentioning the bugs made him itch, so he scratched away while swatting at a rather large one that had followed him from his bed. His entire body felt like one big bug bite.

"Hmm. I hadn't noticed them, the blood suckers. This smoke must be keeping them away." He nodded at the roaring fire, which crackled and popped as if it knew it was being spoken about. "But I can solve that easy enough."

Akari walked over to one of his bags - he had three or four of them scattered about - and dug through it, muttering to himself as he felt around, picking up and dropping a few items before settling on the right one.

"Aw, here we go!" He held a glass jar filled with leaves, twigs, pieces of bark, and other little bits cultivated from the woods. "Nearly forgot all about these guys with everything that's been going on. They won't be too pleased with me, but they'll have a feast tonight for certain!"

"What is it?" asked Jonas, leaning in to take a better look at the contents.

"Spiders, Nephew. I never go camping without them. They are exactly what we need." He held the opened jar up, peered inside, and tapped the side with a fingernail.

Jonas watched as spiders started to pour from the jar, crawling on Akari's hand and down his arm, arranging themselves in a neat line from his elbow all the way down each of his fingers. Jonas strained his ears, hearing what sounded like a collection of quiet, whispering voices coming from the spiders, though he was unable to make out any of the words. Of course he couldn't, he thought. They're spiders! But Jonas watched in amazement as his uncle spoke as if *they* could understand him.

"Now, now spiders, I apologize, but all will be made well. Don't be upset, rush off, and build webs every which place - that won't help a thing." He held out his hand and pointed toward the bedrolls. "Over there, my friends. The mosquitoes seem to have a taste for my nephews, so you will find the hunting excellent. There you go." The spiders left his arm, leaped to the ground, and made a straight line to Mouse's bed.

It was not long before they reached their destination. They worked in perfect harmony to create the net, their legs almost dancing from web to web as they built. In no time at all, a perfect cocoon covered Mouse's bed.

As soon as the webs were finished, mosquitoes flew into the sticky strands, which shook as they struggled against their bonds. The spiders turned and jerked, snagging their prey, rolling them deeper into the webs. Soon the lacy strands were filled with neatly wrapped bug bodies, set aside for the spiders to sink their teeth into later.

"Amazing," Jonas said. "But Mouse won't be too happy when he wakes up - he's terrified of spiders. He'll never get out of bed!"

"Is that so?" Akari replied. "Maybe he just hasn't met the right kind - these spiders are as friendly a spider as you could hope to meet, so long as you're not a mosquito!"

"I don't know, Akari. He's terrified of them all as far as I can tell - friendly, unfriendly, or in between. But he better get over it if he's going to become a great warrior."

"A great warrior? How could that little thing become a great warrior?"

"It's true! A wizard gave him the mark this year on his fourteenth birthday."

"Which wizard told him that? Was he out of his mind?"

"It was Wallary, the Wizard back in Frogpond. If you don't believe me, take a look at Mouse's arm. The mark is there. I didn't believe it either until I saw *that.*"

Akari shook his head. "That old fool. Did Mouse mention that he was probably gassed? Glug glug glug?" Akari made a gesture imitating a man holding a cup to his lips, signifying that the wizard had likely been drinking.

"Well, Mouse did say Wallary acted rather odd, but that's wizards for you. A strange lot, all of them, from what Father tells me."

"Your father was right. They're half-sauced most of the time and yet we let them decide our futures without an ounce of reason. Absolutely deplorable system." He rolled his head around, stretching his neck out to release the tension that was building in his body.

"But didn't you have the mark of a great warrior, Akari?"

Akari stared into the fire and blinked repeatedly, a nervous reaction he had displayed a few times.

"I do have such a mark," Akari said before changing the subject. "So, back to you. What are you afraid of? You say Mouse fears spiders with some contempt, but we all have our terrors, Jonas. What keeps you awake at night?" Akari swatted something on his forearm, and grinned. "Besides mosquitoes!"

Jonas looked into the distance, hesitant to answer. "Well," he replied, "it doesn't make any sense, but if I'm afraid of anything, it's sharks."

"Sharks? You live in the middle of the country, nowhere near an ocean. How can you be afraid of sharks?"

"I said it didn't make sense," Jonas retorted. "But you asked! I saw a drawing of one when I was little and ever since, they've terrified me." He paused, staring into the fire as if debating on whether or not to continue, then deciding he would. "Truth be told what really scares me is being told by a wizard that I won't be a great warrior, that I'll be a blacksmith like Father is now, or a raftsman, or something like that."

"There's nothing wrong with honest, hard work," Akari replied.

"I know that, Akari, but I want to be Chief Knight - like you and Father. Someone important, who can protect the Kingdom."

"I once thought the same way Jonas. I was wrong, for many reasons, but we'll talk about *that* later. For now, you better get back to bed. We're going to have a busy day tomorrow. And I'll have the spiders take care of your mosquito problem."

"Won't you be going to bed too?" Jonas asked.

"No," Akari declared. "I don't go to bed."

"You don't *go to bed?* What do you do, sleep on your feet?" Jonas asked, his eyebrows rising in disbelief.

"No, young Jonas. As I said earlier, I have much to learn about magic, but that doesn't mean I haven't learned much as well. It's quite simple, really. I invented a pill that keeps me awake all the time. I never have to sleep as I never grow tired. It's wonderful!"

"That's absurd! And impossible!"

"No, it's very much possible. Magic is about making the impossible possible. I do it everyday. Stay up with me if you believe otherwise, and tomorrow, and the next night as well. In fact, you're welcome to try one if you'd like. I have plenty more! I just take one every thirty days or so and I'm good to go."

"Why would you want to stay awake all of the time, Akari? I don't get it."

"It's quite simple. You see, I'm a busy man, and I found that there just weren't enough hours in the day to do all I wanted. At first, I simply tried to come up with ways to save time throughout the day - an hour here, a few minutes there - and then I could focus on more important matters.

"Well, the first thing I tackled was cooking. We spend an *awful* lot of time eating and preparing to eat - three meals a day, and of course there's the cleaning up and washing after. Someone once said I should wash the dishes *before* I ate to save time cleaning up *after,* but that was foolhardy, of course.

"So after a good deal of trial and error, and a lot of bad recipes, I created my food pill. It worked wonderfully! Remind me in the morning to give you and Mouse one, unless you'd rather go out and find something to eat, and good luck to you since you can bet all game fled at the first scent of dragon.

"I'm off track. Anyway, that saved me quite a bit of time, but still I needed more. Then it hit me. I had to slap myself - it was all too obvious! Did you know we spend fully one-third of our day sleeping? Eight out of twenty-four hours spent doing nothing. What a tremendous waste of time! And nothing good ever comes of it. I've had some wonderful dreams, absolutely wonderful, but then I wake up - and I can't fly like a bird anymore or swim underwater for hours and hours, so the whole experience ends up being worthless. So I've cut out cooking and sleeping both, and now I have much more time do all sorts of things."

Jonas was dumbfounded. He wanted to know more. "Like what?" he asked.

"Well, learning to talk to spiders, for example," Akari said, pointing to the webs that were beginning to sag as they were overloaded with tiny mosquito carcasses. "It's been the most productive time of my life! Just wait until tomorrow when you see what I'm working on tonight, although I've still got quite a bit more to do. But no matter, as the night is still young. Now off to bed, unless you'd like me to find one of those pills—"

"Not tonight, Uncle," said Jonas. "I'm too tired to *not* sleep, pill or no pill, and since I don't have to worry about those dratted mosquitoes, I'll be able to. Besides, I'm not so sure of your invention. Do you find that it makes you act strange at all? You seem jittery."

"Not at all. Acting strange comes quite naturally for me; I've never needed a pill to pull *that* off."

"I see. Well, good night, Uncle. I certainly hope you have another productive night."

Akari wished his nephew a good night and Jonas went yawning to bed. After he nestled down, he sighed in relief as the spiders went about their work above him. He silently vowed never to clean up a cobweb again if he could help it.

Jonas soon drifted off to sleep, with questions about his uncle drifting in and out of his consciousness, and wondering what tomorrow would bring.

## Chapter Thirteen - Roads Unknown To A Destination Uncertain

Caroline climbed a rock that stood high above the landscape, a lonely sentinel on the High Plains, and searched for a better view to look out across the lands of Azoria. They had watched the stone grow closer for some time as they journeyed, curious about how it had arrived here in the middle of the plains. Had it been standing there for centuries, left by some ancient giant? Or, perhaps it had sprung of its own accord from the earth below.

Caroline used her hands to shield the sun. It was easy to see why Maldazor felt he'd been cheated when his father Renwick had divided the kingdom. From the moment they left the Kin Kara, Caroline and Chupwah were struck by the sheer desolation and greyness of the land. It was barren and rocky, broken up by occasional, isolated patches of crooked trees growing alongside small meandering streams that crossed the country.

Caroline looked at her friend, overwhelmed by the vastness of the wasteland stretching out in front of her. "Chupwah, what are we going to do? We'll never catch the Army on foot," she said, in an unusually whiny voice.

"Don't say that, Caroline. We've come too far to give up. Right now our only option is to walk and think things over. The signs tell us they have come this way, and besides, there is really nowhere else for them to go. If they go west it takes them into the wild lands, and to the east leads only to either the ocean or more uninhabited lands. At least, uninhabited by man.

"So let's keep moving and try to think of something better. This place is a wasteland, but on the bright side we've only got a hundred miles of it!"

His positive attitude did little to cheer Caroline. She groaned at the thought of walking one hundred miles, especially in this terrain. "I never realized how attached I was to the forests, mountains, and rivers of Ambrosia. Everything here makes me feel dead, like I almost wish I was never born. I don't know how anything can stand to live here."

Chupwah nodded in agreement. "There's a reason the Sasquatch no longer venture this way, besides our general hatred of King Maldazor. But we will survive." His voice was confident, putting a good face on things even though he couldn't think of a way to improve their situation. He just needed time; luckily, time was one thing they had plenty of right now.

The only sound they could hear was the constant plodding of their feet on the rocky trail. Chupwah thought the quiet would do them both some good, but it was an eerie kind of quiet. The kind where it felt like any second something could jump out and alarm them, and it did little to make either of them feel better about their current status. Caroline quickly grew tired of it and decided to make conversation.

"Chupwah, you said earlier that Maldazor had attempted to find your kind for years and has never been able to do. How is it that you can go unseen?"

"We have our ways, Caroline. The trees, the plants, the earth, they all conceal the Sasquatch. Nature gives us everything. Food, shelter, life. As it does to all who allow it."

"Well, when you put it like that, hiding does seem easy enough in the forest. But how will you do it out here?"

"Simple. I'm not going to hide any longer! That time has past. Maldazor wanted to find the Sasquatch, so he'll get his wish.

"His plans threaten us all. I believe that we have no choice but to reveal ourselves now, and take the fight to him, or we will simply delay our inevitable destruction. My parents don't agree, nor do most of the others, but it's something I've felt for a long time, ever since I was told about Maldazor and his ways. I'm grateful you came along when you did as you gave me the strength I needed to do what I must."

"This is crazy. How can you be so sure of Maldazor's plans?"

"Well, a lot of it has been guesswork," Chupwah admitted. "But as I mentioned, the secret group of the Watchtower meets often to discuss the goings-on of the world. I trust them. They always said this day would come, when Maldazor would strike out and reach for the whole kingdom of Ambrosia, desiring to rule as his ancestors did before him. But he won't simply settle for the kingdom of his heirs. I bet even now he is working to obtain the entire island, to rule as none of his ancestors did before him.

"Soon, the Wild Men of Mulvaria will not be safe, nor will the beasts that live in harmony with Birdsong of the south, nor the free creatures of the east. Maldazor's aim is to conquer the entire island and rule as king. Or so the Watchtower feels."

"And how does he plan on doing that, Chupwah?" Caroline asked, still leery of all Chupwah was saying.

"There's no telling, but his plot runs deep. First, he needs to get the people on his side, and clearly the threat of another Barbarian invasion is part of it. Your father being taken captive by that type was no coincidence. From what Father said, the capture of one of the heroes of the Ambrosian Army will likely be used to strike fear in the hearts of the people. In other words he can simply say that if Eston isn't safe than nobody is. He will offer the country protection and security, and in the exchange freedom will be sacrificed. My father says it is always that way. And I bet Maldazor will put your father to work in the armory, another asset in the build-up to war.

"I could be wrong, and I'm not much for politics, but my father passed on his theories to me when we were on the way to help you. I just happen to think he's right." Chupwah stopped walking as they came upon a small creek lined with a few scattered trees. Caroline was so riveted by what Chupwah had been saying that she hadn't even noticed them until they were right there. "Let's stop here. You look exhausted, Caroline."

"No, we have to keep going. We don't have any time." Caroline spoke loud and clear, her voice filled with determination, but she was clearly spent and needed rest.

Chupwah looked down at his new friend, noticing that her eyes were being held open by sheer force of will, her features tired and drawn. "Caroline, a little break won't hurt. Even the soldiers will have to rest, so it will all even out.

"And this little grove of trees is perfect. We'll be hidden among the leaves. We're not going to catch the Army on our feet anyway, and it gives us a chance to rethink our plans when we awaken. Besides, neither of us will be any good if we're exhausted - I don't have a single useful idea going through my head right now and won't until I get some sleep. We haven't slept for a day and a half!"

Caroline knew he was right and gave up her protest. She dropped her bag and rolled out her tent. She was not crazy about sleeping in the daylight, but the situation was beyond her control.

While setting up the tent, she noticed there were all sorts of unusual, unfamiliar bugs crawling around, bugs she did not particularly relish sleeping with. She shuddered at the thought of laying amongst their kind and dug through her pack before finding a small cot that would raise her bedroll just far enough off the ground, where hopefully the critters would leave her alone. She set it up quickly and walked out of the tent to say good night to her friend.

She found him carrying armfuls of leaves. "I'm afraid you won't fit in the tent, Chupwah."

Chupwah chuckled. "I think you're probably right. Besides, I'd rather sleep in one of these trees. You're welcome to join me if you like. You really can't beat a tree for comfort!"

"I don't think so - but thanks!"

The Sasquatch shrugged and walked to the trunk of the largest tree among the grove, but before he could climb up, Caroline added a few final thoughts.

"You know, it sure seems that my dad kept a lot of secrets from us. Meeting up with Skunk Apes, forming an alliance against Maldazor - there's no telling what else I don't know!"

"That's how adults are, from what I can tell. Always protecting us, or so they think. Then we get out in the world and find things aren't as safe and secure as we thought, and all this time we were living under a delusion. For example, I once thought *all* animals lived in the shadows and stayed hidden from the rest of the world. Not true, as you know. Then again, seeing the way some humans act, it might not be the worst idea to live so. No offense."

"None taken. Good night, or day, or whatever time it is now, Chupwah," Caroline said, stifling a yawn.

"Night, Caroline," he replied. He shimmied up the tree in a fluid motion and took refuge in the crook of a branch. The leaves he carried up were molded into what could only be described as a nest, not unlike the great aeries of an eagle. Soon, his massive body sprawled out lengthwise along a large branch with his arms and legs dangling from the sides, looking so natural that if one did not know better it would appear to be just a mass of leaves.

"Amazing. And that's comfortable?" Caroline remarked, shouting to be heard with Chupwah so high in the tree.

"Quite so. You should try it sometime. Rest well, Caroline. I sleep light, so don't worry about anything catching us unaware."

"Me too. I've never been much of a sleeper, but it sounds good right now!"

She stretched out her arms, rolled into the tent, laid out her bedroll on the cot, and prepared to drift off into a deep sleep. Caroline hoped what Chupwah said about being a light sleeper was true, because as she lay down, she did not feel confident she would be one herself. She was beyond exhausted, unsure that even Maldazor's army marching by could wake her.

*

As expected, Caroline had no problem falling asleep, snoring loudly when an awful growl snapped her awake. It sounded like a bear mixed with a wildcat, so ferocious it left her temporarily paralyzed with fear, and frozen in bed, not even daring to breathe. She hoped the noise was from a bad dream. But she soon heard it again, a vicious sound and no mistake. It was followed by a low growling noise not unlike the warning yowl of a cat. Caroline wondered what it could be when it hit her - it was Chupwah!

"Chupwah!" she yelled, reaching for her sword. She found it with her fingers and lifted it in the air, the blade brushing against the canvas roof of the tent. Suddenly, there were footsteps stomping all around her, mixed with the whinnying of terrified horses, frightened by the Skunk Ape's roar. Swarthy voices around her tent said things like "it's a bear" and "no, a gorilla more like it."

Caroline prepared to escape the tent when it collapsed from outside. Something had pressed down on the roof, which caused it to fall in, and next thing Caroline knew, a group of people was trying to wrap her in the canvas of the tent. She shrieked as she felt hands grabbing at her.

The tent entwined Caroline and she was wrapped up. The whole world was a ball of confusion, but Caroline's well-honed instincts kicked in. She freed her arms and slashed with her sword, cutting through the canvas and stabbing something in the process, a something which yelled out and instantly retreated. This gave her more room to work with, so she again slashed out with the blade and hacked the tent to pieces, allowing herself to go free. She rose to her feet and into a defensive posture, the sword ready to strike at anything in her vicinity.

She was blinded from the onrush of sunlight, much to her surprise - it appeared to be early evening, though it felt like she had been asleep for days. She tried to shake off the cobwebs that cluttered her mind, and searched frantically for Chupwah. All she had to do was follow the trail, made up of fallen soldiers, with the young Sasquatch standing at the end of it.

He was sending the attackers sprawling, one at a time, in rapid succession. The ones still standing were trying to throw large nets around the giant creature, but so far, he was able to fend off such attacks.

They were all soldiers from the Azorian Army. Chupwah was right - Maldazor could not be trusted. She seethed with anger, furious that a King her father had defended as Chief Knight would turn against him, kidnapping him away from his family. For shame, but the game was afoot and soon the world would be on to his ways. Until then, she would not go down without a fight. She quickly measured them up, thinking over a course of action.

The odds were not in their favor, despite the fury of Chupwah's attacks. Caroline did a quick count and figured there were twenty soldiers still standing while another ten or so lay sprawled out, writhing in pain. Caroline vowed she would bring the fight to them, long odds or not - just like Chupwah.

Crouching low to the ground, she kept her head on a pivot to stay abreast of any attackers. They kept their distance, moving backwards any time she moved toward them.

"What do you want from us, cowards?" she yelled, though none responded.

She looked around more and spied a soldier standing away from the fighting, sitting on a large black horse as he surveyed his troops. He was the general; Caroline had seen his kind before. He wore a silver helmet and armor polished meticulously to a brilliant shine, sparkling in the sun. His helmet held a blazing red plume that rose from the top and swayed slightly in the light breeze. From his perch, he looked at Caroline and responded.

"We don't want anything from you. Overzealous soldiers, young lady. My sincerest apologies." The man bowed while horse bound, trying his best to seem sincere and doing a poor job of it. "I am General Roland, and this is my company. You may not be aware but you were camping near a Skunk Ape, a vicious, dangerous, foul beast."

"I know exactly who I was camping near. Now leave us be, or I'll be forced to kill all of you!"

If Caroline expected them to comply she was mistaken. Laughter sounded out from those not too occupied with Chupwah to pay attention.

"You are no warrior, princess. I wanted to do this the easy way, so please leave me that option. I am giving you a way out and you slap my hand aside, but no matter.

"Yes, we have caught word of your association with this *creature*, and I do admire your foolish bravery during that association. The Tweeners sent tidings regarding your escapades.

"But enough is enough, so please stand aside before someone is hurt. We intend to take this beast alive and it would be a pity if we were unable to. A pity for me, but more so for you."

Caroline quickly surmised that the General was a grim, miserable man, and used to getting his way. She also guessed his assignment was not one of the plum jobs of Maldazor's Army and therefore he was not likely pleased to be assigned to the drab wastelands of Azoria, leaving him more bitter and callous.

"I will not stand aside," she responded. "If you want Chupwah, you'll have to get through me first."

"The creature has a name! Fascinating. I suppose you talk to it too, like a toddler to its baby doll. *Very* cute. But you will step aside or you will be made to. I don't know what possessed a *girl* like you to go stumbling through the Burmian Caves, but you must be rather stupid. Now—"

Before he could speak further the General ducked low in the saddle lest he risk having his head removed, as one of his own soldiers had been flung some twenty yards by Chupwah and was barreling toward him through the air. As General Roland crouched down the soldier landed just behind him, whizzing by the General's head and landing with a teeth-rattling crunch. The General tried unsuccessfully to steady himself, and was stunned to see Caroline running straight toward him. She leaped and yanked him from the saddle, pulling until he fell to the ground flat on his back. Caroline wasted no time and replaced him in the vacated saddle, grabbing the reins.

She pulled her hair back from her face, swung the charge around, and noticed the other horses were unmanned, loosely picketed in a circle while their riders attempted to wrangle Chupwah. It was the break she was looking for. Her hands trembled as a plan formed.

She felt comfortable on the General's horse and realized how badly she missed her horses back home. Being on a horse was second nature, being born with the gift to get even the most stubborn horse to do what she wanted. And with these horses, she knew *exactly* what that was.

She kicked her heels into the horse's ribs and galloped to the others. From the corner of her eye, she noticed that a few of the soldiers were moving toward her, while most of the group continued trying to trap Chupwah. The Sasquatch was still faring well, working with a huge advantage as these soldiers were not used to capturing something alive.

As strong as he was, Chupwah could only fight them off for so long, and Caroline knew it. She had to work fast as net after net gnarled around him. Her plan had to work, and she felt sick to think about what Maldazor might have planned for a live Sasquatch - probably torture and worse.

The horses heard the approaching hoof steps and caught right on, their legs kicking into action to Caroline's great joy. They were clearly used to traveling as a herd from one place to another during their nomadic life in the King's army, which was exactly what Caroline had been hoping. So far, so good.

With the horses willing to bend to her desires, Caroline started a stampede. Her charge led the way, working them into a frenzy as they rushed toward Chupwah. She kicked her horse into a faster pace to move into the middle of the pack, skillfully weaving in and out among the different horses, making quick cuts in between some and narrowly avoiding others. The horse soon shot out in front of the pack, responding deftly to Caroline's every pull of the reins. This was some horse she was riding, deserving of a much better rider than a lout like the General.

The group bore down on the soldiers, who scattered and fled, leaving Chupwah alone to pull free from the nets and ropes wrapped around him.

Most of the soldiers ran to the little brook and jumped into the water. They crashed and landed on top of each other. Meanwhile, Caroline ran herd on the few that had not headed for the stream.

She chased them toward General Roland, who had little choice but to join the group, with the plume of his helmet waving back and forth comically as he ran. Suddenly, the General turned in a complete circle and Caroline had to laugh - the giant red feather had flopped over into his face, covering his eyes and leaving him blinded. He fell, rolled head over heels, and finished only when he landed on his back. He looked pathetic crumpled on the ground, and Caroline pumped her fist in celebration. So far, the plan was working wonderfully.

With the soldiers out of her way, Caroline galloped over to Chupwah, came to a stop, and cut away what was left of the netting with her sword. "Can you ride?"

Chupwah nodded that he could and slapped Caroline on the back in his joy, nearly knocking her from the horse.

"Sorry, Caroline! I didn't mean to hurt you!" he shouted over the hoofs that roared around them.

"I don't know how those soldiers managed to stay standing as long as they did, seeing as you *meant* to hurt them! Whew!" She rubbed her shoulder and moved her left arm in a circle to get the feeling back. "Well, grab a horse, and take your pick! After all, I've taken every last one of them," She was doing a poor job of hiding her pride at her first successful foray into combat. A warrior's wife? Not yet.

Chupwah found one that could hold his massive frame and together they kicked the horses into a gallop, leaving nothing behind but a cloud of dust and a group of ashamed soldiers led by General Roland, who had not even bothered to remove the plume from his face as he watched the horses thunder away.

Caroline and Chupwah were in high spirits, stunned by the turn of events. "I guess we don't have to walk now, Chupwah!" she yelled over the galloping horses. "Woo! Now to find my father!"

"That was incredible, Caroline. That General Roland won't underestimate you again. And neither will I!"

They rode ahead into wide open country. They were grateful. They would have been walking for miles if they had not been attacked by a unit of thirty, ruthless soldiers. They were both euphoric at escaping such a close call.

"What a lucky break that a group of horses just happened to come along. All we had to do was outsmart thirty of the King's elite guard to do it," Caroline declared, laughing as she did so.

"Yeah, some luck! But next time I think I'd be happier with just two horses and no guards, rather than thirty of each. That would be a bit luckier," Chupwah replied, but the euphoria ended abruptly as his eyes opened wide in surprise. "But I'm afraid we're not free yet. Look!"

The horses were brought to a halt as Chupwah leaned forward and pointed to what had seemed to be a limitless plain in front of them. Now, there was a massive column of Maldazor's army off on the horizon, at least two hundred strong. The setting sun cast their shadows in front of them across the plains, making General Roland's force seem a pittance. From this distance they were the size of ants, but there was no mistaking the large red flag of Azoria held aloft in front of the army. Caroline and Chupwah were heading right into their midst and no retreat was possible, if they wanted to rescue Caroline's father.

"Well, Caroline, I hope luck stays on our side," Chupwah said soberly. "We're going to need it."

# Chapter Fourteen - The View Above

Mouse awoke from a good night's sleep and blinked happily into the early dawn light. But he soon was paralyzed with fear. Directly above and all around him was a network of webs, filled with spiders dining on their prey. There was no escape without becoming entangled in the webs. He shuddered at the thought.

He wanted to scream for help but he thought better of it - no sense in looking like a fool to Akari. At the same time, he desperately wanted to escape, and no solution was presenting itself. But before he could go into a full panic, he was relieved to find Akari standing above him with a little glass jar in hand.

"Good morning, Alexander. I apologize for the surprise this morning, but you must admit they did an effective job of keeping the mosquitoes at bay."

"I...I... I didn't feel any mosquitoes," Mouse stammered. "All I see are spiders!"

"Exactly! You didn't feel any mosquitoes because the spiders gobbled them up! Marvelously effective, aren't they? And don't worry. The spiders are quite friendly, especially since they're good and full. Just hold still for half a second and I'll call them in."

He held out the jar and whispered something indecipherable, but it caused the webs to sway and no less than twenty spiders ran down the various strands, heading to Akari. Compared to their earlier dancer-like movements, they seemed sluggish, fattened up from munching on mosquitoes. Soon enough, though, the webs were empty and promptly cleared by Akari with a stick.

"There you go, Alexander. All is well, and I already took care of Jonas's webs. He's down by the river cleaning up," Akari stated, then added with a wink, "You ever ride a dragon before?"

"You really know how to wake someone up! First spiders and now dragons! No, I can't say I have - you must know that." Mouse's eyes bulged. "You can't mean...?"

"But of course! These fellows are wanted back at Dragon Island, so we're going with them. As expected, the elders were none too happy that they were revealed to Ambrosia yesterday. Tidings were brought with great speed last night."

"How is that possible? How could they find us?"

"Bats, young Alexander—"

Mouse interrupted. "I hate that name. Please call me Mouse, Akari."

"Noted, although I find it curious. You really don't mind being called Mouse? Of the two, I'd much prefer Alexander."

"Absolutely. Alexander is the name my father gave me, my *real* father, if that's what you want to call him. I wish to have little to do with it," Mouse said, a touch annoyed at having to explain, as he disliked speaking of his birth father.

Akari could not help himself and laughed. "Fair enough, *Mouse*. "Most odd. You must tell me the story of how you got that name sometime," he said, and held out his finger. "But not now."

"We were talking about bats," Mouse reminded, with more than a trace of annoyance. Akari seemed to have trouble focusing on one thing at a time and it was growing bothersome.

"Oh yes, bats! Outstanding messengers, and since they travel at night few can follow their path. We had a couple visit last night, bringing word that our dragons are wanted for a special Council of the Dragons. I can only hope they won't be too rough on them." Akari looked behind Mouse and his eyes lit up. "A-ha, speaking of, here's Tod. It seems that a huge, fire-breathing dragon has caught us completely unaware. We're going to have to improve our woodcraft, young Mouse."

The dragon came over and stood by Akari's side, towering over them, its head even with the surrounding trees. "Good morning, Mouse," it said in a gravelly voice.

"Umm, good morning, Tod," he replied, before turning to Akari to whisper in his ear. "However did you tame these beasts?"

The dragon overheard the question and laughed, a roaring, strange laugh that sent shivers down Mouse's spine. While this was taking place, Jonas finally returned.

"What's the dragon laughing about?" Jonas asked, running his fingers through his wet hair in a half-hearted attempt to style it.

"Jonas and Mouse, the first thing you should know about dragons is they have an absolutely incredible sense of hearing. There's no use whispering around them - you'd have just as much success keeping a secret by shouting it from the nearest watchtower.

"As to why Tod was laughing, I believe he may have been amused by the very idea of me taming him, or any other dragon for that matter. Tame a dragon! Imagine." He chuckled again. "But Tod, you may speak for yourself if I miss my guess."

Again the dragon laughed, low and wild. "Boys, it might be better to say that we dragons *tamed* Akari. Never seen anything like it in a man. Just as wild and free as can be, and his sister wasn't much better, may she rest in peace." He bowed his head and continued. "But they both were great friends and allies to us. They saved us from our greatest enemy."

"Maldazor?" guessed Mouse.

"No, not Maldazor," the dragon stated somberly. "Not yet. I'm afraid it was your father, Eston Strongheart."

Jonas and Mouse both jumped back, their eyes bulging. "Our father? We've never heard of him killing any dragons before," Jonas stated. "I've only heard of *you* killing them, Akari."

Akari said nothing, waiting to determine how he wanted to proceed. "First off, it's a long story regarding myself and dragons. Most of what you've heard is untrue. Secondly, your father did not kill any dragons *personally*. But you are both aware of his skills with crafting weapons." He rubbed his chin, still deciding on what all to say.

"Have you heard of the Dragon Killer? Of course you have. Well, that was his invention. The only real way that I know of to kill a dragon. Luckily, your mother and I were able to make him see reason and talk him out of ever using it! Remember that, boys - not all wars are fought on the battlefield. Ask any married couple if you don't believe me!

"But dragons aren't evil - well, not any more evil than humans can be anyway - and through a bit of, shall we say, education, we were able to make him see logic."

Both Jonas and Mouse were shocked, Jonas especially, who stood silent for some time when a sudden thought hit him. "Akari, speaking of father - Caroline is after him *right now*, and out there in who knows what kind of trouble. We have to go save them! These dragons will make it easy, don't you think?"

Akari shook his head. "Boys, I'm afraid that will be impossible. The bats brought other tidings as well, and of great import - your sister has made it through the Burmian Caves! And she seems to have acquired a friend, a Sasquatch, from what they tell me. She is doing quite well, and though I desire to do as you say, the dragons have been summoned home, upon pain of death if they do not go.

"To make things worse, it seems that Caroline has riled up the Tweeners in the Burmian Caves. They don't take kindly to someone making it through their caves alive - at least, not without permission. They were so upset they have sealed off all entrances, so there's no catching Caroline from that route. But we will find a way to help her, I promise."

Tod hung his head in shame. "I am sorry, Jonas and Mouse. But Akari is correct. We're already in enough trouble for coming after you, and it won't do to defy a summons by the Dragon Council. But if anyone can find a way to help your sister, it is your uncle. He will find a way."

Akari nodded in agreement. "Yes, I will find a way. I haven't seen my niece in—" He stopped, his lip shaking slightly, overcome with emotion. "I have faith in Caroline. I've heard so much about the kind of woman she's grown in to. It's my loss for having missed it all. But woe to those that oppose her! She sounds an awful lot like her mother, tough and smart. She'll find a way."

He then turned to Mouse. "Mouse, go and clean up for your first and possibly last dragon ride."

Mouse did as instructed and soon they stood in front of the dragons, anxious to board. Both Mouse and Jonas felt pangs of hunger, so they gratefully accepted their uncle's offer and tried his pill. They were wary, but were soon surprised by how *normal* it seemed. It felt very much like they had sat down to a nice breakfast and were comfortably full, ready for the long day ahead. With that taken care of, it was back to the matter at hand.

"So what's riding a dragon like, Akari?" Jonas inquired.

"You ever try riding out a tornado by hanging on to a tree trunk? It's something like that," Akari responded. "But really, there's nothing else like it. To describe it with words would be an injustice. Oh, how I've missed it! These boys just aren't the same when they're transformed into horses!"

Akari sized up the beasts for the best match of rider and dragon. "Jonas, you'll be riding Grayson, and Mouse, hop on Drake, he's a bit more your size."

Both dragons bent at the knees to allow the boys to clamber on to their backs. There were no saddles, so they sat between narrow ridges that ran down the dragons' backs, and clung with all of their might. Mouse felt silly at being so terrified of spiders - *this* was something to be afraid of, riding on the back of a dragon while soaring above the clouds.

"I don't know about this, Akari," Mouse stammered.

"Don't worry. Even if you do slip, they'll catch you before you fall too far. Dragons are uncanny that way. Tremendous reflexes. Remarkable creatures!" He paused and added one last thought. "But hang on anyway, just to be safe."

Mouse looked as if the pill he had just swallowed was going to come back up, but he nodded weakly to confirm that he was ready.

"Yah!" Akari yelled, and the dragons sprung into action, their wings flapping with powerful thrusts, blowing dust and the boys' hair into their faces. Soon, the tops of the trees were at eye level as the dragons hovered; the merciless beating of their wings caused the trees to bend at will.

It was unlike anything they had ever experienced. Exhilaration pulsed through Jonas' body - he had thought of dragons as the embodiment of evil before today, and yet now felt as if his entire life had been building to this moment. This was an adventure, a bold one, one that a great warrior could embrace.

In front of him, he could see Mouse tensely clinging to the dragon's spine, though Jonas could see from his wide grin that his brother was enjoying himself as much as he was.

Soon the forest was far below and the river looked like a narrow blue ribbon. The morning sun was nearly in full bloom and the river sparkled in the sunshine. It was breathtakingly beautiful. They continued to climb and soon they could see the castle of Ambrosia City off in the distance. They had been so close, and yet it was all for naught.

Jonas started at the castle and wondered what kind of activity was taking place there. Certainly there were big doings going on. The King was dead, the Princess would soon be Queen, and if Akari was to be believed, Maldazor was behind it, all part of a plan to put himself in the throne previously occupied by his very own brother. The whole world was being turned upside down, right down to his own family, with his father taken captive and his sister chasing after, with no way for them to help. And yet all those troubles seemed so far away up in the sky riding on a dragon.

They rose higher and higher, and soon they were mingling with a group of white clouds floating in the sky. Grayson snorted, stopped rising, and changed the direction his wings had been flapping, the shift propelling them forward rather than up. They were on their way to Dragon Island and the Council of the Dragons, a place few men had visited and fewer still had returned. There was no telling what the future would hold, but Jonas looked forward to the ride.

Such adventures as this would be part and parcel of his life as a great warrior. Although his Fate had not yet been officially determined, his fourteenth birthday was just a day away, and a Wizard was certain to give him the Warrior's Mark that would confirm such a destiny.

But that was for tomorrow. As for now, there was only the dragon, the sky, and the clouds below. Nothing else seemed to matter.

## Chapter Fifteen - Upward and Onward

Caroline would be the first to admit her plan had little chance for success. After all, how could a Sasquatch and a lone girl expect to make it through a column of Maldazor's troops? It was impossible, irrational, and illogical, short-sighted and far-fetched, a fool's dream and a sane man's nightmare.

But her father was out there somewhere. Exactly where, Caroline did not know. But in order to get there, she had to go through these troops. She had hoped her father was somewhere in the column of soldiers, but as they approached it, it was obvious it carried no prisoners.

The odds of success were slender indeed, but out of the fifteen or so plans Caroline and Chupwah discussed it was the only one that had *any* chance of succeeding. Every other idea had too many shortcomings. It was this or nothing. And doing nothing was not an option.

Caroline's father Eston had a saying that came to mind as they rejected one plan after another: "When in doubt, confuse them."

He had said it many times over the years and the lesson stuck. Her father had explained it simply: "It's not the punch you see coming that knocks you out, it's the one you don't see that does the trick." So with that advice rolling through her head, they inched their way closer to the army in front of them, hoping the punch they were readying would not be seen.

As she searched for some hope that their plan would work, other words of advice came to mind. Her father always said that the greatest strategy could be a simple one that the enemy would rule out as being too easily defended. As Eston would put it when conversing with guests at the campfire, "The obviously wrong ploy could be your best ploy, under the right circumstances." Caroline could only hope these were the right circumstances for an obviously wrong ploy.

The last point her father often stressed was simple: there was no greater weapon than courage, and by that he meant true courage, not the kind that men bragged about while downing drinks at the local tavern. No, what often separated the living from the dead was the kind of courage that allowed one to head face-first into battle, completely fearless, knowing all odds were against them, but clear of mind, in control of one's emotions and actions. "Steady as steel" was the way he put it.

Caroline did not have that kind of courage, or so she thought, as she struggled to control her nerves and sweated profusely, despite the evening's cool air. She even had difficulty gripping the reins of her horse. No, she was not fearless, and she did not have that kind of courage.

But Chupwah did, and if he did, then she would do what she could to have it too, because her father needed her. Perhaps courage was not the absence of fear, but the nerve to act in spite of it. Now she only had to get Chupwah on board with her plan.

"Chupwah, I once read in a book about my uncle, Akari, that there were four rules he tried to follow as a General in battle: namely, there was a time to run, a time to fight, a time to run *during* a fight, and lastly, a time to run *after* you fight."

"So what time is this, Caroline?"

"This is a time to run."

"Agreed. But to where? We can't go backwards without risking a run-in with General Roland again, not to mention the Tweeners in the caves. Or we can skip the Tweeners and climb the peaks of the Kin Kara, which few have survived."

"You misunderstand me, Chupwah."

"You want to go to west? Now there's some sense in that. It'll be a long, hard journey through the desert - we'll want to fill our canteens - but perhaps we can fall in with some of the wild men of Mulvaria and come up with another way."

"No, Chupwah. We are going to run *directly* at the troops."

"I don't think that's what Akari meant by running, Caroline! That would be suicide!"

"Listen, Chupwah. As soon as it turns night, under cover of darkness, we shall make our strike — we'll stampede the horses, and they'll be so distracted we can slip right on by!"

Chupwah looked thoughtful. "That's not bad. It's crazy, but it just might work."

Caroline brushed her hair from her face and looked Chupwah in the eyes, her dark pools locking on to his. "Chupwah, I wouldn't have made it as far as I have without your help, and you know this. But I want you to know, you are free to go at any time."

Chupwah would not hear of this. "Caroline, you are my General in our little army here, and I'll do as you say. I don't know about this plan, but we're not exactly in a favorable position here."

"No, we're not, but we have one advantage. We know they are there, but they don't know we are here. As far as my plan, we've talked over more than a dozen and not a *single* one was any good. We can try to sneak by them, leaving the horses, but why do that when we can use them to our advantage? They'll never expect it, and that is why it might work."

"It's worth a try. When the sun goes down, we will try," Chupwah replied, dismounting his horse and bringing the others to a pause. "Until then, let's rest. We're getting too close anyway - they'll see us if we get any closer. It's a miracle they haven't already."

The sun soon dipped below the trees, darkness overtaking all, as the moon had yet to appear, leaving her grateful for at least one lucky break. When Caroline struggled to make out her hand in front of her face, she knew it was time.

Thirty horses soon galloped at their behest and rumbled through the plains. Caroline clenched her teeth, wincing as the wind rushed through her hair, terrified of what was ahead. She could feel the force of the Generals' horse under her while Chupwah charged forward on his feet.

In an instant, they were upon the outermost guards on duty, who were taken by surprise and ran off in retreat. The narrow light of the stars revealed one guard standing in their way. He held his ground, jerking his sword from its scabbard while pulling a bugle from his side. He placed it to his lips to sound warning to the camp.

Although they were a ways from the main army, Caroline could hear the sounds of confusion coming from the encampment - frantic shouts, calls to action, metal clanging as soldiers pulled on their armor, tents ripped as soldiers stormed out.

Chupwah peeled off from the pack and ran to where he heard the bugle's call. He quickly found the guard with his sword drawn. Before the man could react, Chupwah was on him, sticking his arm out in a straight line and leveling the soldier as he ran by without breaking his stride. The guard went flying, rolling backwards head over heels. He landed unconscious beside his bugle, crumpled beyond repair.

Meanwhile, Caroline and the horses gathered steam. The beasts frothed at the mouth with excitement. She led them toward the middle of the camp, hoping this would cause the most distraction. As she did, she glanced behind and saw that Chupwah had already caught up. It was time to peel off from the horses.

Caroline pulled her left foot from the stirrup and swung it around, all of her weight now supported by her right leg. The horse reacted awkwardly but Caroline held tight to the reins, keeping it in line with the others. She was going to miss this horse. It was a war horse, and nearly leading the charge by itself with only minor direction from Caroline. But for the plan to succeed, she had to leave the mount behind, for they must sneak stealthily past the distracted soldiers.

Caroline was certain the horse would lead the rest of the mounts through the middle of the camp. The only thing left was for her to get off and let him. She hadn't even had a chance to give him a name…

She pushed off the stirrup with her right foot and jumped, landing roughly on the hard, arid ground of the plains. The landing jarred her knees and scraped both of her hands as she hit ground, but otherwise, she was safe. Chupwah ran to her, and they trailed away from the pack, getting as far from the action as they could. It was tough going this time of night, but they found comfort knowing that Maldazor's troops would have trouble, too.

Soon, they heard the clanging of swords, as confused soldiers panicked, fearing they were under attack. Voices shot out, trying to make sense of what was happening. The plan seemed to be working!

Chupwah and Caroline circled wide to avoid the forces. They picked up the pace as they grew more comfortable moving in the pale light, and were making good time until Caroline ran smack-dab, head first, into something large and bulky.

Unfortunately, whatever it was yelled out with the collision. Caroline squinted and a face slowly appeared before her. She had run right into a soldier guarding the perimeter – what awful luck.

The soldier drew his sword and yelled loudly. "Halt! By the order of Malda—" Before he could finish, his words were cut off mid-sentence as Chupwah leveled him with one strike.

"So much for that! Caroline, he has a horse. Take it and I'll be right behind you."

Caroline squinted again, seeing better as her eyes grew accustomed to the darkness. Off in the distance, it appeared that most of the soldiers were occupied by their feint with the horses, still unsure of where the attack was coming from. Well, most of the soldiers...

Unfortunately, trouble was on the way as the guard's scream had alerted others. Caroline could just make out a group of ten or so heading their way, some on horseback. They would likely not be pleased to find a Sasquatch waiting for them.

But they would not find a Sasquatch alone. Despite what he had said, Caroline was not going to leave Chupwah with these soldiers. Never. She would stand beside him and fight, even if it meant their cover was blown with no chance of ever rescuing her father. She could not do that to her friend.

"Chupwah, they're heading this way! You'll never make it alone, but together we have a chance." She lifted her sword and prepared for battle.

"There's no time to argue," Chupwah replied. For the first time Caroline detected panic in his voice, but she knew he was concerned about her safety and not his own, which he quickly proved by scooping her up and setting her on the guard's horse, holding her down as she tried to squirm free.

"Caroline, don't give up. I believe you will save your father, and maybe you'll even stop Maldazor in the process! Maybe I'll be there to help. But right now, this is the best way. I will keep them busy while you escape."

For the first time in years Caroline cried tears of sorrow, not anger, but true tears of sadness, and she did not scold herself or try to stop. She let them fall freely down her cheeks, where they landed in Chupwah's thick hair. "No, Chupwah. No! I will not go! Let me down!"

"Until we meet again, my friend."

He held her tight with one arm, then slapped the rear of the horse sharply with the other and roared, as loud a roar as she had ever heard, so powerful that her ears rang.

In a flash the horse was gone, gone before she could even say good-bye, and it flew so swiftly that it would have been suicide for Caroline to jump off, as much as she wanted to help Chupwah. Caroline heard Chupwah roar again, quieter from this distance but still powerful enough to shake the earth below. She could only imagine how terrified the horse was as it ran even faster. It was as if it knew it had already placed some distance between itself and the Sasquatch, with its only wish to increase that distance. There was no safe way for Caroline to even attempt to jump, and to do so would dishonor her friend's sacrifice, but it felt wrong and Caroline felt sick about it.

Over the footfalls of her horse's feet she could hear the furious roaring of Chupwah as he fended off his attackers. The roars came to her on the wind, so strong they sent chills down her back and goose bumps down her arms. Over and over he roared, which further encouraged the horse to keep moving, again and again, until finally Caroline heard one last roar that was silenced halfway through.

She listened desperately, her ears straining to hear Chupwah's roar again, knowing that she was still within range. But she heard nothing but the wind in her ears and the hooves of her horse as they took her further and further away from her friend.

Caroline had managed to make it past King Maldazor's Army. Her plan had worked, but it had cost her everything.

## Chapter Sixteen - The Council of the Dragons

Akari looked down with glee from his perch atop Tod. He sifted a chalky white powder through his fingers and watched it fall toward the ground, where it mixed with the air below to create a puffy white cloud.

His face lit up each time a new cloud appeared. No matter how many successful inventions he created, he still got a thrill when he perfected another. This particular experiment was especially thrilling as it went from just a wild idea, to a test, to a completed project in the span of a single night. It was rare to conduct experiments with such efficiency, and the effect was rather exciting.

The clouds were amazing - anyone looking up from the ground below would be unable to see through them and would have no idea that dragons were soaring above them.

Enough trouble had been raised by the first appearance of the dragons; there was no need to stir up more. He also had no intention to alert the town that they were flying to Dragon Island. Most Ambrosians thought Dragon Island had long been vacated. It was probably best to leave it that way, though some would likely realize that they'd been duped.

Dragons had not been seen for some ten years, perhaps longer. However, they officially were missed when they failed to retrieve their annual tribute during the Dragon Festival - and good riddance, thought most Ambrosians.

The three dragons flew in a V-shape similar to geese, with Tod in the lead and Akari on his back. Behind the leader, both Mouse and Jonas hung on to their rides with broad smiles, though they both were filled with a bit of fear. It was an unbelievable thrill riding such amazing beasts, and they wished it could go on forever. But Akari had warned them the ride would be short, only two hours or so, so they savored it while they could.

They both wished they could look down at the world below, although they understood why Akari was concealing them. After all, if someone had told *them* a few days earlier there were dragons flying around Ambrosia, they would have made battle plans that same day. But now they were having the thrill of a lifetime, and felt let down as the Dragons descended. Their ride was approaching its end.

As they dropped further, the clouds dissipated as Akari ran out of his supply of chalky powder, and Mouse and Jonas gasped as they finally could see beneath them. It was a sight to behold, soaring over the Dragon Sea high above the choppy water. Their eyes then turned to the infamous Dragon Island, which seemed to spring from the sea itself, a small island with a large smoking volcano. Dragon Island, a name that made up in accuracy what it lacked in creativity.

It was both stunning and terrifying to see the island looming ahead. As the volcano drew closer, the terror began to take complete hold of the boys, Mouse in particular, as they realized by the Dragons' flight path that they were not only heading to the crater, but they were preparing to fly *into* it.

"What are you doing?" yelled Mouse, not attempting to disguise his terror.

"Nothing to worry about, Mouse," Akari yelled over the onrush of air that muffled his words and blew back his hair. "This is their home. All is well."

"Are you crazy?" Jonas yelled as his hands dug deep into his dragon's spine.

"We've covered that, Jonas! Like I said, these dragons are going home, nothing more. Now hang on!" Akari shouted, his voice trailing away as his dragon suddenly shot down into the crater and disappeared from view.

With that, the other two dipped, one after another, and flew gracefully through the crater and straight down into the volcano. But they were stunned to find they were not in the belly of a volcano after all, but a hollowed-out mountain that housed a great dragon city.

"Welcome to Verrigo, my friends. The home of the dragons," Tod roared.

They looked around in wonder. There were dragons everywhere: some flying, others walking, young ones engaged in playful wrestling matches, while older, larger ones stood around and talked. Giant lanterns hung throughout the city, mounted on the inner walls of the mountain. Jonas saw a dragon flying around to relight the lanterns as needed, aiming balls of flame from his mouth to accomplish the task.

Mouse looked back to the crater they had just flown through and saw a large fire set over a huge pot of what appeared to be water near the opening, with steam rising out the exit. It was ingenious. The steam gave off the illusion of an active volcano. No human would ever suspect that inside the volcano was a lively dragon city. Who, in their right mind, would ever venture into a live volcano? He wondered if Akari had come up with the ingenious scheme.

A buzz was flowing through the city and in short order they acquired escorts, grim dragons who wordlessly flew by their side, occasionally nudging them toward a large chamber that held the Dragon Council. If the three dragons had expected a welcome reception, they were gravely disappointed, and even the slightest deviation off course by Tod, Drake, or Grayson caused one of the escorts to helpfully shove them back into place. The three dragons silently accepted their fate and flew toward the chamber while their human riders watched nervously.

They glided to their destination. Upon landing, Akari leaped down, landing gracefully on the ground. His demeanor belied his nervousness, yawning as if he did not have a care in the world. He stretched his arms and legs as if he had just awoken from a long and rather comfortable nap.

Mouse and Jonas also dismounted but with none of the apparent assuredness of their uncle. They were clearly nervous and on edge, a million thoughts running through their minds. They had no idea on how to act in the middle of a dragon city and figured – correctly - that they were better off staying near Akari, who had been in the city before. Meanwhile, the dragons walked into the chamber without saying a word, not even a good-bye to their riders, their heads bowed in shame.

Akari noted the restlessness of Mouse and Jonas. "Relax, Nephews. We couldn't have expected a hero's welcome under such circumstances, and seeing as they didn't eat us the second we touched ground, all in all, I'd say we're doing quite well."

"Akari, this is madness! Is there any way we can escape?" Jonas asked, looking around for an exit.

"Yeah, Akari, I don't care for this place," Mouse added. "It's hot, smells of sulfur, and call it a hunch, but I don't think we're wanted here."

"I can appreciate that, fellows, but you don't seem to understand what we are about to witness." He pointed into the chamber. "My kin, this is a Dragon Council, something very few humans can claim to have seen! It is a sight to see, and a story to tell your grandchildren when you have reached old age."

He walked toward the entrance, turning to beckon Mouse and Jonas to follow. But as soon as he turned back toward the chamber he was forced to stop, as the large granite doors slammed in his face.

"Oof," Akari grunted. "Rather rude, but I'll let you tell them so, if you don't mind." Akari straightened out his shirt and turned to the boys. "Well, I guess we weren't invited after all. No matter. To tell the truth a Dragon Council is an awfully boring thing, with that old bore Rausten going on and on about how they did things in his day. Not much different than *our* politics, really, though the dragons actually *elected* Rausten to serve them. So they only have themselves to blame, alas."

"Well, what do we do now, Akari? I really want out of here," Jonas said.

"Boys, we shan't stay long, but I must insist we wait this out. It is *your* fault they are in this predicament after all, seeing as the dragons came to your rescue. It wouldn't be right to duck out now."

Jonas looked like he was ready to explode with anger at that remark, but Mouse held out his arm to stop him. "That is true," Mouse said, just getting the words out when the great door swung open behind him. It was his turn to jump, as he was nearly knocked over as what appeared to be a female dragon shuffled through the door and beckoned them to enter.

"Certainly," Akari said to the dragon. Turning to the boys he added, "Look lively boys - dragons can sense your vibrations. Puff your chest up and show a little confidence, all right?"

"We don't want to go in—" Jonas started to reply before being interrupted by Akari.

"Exactly! We don't want to go in looking like idiots, Jonas. Right what I was getting at but you said it so much better. Remember - lively, boys!"

Akari grabbed them both by the arms and pulled. Not wishing to look foolish, they picked up their steps and Akari loosened his grip, leaving them to trail behind slowly.

They made their way toward the chamber, growing nervous as they neared the door. A group of eleven dragons were seated, arranged in a tight circle perched high above the floor so that they looked down on anyone who entered. The dragons were all different sizes and colors. Many of them wore rings through their noses, there were older-looking ones with white hair sprouting from their ears, and others with gold bracelets wrapped around their arms. An elderly dragon with especially hairy ears and graying skin sat in the middle with five dragons gathered on each side, and both boys correctly guessed that this was Rausten, the speaker of the council.

Tod, Drake, and Grayson stood below, their heads bowed in either shame or reverence for those seated above, or perhaps a combination of the two. But as soon as Akari entered, the chamber the door again slammed, right in the boys' faces, as if they were not there at all.

"Guess we won't be witnessing a Dragon Council after all," Jonas remarked, far from disappointed.

Mouse shrugged his shoulders and placed his ear against the wall to attempt to hear what was taking place in the council.

Jonas' curiosity was piqued. "What's going on in there?"

"Let's see. Right now Akari is thanking them for the warm welcome to the Dragon Council." He paused before continuing. "He also wants to thank them for not making it warmer in the way only dragons can." Mouse chuckled softly, unable to help himself.

"He's making jokes? And awful ones," Jonas said, his eyebrows arched. "Did they laugh?"

"I think so. Either that or they all growled at him. Hard to tell with dragons." Mouse kept his ear pressed to the door, but was unable to make anything else out as other dragons carried on the discussion in low voices.

Jonas walked to the door to try to listen in as well, but before he could get there, the doors swung open yet again. "Do they always do that?" he exclaimed, leaping backwards.

Akari rushed through the door with a large dragon claw roughly shoving him through. "Well, that was fast," Jonas deadpanned.

Akari did not look amused in the slightest and ignored Jonas' comment, instead stopping to yell back at the dragons. "You'll have to pick a side at some point! Be sure you make the right choice!"

A gruff voice called back. "We already have. We are for the dragons, as we always will be. Now go!"

Akari lifted his hands up, exasperated. "Well boys, we aren't wanted here, in case it wasn't made obvious. But I have news."

"About our father?" Mouse asked hopefully.

"Exactly. Your father has been sent to Maldazor's dungeons. It's just as we figured. Maldazor's plot is unfolding quite well, as it were. And revealing the dragons played rather well into his plans, I'm afraid. I figured as much, but it caused him to move faster than he anticipated, which ultimately may benefit us."

Seeing the confused look on his nephews' faces, he clarified. "He's moving so fast he's bound to make some rather serious mistakes in my estimation. He's now en route to Ambrosia, presumably to accept the crown that has likely been offered to him by the Princess. But here's the thing. Maldazor wanted to create a fake invasion to scare everyone to death, and now he's worried that he's gone and started the real thing."

"Unreal," Jonas said.

"Yet very real," Akari replied. "There's more. It seems I am not the only one blamed for murdering Wilhelm. They have sentenced to death a consort from Wilhelm's court, claiming she was an accomplice to the crime. She is set to die in two short days."

"Terrible," Mouse said. "I wish there was a way I could help her."

Akari's face broke out in a broad grin. "Just what I knew you'd say Mouse, and I never doubted it. You *can* help her! More than help her I'd say. Mouse, *you* are going to save her."

"Impossible," Jonas said. "You said they're going to kill her in two days! There's no way we could ever make it there and to my reading without the dragons to fly us, and I'm guessing that's out."

"A good guess, and correct. Well done, Jonas. And here I was, worried you weren't paying attention," Akari said. "Nonetheless, we will get there. I did not forget it was the eve of your birthday. The dragons have promised to take us to the shoreline, which will help considerably as I don't much feel like climbing the inside of this mountain. They don't do it out of any kindness, mind, but solely to be rid of us."

"Well, then let's be off," Mouse said while Jonas looked on skeptically, smirking. He realized he didn't have any other options, but that didn't mean he had to be happy about it.

They had hoped for the familiar faces of Tod, Drake, and Grayson, but instead three other dragons emerged. They said nothing but bent down, indicating the trio was to mount them. Akari, Jonas, and Mouse did so and the dragons silently rose in the air, going about their business solemnly. It was very disconcerting, and the ride was much rougher than the one that brought them to Dragon Island.

Akari looked backwards to catch a final glimpse of his three friends. He was not even given a chance to say good-bye, simply ushered out the door and sent away. But he couldn't find them, and just like that they rose from the same crater they had just entered. That was that.

Although Jonas and Mouse were impressed by the city in the mountain, they were not sad to leave - knowing you are in the middle of a dragon city and not particularly wanted there was unnerving.

As soon as their riders dismounted and touched the ground, two of the dragons took off without a word. But the last one, a younger looking dragon with dark red scales, paused briefly to mutter under his breath. "Many of us support you, Akari, and are doing what we can. Stay strong." With that, he too sprung from the earth and flew away.

"Well, that's good to hear, and I suspect many will come around shortly if Maldazor does what I expect. But nothing we can do about *that* right now," Akari said.

"No, there's not," Jonas said, cutting his uncle off. "So how do you propose we get to Ambrosia City? Tomorrow is my fourteenth birthday and I need to be told my Fate, but you've got us stuck in the middle of nowhere!"

"Still on that, are you? Well, that's fine. But I never proposed anything about *us* going to Ambrosia City. Maybe you didn't hear me earlier. *Mouse* is going to save her, and we will get you to your reading."

Mouse looked as if his stomach hurt. "Me? Alone? I can't go alone, Akari."

Akari walked over and put his hand on Mouse's shoulder. "Young man, let me see your arm. Come on, roll up your sleeve." Doing as instructed, Mouse revealed his mark, indicating his fate of being a great warrior. Akari did the same, revealing the same mark. "Now Mouse, this indicates that we are great warriors. Does it not?"

"It does," he replied, not sounding entirely convinced.

"Now I happen to think it's all nonsense, as I've told your brother. But it doesn't matter what I think. What matters is what *you* think. Now, do you believe you will become a great warrior, just as the wizard said and as the mark on your arm signifies?"

"I guess I do," Mouse said. "But why do I have to go alone?"

"Because you're the only one who can make it in time," Akari responded casually.

"That's ridiculous, Akari, I'm much faster than him," Jonas declared.

"Yes, that's probably true, but could you squeeze through the entrance to the tunnels that run beside the Great Falls on the Hyrax Cliffs?"

Jonas gasped, while Mouse looked on with an expression that indicated he was going to be sick and was trying desperately not to be.

"Surely you don't mean to send Mouse up *that* way to Ambrosia City?" Jonas added. "All manner of foul creatures reside there."

"I surely do, as there is no other way, not with the limited time we have anyway. I know those tunnels well, having explored them when I was quite young. I've scaled those cliffs with the proper gear, but I assumed you hadn't brought along any mountain climbing gear - did you?"

Jonas nodded, confirming that he had not. He was still having trouble reconciling what he was hearing.

"I figured. See, Jonas, this is the only way."

"This is folly!" Jonas shouted. "Not to mention we don't even know this woman. It's not like we're talking about saving the Queen or something, we're talking about a consort. You want to send Mouse through the Hyrax tunnels, tunnels filled with deadly Giant Rock Hyrax and who knows what else. It's insane. Enough of this, and let's concentrate on saving my father and sister."

The disappointment was evident on Akari's face, but before he could retort, Mouse spoke. "I'll do it, Akari. If you think I can do it, then I will."

Akari's disappointment vanished. "I don't think you can do it, Mouse, I know you can! And I'm proud of you.

Jonas, I didn't say it would be easy, and you're right, it's a hundred to one shot if you're the type of person that pays attention to those things, but there's an innocent life at stake. It is imperative we at least try."

Jonas remained unconvinced. "So tell me about this girl, Akari. Something tells me there's more to it than simply trying to save an innocent life."

"I don't know her at all, Jonas. But I will always stand up for someone who is innocent."

"So you say, but you know *of* her. How does she look? She must be something if you'd reject a Princess yet have an interest in *her*."

"She's stunning, Jonas, but that matters not. If she looked the way you're acting, we'd still save her, and you can believe that or not. Mouse has made his decision, and I applaud him for it. As for you, I'll get you to your wizard, and we'll learn your Fate, but for your sake, I hope he doesn't tell you you're going to be a consort, lest someone look upon you unfavorably."

"Fine, Akari. Mouse, I believe in you as well, because it is your Fate after all, and you will prove it. But there remains the matter of getting across the sea here. Any plans on that, or do you have a pill that will materialize a raft from thin air? Or maybe you know some magic clams that can transport us?"

"No, I haven't managed to pull a raft from thin air yet, and besides, we'd never get there in time. A raft is no good on choppy seas, and magic clams are something I've never considered - you'll have to discuss your idea further when we have time - but everything is under control."

"What do you mean, *everything is under control?* How are we going to cross the ocean? Will we swim?"

"Well, we could build a boat," said Mouse.

"Very true Mouse, and thank you for offering a solution rather than simply restating the problem..." Akari began, but Jonas interrupted his uncle yet again.

"Build a boat! From what? This island is barren. We're completely powerless here, trapped, with no control over anything!"

"Jonas, one can wish they were in control of all situations, but such a possibility does not exist. Take this turtle here." He pointed to a sea turtle burrowing in the sand nearby, preparing to bury its eggs. "An extraordinary swimmer, capable of covering vast distances swiftly, unlike its slow-moving cousin on land. Completely in control of where it goes and when, master of its own destiny. That is, until a storm comes along and takes the turtle wherever it pleases! Such is life."

Akari then pointed to the waves that crashed against the beach. "Now look at these waves. We often have a choice in life. We can ride on the crest of the waves, letting them take us where they will. Or we can swim, and fight the current to go where we'd like."

"How is this lecture helping us Akari?" Jonas blurted, completely beside himself.

"Have patience. If you'd stop interrupting, I could get to the point. See, often we are riding the waves, or fighting them, but every now and again there is a third option."

"What would that be, Akari?" Mouse asked, hanging on to Akari's every word, unlike his brother.

"As I was saying, often we are riding the waves, or fighting to swim against them." Akari stuck two fingers in his mouth and whistled, a sharp shrill sound. "And then there are other times, such as now, when we have *sea horses*."

"Sea horses? I don't see any sea horses," Jonas leaned over the beach and peered into the ocean, looking back at his uncle with a puzzled expression. "Did you tell some sea horses to come here?!?"

"My dear Jonas, you never *tell* a sea horse to do anything, you can only ask."

"Akari, I've never seen a sea horse that you could ride before. Aren't they just little itty-bitty things?" Mouse asked.

Jonas threw his hands up. "Exactly. This man is insane, Mouse. You still want to follow this guy? Riding sea horses! I've never seen one bigger than my hand, and yet he talks of riding one!"

"Not all of them are so small, nephews. Besides, what else would you use to get across a sea? When on land, use a land horse, and when at sea, use a sea horse. Pretty simple." He cleared his throat and went on:

"I know you're probably thinking we should go with dolphins, but I don't hold with them myself. They are unable to stay focused at all - flighty little things, awfully hard to keep on a straight path - and they get so caught up with jumping through the air, racing each other and whatnot that it adds a good half hour to your journey. And I didn't even mention how they chirp about everything and anything. No, sea horses are much better for *this* sort of thing, and luckily I happen to know quite a few in this particular sea."

As if on cue, three shapes emerged, dripping water as their bodies rose from the waves. One was a brilliant yellow, almost as painful to the eyes as staring straight into the sun. Another was spotted brown and orange, large splotches of each color alternating along its body. The last and smallest was green with yellow stripes. As Akari promised, they were nearly as large as a "land" horse and what's more, they were already saddled, ready to ride, with their tails floating just below the top of the sea, supporting the rest of their bodies above the surface.

"Good evening, fellows!" Akari called out. "Thank you so much for your service. We are greatly honored."

Akari bowed as the sea horses chattered with a strange combination of sounds. They chirped and neighed and seemed impossible to follow, but Akari managed. He nodded in response to their strange chatter, then patted the first one on the head and held its reins, motioning for Jonas to mount. Jonas walked over and allowed Akari to help him board - clearly he had lost the argument and thought it best to pretend it never happened. But Akari was not ready to let him off the hook.

"Can't believe you've never heard of riding sea horses before. Such a sheltered life on the homestead in Frogpond, Jonas. Eston really should have taken you out more. No matter. Now that I'm here, you'll learn!"

"Unbelievable," Mouse said, and Jonas was inclined to agree. Once again he had to admit he was wrong, which only made him more determined to be right during their next argument.

Akari made his own chattering noises, which sounded similar to a squirrel chirping and the sea horses clearly understood. Akari hopped on the yellow one and pulled its reins, forcing the sea horse to turn and face away from Dragon Island. He called for his nephews to follow his lead.

Mouse did as instructed while Jonas hung back. "That's it, Mouse. Come on, Jonas, no time to waste as the sun will be setting soon. We're going to head to the base of the cliffs first and give Mouse a proper send off. Then we'll head north to pay a visit to your wizard."

Jonas swung his sea horse around while Akari nodded his approval. "Just hang on to their necks. That's it. It can get a little bumpy, but if you can handle a dragon, you can do this standing on your head. Now, go!"

With that, the three sea horses were off, their little tails spinning to propel them through the water. They made good time, and luck was with them as the tide was heading in, which sped matters along immeasurably.

Mouse found it difficult to fully enjoy the ride, despite its inherent thrill. His self-confidence, which seemed so strong only minutes earlier, was already waning. How was he going to climb up tunnels that would soon go dark in the deep night? How would he make it through these dangerous places, where animals lurked, welcoming a change from the normal fish dinner they clawed from the sea each night?

Mouse held on tight to his sea horse's reins as they approached the cliffs, foreboding in the evening sky. But Mouse knew that Akari was right. If he was going to be a great warrior, it was time to prove it - providing he did not die in the process.

# Chapter Seventeen - Second and Third Guessing

Three days of monotony had passed since Caroline had slipped by Maldazor's Army, yet she still felt the heavy weight of depression from leaving Chupwah behind. As awful as it was to lose a friend, it was far worse because she knew that choices she made had led to the loss, a loss she felt certain could have been prevented.

Over and over the scenario replayed in her mind. It was a pointless exercise, but she tried to think of a way they could have made it through the line of soldiers without Chupwah suffering harm. No matter how much she thought it over, she could think of no other way she could have escaped the soldiers. Her mood darkened further when she realized that Chupwah had likely reached the same conclusion before they had even embarked on the plan. There was no question in Caroline's mind that he had planned on sacrificing himself all along, if needed - anything to help Caroline continue her journey.

Instead of feeling honored that he would do such a thing for her, it made Caroline feel small. She wanted to be a great warrior, not someone that great warriors like Chupwah sacrificed themselves for. Maybe she really was only cut out to be the wife of one as her Fate had foretold. After all, how could she claim to be a great warrior if she could not help a friend in need?

Worse, she knew that her father would be gravely disappointed. He never would have approved of this rescue mission in the first place. She had hoped to stifle his objections by rescuing him without a scratch to show for the effort. But the loss of Chupwah would enrage her father. He never would accept that a life was sacrificed to save his. He would not stand for such a thing. And that was assuming that Caroline would be able to save her father. Even her best-case scenario would result in her father's eternal disappointment.

Find her father? She laughed out loud at the possibility. How would she ever find her father? She was in a land she did not know, facing enemies led by the evil Maldazor, and she was a sixteen-year old girl. Perhaps she had let the idea of being nothing but the spouse of a great warrior color her thinking. Perhaps fighting that Fate would lead her to an early grave.

Caroline was unsure of what to do next. She might as well have been traveling blind. Chupwah had guessed that her father was taken to the castle dungeons at Azoria City and Caroline had agreed, setting them off in that direction. Still, there was no way to know for sure. There was also the question of what she would do once she got to the castle. How would she get in? How would she know where to go, even if she did manage that?

On top of all of that, she was riding through a cold, hard rain rarely found on this side of the Kin Kara mountain range, made worse by a brisk wind. What good was a desert if it poured rain at the exact time you happened to be traveling through it? She was miserable and soaked to her bones.

But at least the horse she had taken from the soldier was a good one, strong and stout. The rain didn't bother it in the least. The soldier had packed well so there were plenty of supplies, including beef jerky and a blanket that made things a lot more comfortable as she slept under the stars. Still, today's falling rain made her desperately miss her tent – the one shredded by General Roland's soldiers and left to blow off in the wind.

Not knowing the horse's name, she had called her Lizabell, in honor of her mother. In truth, Caroline rarely thought of her mother. She had been so young when her mother died. So young she didn't remember her. And, after all, it is impossible to miss someone you do not remember. Everything she knew about her mother came from her father's stories. She often wondered what it would have been like if her mother had lived, but it was not something she dwelled on.

What mattered was what she *did* have. No sense in worrying about what she did not, and her father said the same. While there was nothing she could do for her mother, she could still help her father and she was determined to fight for his freedom, whatever that might require. With that thought in mind, the rain, the misery, and helplessness became secondary to her true purpose.

"Drat this rain," she said to her horse, perhaps a slight bit delirious from her arduous journey. "But it won't hold us back, will it Lizabell?" She patted its mane and the horse glanced back at her.

The sun had fallen some time ago, yet Caroline pushed on. With the steady rainfall, she didn't think there'd be much chance of sleeping and the horse was going strong. Most impressively, Lizabell seemed to know the way. Caroline guessed the horse had been down this route before, during its life as a soldier's mount – riding back and forth from the field to Azoria, from peace to war and back.

At least Caroline hoped they were heading toward the castle. Her sense of direction was uncertain. She figured they were just a couple of days away from the castle, meaning she must stay vigilant to avoid coming dangers. So far, she and Lizabell hadn't encountered anything besides wild animals that scurried away as they approached.

These thoughts faded, though, as she was overcome by fatigue. She tried to fight it, but eventually her chin fell forward and pressed down on her chest. A few moments later, she was slumped over, sleeping in the saddle with her head resting on Lizabell's neck. The horse's even pace was relaxing and Caroline slept deeply, her head buried in the horse's mane.

*

Caroline did not know how long she had slept, but when her head snapped forward, she was jolted awake. Lizabell was bent over, munching on grass in the early morning sun. The rain had gone and the sky was a perfect shade of blue. It was shaping up to be a beautiful day, and it was obvious they had covered a great deal of ground. The capital of Azoria City must be close now, perhaps only a day away.

Off in the distance she could see the outskirts of civilization. Small huts with thatched roofs stood at the edge of the town. It was time to leave Lizabell behind, to help her blend in more easily. Caroline knew such homes were the beginning of Azoria City, a large city surrounded by a series of smaller towns for protection. The closer she came, the larger the buildings became and ultimately they would lead to the towering spires of Maldazor's castle that bordered the Green Sea.

Caroline knew that the Renwick River, renamed by Maldazor to honor his father, flowed into the sea. There were stories that sea serpents inhabited the chilly waters, but no one knew whether that was true or just a rumor that Maldazor perpetuated to keep people away.

Caroline dismounted and led the horse into the trees, patting it on the neck as she did. It was really a lovely horse. She sighed at the thought of losing the companionship of a fine animal, nearly as fine as the General's horse, or perhaps even finer given its sweet disposition, so rare to find in a seasoned war horse. Caroline felt remorse for the beating the guard that owned this horse had received. He must have had some good in him to have raised such a fine animal as this. Well, Caroline thought, maybe the horse and the soldier will ride together again.

Caroline did not feel hungry but knew she should eat some breakfast to sustain her strength. But she had no desire to eat beef jerky. She dug through the soldier's belongings, hoping she would find something different. She found a bag that looked promising - one she had overlooked in previous searches - but her hopes were dashed as she uncovered more of that dratted beef jerky. Does everyone only eat beef jerky on this island? She looked at Lizabell with envy. If only she could eat *grass* like the horse then she'd have something different to eat.

With no other option, she chewed on a piece of jerky and watched the river. The river was full and carried along flotsam in its swift current - mainly driftwood of all shapes and size.

Driftwood. That gave her an idea.

Suppose she could hang on to a tree branch and use it to float down the river? Drifting in the current would be faster than walking, especially since she would use great caution to go undetected.

The river sounded better like a better option. But what to do if soldiers came along? What if the river was heavily guarded? After all, it ran right past the castle, so they were not very likely going to allow some girl to just float on by.

The more Caroline thought about it, she realized her chances of making it through Azoria without being spotted were slim. She knew she would need to be cunning to sneak in without being caught.

Following her brief breakfast, she paced back and forth trying to think of a solution. With her mind racing, she didn't pay attention to where she was walking and she soon stood in the middle of swampy marshland, sinking to the top of her boots.

The marsh was soggy with brackish pools of water, a haven for bullfrogs and dragonflies, but not such a great place to walk. In fact, it was downright disgusting. She yanked her feet from the muck. The swamp did all it could to swallow her boots; it was all she could do to escape. Free at last, she sat on the ground and used a stick to scrape off the mud from the soles, feeling dejected as she had not thought of a plan.

Then again... She stood among tall cattail reeds; in fact, they grew throughout the swamp. The reeds brought to mind a story of her father's, where he was being chased by an enemy and forced to take refuge in a swamp. With nowhere else to go, he broke off a reed and used it to breathe under water, waiting many hours until he was certain his enemies had moved on.

She broke off a number of reeds and slid them into her scabbard where they pressed tightly against her sword. These reeds could prove useful, but still, she needed more. Staying in one place with a reed in murky swamp water would be easy enough to hide in, but how could she do so while floating on a log down a fast river?

She left the swamp and walked along the river bank, still desperate for an idea. She made her way up and down a narrow slope, where she tripped on an exposed tree root. Caroline flailed her arms in effort to regain balance. She just managed to stay on her feet when her eyes lit up. That was it! The idea she had been looking for! If she could find an old stump, one with its roots still attached, it would be perfect. But where?

Luckily, this river was popular with beavers and there many chewed stumps strewn about the forest. That was all well and good, but getting one from the ground, roots intact, would be tough indeed. "If only Chupwah was here," she thought. "He could pull a stump right out of the ground, roots and all!"

She sighed. "OK, Caroline, enough," she warned herself. "No reason to focus on *that* again. Think of the here and now."

With her focus back to reality, she noticed some trees that had the misfortune to take root on an eroding hillside. Years of rain had left roots exposed, leaving entire trees in a precarious position, destined to topple over as eventual erosion would wash away all of the soil that held the roots tight. But these trees were small and ill-suited for her purpose.

She traveled deeper into the forest and found a small creek that had cut a nice ravine through the woods over the years. Frogs and otters dived into the water as she moved, and soon, she found exactly what she was looking for. She ran toward it. Yes, this would work, a big trunk chopped down to size by beavers.

She arrived at the stump and shoved as hard as she could. It was hard work, pushing with all her might again and again, every muscle in her body straining with effort. With her face covered in sweat, she gave one last shove and felt the roots give way from the earth. She drove forward with all she could give until she felt the roots pull entirely from the ground, and with a final burst of effort, it skidded down the side of the ravine and fell into the creek.

Caroline nearly shouted with joy but bit her tongue, not wishing to attract attention. She went into the water after the stump, dragging it down the creek to the river. Once there, she beached it to go back to Lizabell.

"Sorry, girl, but I'm afraid we must part," she whispered to her mount, stroking its mane one last time. She kissed the horse on its nose. It was a much more peaceful good-bye than with her previous horse. She loosened the reins and saddle, tugging them free and dragging them into the woods - no sense in leaving any sign that this horse was once a soldier's. She covered the saddle with leaves, but not before using her sword to cut off the leather reins and removing a few other items of use before returning to the horse one last time.

"Now Lizabell, you take care of yourself. Try not to get mixed up in any more wars if you can help it. Go find some little old lady with nothing else to do but take good care of you and take you on quiet rides in the woods. Won't you, girl?"

She patted her one last time and left the horse to go where it may. She figured it would continue on its course and head back to its stable. But there was always a chance it would find a better life, away from being the target of arrows and swords, forced into battles it little understood. The life of a war horse seemed to be a sad one, but such was Fate.

Caroline returned to the mouth of the creek. She took the leather straps and tied them around her wrists so they would not come loose, then pushed the stump into the water with the roots facing the back. She hopped into the river, finding it cold but tolerable, and looped the leather around the stump.

She was pleased to find that the stump seemed to conceal her fully. But the celebration was short lived as she was swept into the river current, gasping, grasping each end of the straps tightly to float with her face hidden in roots. Caroline could not resist congratulating herself; she was making great time and watched as she flew past the houses on the shore.

It was almost relaxing floating, if only she knew more about where and what she was heading for. Of course, she could not fully judge how good her plan was until she actually made it through unscathed.

After some time passed, she pulled her head above the roots for a better view and was able to see above water level. There were rows and rows of houses still ahead, built along the banks of the river, raised with stilts to keep them safe during floods. They were coming up quickly, so she sunk back into the water and crossed her fingers she would stay concealed.

She placed a reed between her teeth and breathed through it a few times above water to get a feel for it and dipped into the water. She hoped it looked natural, with the reed appearing to be just another root.

Caroline could rest easy, as to anyone who happened to look out at the river, it would appear that a stump was floating by, one stump among a thousand other branches and logs that would pass by that day, never revealing that a young girl - who intended to rescue her father from the King - was floating underneath. In two or so miles, if all went to plan, that girl would find herself in Maldazor's backyard, ready to prove she was a great warrior, once and for all.

## Interlude - Maldazor

Fritz tapped lightly on the door, hoping his announcement would go unheard. They had traveled a long way to meet the person behind the door, never uncertain their plan would work, yet now that they were here, his confidence wavered. There would be a rich reward if the plan came off, but a voice inside Fritz kept reminding him that there were more important things than money, and he was starting to believe it. There were much more important things.

Like breathing, for example.

However, the voice next to him, which belonged to his partner Frederick, had been telling Fritz throughout their entire journey that money was the *only* thing that mattered, and thus they had to see this through. Fritz had been convinced, yet noticed that *he* was the one carrying the bundle of bones and small treasures removed from the grave atop Cemetery Hill, not Frederick, and more, he was carrying them at Frederick's insistence.

Fritz looked toward his co-conspirator as the door remained closed and unanswered, hoping that they could turn around and leave. Instead, Frederick gestured with his hand in a fist, air motioning for Fritz to knock again.

"Harder this time," he whispered, his face wrapped in a nervous mask. It didn't help Fritz's unease to see that Frederick was as frightened as he was, and only pretending not to be.

Nonetheless Fritz sighed, shrugged his shoulders slightly, and rapped on the door again, harder this time, as instructed. The sound echoed off the stone walls behind them, seeming to reverberate throughout the entire castle. Too hard.

But there was no question *this* knock would be answered as they could hear shuffling noises in the room behind the door. Fritz felt his hand shake violently as they waited, his senses lessened as his breathing rate increased. It was all he could do to not drop the bundle, turn, and run. And he might have if Frederick had not been gripping the bottom of his shirt, a safeguard against just such an action.

"It's not going to work," Fritz whispered. His slender body rocked back and forth while his dark eyes bounced across the hallway, honing in on a tapestry designed to mark the reign of the current King.

"We've been over this, Fritz. It will work. Just leave it all to me," Frederick replied, before adding sternly. "But hold on to that bag until I say so."

Fritz looked to Frederick and noted the sudden calmness in his voice and body, but with an underlying edge. Suddenly Fritz had the faint notion that what might be good for Frederick would not be so good for him, yet he continued to resist the urge to flee.

Finally the door swung open, creaking on its hinges. Standing in the doorway was a man around the age of fifty, a handsome man if Fritz could be honest. His beard was trim and immaculately groomed, his dark hair pulled straight back into a pony tail, and he was in impressive physical condition, slim and fit, the contrast to his slovenly brother Wilhelm.

It was Maldazor, King of Azoria. And he did not appear to be in a particularly good mood, although his visage softened slightly when he saw who had been knocking.

"Aw Frederick, and, um," he said.

"Fri....Fri...Fritz, sir," he said, bowing "Your highness."

"Yes, Frederick and Fri...Fri...Fritz," he replied, imitating Fritz's stuttering, then laughed, heartily and richly. "Please, come in, come in." He held open the door and quickly shut it behind them as they entered, taking good care to ensure they were not watched as he did.

"Do you have the ..." Maldazor paused as if what he was saying was wrong, before dropping the act. "No sense in being proper about things now. We're among friends. Do you have the bones and such? Or what's left of them?"

Frederick stood tall and proud. "We do, sir. Course we do. Fritz, out with it."

In his nervousness, Fritz nearly tripped over the bag while he dragged it to Maldazor. He dumped the contents at the King's feet. A cloud of dust appeared, then settled to reveal a scrambled assortment of bones and trinkets. But with such anxiety, Fritz hit the skull with his foot, which rolled off, to Frederick's embarrassment. Maldazor stooped to pick it up mid-roll, stared at it briefly, and placed it back in the pile. He then fished out an ornate dagger from among the bundle and ran his finger along the edge of the blade.

"Still sharp," he said, holding his finger up to reveal a tiny cut. "As sharp as the day our family presented it to *Osirah*. And as sharp as it was on the day we buried *Osirah* with it."

Fritz gulped at the emphasis on the name Osirah while Frederick outwardly remained the image of calm. "No, your majesty, those are the bones of Akari, just as you requested," he said. "Fritz here removed them himself."

"Is that so?" Maldazor quizzed, turning to Fritz and looking him in the eye. The nervous man tried to return his gaze but failed. He stared at the floor, just managing to spit out a reply.

"It's so," Fritz said unconvincingly.

Frederick knew they were on thin ice and stepped in. "Your highness," he said. "May I ask you a question?"

"You may," the King replied curtly.

Frederick assumed the posture of one who is pretending to be in control of a situation, hoping to bluff his way through. "Does it really matter whose bones are in that bag? I mean, either way they belong to a great warrior and a former Chief Knight. I daresay you *are* planning on resurrecting a Chief Knight, since the ones you've had over the years have all been worthless. Am I correct?"

Fritz waited for Maldazor to explode, but strangely the King seemed to be curious rather than angry. "Whatever gave you such an idea, Frederick?"

"Well, I've mostly pieced it together through some of what you said along with what you've had us do," Frederick said casually, while Fritz resisted the urge to shout him down. He was acting the fool and cocky to boot, and surely Maldazor would be displeased. Yet his partner continued in the same tone. "I know much of such things. You don't end up in my business of grave robbing without learning a thing or two.

"And when we opened up Akari's tomb, your majesty, the truth is, it was *empty*. Not a bone, not a skull, not a finger nail. Now anyone else would've come back here with naught but an empty bag, and poor Fritz was ready to, but I said 'Now hold on, we've got a full graveyard here we can pick from. And none would be better than old Osirah, the most feared Chief Knight we've ever had. That's who we need, Fritz, and won't Maldazor be *pleased?*' So that's what we did, your highness."

Maldazor looked slightly annoyed as he twirled the dagger between his fingers, mulling over Frederick's words. Fritz felt his heart leap as he had the notion that Maldazor seemed to be agreeing with what his partner had said. Finally, he shook his head, indicating he did agree, and Fritz was joyous beyond belief.

"That's good. Solid reasoning all around, and I salute you for it, Frederick. You've done well. Now you say Akari's grave was empty? Not a sign of anyone or anything? You're certain of this?"

"Not a thing," Frederick replied. "Right, Fritz?"

"Yeah, yeah," Fritz stammered. "Nothing at all."

Maldazor looked distracted as he mumbled to himself, though loud enough to be heard by the grave-robbers. "Strange. Explains a lot, but still, this is most unexpected. I'll have to deal with Natalia, she won't be happy. But a new Chief Knight—" His voice trailed off without completing the thought out loud.

He raised his eyebrows and spoke louder, directly to Fritz and Frederick. "Very good then- Osirah it is. The twists of Fate can be a winding road indeed, but never question them. Osirah is perfect." He smiled broadly, speaking even louder. "Gather up the bones, with all of his personal effects, and put them back into the burlap sack."

They did as instructed while Maldazor reached for a vial filled with a green liquid. "Good. Now Frederick, if you could lean in and place this all the way at the bottom of the sack, underneath the bones and such." He lifted the stopper on the vial and smoke poured out. He gave the vial to Frederick. "Just pour it on in there, all the way to the bottom now."

Frederick leaned into the bag and soon Fritz could hear liquid pouring. He watched as a hint of green smoke lifted out of the bag.

Maldazor nodded with satisfaction. Then, he acted as though he had missed an important detail "Oh. I almost forgot. It won't work if we don't put this in there." He held the dagger up high. Fritz could see the King's eyes in reflection on the dagger and jumped back. They were manic, the eyes of a crazed man, and Fritz wanted no part of it. He ran to the door but it was locked, and try as he might, was unable to unlock it.

There was no escape, so Fritz turned and watched as Maldazor took the dagger and drove it deep into Frederick's back, swiftly, and with great force. Fritz couldn't see Frederick's face, which was concealed by the bag, but he heard him gurgle in pain. Then Frederick shook and died, his last words cut off by the choking. Maldazor then shoved Frederick's body in to the bag with the dagger sticking between his ribs.

"I thought I mentioned this when we spoke before," Maldazor said. "The secret of resurrecting a life is giving one to bring it back. There's just no way around it! Maybe you forgot, Frederick, or maybe you thought I would simply sacrifice your friend here."

At that, he winked at Fritz with an evil look in his eye, an expression that gave him the chills. Maldazor tied off the bag with a rope and shoved it in the corner, where it lay motionless. He peered over at Fritz, who was frozen in place, stunned. "We'll see how it goes. I've never done this with a human before. Just rats. I'm dying to see how it turns out!"

Fritz said nothing, his eyes bugging out. Maldazor walked over and placed his hand on his shoulder, which caused Fritz to squirm.

"Relax, Fritz. If I had wanted to kill you, I would have. But I like you. You were smart enough to know that you couldn't *outsmart* me, unlike your friend here. There's something to be said for such a man."

Fritz said nothing as he had no idea how to respond. So he stood motionless and watched as the bag twitched, lightly at first, then violently. That grabbed Maldazor's attention, to Fritz's great relief. Suddenly, the bag ripped, with the dagger tearing through the canvas. A man stepped out, leaving tattered rags behind. Fritz was gone. Standing before them in his place was a fierce looking man with a ghostly pale face and unkempt eyebrows that jutted from his forehead. His eyes were all white, with no pupils. His skin was ashen, creating the distinct impression that he just stepped out of a grave.

He opened his mouth to speak, but nothing came out. So, he looked around the room, confused. Fritz was unsure if the man could actually see.

But Maldazor, on the whole, looked quite pleased. "It'll take him a few days to sort things out - if he's anything like the rats. But I am happy to announce that I have a new General for my army! I will inform Chief Knight Gobie that his services are no longer required." He then turned back to Fritz. "See, this is all working out rather nicely after all, Fritz. I'll see to it that you get your reward." With that, the King grabbed him by the arm and ushered him toward the door and unlocked it.

"There is one last thing. I want you to tell everyone you come across this. You see, I have business to attend to down south and I need someone in charge here. I couldn't have asked for a better man than Osirah. So I want you to tell them - tell them all now! - that Osirah is back."

At this, Osirah seemed to recognize his name and let out a nasty, guttural growl.

"Now, now big fellow," Maldazor counseled. "No need to get excited. Not yet anyway. There will be plenty of time for *that*."

The King turned again to Fritz. "Like I said, spread the word." He snickered as Osirah growled again. "He's apt to keep things in line here, while I attend to Ambrosia. You see, before the week is through I shall be named King of Ambrosia, and I will finally rule two-thirds of the kingdom that *properly* belongs to me.

"But Fritz, don't tell them all of that, yet. Just tell them about Osirah. That should be quite enough for now!"

## Chapter Eighteen - Becoming a Warrior

Mouse was having the time of his life riding the ocean waves on a sea horse. It was amazing, feeling the wind rush through his hair and sea spray splash on his face. But that fun was tempered, substantially, by what he was about to get himself into.

Soon he would climb through a steep tunnel, up a cliff, moving past creepy, crawly things in an attempt to save a woman he had never even met. And he would be taking on this dangerous mission all on his own. How had he reached the point, where a great warrior like Akari, would entrust him, little old Mouse, to pull this off? Sure, his small frame was the only one that could fit through the narrow entrance of the tunnels. And, yes, he had the mark of a great warrior, but what really brought him here? And then it all came crashing back. He was instantly transported from the back of a sea horse in the middle of the ocean to the day that had changed his Fate.

It was his fourteenth birthday. As was the custom of Ambrosia, his father took him to the monastery of a wizard named Wallary. The wizard would do a reading to determine how the remainder of Mouse's life would unfold. When he gleaned enough information, he would make a *mark* on Mouse's upper arm. From that day forward, Mouse's Fate was sealed. The mark would determine what Mouse would do for a living, which would affect other parts of his life.

In many ways, the system worked. Everyone had a role in life and a job to perform. Few rebelled against their Fate, and those who did were typically shunned - Mouse's "real" parents, for example, were shiftless lay abouts who had forsaken their duty to serve the King as prescribed. As long as the majority accepted their Fate, the system kept things in order.

There was work. There was reward. And, you were part of the Kingdom of Ambrosia.

Mouse had gone into his reading with a great deal of trepidation. He was understandably nervous, but no more than what would be viewed as normal. Anyone about to learn the fate of his or her life would have a degree of excitement, but this was tempered by his opinion that he had no chance of becoming a warrior. He loved training alongside his brother under the tutelage of their father and learning their ways, but he knew he had not shown any particular skill for battle.

The wizards, with their insight to the Fates, would certainly realize he was not cut out for such a life, even if it would be unusual for the son of a great warrior to not be chosen to follow his father's footsteps, even if his father had adopted him. Mouse knew it was more likely he would be chosen to become a farmer, or perhaps, to work with his father in the foundry. But he hadn't shown much promise in the foundry, either.

Being marked as a warrior was surely out of the question. Mouse made mighty efforts to learn how to fight. He trained hard, too. But it did not come naturally or easily to him. He also was short for his age. He and Jonas were around the same age, but Jonas was nearly a foot taller and much broader in his chest and shoulders.

So when marking day came, Mouse left his father behind and walked the lonely dirt path to the wizard's hall and climbed the steps to reach the front door. The house appeared humble from outside, simple and plain. The door was propped open, so Mouse cleared his throat to draw attention and waited. When that failed, he coughed to make himself known. When that failed, too, he took a few cautious steps and peered inside.

Mouse was stunned to see the wizard fast asleep at this midday hour. He was lying on the ground, wrapped in a rug and snoring in front of a barely flickering fire, which gave little warmth. The room was chilly and Mouse shivered.

Unsure what to do next, Mouse coughed again, hoping to rouse the wizard. He tried again and again, louder and louder. Still, no response but snoring. Next, he walked over to the wizard, looked down at the old man with his unkempt beard and hair, and hoped he would find a solution without offending him. The wizard held a great deal of sway over Mouse's future and Mouse didn't want to anger him.

Despite its simple outward appearance, the home was furnished with chairs covered in beautiful fabrics and tables made of fine wood. But the beauty of the furnishings was diminished by its lack of order and neglect. Mouse searched the room for something of use, and found an open bottle on a table, containing a red liquid. A silver goblet was leaning precariously next to it. Mouse smelled the liquid. It was wine, just as he'd suspected. He picked up the goblet and examined it. He admired its encrusted jewels that were arranged in an ornate dragon pattern. It was a fascinating piece, and obviously used often, judging from the oil stains on the sides of goblet left there by the wizard's hand.

He placed the goblet back on the table, but lacked the proper care. The goblet tipped over and rolled off the table, clanging loudly against the stone floor and echoing off the walls. He had not planned that, but his problem was solved. The wizard sat up and was instantly wide awake.

"Suh-suh-sorry," Mouse stammered, though secretly relieved the wizard was awake. "I didn't mean to do that."

Wallary looked around, seemingly confused about where the voice had come from. He finally laid eyes on Mouse and stared hard, though he still seemed baffled about what was going on. The wizard tried to stand, but fell back down, with the rug unrolling. He laid on his back, wearing only a bath robe, a tattered garment that looked to be as old as the wizard.

"Sir, my name is Mouse, err, Alexander. Alexander Strongheart, as it were. I'm here today as it is my birthday. My fourteenth birthday, that is. I'm, um, here for my reading." Mouse then bowed, trying to show proper respect though completely clueless about how to do that.

The wizard didn't even sit up. He stared at the ceiling. His hair and beard went a thousand directions. He made half-hearted attempts to straighten them with his fingers. He coughed, rather violently, then cleaned something from his ear, held it out in front of his face, and admired it briefly before wiping it on his shirt. It was known that wizards took a vow to avoid marriage, but it seemed to Mouse that this particular wizard need not have bothered.

Mouse hid his repulsion and spoke up again. "Um, sir, I had an appointment today at eleven, for my reading? I believe I mentioned I turned fourteen today. I do believe the reading, ahem, has to be done today?"

The wizard slowly turned his head and cleared his throat, finding his voice at last. "Yes, yes, just hold on a second. I'm not feeling too well at the moment. It seems someone spiked my wine. I believe there was alcohol in it. Can you believe that? Who would do such a thing?" At this the wizard giggled, then laughed uproariously at his own joke while Mouse watched on silently, too nervous to find it funny.

"Um, isn't all wine that way, sir?" Mouse finally spat out.

"You know, now that you say that, I believe you are right! Why, I think that's been my problem all along!" Now the wizard outright cackled, which was rather unnerving. The wizard regained his composure and managed to shakily pull himself to his feet with the aid of a chair. "I'll have to talk to someone down at the winery. Something must be done about this, I won't stand for it!" He then fell back over and cackled away while Mouse looked on, bewildered.

When the laughter finally died down, Mouse spoke up yet again. "Sir, about my reading?"

"Aw yes, well, about that. I suppose I should sit up." As he did, he promptly fell over on to his side. The wizard sighed. "Well, I guess standing is just not meant to be right now. So let's see. Anyone looking at you could get a feel for you rather quickly. A Strongheart! And simply a hulkish brute of a boy, aren't you? Fearsome!"

Mouse was unable to discern if the old wizard was joking or not.

Wallary then held out his left hand in front of his eyes and started counting his fingers, getting all the way to eight before giving up. "That's strange, very strange. Why, I only had six fingers last night!" With that he cackled again, laughing so hard that tears streamed down his face. His cheeks were red and he gasped for air before settling down. "OK, boy, time to get this over with. Could you do me a small favor and bring over that goblet - yes, that's the one - and don't forget the bottle! I'd like to test it again, if you don't mind, make sure they really did lace it before I go around making false accu-stations."

He froze, thinking over what he said. "Accu-stations!" he repeated, while Mouse did as instructed, doing his best to ignore the old wizard, who again was howling with laughter.

"There, that's a good boy. Go ahead and fill the bottom of that cup, just need a taste right now." Mouse did so and handed it to him. The wizard promptly held the vessel to his lips, spilling most of the wine down his neck. His hand then fell to his side while the goblet rolled across the floor, echoing off the walls while Wallary felt his neck and tried to wipe the wine off with his bare hand.

"Oh, dear me. Seems I must have a hole in my neck. Ha ha! Well, son, do you see that barrel over there? With those metal bars? Looks like they have stamps on the end of them? Go grab one, the one with little swords, if you please."

Mouse raised his eyebrows in shock, knowing this was the same brand his father bore, but went and did as he was told. This couldn't be the way one's Fate was determined, could it?

"Are you certain, sir? Don't you want to ask me some questions or something?"

"No need. None at all. I can see exactly who and what you are. I'm a wizard!

"Yes, sir," Mouse replied, stalling for time. He looked over the various brands in the barrel before selecting the one that depicted swords locked together in an x-pattern, as ordered. "Yes sir, I have it."

"Good. Now go throw a couple of logs on the fire for me, and once you do, go ahead and place it in there. Let it get real hot, see, and when it's good and ready, you let me know. I'm going to take a little nap. It's been a long day and it's not even noon yet!" With that he closed his eyes, and within seconds, Mouse heard the old wizard snoring.

Mouse did as he was told and stoked the fire until it was roaring. The hair on his arms was getting singed as he stood in front of the fire. He stuck the iron deep into the hot coals. While doing this he thought of his father outside, who had been such a great warrior, and then his brother, already a fine swordsman and excellent shot with a bow and arrow.

How would things change if others looked at Mouse as being their equal? It would certainly make life different, even though his father had never looked down on him for his lack of ability in fighting or weapons-making. So long as he tried his best, his father was satisfied. But he was the exception. Everyone else treated him as the runt of the family, a tag-along, and not a true Strongheart. Today, that could change.

With the wizard sound asleep, Mouse wandered over to stare at the other brands. It was an interesting mix. There were some with pitchforks, others with pots and pans, one with an ax, and another with simply a book on it. He was unsure of what the symbols really meant, though some were easy enough to guess.

Mouse's heart began to race as a thought dawned on him. By simply choosing one of these other brands, he could pick the course of his life. Figure out what all of the symbols meant and he was master of his own Fate, of his own future. It was fairly obvious Wallary was too sauced to notice the difference, no matter which one Mouse chose. He could do anything he wanted with his life, an opportunity rarely, if ever, afforded Ambrosians.

Mouse rifled through the barrel and removed one of the brands, the one with a pitchfork. Clearly this would lead to him becoming a farmer. He eyed it for some time, feeling the brand with his hands, running the pitchfork against his fingertips. There was no shame in being a farmer. He would live a good, safe, productive life, and one he could do quite well at.

His eyes shifted back and forth between the brand in hand and the one hot in the fire. There was something to be said for either Fate. The quiet life of the farmer or the constant struggle of a warrior in the King's Army. He weighed the pros and cons, went over them again to be sure, then sighed and plunged the pitchfork back into the barrel.

There really was no choice. His Fate had been decided. It may have happened in a rather strange way, from a rather strange man, who in his delirium decided that Mouse was destined to be a warrior, but who was he to argue with a wizard? Who was he to question the way of things? If being a warrior was his Fate, then he would embrace it with open arms.

Little time passed before the wizard awoke and drove the brand into Mouse's right shoulder, searing his flesh and leaving behind the mark of the warrior. His Fate.

Now here he was, six months later, having to prove to himself that he had made the right decision to accept that Fate. They had arrived on the mainland, where Jonas and Akari left Mouse behind. He was on a narrow shoreline that ran under the cliffs, just a short walk to the place where he would squeeze through tunnels that would lead him to rescue someone he had never met, with few instructions from Akari and no help expected.

He held a sword in his right hand and a glass jar that Akari had given him in his other hand. He approached the narrow and dark hole at the base of the Cliffs. This was his Fate - to be a warrior — even though he could not completely wrap his head around it. No matter. His Fate was sealed. He could no longer choose the life of a farmer. That was fine, Mouse thought, because he *was* a warrior. He could feel it in his bones.

Now it was time to prove it.

# Chapter Nineteen - The Best Plans

So far, everything had been going smoothly for Caroline during her trip down the river.

She knew it wouldn't last.

The young girl had almost been enjoying a leisurely trip down the river, simply drifting along without anyone noticing and making good time as she soared along the river bank. It was peaceful and quiet, and she felt quite confident in her scheme. Suddenly, a panic overtook her - she hadn't bothered to actually breathe underwater with the reed! It would not be a good idea to test it for the first time when she needed it to work, so Caroline decided to give it a go while it was safe to fail. Sure, it *seemed* like it would work, as it had worked for her dad, but when she dove into the river and tried to draw in a breath of fresh air, it did not work well at all. In fact, it nearly killed her.

Caroline came up from under the water coughing, spitting, and gasping for air. This was no good - what little air she did pull in through the reed was far from enough. Why did this seem to work for everyone else?

Caroline cursed herself for not testing it before she went downstream. It had seemed to make so much sense, she had not suspected that it wouldn't. Now, she was stuck. Her mind raced, desperately trying to think of a solution. All she could do was to keep floating behind the stump and hope for the best. Maybe if her head stayed tangled among the roots and the rest of her body hidden under the log, she could blend in well enough. Her hair certainly felt dirty enough to be confused for a root.

But the pressure was overwhelming and her hands were shaking, making it difficult to hang onto the slippery roots. This was going to be a long ride to the castle, and far from the leisurely trip she had hoped for.

Even worse, she now could hear people talking on the banks of the river. The channel had narrowed, so anyone walking by was almost right next to the water. On the plus side, this also caused the current to gain speed, which was a relief to Caroline. The less time she spent in the water, the better. Caroline was thankful that mud had dyed the water a dark brown. She tried to make few movements as to avoid being discovered.

Each new voice raised another panic in Caroline - but they walked right on by, minding their own business. Her arms were growing tired, though, and she struggled to continue clinging to the log. How much longer would this last? Then again, it didn't matter. She would remain strong, no matter how long it took. She had to find her father.

As she drifted along, Caroline noticed that the tone of voices and conversations was changing. At first, it was farmers talking about crops. Then, it was soldiers using stern voices as they talked about warfare. She knew about this type of talk. She had heard her father carry on similar conversations with old friends. In the middle of the chatter, her heart leaped when she heard the word Sasquatch. Could they be talking about Chupwah?

Caroline strained her ears, almost revealing herself as she raised her head from the water. But she could not quite make out what was being discussed, and before she could get any more insight, she drifted out of range.

*

An uneventful couple of hours passed when suddenly the river began swirling, spinning Caroline in circles. She was bobbing up and down in the angry river. Heavy waves lashed at her. It took all of her power to simply hang on.

She came around a bend in the river and gasped at what she saw. There it was - exactly what she both hoped and feared to see - the towering castle of Maldazor.

It was beautiful and terrifying, with deep red flags waving above the gray, foreboding towers and spires that blocked out the sun. Caroline was awestruck, but at the same time her mood darkened. She knew it would not be easy to penetrate such a fortress.

The water was still swirling, so Caroline's view of the castle was spinning all around her. It seemed that the castle grew more imposing with every rotation. Caroline feared that a soldier would snatch her from the river at any moment. She was getting dizzy, too. But she gritted her teeth and hung on.

Just when she felt she had reached her limit, the river calmed and she floated lazily into the Green Sea directly behind the castle. It was not a moment too soon. This adventure business, as it turns out, is hard. And, it was about to get even harder.

Caroline untied the leather straps from her wrists and yanked them off. It was time to make an exit strategy.

Guard towers surrounded the shore, looming large in both the sky and her mind. Caroline expected to hear yelling, shouting, and the ringing of warning bells from the towers any second now. How was it possible she had not been spotted?

She released the tree stump and found she was fifty feet from the shoreline, so she took a deep breath, gathered her strength, and swam inwards. It was a good thing her brothers were not on this mission, seeing as they could not swim. *Her brothers.* She was so caught up in her mission she had hardly given them a passing thought over the last few days, and now, she found that she missed them greatly.

She longed to see them. She missed the way Mouse made her laugh, often quite unintentionally. She could really use Jonas and his sometimes irrational confidence. Indeed, some of *that* would go far right now, for she wasn't feeling confident, irrational or otherwise. She was at the castle, but had not figured out her next step. How would she break into a castle and make it all the way to the dungeon, she wondered. And, even if she did, there was no guarantee she would find a prisoner, or more particularly her father.

If Jonas were there, he'd have a plan – even if the plan had flaws. Fortunately for Caroline, this was one of those times when doing anything was better than doing nothing. Strangely, knowing that helped put her mind at ease. As long as she was doing *something*, she was a step ahead of doing nothing. After all, all she could do was give it her best shot. To her tired mind and dulled senses, that sounded pretty good.

Her last strokes took her to the shore. Soon, she felt sand on the soles of her feet. She was relieved to finally stand on her own two feet, but she crouched low to avoid detection. When she reached the beach, though, she collapsed. She'd run out of energy completely. She lay motionless and let the waves gently lap at her, begging her to take a nap.

After some time, she raised her head and noticed an evergreen tree up the shoreline, with branches that hung low to the ground. That looked like a much better place to recover, instead of out in the open. Still, she wondered why no one had seen her. But she was too tired to think about it. She crawled under the tree and passed out.

When she finally stirred again, a thousand plans came to mind. But the only thing that made any sense was to walk, sword held high, and try to force her way through. Was there any other way? She probably would be captured, but maybe that was not the worst thing - perhaps in the dungeon she could find a way to escape, and bring her father along.

That was it! What easier way could there be to find the dungeons? If she became a prisoner, why, they would take her right to them! It was too easy - her enemies would take her exactly where she wanted to go. Of course, she would have to deal with being imprisoned, possibly tortured, and who knows what else, but what was an adventure without complications? And just as the plan started to sound good, irrational as it was, with the will of her mind raising her body to action and overcoming all of her doubts, a voice suddenly rose from a branch hanging above.

"How do you do?" the voice asked, quietly, not quite a whisper but in the sort of voice someone uses when they want to be quiet but not unheard.

"Who said that?" Caroline asked. Her head swiveled around, but all she found was a bat hanging upside down. She narrowed her eyes. Could it be? Caroline had heard tell of bats that could speak, but from what she knew, most were treacherous and likely in league with Maldazor.

"Yes, I said it," said the voice, clearly coming from the bat, no question about it. "My name is Jomey. And *you* must be Caroline."

Caroline's face sunk. She had been spotted; it was all over. The bats knew she was here and it would be just a matter of time before she was taken prisoner, forgetting in her addled state that such a thing was exactly what she wanted only moments earlier. Now it seemed like an awful idea. But before she could reply, the bat spoke again.

"Relax. I'm your friend." The bat flapped its wings and flew over to another branch, landing with its legs upright so that it no longer hung upside down.

"Bats are no friend of mine," Carol snarled.

"Nor mine, and it's been positively awful pretending that they are. Nasty, vile, little things," the bat said. "Most of them anyway."

"Umm, you're a bat."

"So I am," Jomey responded, and rather cheerily Caroline thought. "For now. But you're wrong there. I may look like a bat, and I can certainly pass myself off as one - even fooling other bats - but I am no bat. I am a dragon."

"Dragons are no friend of mine either, bat," Caroline snorted. She then laughed. The poor thing was delusional. It thought it was a dragon?

"Well, Caroline, don't take offense, but as I said, you are wrong, and on two accounts. I am a dragon, and I am also a friend of yours.

"See, I've been posted here for many years disguised as a bat to spy on Maldazor and his Army, yet I remain a dragon. But instead of talking more about it, I'd rather prove it."

"And how will you do that?"

"You are here for your father. Together, we're going to rescue him."

"Is that so? I appreciate that," she stated, growing serious. "But let's cut to the chase. The lies do you no good, so enough. Go tell the soldiers and Maldazor I'm here so that they can come arrest me."

"I will do nothing of the sort, though not all of the soldiers are bad. In fact, many of them are not bad at all. But I certainly wouldn't tell Maldazor—"

Caroline cut the bat off. "Lies, lies. Go on. I'll just wait here until the soldiers come along to take me to the dungeons." She flopped to the ground, pulled her sword from its sheath, and cast it aside. The bat saw this and had seen enough.

"As I was saying, I certainly wouldn't tell *all* of them, only those sympathetic to our cause. Besides, if I had wanted to, don't you think the sentries would've sounded an alarm by now? But I took them out hours ago; they're still sound asleep. Now get up."

"What are you talking about, bat? You must not be too popular with the other bats. It's really a shame they don't have help for someone as disturbed as you."

"My name is Jomey, not 'bat,' Caroline. And, I wasn't finished showing you my sincerity. So, how about this?"

The little bat left its branch and flew to eye level with Caroline, hovering in place for a few moments when all of a sudden, a tiny cloud of smoke appeared, which quickly blew off, leaving behind a little dragon equal in size to the bat. But it was clearly a dragon, albeit in miniature.

Caroline's eyes grew big at the transformation. "Well, you are a dragon, sure enough," she said. "Amazing! But you're awfully small. I suppose you might come in handy for campfires, or maybe lighting pipes and such, but if I had a dragon on my side I think I would have preferred a full-sized one, all things considered."

"In due time you shall have one, but not yet. We dragons are all born with different abilities. In my case, being able to shrink in size does have its occasional uses. Of course, *all* dragons can transform, with the right magic. But when the time is right, you will have your full-size dragon."

Caroline looked confused, so Jomey explained further. "You see, Maldazor isn't here, and he's taken a legion of his best soldiers with him. This place is ripe for the taking. So we are going to take it."

"Who is going to take it?" Caroline asked. Her joking manner had disappeared now.

"*We* are. And your father, for another. He's not the only prisoner friendly to our cause, either. I'd even dare to say many of Maldazor's own soldiers, who know your father well, will fight alongside us when it comes down to it. But most importantly, we hope to enlist the Mulvarians of the west, the wild men, who despise Maldazor."

He then flew in closely to Caroline's ear. "I believe we are going to have what they call a *revolution*."

Caroline's jaw dropped. How to respond? But the thought vanished as her focus turned to her father, and she desperately wanted to see him. "My father? Will you take me to him? That's why I came all of this way. Please, Jomey!"

"Not yet, Caroline. For starters, he's not here. He's off working. You see, the reason Maldazor captured him was because of his skill with weapons. He has him at his armory making weapons." The little dragon shuddered. "Specifically, his Dragon Killer weapons." The little dragon shuddered again; he couldn't help himself.

"Now, he's not done with them yet, as far as I know, though we haven't really spoken since he arrived days ago. But I've talked to others and they all say it won't be long. We cannot let your father finish the weapons, as it will spell trouble to dragons everywhere."

Caroline nodded in agreement. It was odd. She had grown up her entire life thinking dragons were evil and dangerous, yet now that she was conversing with one she found them rather agreeable.

"We will set your father free. But we can't go in the castle. Maldazor has put some kind of spell on it, one that keeps us dragons out. And I'm sad to say the spell works very well. He's quite powerful. He did it as soon as he heard about what happened down south."

"What happened down south, Jomey?"

"Oh!" the dragon exclaimed. "I should've told you first thing. I do apologize. Your uncle and your brothers escaped from Ambrosia on three of my cousins, dragons like me who were in Ambrosia to spy on *that* King - see, we don't trust any of them.

"It's a long story, and I've only gotten third-hand accounts up here, but their appearance has stirred up all kinds of trouble, of course, so Maldazor went down to Ambrosia City to handle things, or so he claims. Nobody seems to be sure as to what he's going to do, but clearly he has business with the new queen."

"So what happened to my brothers?" Caroline asked. "And, I don't have an uncle - just a bunch of aunts. My only uncle died years ago."

"Well, Caroline, I'll let him explain all the details to you, but your uncle Akari is alive and well. All I know is that they went to Dragon Island and were told to leave. The last anyone saw of them, they were riding sea horses back to the main land."

Caroline was quiet for some time - there was a lot to process. On one hand, she was ecstatic to have news on her brothers. On the other, the news was stale and there was no telling where they were now. And she didn't even know how to react to the news about Akari. Alive? Impossible.

Then Caroline thought of Chupwah. "Jomey, have you heard any talk of a Sasquatch, maybe something about one being taken to the dungeons? Goes by the name of Chupwah?"

"I have not, but it's a big dungeon. I would think I would have heard about a Sasquatch, though. And with the dungeons so full, I don't know where they'd put a creature like that - it's going to be a lot of fun once we open the dungeon up! Inside, we'll find nearly a full army of people that hate Maldazor, and all waiting for him in his very own basement!" The dragon did a little flip in the air before continuing.

"Now, you say this Sasquatch is your friend?"

"Yes," Caroline replied, her eyes tearing up. "He sacrificed himself for me. I hope somehow he's alive, but it didn't look good when I left."

"I hope so too. I've wanted to meet a Sasquatch for some time, but they've never felt the same way about dragons, from what I hear. We've been pretty well misunderstood for some time, hated by most and loved by few."

Caroline nodded. "What now, Jomey? I don't want my father to wait a second longer."

"Patience, Caroline. It won't be long. Soon we will have our revolution. While Maldazor is off strengthening his hold on Ambrosia, Azoria will slip from his grasp, just as soon as a few events fall into place."

"Do you think we will be ready in a few days?"

"Oh no, Caroline, certainly not days. Tomorrow morning it begins! We've only been waiting for you, and here you are! You will get a good night's sleep and will be good and fresh."

Caroline was dazed by this turn of events. Was this dragon delusional, or was her adventure bigger than she ever imagined? All Caroline wanted was to bring her father home, yet here they were talking of a revolution. But something told her he was in earnest, and in response, she picked up her sword, the steel feeling powerful in her hands. *A revolution.* If Maldazor was as evil as many believed, they had no choice.

"Caroline," the dragon continued. "Your father has been expecting you. We heard you were on the way some time ago from an owl, though they lost sight of you shortly thereafter. So your father told us to wait, that you would be along shortly, and then we could carry out our plans.

"You can only imagine how pleased I was to see you coming down the river this morning. I went and took care of the sentries right off, and I've been following you ever since, right up until when you crawled under the tree. You are most important to our plans, as your father said you were the bravest person he knew. In fact, he said you were braver than he even thought once he heard you were attempting to rescue him. Don't get me wrong, he wasn't pleased at first - but he was proud."

Caroline's eyes watered and she choked up. She couldn't help it. Not only was her father alive and well, but he was proud of her. It was beyond her wildest hopes.

"So are you ready?" Jomey asked.

"I'm ready," she declared.

"Good," the little dragon replied. "But first, we must sleep. Well, you must. I've become rather accustomed to the bats way of doing things and I'll likely be awake all night, unless the urge for a nap comes me way – you never can tell! I'll take care of the next shift of guards so that you can rest easy, and come morning, we will begin our revolution! Not that it's going to be easy."

Caroline chuckled. "Why would things be easy now, when nothing has been so far? I wouldn't expect things to change, so near the end!"

## Chapter Twenty - Fast Asleep

By the time Jonas turned around, Mouse was gone. He'd already slipped into the tunnel and was off to save the prisoner, Abigail. The only sign that he had ever been there was his sea horse, which waited patiently on the shore in case it was needed.

Sadly, Jonas was getting used to these abrupt departures. After all, he hadn't had a chance to say goodbye to his father, either, because he was snatched away while Jonas, Mouse, and Caroline waited for him to return.

Next, he watched as Caroline left with just a moment's notice. There was barely even time to give her a hug, let alone a proper farewell. Just like that, she was gone.

Now he had just said good-bye to Mouse, who Akari had sent into a death trap – the way that Jonas saw it. He wanted to cry, knowing that it was quite possible he would never see his father, brother, or sister again. But he didn't dare, lest his uncle think less of him.

All he had left of his family was Akari, and frankly he was having a hard time warming up to him. He didn't understand why this so-called great warrior would send little Mouse to do his dirty work. Some great warrior! Worse, his dirty work consisted of rescuing a girl they had never even met, and for no other reason than her presumed innocence. Jonas felt bad for her, but how could they afford to waste time on such folly? Why send Mouse on this mission – risking two innocent lives instead of just one?

Of course, Mouse's Fate was to be a great warrior. Was it possible that Akari knew what he was doing? Was he simply preparing Mouse for the first of many adventures? Perhaps. But Jonas was also certain that Akari was out of his mind, and to even attempt to find logic in his ways would be, well, illogical.

With all of these partings, Jonas felt completely helpless, totally and unequivocally. The only thing he seemed to be good for was waving good-bye to those he loved without lifting a finger to help them.

But he reassured himself that he would not be useless for long. Tomorrow would be his long-awaited fourteenth birthday, the day his Fate would be revealed. Jonas was certain to be told he would be a great warrior like the rest of his family. Then he would be able to show the world that he, too, could be a hero for Ambrosia.

They took the sea horses north along the coastline, making good time to their destination. With much regret, Jonas watched them disappear underwater. Tomorrow, they would walk.

*

"Happy birthday, Jonas!"

Jonas rubbed the sleep from his eyes and yawned. It was the day he had been waiting for! "Thanks, Akari," he stammered out.

They soon began their journey, moving inland to the home of a wizard named Barini. Jonas sorely missed the sea horses as the terrain was rough and rocky, and soon blisters burned on his heels. They had traveled in virtual silence their entire walk, and the silence was unnerving. Could it be that Akari was not as confident as he appeared to be regarding Mouse? Jonas was unsure. But it had made for an awkward journey. So, Jonas was pleased to be ending this part of the journey – and to be just steps away from where he would learn his Fate.

Barini the wizard. Jonas had heard the name before. He was a wizard of little renown who had been assigned to a sparsely populated outpost of Ambrosia. The wizard received few visitors and those who did come from readings generally were the children of miners living in the area. Jonas knew there were doubts about this wizard's abilities. When he mentioned that to Akari, the warrior merely downplayed them, saying Barini was just as bad as the rest of them. In other words, he'd do as well as any. Aside from that, there had been no conversation until now, when Akari broke the silence.

"Jonas, forgive me for my doubts, but what will you do if this wizard tells you that you are to be a miner, a farmer, or have a life along those lines? Not everyone is destined to be a great warrior in the King's world - your sister, for example. I see no guarantees for even the son of one such as your father. There are other options."

"I'm not worried about it, Akari," Jonas replied. "It would be folly for a wizard to choose otherwise. I am certain that my Fate will be to follow Dad, and you."

"I, too, was certain, nephew. So sure of what I wanted my Fate to be that nothing else ever crossed my mind," Akari said grimly. "But I was in for a shock! My wizard, an old fellow, determined I would be a dishwasher at the castle.

"Can you believe it? A dishwasher! He said that if I worked really hard, and did everything I was told, then I could rise to the level of cook."

"What are you talking about?" Jonas scoffed. "You have the mark of a warrior on your arm! A great warrior, in fact, two swords crossed together, just like Father and Mouse."

"So I do. But that is because I came prepared." Akari rolled up his sleeve, exposing his shoulder to reveal the symbol imprinted in his flesh. "There it is. Same as anyone else with the mark of a warrior."

Jonas stopped walking and looked his uncle in the eyes, completely baffled. "I don't follow you. How were you *prepared*? Didn't a wizard read the signs and then brand you?"

"He read my signs, yes, but he never branded me. No, your mother did that."

"My mother?" As eager as Jonas was to visit the wizard, his interest temporarily waned as he listened to what Akari was saying.

"Yes, your mother. What a woman she was! And what a shame you didn't know her. But she helped me pick my so-called Fate, wishing for me to avoid what had befallen her."

"You mean she didn't want to become the wife of a great warrior?" Jonas asked.

"Exactly! Like Caroline, your mother desired to be a great warrior herself, not the wife of one. Don't misunderstand me. She loved your father very much. Truth be told, she loved him so much she kind of came around to embracing the concept of Fate, but that's not important right now. Let's climb this hill, and as we do I'll tell you my story.

"You see, Jonas, more than anything I wanted to be a soldier in the Ambrosian Army, no different than most boys who grow up in our lands. But I was determined that it would happen, so much so that as my fourteenth birthday approached, I was awfully shook up about what a wizard would tell me. Would I be a servant? A farmer or sailor? It was driving me crazy! I couldn't even sleep at night.

"Then one restless night an idea came to me. If a wizard didn't tell me what I wanted to hear, then I would find my *own* way to get what I wanted. After all, why leave it up to some silly old lout? The trouble was I couldn't find a way. I searched and searched for a spell, but there's so much more to learn about magic and we've barely scratched the surface. I couldn't find a thing. So that type of magic, the spell-type, was out.

"And that's where your mother came in. Oh, she was smart, and she knew how it felt to be denied the Fate you deserve. So we came up with a plan together, racking our brains for some time. The answer was so simple we could hardly believe it. It was right there in front of us! Why, if a wizard didn't tell me the Fate that I wanted, no problem! I'd just make my own mark."

Jonas whistled softly. "That's against the laws of Ambrosia, Akari."

"I didn't care. A bright mind such as yours may be able to discern that laws mean little to me. Any old idiot can obey the law. It's much harder to do what is *right,* especially when all else tells you it's wrong. Now that takes a *special* kind of idiot.

"So I sat down to have my reading, and you know what this wizard tells me? I guess I said it already, but it bears repeating. The old codger tells me that my Fate is to be a dishwasher. A dishwasher!"

Jonas listened intently, stunned by all he heard. How could someone choose their own Fate? It was unbelievable, and seemed so wrong -- but then again, the idea was tempting. Jonas pushed for more details. "What did you do next?"

"Well, your mother and I had devised a little sleeping powder. As soon as he said the bit about washing dishes, I reached into my pocket and blew a little into his face. He breathed it right in and staggered around, then fell to the floor face first, snoring. It worked like a charm, just as we knew it would – we'd already tested it on Tess, our little dog.

"With the old guy in a deep sleep, your mother entered and gave me the mark of a great warrior. Nobody was the wiser, and we made sure to tip out quite a bit of that old wizard's liquor supply, so he chalked everything up to drunkenness. He never told a soul, lest he get himself in trouble. We came to find out that he *was* drunk most of the time. We just caught him on a rare occasion of sobriety. It all evened out."

Jonas started at this. "So *that's* why you mentioned the wizard having too much to drink earlier."

"No, I said that because most of them *do* drink too much," Akari replied. "Yet their wisdom is not to be questioned! The mind boggles."

"And he said you were to be a dishwasher? You? But you are one of the greatest warriors Ambrosia has ever had!" Jonas held his head in his hands and looked like he was going to be sick.

"That's what he said, the fool. My whole life left in the hands of a wizard who didn't know a thing about me."

Jonas was still in denial. "Wizards know the key to the Fates, Akari. There's no telling what damage you did to things by bypassing that! You can't choose your own Fate. It's wrong."

"You know, there may be some wisdom there, Jonas. Looking back, maybe I would've been happier washing dishes, instead of getting mixed up in wars and such, associating with dragons, having to rescue you, and so forth and so on. I'll never know. This life has certainly brought me my share of pain and misery.

"But I deserved to find that out myself, young Jonas, instead of having some wizard marking me with a brand and plotting out my life's course at the snap of a finger."

"Those are our laws, Akari, and they've worked for a thousand years!"

"Yes, they have worked very well, if you happen to be born to a King or a Queen. For the rest of us, that's debatable. I've thought this over for years and years, Jonas, and it's clear to me that the system is a sham. Now I can't say I don't have my regrets, but all in all, choosing my life's course isn't one of them."

"I can't believe it. This is so wrong." Jonas' face was still flushed. He had never heard of such a thing nor contemplated doing the same.

Akari took hold of his nephew's shoulders and looked him in the eyes. "Jonas, is it possible that an individual may be right and an entire government wrong?"

"I don't believe so, Akari. We all follow our Fate. To do otherwise could risk everything!"

"Kings don't follow any *Fate*. Do you think it was Fate that made Renwick divide his kingdom in three? Did Fate cause Renwick's own brother to attempt to kill him to steal his throne?"

"Well, that's why they're Kings, Akari. The Fates have chosen them to rule for a reason," Jonas retorted. "They take care of the big things, not small matters."

"Aw, but what is small to a King might be awfully big to one such as you or me. I refuse to believe Fate controls everything, and that there's a reason for all that we do. I don't believe that our life has been laid out, neat and tidy. Is that what you believe?"

"Exactly. Of course!"

"I see," Akari replied. And with that, he stuck his leg out and tripped Jonas, who fell to the ground and crashed into a small shrub. He scrambled to his feet and dusted off.

"What did you do that for?" Jonas asked, his voice rising.

"It was my Fate to trip you, Jonas, and yours to fall!"

Jonas looked like he was ready to crack Akari's head open. "I told you! Fate determines the big, important things! Not *literally* everything."

"I see. So when the King decides to go to war, that's Fate."

"Exactly! Now you see what I mean." The relief in Jonas' voice was evident.

"Let me make sure I understand. It's important we have it all straight," Akari said. "So what if Maldazor comes down here and decides to become King of Ambrosia? Would that be Fate?"

"I suppose so. What else could it be?"

"Got it. Now what about this poor girl that Mouse went off to rescue? Was it her Fate to die for something she didn't do?" Before Jonas could respond, Akari stopped him. "Hold your thought, we're almost there. We should have talked about this earlier."

They were steps from the small rundown hut with a slender curl of smoke rising from the chimney. The shutters hung limply from the windows. The door was torn off its hinges. The yard was choked with thistles and vines. "This wizard likes to live plain, doesn't he?" Akari remarked.

"That's one word for it," Jonas said, then took a deep breath, the uncertainty he was feeling all too clear on his face. But he stood up straight and tried to project confidence.

Akari moved in next to Jonas and held out his hand. "Here, take this," he whispered. Jonas looked at him with a confused expression, but did as instructed while Akari dropped a small cloth bag into his hands.

"It's sleeping powder. You know, in case you need it." Jonas looked annoyed, exasperated even, but Akari continued. "Just in case. You never know. If you need me, I'll be back there among the trees."

"Well, here's to it," Jonas said, knocking on the door. He tapped lightly to account for its poor condition, but the door still rattled loudly and nearly fell off.

Akari concealed himself in the trees to avoid being seen. He watched as Jonas stuffed the bag into his pocket. Soon the door opened and an old, hunched wizard shuffled into the doorway. He and Jonas exchanged a few words and shook hands. Then he led Jonas in, closing the door behind them.

Akari sat down and stretched out his exhausted body. He wondered what fatigued him more, having to deal with his stubborn nephew or the lengthy journey. He sprawled out on the grass comfortably, and listened to the peaceful sound of the wind blowing through the trees.

After a few restful minutes passed, a clatter arose from the hut. Akari instinctively drew his sword and ran to the wizard's home, bursting through the door to find his nephew clutching the now-empty pouch of sleeping powder. Akari was stunned to see Jonas standing over two, snoring bodies; the wizard and a soldier clad in the armor of an Azorian soldier, out of place here in Ambrosia.

"What's going on here?" Akari asked as he looked over the scene.

Jonas did not even bother to lift his head as he mumbled a garbled reply. He was panting heavily.

"He asked who my father was, and I told him. Soon as I did, he said that was good, and that Maldazor - *King* Maldazor - had something special for me. Said I was going to work in father's foundry, that it was my destiny. So when he grabbed the iron to mark me, I panicked. I reached into the pouch and tried to use the sleeping powder, but he knocked it from my hand. He seemed to be expecting it! Next thing I knew a man came out from behind the curtains - that soldier - and he held me while the wizard branded me."

He held out his arm and showed Akari the proof, two blacksmith's irons crossed together on his shoulder.

"After that, I slipped free and grabbed the powder from the floor. This time I threw it in both of their faces, hoping that I could adjust the branding to something else. But it's too late! Akari, what can I do?"

"Well, they're going to be out for some time. Listen to them snore! But I am sorry, Jonas, and I was afraid of this. You should hit him with the powder right off. No matter. I'll figure something out. Trust me!"

Jonas simply put his head in his hands and rocked his body back and forth.

"Get it together, Jonas. There's sinister forces at work here, namely Maldazor. I bet he's sending Azorian soldiers to every wizard, picking off all the fourteen-year olds who come for readings to send them off for hard labor. Tell every fourteen-year old they're Fate is to work in the foundry and boom, you've got a workforce. The Fates work in mysterious ways, indeed."

Jonas did not respond. This was a hard blow for him to take, and it was all happening so fast. He held back tears and stood off to the side while Akari tore through the hut.

The inside was shockingly in worse shape than the outside, with buckets scattered along the floor to catch rain water that leaked through the roof, dirty pots and pans piled high, overtaking the kitchen, and a bed that looked like it hadn't been made in a decade, covered in tattered and torn blankets.

Akari stood over Barini and shook his head sadly. "Some wizard. Think he'd conjure up a spell to get this place in shape." He then turned to the soldier. "Sure enough, that's the armor of an Azorian. Strange. I can only wonder how many Azorians have been called to help Ambrosians stay *loyal* to their new King. And I wonder how many are left to defend Azoria?"

Jonas ignored him, remaining focused on the news he had just received. He mumbled quietly to lament his misfortune. "I've trained my whole life for this, Akari, and now, nothing."

"I understand, Jonas, but not all is lost. Not yet. It's a shame someone decides your entire life for you when you're fourteen, but until things change, it's the best we can do, isn't it?

"But don't fret. You're on your road to becoming a great warrior, Jonas, and I'd say you've been on that road for some time no matter what was branded on your arm. It's an awful system. And there's only one thing to do when you're stuck in a system you don't like."

"What's that, Akari," Jonas sniffled, trying his best to choke back tears.

"You *change* it."

Jonas was incredulous. "And how do you propose to do that?"

"A few things are coming to mind, Nephew. Let me work it all out in my head. In the meantime, we better head to Cemetery Hill and see if Mouse's chosen Fate as a Great Warrior was accurate."

"Do you think he will make it, Akari?"

"I don't know. There's more to that little guy than meets the eye, certainly. But if you ask me, Mouse needed to try something daring, to put himself to the test, or he'd never truly live. You see, it doesn't much matter what I think about Mouse, or if he's been branded - what matters is what Mouse thinks. And I'd say the same for you.

"As I've said, I do not share your trust in the Fates. If Mouse pulls off this escape, it's because he did it on his own, with no help from the stars or moon or some wizard, or whatever it is that people seem to think controls us."

Akari continued searching the home until he found a bottle on the table in plain sight.

"There's only one thing left to do, Jonas. Would you please fill that cup about halfway with some of that wine? There, that's perfect. That will cover our tracks a bit, and then we'll find some horses to steal - ahem, borrow - to take us to Cemetery Hill, where we will meet the conquering hero Mouse!"

Jonas felt ill. He had lived his entire life assuming that Fate would take care of everything. He had truly believed his Fate was to be as great as every other male in his family. Now, he was not sure.

Maybe everyone was on their own in the world. Maybe each person was the master of his destiny, capable of choosing their own way. Maybe.

Yet, even though he had worried about Mouse, Jonas had believed that Fate would empower Mouse to complete the rescue and meet them at Cemetery Hill. Now, he was not so certain, and their only option was to go to the hill and wait.

## Chapter Twenty-One - Onward and Upward

Mouse wrapped his possessions into his blanket and tossed them into the tunnel ahead of him. Then he squirmed through the small hole at the base of the cliffs. Even with his tiny build, he had difficulty squeezing through, feeling as a snake must.

He held his sword in one hand and the small glass jar that Akari had given him in the other. He knew that Jonas and Akari were still there, but he refused to go back for another good-bye. Onward and upward. He was on a quest to save a prisoner he did not even know, but first he must navigate through a winding tunnel that rose to the plateau above. He was doing this, in part, to push past the doubts in his own mind and to prove to himself that he had made the right decision when he accepted his Fate.

He came through the entrance and the tunnel widened, allowing him to stand. Thank goodness, Mouse thought, as he certainly did not want to crawl the entire way to the plateau.

Akari had left Mouse's sea horse behind "just in case." Mouse had protested vehemently, swearing to Akari that he would not need it, but Akari refused to budge. Mouse would be lying if the thought of turning back to the sea horse was not a huge temptation. After all, his feet were pressing down on a spongy, moist surface, and the tunnel reeked of a foul stench that wafted through the chamber. He stopped in his tracks. All he had to do was turn around, wait for a short time, and when he caught back up with Akari and Jonas he could simply tell them he was too large to make it. They would never know the difference.

Each step he took seemed to land on something crunchy and perhaps alive, and each time he did, turning back to the sea horse sounded better and better. Then he stepped on something that hissed. That did it! He jumped back and returned to whence he came, with only one thought in mind. He had no choice.

So he crawled backwards through the tunnel and felt the cool sea air rushing at his face. He had only been in the tunnel for a short time, but his face was covered in sweat and the fresh air felt good. This might not be the smartest thing he'd ever do, but nonetheless, he felt relieved - he knew he was making the right decision.

So he walked over to the sea horse and made a clicking noise, a poor attempt to imitate the sounds Akari had made earlier. The sea horse gave a curious look, its head tilted sideways. But it seemed to puzzle it out and as Mouse drew near, it rose from the water to allow Mouse to board.

But Mouse would have none of it.

"Go on," he shouted. The sea horse stared, confused, and stayed where it was. So, Mouse shouted again, only louder: "Go along! I won't be needing you. Thanks for everything, but move along."

The sea horse still didn't budge, so Mouse yelled again and this time lightly shoved it. That was all it took. The sea horse slipped into the sea and was gone. There would be no catching up to Akari and Jonas now. He would have to see the mission through, one way or another.

"I don't need a safety net," the boy said out loud, steeling his resolve.

Now, he was truly on his own. He went back to the hole with renewed determination and again squeezed through. Akari was right about one thing - there was no way that Akari or Jonas could ever fit. It was up to Mouse and Mouse alone.

As soon as he was able, he reached into his pack and found a glass jar given to him by Akari. But he quickly pulled back, as he could feel a swarm of bugs crawling up his arm. His hand shot back and he shook them off. "Gross!"

He sighed. He had to be tougher than this. He took a deep breath and cringed as he tried again, shuddering as little legs tickled the hairs on his arm.

He unscrewed the lid and thought back to what Akari had told him. "As soon as you get in the tunnels, open this up. It will light the way."

Mouse did as he was told and was greeted by the sound of little wings pouring from the jar. Well, that was no good - what did he need with more bugs?

Just as soon as that thought was finished, little lights started to pop up. Of course! Fireflies! In fact, extremely bright fireflies. They were so bright, Mouse had to cover his eyes, which had become accustomed to the darkness. It took some time to adjust to the piercing light.

It was incredible. Fireflies formed a row along the roof, creating a chain that lit all the way to the end of this tunnel. Amazing! Mouse was grateful for the light. But he soon had second thoughts, as the light revealed that the tunnels were filled with bugs. Thousands of bugs. The floor was covered with centipedes, millipedes, beetles, wood roaches, cockroaches, and big, hairy, nasty spiders. They crawled through the damp clay floor and made the entire tunnel move as if it were a living, breathing thing. Mouse once again backtracked, scooting feet-first from the cave.

He couldn't help himself. His entire body was in the throes of panic. He yelled out a single word over and over - "disgusting" - and shifted his weight from foot to foot while brushing his shirt and pants off. He finally whirled around in a circle to try to throw off the bugs. When he finally felt free of insects, he took a moment to catch his breath.

He could deal with beasts, snakes, and whatever else was in there, but not spiders. Repulsive. His encounter with Akari's spiders had done little for his arachnophobia, as everything about him wanted to turn around and find a way to bring back the sea horse. Yet, he held strong. Turning back was not an option.

Mouse thought about what he had to prove. In theory, it sounded good. But he did not move an inch. He kicked himself for chasing his ride away but could not bring himself to return to the tunnels. He was sickened by his cowardice.

Then, he thought about his father. His father, who believed in him. His father, who didn't laugh when he learned Mouse was to be a great warrior. Jonas had laughed, but his father had not.

His father always had good advice when asked. His father took him in and made him one of the family. His father loved him like a son because Mouse *was* his son and was never made to feel otherwise. His father would want Mouse to gather all of his courage and rescue this Abigail, a woman who was innocent of the crime for which she'd been sentenced to death.

He recalled that his father had told him: When faced with a decision, decide the right thing to do and do it – no matter the difficulty. On the other hand, if you do something for the wrong reasons, even if you succeed, you would have a hollow victory, without true value. When doing things for the right reasons, Mouse's father had told him, you will have your heart, mind, and soul working together, committed to seeing the job through. And when you succeed in those ventures, victory will be sweet.

Saving this woman was the right thing to do. Mouse knew it. Jonas might say it was a waste of time, but Mouse knew better. He knew that Jonas knew better, too. Saving Abigail was the right thing to do, and for the right reason. Simply doing it to prove to himself or anyone else that he was a great warrior was self-serving – and not the right reason. But Abigail was innocent and must be saved. It would not be easy, but no crawling creatures would stop him, no matter how many shivers they sent up his spine.

Mouse walked back to the tunnel, feeling confident, ready to charge head first into any challenge, with nothing to stand in his way.

As he made his way to the entrance, the chain of fireflies exited. What were they doing? Mouse couldn't believe it! It was a magnificent sight, as the fireflies hovered slowly, one after another, with nearly every bug from the tunnels following, irresistibly drawn to the light. The bugs exited in droves. Some crawled, others flew, and a few hopped, but all followed the light emitted by Akari's lightning bugs.

To Mouse, it was one of the great mysteries of the natural world - insects that preferred the darkness of night, sleeping while the sun shined, were strangely attracted to lights that shone in the dark, even if it meant flying head first into a campfire or drowning in candle wax.

Mouse was so happy that he started thanking the fireflies out loud, unsure if they even understood him, although he almost thought he heard a tiny collection of voices respond. But whether they understood him or not, it was the right thing to do. One last time, he knelt in the dirt to crawl through the entrance.

The fireflies flew speedily ahead to light the way, leaving the other bugs behind. Mouse was relieved to have a path free of dreaded spiders, but was slightly disappointed he wasn't able to look his fear right in the face and overcome it. Then again, he figured this trip promised to have ample opportunities to face his fears, so what was the harm in skipping a few spiders along the way?

In no time, Mouse came to the end of the first tunnel. There was nowhere to go but up, to the next tunnel, a little bit higher up the cliff side and closer to his goal. There was just one problem. The way was blocked.

There was nowhere for Mouse to go. Boulders were piled high and there was no getting by them. Even the fireflies couldn't squeeze through.

The sea horse was gone, he was stuck on a beach that was surrounded by a rocky harbor and he couldn't swim, and the tunnel that led up the cliff was impassable. Mouse simply stared at the pile of boulders with his jaw wide open, unable to comprehend his next move. Now what?

He double checked to make sure there was no way through. Finally, with his shoulders slumping, he trudged back down the tunnel he had triumphantly marched up only moments before.

Once again, he kneeled and crawled out the exit. He ripped his pack from his back and rifled through it, hoping to find anything that could help. But there was nothing.

He was stuck. He had failed.

Rather than break down and cry, Mouse simply held his hand to his head and stood frozen in disbelief. How could Akari have failed to realize that the tunnels could be blocked? And how long would it be before they realized he would not be joining them? Would they leave him behind, or come after him? Mouse had no idea.

Mouse looked up the cliffside, a face of rock that towered nearly some hundred feet into the air. In a few places, the stone was cracked, and from these fissures, hearty little plants sprouted out. It was difficult to see, but it appeared that such features rose all the way to the top.

A strange thought came to mind. It seemed impossible, yet there weren't exactly a lot of options at hand right now. In fact, there were none.

A cluster of fireflies flew to the first plant as if they were having the same thought as Mouse. Perhaps his idea wasn't as crazy as he thought.

He reached out and grabbed hold of the bunch of plants, pulling hard. He used all of his strength to try to rip it free from the wall, but it held firm. He then did the same to another clump, which was a little higher up the wall. It too held true.

He used it to pull himself up and his feet were soon dangling from the ground. The fireflies flew ahead to the next clump, which was higher still.

Mouse didn't know how, but they seemed to catch on instantly to what he was doing and were doing their best to guide him up the surface by shining their light on his next handhold. Mouse reached for another and pulled himself still higher.

Some of the cracks had yet to have any plants take root, but he dug his hands in and used them in the same manner. Each grab moved him further up the cliff.

It was tough work, and already he felt as if his shoulders would be pulled from their sockets. His arms burned and his fingers ached, but Mouse would not be denied. Slowly but surely he scaled the wall, piece by piece, crack by crack.

The wind started whipping around, growing ever stronger, and if he wasn't mistaken, a storm was blowing in – the last thing he needed. As if climbing wasn't hard enough, now time was of the essence. He had to beat the storm or the rain would send him falling from an untold height.

Mouse didn't dare look down. It would do no good, but he was well aware that he had climbed a considerable height and didn't need to have it visually confirmed. That was the last thing he needed to think about …

Finally, when he thought his arms couldn't last another second, he came to a narrow ledge that had been eaten away from the cliff wall. He scrambled onto it and lay for some time to allow his arms to rest.

He then decided to chance a look down below. He couldn't even see the beach where his journey had started, and he judged he was near the top. His nails were cracked, his fingers were bleeding, and he didn't know if he'd ever be able to lift a sword again, but he was nearly to his goal. Mouse was beginning to feel like a true warrior.

The wind gained in strength and a peal of thunder boomed, nearly causing Mouse to jump out of his shoes. Then a bolt of lightning flashed and Mouse realized he was back in the tunnels. The wall had eroded, leaving the tunnel exposed, but he found himself at the top after all. But this was no place to take a wrong step; if he did, he was a goner.

So he cautiously walked down the pathway when suddenly something popped out and shoved him, hard. Mouse nearly tumbled over the edge and just managed to hang on. The fireflies scattered and flew all around as they searched in vain for a way to help.

The creature, whatever it was, had been pressed against the wall, nearly invisible, its body covered with mud. There was no telling how long this *thing* had been waiting for something to come along, but one thing was certain, it was ready.

Mouse screamed, terrified, desperate to escape. He had not mentally prepared for a creature such as this, almost human in appearance. It was filthy, clad in rags, and nearly emaciated.

Mouse scrambled to his feet and nervously waved his sword in front of him. "Don't move!" he yelled.

"What's that? Who are you?" an elderly-sounding voice responded.

"That's no matter. Who are you?" Mouse inquired, doing his best to sound brave while struggling to hold the sword level.

"I'm Rigby. I thought you were a critter of some sort... Say, can you get me out of here? I'm stuck!"

"You mean, you're not a monster?" Mouse replied.

"Oh no, not at all. I fell down here a few days ago, or so I think. There were dragons flying about and next thing I knew, I rolled off the cliff and fell. I don't know how I managed to save myself and land in here, but I haven't found a way back up. Even if I did, don't know that these old bones could carry me anyway."

"So you've been down here all alone?" Mouse asked while the fireflies regrouped and revealed the old man, who was clearly a man after all, although almost unrecognizable due to the filth that covered him.

"Yes, I have, and I'm about starved half to death. Don't suppose you've got anything to eat?"

Mouse fished through his pockets and took out one of Akari's pills. Akari had given him a few before he set out, in case of emergency

"Try this, sir," Mouse said, handing him the pill, but the old man simply stared.

"What is it?"

"Well, it's food. Sort of," Mouse responded. "Trust me. It will fill you right up."

The man stared harder, a crazed expression on his face, so Mouse changed the subject.

"You said you fell in here after a dragon attack?"

The man stopped looking at the pill and responded. "Well, I don't know if *attack* is the right word, as I don't really know what happened. I just saw three dragons flying and didn't wait around to see exactly what they were up to. I didn't really do much but panic. Silly of me, I suppose, but I find it's best to be heading the opposite direction the dragons are going."

"Makes sense to me," Mouse replied. "So you just kind of tumbled over the side and landed in here? You're lucky."

"I certainly was. These are old tunnels- used to be for the King and his family, where they could go down and have their own private beach from what I hear tell. But after some Barbarians found out about it and made their way up, they were sealed off and been untouched ever since. Say, how'd you wind up here?"

Mouse stammered for an explanation. "I, well, um, I got lost. My boat was sinking and I made it to the beach down below. The tunnel was blocked, so I climbed up."

"Is that so? Darn awful luck that is. Well, boy, you can look for a way out if you want, but I'm stymied." He stopped and rubbed his stomach, finally taking the pill after all. "Say! That's pretty good! I feel like I just had extra helpings of everything. What kind of vittles was that?"

"It's a long story, sir," Mouse said. He began examining the ceiling of the tunnel for a way out. The fireflies did the same, swarming to a section near the end of the path, with Mouse following.

"Hmm. Looks like an old wooden door," Mouse said quietly, while the old man looked on. Mouse stood on his tip toes and felt the surface. "It is wood. Looks like its rotting away. I might be able to break it apart."

He was able to pull free rotten pieces from the door and used his sword to chop away the rest, knocking out big chunks with each blow. Dirt started falling through the cracks, and a rather large section of earth crashed down on Mouse's head. Once he brushed the soil away, he looked up and a flash of lightning above revealed that the exit to the tunnels had been opened up. He was just steps from the top off the cliff and Ambrosia Castle.

It was all Mouse could do to not climb free, but it wouldn't do to leave the old man. He went to Rigby and guided him to the exit. "I believe I've found our way out, sir. Come with me."

"That's great," he said, waiting while Mouse pulled himself through the hole first. Mouse was now smack dab in the middle of a thunderstorm, with rain pouring, thunder booming, and lightning filling the sky.

He extended his hand to Rigby, using all of his muscle to pull the old man free, who was much heavier than he appeared. But in short order, he clambered out of the tunnel.

"See ya, sonny!" the strange old man exclaimed. "I'm going home! Good luck to ya!" With that, the old man was gone without even waiting for Mouse to reply.

Mouse shrugged and admired the castle that towered above all. It was truly impressive, even at this hour, with each flash of lightning revealing its magnificent features. He stared for some time before turning his attention to the large gate in front of the castle. His hands shook as he was just able to make out the dim outline of what appeared to be a person tied to a pole. Abigail. Had to be. His heart leaped; this is why he was here.

Mouse looked around the courtyard and noted all that he saw between flashes of lightning. As far as he could tell, she was all alone. All he had to do was walk up, set her free, and race off to meet with Jonas and Akari. It seemed too simple.

But first he would need horses. Akari had instructed him on exactly where to find the stables, and Mouse's pulse quickened as he found the very ones Akari and the dragons had fled only days before. Perfect. He ran to them, smelling the barnyard scents that reminded him of home, and he was ecstatic to find an outside corral filled with horses some of which were already saddled, likely left there by Knights too tired to bother with them.

He ran to the corral gate and used his sword to slash through the rope that held it shut. But as he opened the gate, he suddenly felt a sword at his back. He turned slightly to find a young, slender soldier behind him, a little guy just a few inches taller than Mouse. He looked like a strong wind could blow him away.

The slim soldier put his finger to his lips. "Shh. Don't you say a word and spoil this for me! All the other guards are fast asleep, as they are every night, always derelict in their duty. They make fun of me, Harvey, for doing my job. Well, the joke will be on them! Put your hands up and drop your sword! Do it!"

Mouse felt as if he would faint. His plans were unraveling quickly, and he knew if he dropped his sword, then it would be all over.

"Sir, I'm just hear to bring a treat for the horses. This is my dad's horse, see…"

"Uh-uh, I know exactly whose horse that is. I watch everything that goes on around here. That's Cyril from Azoria's horse and he came here all alone. Nice try! You were going to steal it, I bet. Now are you gonna drop that sword?"

"No, I will not," Mouse replied. A plan was coming to mind, though it was risky. "If you want to really show the other guards something, why don't we duel? Then you can show them!"

The soldier named Harvey considered this before working his lip into a snarl. "No, that's no good. Drop your sword, now! Hurry before the others wake up and take credit for my arrest!"

"Oh, that would be a shame," Mouse replied. "Have it your way. If you won't duel, then I'll just make enough noise to wake the dead. OK, here we go…"

The soldier's eyes bugged out and he started to shake. "No, no, don't do that! Just wait." He put his hand on his forehead as he considered the offer, but before he could make a decision there was a loud clap of thunder and the young soldier nearly jumped out of his boots. He was so shaken that he fumbled his sword and nearly dropped it.

And that was the opening Mouse needed. He was on him in a flash, swinging his blade, which Harvey just managed to deflect. Harvey then swung back, but Mouse easily countered the blow. Whether Harvey liked it or not, he was in a duel with the younger, smaller Mouse.

"So be it," Harvey said. "I'll show you! You're going to regret this!"

He growled, then charged at Mouse and slashed at his neck, but Mouse easily ducked. Harvey swung over the top of his foe and fell to the ground, slipping on the rain-soaked grass. He scrambled to his feet only to try the same move, which Mouse easily dodged as Harvey again fell.

Harvey rose to his feet, but this time Mouse swung his sword around, clashing against Harvey's in a clang of steel. Adrenaline surged through Mouse's body as he realized it was now time to prove he was a great warrior, and they exchanged heavy blows in the pouring rain while lightning flashed and thunder rumbled.

As the fight went on, Mouse was struck with a realization: his brother Jonas was good. Really, really good. This Harvey was a trained soldier, albeit a poor one, yet a trained soldier nonetheless. But compared to training with his brother, this was downright easy, even with his arms exhausted after his harrowing climb moments earlier.

Mouse was a whirl of motion, first fighting defensively, tentatively growing comfortable with his first real fight. Harvey struggled to parry the strikes, each time barely getting his sword in position to defend himself. Again and again Mouse struck, and again and again Harvey narrowly saved himself, although in truth Mouse was holding back, not wishing to kill this man, who was only doing his job, after all.

Mouse struggled to find an escape from this predicament, not wishing to bring harm to the soldier. He thought about working him over to the ledge, but a fall from that height would leave Harvey just as dead as a wound from a sword, so that was no good. So he continued to back Harvey up with each mighty blow when suddenly the soldier fell backwards and disappeared into the earth.

"How?!?" Mouse exclaimed. He stepped forward to examine where Harvey had disappeared. Of course! He had stepped right into the hole that led to the tunnels, the same hole Mouse had emerged from only moments earlier. The guard was laying prone on the ground, out cold. Mouse couldn't believe his luck. He took a moment to wipe the sweat from his brow, but only a moment, as there was still the small matter of rescuing Abigail.

Mouse had done it. It was far from easy, but he had climbed all the way up the cliff and was just steps from rescuing the prisoner. The young warrior could only hope his luck would hold.

# Chapter Twenty-Two - Trapped

The sun had not even thought about rising at this early hour, yet Caroline was already awake and ready to go. She was sharpening her sword after just a few hours of sleep – if tossing and turning could really be called sleep.

Sleep had been nearly impossible. Today was the day she would rescue her father. This quest had propelled her travels across the island, at great peril - over the Kin Kara mountains, through the Burmian Caves to the dry plains of Azoria, and finally down the Renwick River.

As the sun sent its first rays over the horizon, Caroline sprang into action. It was still dark, but the sun was up – and she vowed to wait only until then to start the day.

Caroline went searching for Jomey and found the little dragon hanging upside down in a pine tree, again disguised as a bat. Caroline shook her head. So much for him not needing sleep!

"Psst, Jomey," she whispered. "Wake up."

The little creature was unaccustomed to being awoken in such a fashion. It dropped off the branch and fluttered around like a moth caught in the daylight, confused and disoriented.

Caroline could not help herself and playfully swatted at him. Watching Jomey comically fly around seemed to ease the tension that had been building. She then hooked Jomey's wings and stretched him out in front of her.

"Why are you a bat again?"

Jomey looked annoyed but squeaked out a response. "Well, I found that I rather like sleeping upside down. It's a lot easier as a bat then as a dragon, unless, of course, you like falling on your head in the middle of the night."

"But look at yourself! Why, you're only as big as a mouse! I could squash you right now. Imagine, squishing a dragon with your bare hands." She giggled at the thought and let Jomey go. She then held out her index finger and thumb, and pinched them together. "I might even be able to squish you with just two fingers," she said, playfully. She giggled again, then regained her composure. "I'm sorry. I must be delirious - didn't sleep a wink. I'm too nervous."

"I understand, Caroline," Jomey responded, though a bit huffily before taking a moment to fully see it her way. "I mean, it's not like we have anything major to get worked up over. Just freeing your father and kicking off a revolution, little things like that." He circled around her head, then continued.

"But, you're right. There's no sense in wasting any time. I'll tell you what, I need to take care of the guards arriving soon for shift change. After that, I'll do a quick fly-by to scout the area. It's just a few miles from here. They usually have the prisoners at the foundry ready to work before sunrise, so your father is probably already there, working hard with the other prisoners to make weapons. They do so every other day, though I suppose it would be wise to make certain."

"So what are we going to do? I can't imagine we can just walk over and take him home," Caroline said.

"Of course not. The prisoners are heavily guarded, although – to our advantage -- the guards are a bunch of nitwits," the dragon replied. "As far as having a plan? We'll have to make it up as we go."

Caroline chuckled. "Well, that approach got me this far!"

Then, she turned serious. "As far as this morning, I am sorry I woke you up so early, Jomey. I'm sure you haven't had much in the way of sleep, and here I go waking you up first thing."

"True, it was the first enjoyable sleep I've had for awhile, up in the pine, listening to the waves. But now is the time for action. We'll have plenty of time to sleep later."

Caroline smiled as the dragon flew away to do reconnaissance. She cringed at how dirty her teeth felt. She feared they matched the brown tone of the river's water by now. She rubbed her face and held up her sword to see herself in the blade's reflection. But her reflection was a diminished by the coat of dust the sword. Oh, how she needed – and wanted – a hot bath. Floating down the river had not made her cleaner. In fact, she felt downright filthy.

Caroline walked down to the river to use the bathroom and try to clean up. Upon arriving, she again looked at her reflection, such as it was, in the muddy water. The image looking back was rather chilling. She seemed tougher, harder, and somehow wiser than just a week before. It was hard to reconcile the image looking back at her with the girl who had left her family home. She sighed - adventures sure didn't do much for one's looks. Just because Caroline was not one to spend much time on her appearance did not mean she didn't care at all. She was taken back by her reflection.

The young girl smirked. Guess she would have to sit out next year's Frogpond beauty contest. Ha! She had never entered before, so why start now? Caroline smiled as she thought back to such simple times. She would make fun of her brothers for being enchanted by the ditzy farm girls who traveled from across the land to enter the contest. Oh sure, it is true that many of them seemed beautiful and perfect. But, Caroline wondered, could they have survived the journey she'd experienced? She doubted it.

Enough of that. She bent down and cupped her hands, filling them with water and splashing it on her face. She made a half-hearted attempt to clean herself. For some reason, this made her feel as silly and vain as she had believed those beauty queens to be. It also seemed a strange time to worry about her appearance. She closed her eyes and continued splashing water on herself, in an effort to get clean.

She opened her eyes and her heart nearly leapt from her chest. A large stump was floating down the river with a large pair of eyes looking out from among the roots that trailed it. She gasped as the large creature that owned the eyes let go to swim toward her, his massive arms pulling him through the water, quickly bringing it to the shoreline.

Caroline couldn't believe her eyes. Could it be true – was the moment she had not even dared to hope could happen indeed happening?

It was.

Chupwah was alive! Not only was he alive, he was swimming right toward her.

Caroline could hardly contain her excitement as the young Sasquatch emerged from the water, dripping on to the banks of the river with bits of twigs and weeds entwined in his fur.

Caroline rushed at him, excited beyond words. Speechless, all she could do was hug him, her arms stretching to wrap around his massive body. Her nose burrowed in the wet fur. He smelled rather awful but Caroline did not care. He was alive!

"Is it safe, Caroline? Are we being watched?"

"I think we're fine. The dragon is taking care of the guards in the watchtowers right now. They'll be out cold for some time. Chupwah, I can't believe it!"

"Me either! It's so good to see you, Caroline. I didn't think I would ever catch up, but here we are!" They let go of each other to stand back and beam at one another.

"You might want to take a few steps back," the Sasquatch advised, a bit later.

She did, and Chupwah shook his entire body, water spraying in all directions from his thick fur coat. When he finished, Caroline took a closer look at her friend. He looked awful. His fur was missing chunks here and there, leaving many bald patches. He had gashes on his arms and legs, and a ghastly cut across his chest. One eye was red from some kind of trauma, and his ear was missing a small chunk.

"Goodness, Chupwah, what happened?"

"It's a long story, Caroline, a very long story. To be brief, once you escaped, I fought off the soldiers as best I could. Did pretty well, too. I was cracking heads as they say, though I took some shots, as you can see. But all I had to do was fight them off long enough to buy you some time. So once I did, I took off, running the opposite direction you went until I knew they were completely off your track. Even on horseback they couldn't catch me. I reckon I know now why Maldazor fears the Sasquatch such as he does. We're too much for *his* army. I can't speak for any other armies but the Azorian Army will like us even less when next we meet. I have some scores I'd like to settle..." He cracked his knuckles and continued.

"Eventually, I circled back toward Azoria, hoping to follow you, and by a stroke of luck I happened to find a stray horse. I'm fairly certain it was one we had used to distract Maldazor's army. Speaking of him, I heard some talk as I sneaked through a village that he has left for Ambrosia and likely been declared King there by now."

Caroline nodded, confirming the story. "I heard that, too. The good news is he took a massive contingent of soldiers with him. There's just a fledgling crew protecting the castle, according to Jomey, the dragon."

"Well, that's another lucky break. I hope they keep piling up," Chupwah replied. Then, he resumed his tale. "So I eventually came across your tracks, seeing where you tripped over the tree root, then where you kicked a dead stump from the ground, and I even found the reeds you broke off for breathing. Did that work for you?"

Caroline sadly shook her head no. "It nearly killed me!"

"Me too," Chupwah responded. "Oh well, the rest of it was brilliant, so I did the same thing. I thought for certain I'd be caught, but nobody paid any mind. I hung onto the tree trunk and floated all the way down. Great plan, Caroline."

Caroline looked down at the ground, uncomfortable with the praise. "Thanks, Chupwah. Oh, I'm so happy you're alive! And just in time, too. My father is here, just like we thought, and we're going to free him!"

"Well, that sounds great, but what is all this talk of a dragon?"

"His name is Jomey. He's been living as a bat, as a spy. He is going to help me, or I should say, us!"

"A dragon, eh? Never met one. Never heard much good about them, either," Chupwah declared. "I suppose I'll give this one a shot though."

"Please do! He's been so much help already."

Chupwah nodded. "So Caroline, how did you happen to come along the river this morning? I was afraid I'd never find you!"

Caroline looked a bit sheepish. "Well, I wanted to clean up a bit. I'm filthy!"

Chupwah laughed. "I suppose it is important to look good before you rescue a prisoner from an army," Chupwah teased, mussing her hair with his giant paw. "It's good to see you, Caroline. Now we can finish what we started!"

"Yes, we will," Caroline said. From there, she explained the situation while Chupwah listened and occasionally asked questions, expressing amazement at the tales of Jomey the dragon, and offering advice on how they could pull off their rescue.

They hashed out what seemed like a pretty good plan when Jomey fluttered in to see what the delay was. He let out a low whistle when he saw Chupwah.

"This must be Chupwah, the skunk ape," Jomey said, sniffing the air. "Doesn't smell like one, although he's not too far off."

Chupwah growled. "Just wait and I can change that. I dare say you don't look much like a dragon. You might come in handy for lighting candles or cooking an egg, but I'm not really sure what else good you'd do."

Though Caroline was unaware, dragons and Sasquatches had an ancient disliking of one another, which had apparently been passed to this generation. Neither Chupwah nor Jomey had even been alive the last time the two species had any kind of run-in, although the stories and legends of each species were rich with such tales. These two were far from making nice.

Caroline sensed the hostility pouring from the two and moved to end it with a simple introduction. "Chupwah, this is Jomey; Jomey, this is Chupwah."

Both nodded at each other but offered no other greeting, leaving Caroline to take charge. "OK, we can stand here and glare at each other or we can do what we came here for."

After that, Chupwah looked ashamed. It reminded Caroline of their first meeting, when he apologized for scaring her in the woods.

"You are exactly right, Caroline. Your father has waited long enough." He then tore a limb from one of the pine trees and broke it in half, creating a staff. "Let's go. This is all I need to send the Azorians packing."

"I'll lead the way," Jomey said. "Caroline, your father is at the foundry, just as we figured."

Chupwah and Caroline walked while Jomey fluttered over their heads. Though Jomey had already cleared the way of any guards up above, they were still wary of finding enemies, so they moved cautiously.

Caroline was trembling, feeling a mixture of fear and excitement. She thought back to the long journey she had made so far, and how many challenges she'd faced. She also thought about nearly losing Chupwah, and she knew that without him, she would have failed.

With him around, it felt like she could do just about anything. There was a quality about him that filled her with faith in their collective fate. She looked up at the Sasquatch as he walked alongside her, admiring his noble face while struggling to keep pace with his large steps. She turned her gaze to his wounds, which still looked raw and painful. Caroline vowed she would take a better look at them when they were finished. She also hoped there would be no further injuries during this mission. Her uncle Akari was known as a healer; perhaps she had inherited some talent in that area, though she couldn't remember showing signs of that yet.

Jomey led them through heavy woods, and soon both castle and ocean were behind them. They went up a slope through a forest of pines and halfway to the top Jomey signaled them, indicating a need for quiet. They were getting close, and now Caroline was really shaking. She was so nervous that her legs were quivering and they felt like they would give out at any step. Chupwah tapped her on the shoulder and made a motion to indicate their goal was just over the hill. They were almost there.

They concealed themselves in tall grass at the top of the hill and looked down upon an immense foundry. It was just as Jomey had said. Caroline had to hold her hand over her mouth to restrain herself from calling out to her father. Somewhere among the mass of workers and soldiers, he was there.

It was almost as if looking at their home in a shattered and cracked mirror. But this place was much larger and lacked the charm of their Frogpond homestead. There were no stables for horses. There was no campfire. There was no dock for boats. Worst of all, there was no home. There were just people, working hard while soldiers armed with swords and whips threatened them to keep pace and stood ready to lash out at anyone who fell behind.

The broken stumps that dotted the landscape were proof that a forest had been razed to make room for the site. The thought of such beautiful woodlands being leveled made both Chupwah and Caroline shudder.

In the center of the clearing stood a long narrow building that Caroline instantly knew was the foundry. It was surrounded by propped up work tents with smoke billowing out. There were puddles of brackish water scattered about, and men working wherever the eye could see. You could hardly find a square foot not occupied by someone pounding away with a hammer, carrying wood to light the fires, or bringing drinking water to the workers. It was a gloomy, depressing site.

The figures that stood out most to the onlookers were the Azorian guards, with their swords and whips. They bore cruel expressions as they rode about on horseback. They appeared only too eager to lash a prisoner with the crack of whip, which echoed through the hills.

Caroline searched in vain for her father. From where they stood, the workers all looked the same. They were well hidden and quite a distance away, so she asked Jomey:

"Jomey, do you see my father anywhere?"

The dragon hovered down to ear level. "I don't see him now, but I'm certain he's inside of the foundry. That's pretty much where he always is. Bad news though. See that big thing sitting behind the foundry, looks kind of like a catapult? It seems they've come along further than I imagined. It wasn't even there earlier this morning!"

"What is it?" Chupwah asked.

"The Dragon Killer," Jomey replied tersely. "And it looks to be completed."

He whipped his tail around and used it to point at the object, staring at it long and hard as if awestruck by its power. Jomey had always hoped that such a weapon was simply a rumor, a tale used to strike fear in the hearts of dragons. But there it was, in all of its wicked glory.

They watched as a group of Azorian soldiers rode out to the weapon while a few prisoners wheeled it into position. Jomey cringed as a ball of steel was loaded into the weapon. With the round loaded, the weapon was sprung and the metal ball flew through the air, landing in the woods, pulverizing tree branches as it caused a huge splash of water from its impact. The soldiers shouted and shook their raised fists in the air, in a show of celebration. They had accomplished what had only been rumored possible. They had completed a weapon specifically designed to kill dragons. They felt certain they would be richly rewarded by King Maldazor and they were feeling drunk with success.

A few men rolled out great kegs of drink to the field, which soldiers drank greedily to slake their thirst. They raised their glasses in the air, chugging, as suds spilled down their chins.

"Aye, this is a break. They soon won't be able to stand the way they're pouring it down," Chupwah declared.

Caroline nodded in agreement. "Discipline sure takes a hit without Maldazor watching them. A bunch of sodden babies, if you ask me."

While Chupwah and Caroline watched the soldiers celebrate, Jomey suddenly flew toward the field. Caroline and Chupwah both stood up, shocked.

"What are you doing?" Caroline yelled.

"It's time, Caroline, it's time," he sang back. "As soon as I'm of size, hop on! I'll take it from here!"

Caroline and Chupwah were stunned. This was a rash and unwise move. The drink had not even had a chance to take effect on Maldazor's soldiers, yet Jomey was already rushing off. Caroline felt terror filling her. She was so close to achieving her goal she could hardly stand it, and Jomey was throwing it all away.

But it was a magnificent sight to watch, as the dragon quickly doubled in size, and then tripled before it grew immeasurably. They jumped on his back and soon its wings cast a shadow over the first bastion of soldiers and prisoners. Screams of terror rang out from soldiers as they scrambled for safety. They spilled their glasses and chaos spread throughout the work site. Tents were toppled and run over while firewood spilled and rolled through the glade.

Caroline drew her sword and held it high over her head, yelling as loud as she could.

Chupwah roared back in the way only a Sasquatch can, adding to the soldiers' terror. The dragon quickly swooped down the hill.

Caroline's father emerged from the forge after hearing the clamor. He wondered at what caused it when he felt a great shadow pass over and looked up to see the outline of a dragon. *Jomey.* Eston was stunned. It was not yet time for an escape attempt.

Eston soon heard a soldier yelling orders to go to his assigned post at the Dragon Killer weapon, and at the sharp sting of a whip he did as instructed.

But on his way, he was stunned to see his only daughter on the back of the dragon. It was time to escape after all — she was here sooner than he had expected. Eston's joy at seeing Caroline was quickly overwhelmed by worry. A thousand fears raced through his mind.

She had made it! It was no surprise, given all that he knew of her. And with that thought, it was no surprise to see a Sasquatch right alongside her.

Though his right leg was shackled, Eston leveled a panicked soldier that ran by, knocking him out quickly and ripping a sword from his unconscious hands. Eston's guard was dumbstruck but managed to strike with the whip, but Eston easily chopped it in half with the sword, then pulled on what remained, wrenching the soldier from his horse.

It was time for bold action, the kind only a great warrior like Eston could deliver. His daughter and her friends were heading into a dangerous situation as the Azorians, thanks to Maldazor and his lifeless general Osirah, had known that a dragon was in their midst. They were waiting for it with intent to kill. In the madness that would ensue, Eston could only shiver at what terrible things might happen to Caroline.

But Eston would not let that happen.

# Chapter Twenty-Three - Cemetery Hill

Akari stood at the grave and stared, his face impassive. How long had it been? Careful examination of the date on the tombstone revealed it had been over ten years, but it felt much longer. In fact, it felt almost as if he had not lived through it but had merely read about it in a book, such as those written about him.

It was strange to stare upon his own grave, though he had been a brief occupant. He had every intention of remaining above ground for some time longer. The spell he used to trick others into believing he had died had taken all of his powers to accomplish, but he had done it. It was the single greatest accomplishment in the history of magic, and yet barely a single soul knew of it. But Akari rarely did things to gain the admiration of others. He believed that knowledge and discovery were their own rewards, and if that meant few knew he had accomplished something great, well, so be it.

Well, it had been the single greatest accomplishment in the history of magic, but as Akari looked over his grave site, he suspected he was seeing evidence that his accomplishment had been supplanted. Still, he needed to investigate more before he could reach that conclusion.

Cemetery Hill. This was hallowed ground for Ambrosians. It was the final resting place for Kings, Queens, the great warriors of the land and other notables. This is a place to pay tribute and remember those who were chosen by the Fates to rule and defend the kingdom. But at the moment, for Jonas and Akari, it was the place that they had arranged to meet Mouse.

Upon arriving on horseback, Akari had immediately gone to his tombstone while Jonas remained silent. He was still dejected from his reading and he was not hiding it. But he dismounted and made a good show of being interested in the cemetery by walking the rows of monuments and reading the names of the various Kings of Ambrosia.

Still, it was abundantly clear that Jonas was beyond depressed. His dream of being a great warrior had been snatched from him at the whim of a wizard. He was sincerely attempting to move on from his disappointment by exploring the Cemetery during what was his first visit there.

So far, it wasn't working. He had begun by walking down the row dedicated to the Kings, starting with Percival the First and ending with his descendant Renwick, the father of Wilhelm. As Jonas stood in front of Renwick's grave, it occurred that soon Wilhelm would be buried alongside his father, many years before anyone would have rightfully expected it. So far no ground had been broken, but Jonas imagined that it would soon be dug up with much fanfare and ceremony, and craftsman would work around the clock to create a monument worthy of a King, in spite of Wilhelm's rather useless reign.

He found momentary distraction in the cemetery, but soon enough Jonas was again taken over by darkness. His so-called life had lost all meaning. What was the point? A life spent making weapons for King Maldazor? A life without daring adventures or duels to the death? Despite his valiant efforts, Jonas couldn't shake the bad feelings that overwhelmed him. He could not see beyond the lack of control he had over his life, no matter how great his desire.

Despite these feelings, Jonas could not make the leap that Akari had made. He was not ready to believe that humans should choose their own path and make independent decisions.

After all, what did Akari know? Akari thought he was so clever for picking his own Fate, but all that made him was a fraud. It was no wonder he couldn't handle being Chief Knight, even going so far as to fake his own death. *Pathetic.* Akari had been living a lie and the lie finally won. At least that's how Jonas saw it. He seethed with anger at the very idea of Akari trying to get him to follow that path, one that led to ruin.

Jonas turned to visit the graves of the departed Chief Knights on the other end of the cemetery, when he suddenly realized that Akari would have a tombstone here – that could be interesting. Perhaps he could even point out the failure of his uncle's plan by turning his attention to the marker bearing his own name.

But he noticed Akari was already there, kneeling in the dirt in front of a lonely tombstone at the end of the line. Jonas made his way to stand beside his uncle, and read out loud the name etched on the grave marker.

"Akari Dragonslayer. Chief Knight of Ambrosia, died from a dragon attack," Jonas read out loud. "So this is where they buried you, huh? Wow. That's some Fate you chose!"

He kicked at the ground, which lifted a chunk of grass that was chewed up as if a mole had taken a turn through it. Part of Jonas wished that Akari *was* buried in his grave, though he scolded himself for thinking such thoughts. That was too far, even as miserable as he felt.

Akari looked at Jonas, appearing distracted and flustered, and for a moment, Jonas was terrified that he had been reading his mind. Of course, that was impossible, even for Akari - right? But it was not the case.

"Look at this," Akari said, pointing at the ground. "You see that?" He pulled at the grass in front of his grave, revealing seams where the sod had been carefully laid after being removed. "Someone was here and dug up my grave. You can see quite clearly where the grass was patched back together."

Jonas followed Akari's fingers with his eyes, and had to agree. The turf had been dug up recently, and clearly not by moles. Akari slipped his fingers through the seam and lifted it up, peeling back the grass to confirm his theory.

He let the grass fall back in to place, then stepped back to stand thoughtfully as if trying to decipher a puzzle. "This is strange. What could someone be looking for in my grave? Any theories, Nephew?"

"Maybe they were trying to figure out why you weren't in it?" offered Jonas. "You did just pop up alive and well in Ambrosia City recently."

"True. You might be right, and that makes some sense. If they were looking for an empty grave, they found one."

But he did not seem convinced by this simple solution and looked for further clues while Jonas walked over to the marker next to his uncle's. It was his father's.

Jonas soberly read the name, Eston Strongheart, a blank space remaining where his date of death would be etched when the time came. It sent chills up and down his spine, made worse by the knowledge that as far as Jonas knew, his father could already be dead at this point, just waiting to be placed in this very grave. He only hoped that it would remain empty for some time, with an unused space next to his date of birth.

"I see they got a head start on my father."

Akari nodded. "Yeah, they like to keep the graves in order, and since your father didn't have the courtesy to die before me, that's what they came up with. I used to stop here on my way up north and it would always give me the creeps."

Akari walked to Eston's grave and looked it over briefly before moving on to another.

"Strange. Jonas, take a look at the other grave stone, next to your father's. It's been dug into as well."

Akari was right. It too bore the same signs as his tombstone, with the grass carefully replaced to avoid suspicion. It was rather difficult to see that the graves had been tampered with unless you were looking for it, clearly done by someone with experience.

"Not good. That grave belongs to Osirah Stone-Thrower," Akari said. "Oh, he was an awful Chief Knight, just awful. And a worse human being. Ruthless, with no morals. We hated serving under him. I don't know how other Chief Knights were killed, but I'd venture that not many died from five arrows in the back from their own soldiers the way Osirah Stone-Thrower did."

He looked over at Jonas, who was smirking. "Hey, *I* didn't do it! Though I felt no pity when the deed was done," Akari said, then smirked himself. "Friendly fire, they call it. Some friends, eh? But he deserved it."

"But what could someone want with his grave?" Jonas asked. "Surely he didn't fake his death too?"

"Simple, Jonas. Grave robbers! Although, I've never known any with the guts to rob Cemetery Hill. But there is a first time for almost everything.

"But I don't think these robbers were after jewels and such. No, they wanted the body itself, or the bones, which is all that would remain of the, um, remains. But it can't be—"

Akari wore a baffled expression as he puzzled out the mystery. Jonas looked on impatiently.

220

"What are you getting at, Akari? Spit out whatever it is you're trying to say."

"I'm working on it Jonas. Wouldn't do to jump to conclusions. First off, they're supposed to have enchantments to stop this sort of thing. Not sure how they made it past those, unless they had help. Well, who would know the royal secrets better than Maldazor? Of course.

"Now, it seems they found my tomb empty and decided to go for Osirah's, though I'm not sure as to *why*. That's what I can't figure. It's all clear but the *why*!"

Jonas decided to investigate himself as Akari's insistent babbling was getting them nowhere. He peeled back the grass and used his hands to start scooping dirt from the grave. He quickly tore through the recently loosened soil, digging deep enough to see the top of a coffin, made from wood that had been polished to a dull shine, still smooth despite its time spent in the earth. He uncovered just enough to get his hands on each side of the lid.

"Give me a hand, will you Akari?" he barked, but Akari let it slide, knowing his nephew was under duress.

"Good idea, Nephew. This shall be most interesting," Akari said.

Together, they managed to raise the coffin, surprised by it's lack of weight as they set it down on the grass. Jonas ripped the lid off, causing dirt atop to spill to the ground below.

They peered inside. When the dust cleared, they were amazed to find that the coffin was indeed empty, stripped bare of its occupant and any belongings that may have been left with the departed.

Akari used his foot to shove the coffin back into the grave. He sat on the ground with his arms crossed and folded on his legs, mumbling to himself. Jonas couldn't be sure, but he was afraid his uncle was losing it, and fast.

"I don't get it. What would they want with the bones of a dead man?" Jonas asked.

Akari either didn't hear his nephew or ignored him. He continued to mutter incoherently, shaking his head in disbelief, before pulling himself together to stand straight up with fire in his eyes.

"Well, I have no real evidence to support this, and I'm probably wrong. But in this world, when nothing makes sense, find the theory that makes the least amount of sense and go with that one. In summary, my conclusion is that Maldazor has discovered a way to bring back the dead. What else could someone want with a pile of old bones? For decoration? Doubtful. And who else could want them?

"You see, I tried to resurrect the departed myself until I realized it was an impossible dream. But I was wrong. Maldazor has done it, or at least he thinks he has found a way, and seldom does Maldazor waste time on mere hunches. And if he has, he beat me fair and square, there's no getting around it." He said this calmly, but it was clear he was quite upset.

"Whatever are you talking about, Akari? You're not making any sense. Bring back the dead? That's insane."

Akari stared directly at Jonas with his eyes wild. "My boy, what I said seems clear enough, but very well, I will explain. That scoundrel Maldazor has likely found a way to bring back the dead. For some reason, they went for my remains first; of course, I wasn't home, so to say. Whoever was grave-digging skipped past your very much alive father's grave and raided the very much dead Osirah's body. Simple as that. As to why? The *why* is what gets me. What could he want with my bones, and failing that, move to Osirah's?"

His shoulders shook as a chill crawled down his back. "I cringe at the thought of that vulture of a man being back among the living. I can only guess at Maldazor's angle, but it won't be good for any of us."

Then it hit Akari, and he could have kicked himself for not seeing it sooner. His jaw dropped and his eyes bugged.

"The Princess! Darn her. When I was revealed in the castle, she said she had brought me back. It didn't make any sense, but now... She murdered her own father! She was in on it with Maldazor! Had to be. They must have made a deal. That crazed woman wanted me back alive, except, well, you know. What a strange turn of events! But why move on to Osirah?"

"Seems far-fetched, Akari. You might want to think this one over."

"Dear boy, perhaps you are right, but there is much to do before I can determine that."

"What can we do, Akari? There's nothing *we* can do."

"At the moment, you're right, there's nothing we can do. So, for now, we wait. Akari looked up at the sun, judged it's placement in the sky, and gritted his teeth, the worry on his face all too evident. "But it seems to me we should have heard from Mouse already. I'm worried that our plan may have failed."

"I was afraid you'd say that," Jonas replied, his fingers nervously feeling the hilt of his sword. He stared down Cemetery Hill and wished Mouse would soon be riding up it.

## Chapter Twenty-Four - Still So Far To Go

Mouse had come a long way since leaving Akari and Jonas, perhaps further than he even thought possible. He had safely made an impossible climb and repelled a foe from the Ambrosian Army. Since then, he had remained out of sight of the castle guards and was free and clear to move about the kingdom on his mission.

All was going well, so far. However, much remained to be done like, well, rescuing Abigail. But first, he needed horses for their getaway.

Mouse knew he had to move fast, causing him to race to the stables with the fireflies leading the way. He wondered if Abigail was despondent by this time, with no way of knowing that someone was coming to the rescue. As for himself, he was filled with nervous energy. Being branded a great warrior sounded like a great Fate, but he was beginning to realize how truly difficult it was.

Mouse returned to the corral and found it challenging to loosen the ropes that tethered a large horse. He struggled in vain for some time when he realized how dumb he was being - he had a sword! How could he be so oblivious? No need to fool around with untying ropes when you could hack it away with one strike. He drew the blade and slashed the rope, steeling his nerves as he did. The small success gave him a boost of confidence.

In no time, Mouse successfully liberated two horses. They were impressive animals that would serve them well. Traveling Knights, who were too exhausted to take off the reins and saddles, had left the horses there for the night. All seemed to be going according to plan, when suddenly the fireflies flew off, leaving him in darkness. He watched with no shortage of disappointment as the bugs flew in three separate clusters toward the castle.

Mouse sighed, but he had no choice other than to carry on. It would do no good to dwell on their absence, but the lack of light made his task more difficult. He struggled to feel his way around the pasture in the darkness, as he led the horses from the corral. The horses snorted and stomped their feet. They weren't happy, being awakened at this hour.

"Strange things, those fireflies," Mouse muttered. "Leaving just before the job is done, and I'm out here as blind as a bat!" he said, and then WHAM, he ran right into a fencepost.

He fell to his back and had to work quickly to regain his grip on the reins. They slipped in and out of his fingers, but he again took control. Once he did so, he kicked the post in frustration before feeling his way around to avoid hitting it again.

Mouse knew from the feel of the ground beneath his feet that he was going through the gate, as the surface changed from the green grass of the pasture to the hard dirt of the road. The road would lead him to the front of the castle, and more importantly, to Abigail.

He was having trouble seeing on this cloudy and thus moonless night, but thankfully the storm had passed and the rain had stopped. Still, he wished the fireflies would return. Where did they go, anyway?

His question was quickly answered as he saw their dim lights appear in the guard towers that fronted the castle - three of them, rising high in the sky to loom over the castle walls. He cringed as the bugs flew directly inside the watchtowers - what were they doing? The last thing he needed was to disturb the guards!

The light of the bugs lit up the towers and Mouse watched as the guards posted within swatted at the bugs, missing comically. Soon their attention was completely diverted, and more, they all had their backs turned to Mouse as they tried in vain to smash the crafty creatures. *Brilliant!* Once again the fireflies had lit his way, and in a way he did not expect. Akari was really thinking when he handed him the glass jar.

Mouse tied the horses to a tree off the side of the road, and then ran to where Abigail was tied up. The Ambrosians had left her all alone, bonded to a pole with the guards stationed high above - and they were, of course, too occupied to see their prisoner being set free by a daring rescuer down below. It seemed too easy.

Mouse crept over to Abigail and whispered in her ear, explaining his mission. It was unclear if she understood, and she offered no response. She was clearly in rough shape. From the small light given off by a lantern hanging from a wall behind them, Mouse could see the effects of her punishment - her face was rubbed raw from the blowing wind and scorching sun, and her eyelids were nearly swollen shut.

Even so, vestiges of her beauty remained. Mouse resolved to save this woman. While Mouse knew that outward appearance mattered little, he also noticed there was something about Abigail that radiated an inner beauty. He wondered if that had influenced Akari's big scheme to rescue her, even though Akari had claimed otherwise.

Mouse wasted no time in slashing through the cords that bound her arms. As soon as they were broken, Abigail tumbled to the ground, her legs still tied at the ankles. Mouse soon slashed those cords as well, and tried to lift Abigail. She was not particularly heavy, but in her nearly comatose state, she was dead weight. Mouse carefully let her fall to the ground and tried to think of how to lift her to a horse.

Mouse looked up, grateful to find the guards still distracted. So simple, and yet he would've never thought to try it. Then again, even if he had, how would one go about telling a lightning bug what to do? They seemed to have minds of their own that they were using quite well - it was best to stay out of their way. So with that problem covered, he turned back to Abigail, only to find a hand around his throat.

It was Abigail.

"I'll kill you," she seethed, shouting loudly in his ear, perhaps mistaking him for one of her captors. "Let me go, or I'll have your throat!"

Mouse was stunned. She was conscious after all, and not in the mood for company. Understandable, Mouse supposed, but he needed to talk her off the ledge quickly.

*If* he could speak seeing as her cold hands were gripping his throat. "Shh. Be…quiet. I'm here…to…save…you."

"Is that so? You're here to save me? A little thing like you, and all by yourself? What good can you do?" Her eyes were wild, her nostrils flaring, and jawline tense.

"My uncle is waiting...Akari," Mouse managed to spit out.

"Him! The one that fled." Her eyes narrowed as she considered the truthfulness of Mouse's words. "So he didn't forget about me. Never expected that. Well, young one, then save me before I put you out." She released him and shoved him aside roughly. What other choice did she have but to follow this boy?

This was far from the triumphant welcome that Mouse had expected.

He shrugged it off and ran to catch up to the crazed woman, who was wandering away.

"Follow me, Abigail. Can you ride?"

"Ride what?" she snapped.

"Horses. What else?" Mouse asked, recoiling at her sharp tongue. No, this was not going the way he expected at all.

"I was hoping for dragons," she replied, without any hint of sarcasm.

"Yeah, me too," he responded. But before he could say more, a great horn sounded from the guard towers, filling the air with its call, causing Mouse's hair to stand on end.

"We've been spotted!" His body tensed as he struggled to stay in control of his nerves. There was no time to lose. "All right, hurry up, Abigail! Follow me to the horses!" Mouse ran off, not even bothering to see what had come of Akari's fireflies. He hoped that Akari would forgive him for not returning them.

Abigail followed his lead. When they reached the horses, they jumped on and galloped away, as voices rang out from all around.

They had a head start, but it didn't last long. Soon, the sound of hooves pounded on the earth in pursuit. From what Mouse could tell in the pitch black, they were being chased by two other horse and riders. If only Abigail hadn't been delusional and screaming at him, Mouse thought, they might have had a greater lead. No one ever said it would be easy.

Mouse strained his eyes and was excited to see the first rays of light to the east - morning was on its way, a relief as it was difficult to see, and Mouse and Abigail could only trust to luck and their horses' knowledge of the road that they would make it. The creatures seemed to know the way, galloping quickly as they carved through the forest.

They dashed through creeks, kicked up stones, and leaped over fallen branches, winding their way around trees and small hills. Mouse hung on tight, hunching down and burying his face in the horse's mane. He could feel the tense muscles of his mount's body under the saddle, straining and pulling with every step. The sweat beaded out from under the leather saddle, and every now and again she would snort, and Abigail's horse would respond. It was just another day in the life of a war horse and Mouse was pleased he had managed to select horses of such high quality in a tight spot.

Mouse wondered how long the horses could maintain this pace, hoping they were nearing Cemetery Hill with Akari and Jonas waiting. But their pursuers were gaining ground, the hoof steps thundering louder and louder as they closed in on them.

Suddenly, he felt his horse take a bad step and nearly topple over. Whatever the cause, the horse was clearly slowed, and their pursuers gained even more ground.

It was decision time. Their horses were wiped, and Mouse couldn't stand running anymore, running like a coward when everything inside told him to stand and fight - even if it was unlikely to end well. He could either keep running, or he could fight.

Then the decision was made for him. Abigail's horse, running slightly ahead of Mouse, tripped on a tree root and its legs went out from under it. Its hooves stuck into the ground and flung Abigail clean off the saddle. She flipped head first into the air, but twisted her body to land cleanly though roughly on the forest floor. Mouse watched and brought his horse to a stop, leaping off to help Abigail, knowing full well he was also running toward their pursuers.

Abigail scrambled to her feet, but she had no weapons, and Mouse doubted she would know what to do with them if she did. So he drew his sword and prepared to make his last stand.

The soldiers slowed their horses, calmly dismounting and drawing their weapons. The two guards, wearing helmets that covered their faces, realized the odds were overwhelmingly in their favor - and they were enjoying it. So they slowly moved to strike, holding their swords overhead, when one of them stopped in mid-movement - he had expected a warrior, and instead...

"A boy? What are you, her son? A misguided soul with a crush?" The guard lifted his visor, revealing a face that was twisted, ugly, and unshaven, with gaps where there should have been teeth. "Tell me what is going on before I'm forced to cast you down, boy."

"She's innocent," Mouse stammered. "And I'm setting her free! She didn't kill the King!"

"I don't care," the guard replied. "It matters not. Maldazor has ordered her dead and that's good enough for me. Now step aside, boy, and put your sword down, before I have to hurt you." He ran his index finger along the edge of his blade. "Not that it would bother me."

At this Abigail took off, scrambling into the woods. She bent down and reached for a stick, as there was nothing else to defend herself. If she was going to be recaptured, she was at least going to inflict a little damage.

The soldiers both laughed. "Fine," the leader said. "We'll do it your way. It's easier to carry a corpse than someone thrashing about anyway." He wore a broad grin, exposing his rotten teeth, and was already looking forward to the reward that would come with the successful capture of both prisoner and rescuer. Certainly Maldazor wouldn't mind if said prisoner and rescuer were dead, would he?

Mouse and Abigail both prepared to fight, standing in front of the soldiers with weapons ready, when they heard the steady clip-clop of horses coming from the north.

Who could it be?

Mouse hoped for a miracle and – judging by the terrified look on the soldier's face – that's what he was getting. It was Akari Dragonkiller, the legendary warrior, riding tall on a great black horse.

Mouse knew not who was approaching, but he saw his opportunity to spring into action. He jabbed with his sword and drove it into the soldier's leg until it hit bone, causing the soldier to yell in pain. He reacted fiercely and slashed back at Mouse, who ducked the attempt and scattered backwards. It was a brave try by the young boy, but it had enraged the soldier, who charged on his horse at Mouse. Before the soldier could hurt Mouse, though, Akari was attacking.

Mouse could hardly contain his excitement when he finally saw it was Akari who had come to the rescue. Before the soldier even realized what was happening, his sword was struck and he was knocked from his horse. He flew to the ground, hard.

On The Backs of Dragons

But Akari was not alone. Jonas was right behind him, roaring through on a large brown horse with a white spot on its nose, heading right at the soldier challenging Abigail. Jonas swung his blade at the attacker, which the soldier blocked. Jonas wasn't strong enough to knock the sword from his arms, but his attack distracted the soldier, who never saw Abigail attack from behind.

Abigail cracked his arm with the stick, a mighty blow which knocked the guard's sword from his hand. Before he could recover, Jonas was there, jumping to pull the soldier down from his mount. Together they fell, with Jonas landing on top, and they hit the ground with a thud. The soldier was stunned, and in no time he was tied and bound through a joint effort of Jonas and Abigail, an interesting way for the two to make their acquaintance.

"Pleased to meet you," Jonas said, while Abigail simply nodded back. She wore a puzzled expression, unable to understand why these people were helping her.

Meanwhile, Akari bounded from his horse and stood over his defeated opponent, eying the wound on his leg that was spilling blood on the forest floor. "So it's you, Eli. I see you've met my nephew Mouse. How's the leg?"

"How do you think, traitor," he snarled back. "Still, it beats having your neck stretched, as you will soon learn."

"Traitor? That's an interesting opinion. Your country is being stolen out from under you by an interloper to the throne and yet *I'm* the traitor. Yes, very interesting. But I don't have time for your nonsense nor to argue politics." He looked to Jonas, also standing over his captive, and saw that his nephew was preparing to use his sword on the hapless soldier.

"Stop it, Jonas! No!" he yelled, leaving his foe to run to his nephew, wrapping his arms around Jonas and pulling him from the soldier. "You don't want to do that. Trust me!"

Akari pointed to the captive squirming on the ground. "This is Christophe. He's a good man, and just doing his job. We're all on the same side here, though most don't know it yet, and some may never know."

Jonas was breathing heavy, confused by the emotions running through his body. Akari hugged his nephew, doing what he could to calm the boy down. "This isn't the way, Jonas. We're not here to hurt anyone, if we can help it."

Eli heard this and shouted. "I can see that! So what are you going to do about *this*," he said, pointing at his leg and wincing in pain. "You boys surely hurt me, let me tell you!"

"On the other hand, unlike Christophe, this Eli is not such a good man. Still, we're not going to kill him… Unless he makes it too tempting!"

Eli toned down, gulping while Akari made sure that Jonas was OK. He then walked back to the whining warrior and removed something from his pouch, bending down to examine the wound more closely.

"Oh, this is barely a scratch! You're whining about this? You always were next to worthless, Eli. I bet that's why they partnered you up with Christophe. Let him carry the load while you most likely take all the credit." Eli started to talk back, but Akari wouldn't hear of it. "Just shut up and let me work. We'll have you back on your feet and doing nothing worthwhile soon enough."

With that he sprinkled some powder into the wound, muttered an incantation of some kind, and stood back. In a flash, the leg was miraculously healed, as good as new. "See? Nothing to worry about. But someday, I may figure out how to remove your leg and give it to someone who can use it properly, you lazy buffoon."

Akari then walked Eli's horse over to the soldier, lifting him into the saddle with his arms still bound. "Now go on back to whence you came. Christophe will be right behind you." He used the broad side of his sword to smack the horse on its rear end and watched as it took off in a blaze.

Christophe stood by, his face mystified. "I don't get it, Akari. Why fake your death and return after all these years? What's your game? Have you lost your senses?"

Akari smirked. "Lost my senses, Christophe? No, I *came* to them, my friend. Lucky for you I did, or you'd be dead." His face turned grim as his mood darkened. "Now get on your horse and go on. I'm going to *accidentally* kill someone with the way people keep attacking me, and that's the last thing I need on my conscience."

The soldier did not wait to be told twice, grateful to be freed. Soon the sound of hooves pounded off into the distance as the soldiers rode out of view. Akari watched them disappear and turned to face his nephews. His face was drawn tight and he was breathing heavily, dabbing at sweat that had pooled on his brow.

Jonas walked up to him with his eyes bugging out. "Why'd you let them go? They were trying to kill us, and you just let them go!"

Akari glared, not in the mood to answer questions. A darkness had overtaken him as old memories were stirred up, and it rather frightened Mouse, who watched on in silence.

"We can't take them with us, Jonas, so what would you have me do? They're no harm to us."

"No harm? Didn't you hear me? They were trying to kill us!"

"Yes, but *trying* is the key word. They had no better chance of killing me then does a fly. We have just liberated a prisoner of the King, Nephew, and they were soldiers, doing what soldiers do - following orders. Get used to it, if that's what you strive to be."

Jonas was not soothed by these remarks, and the last remark cut deep. It mattered little what he strove to be, as his Fate had been decided and Akari knew it. Rage boiled over. "Akari, you're going to get yourself killed if you insist on not killing anyone trying to kill us."

Akari smirked yet again. "You're a boy, and I once felt as you did. But listen to me. Taking a life is never easy. It will eat at you, rotting your soul to the core, and you must avoid it, if there's anyway you can.

"And so far on our little journey, it has been very possible. There's not a scratch on any of your heads, or on mine. So I'll keep my own counsel on whom to kill and who not to, lest you would like to lose as much sleep as I have over the years."

Jonas appeared to be unmoved and crossed his arms, but Mouse noted he offered no further response.

Akari then turned and looked to Abigail, who had been watching with a confused expression. Now it was her turn to seek answers.

"Why did you save me? I don't understand."

"Madam, were you not innocent of the crime you were accused?" Akari asked.

"I am. Of course I am!"

"I know it, and told these boys, my nephews, the same. They insisted we rescue you as soon as they heard the news, fearing the loss of an innocent life," Akari said, stretching the facts quite a bit to no harm, though perhaps projecting how he had hoped for Jonas to respond. "I must say this little one we call Mouse pulled it off with some flare, would you not agree?" The grim expression was washed from Akari's face as a look of immense pride took over.

She nodded, somewhat shyly, and looked at her rescuer. "I'm sorry for the way I acted. I was rather out of sorts, um, Mouse."

"No problem, Miss Abigail," he responded, bowing deeply to her. "I'm just happy to be of assistance."

"Well said, Mouse," Akari said. "Abigail, you can come with us or you can go your own way, it is your decision, though I'd rather you did not return to where you just now escaped!" He then introduced himself formally and explained their mission.

Abigail stared into the forest as she considered her options. "For now, I will ride with you while you make your way further north, for it is on the way to my home, the small town of North Star. After everything I've been through, I do wish to see my family again."

"Very well," he responded, and then he addressed the entire group. "We will now return to Cemetery Hill, for our business is as of yet unfinished there. Then we're off to Azoria, to find Eston and Caroline."

He climbed on to his horse, took the reins and sauntered off, shortly thereafter rising up the famous Cemetery Hill with his nephews and Abigail, with the new morning sun shining bright on their faces.

They had come a long way, but their adventure was far from being complete.

# Chapter Twenty-Five - Hanging On

For the first time since his resurrection at the hands of Maldazor, Osirah felt alive. All it took to finally feel part of the world again was to have a fire-breathing dragon bearing down upon him, its mouth open and roaring, its wings spread wide as they pushed through the air, its dangling claws so sharp they could rip through a suit of armor. Most people would cower in fear from such a sight, but not Osirah. Run from danger? Never.

In fact, he was walking *toward* the fell beast, for he was going to kill it. It just so happened that between him and the dragon stood one of the weapons they had spent the last week building - the infamous Dragon Killer.

Though it pained him to utilize the expertise of Eston Strongheart, a name so foul he could scarcely utter it, his distaste had been worth it. Today, he would taste the triumph of triumphs. When Maldazor had informed him that they had imprisoned Eston, Osirah was beside himself with joy, anticipating the great pleasure he would derive from torturing the hobbled Chief Knight.

It was strange the way the world worked. When Osirah died, Eston was in the prime of his life; now, Osirah remained the same while his rival had aged significantly. Yes, Osirah had been resurrected into a strange world, but one he was learning to enjoy, in his own brutal fashion.

Though Osirah walked into danger, the same could not be said for the army he had recently been ordered to lead. Those soldiers - in the loosest sense of the word, as far as Osirah was concerned - were running from the dragon. Worse, they were getting in Osirah's way as they did. He fought hard against the tide of deserters on his way to the weapon. *Cowards,*

Osirah thought as he lowered his shoulder into all who obstructed him, sending them flying as he purposefully marched. What a *disgrace*.

Quicker than anyone thought possible, the dragon was upon them. Though Maldazor and Osirah had warned the Azorian Army that a dragon attack was imminent, their reaction was disappointing. Osirah shook his head - some things never change. Most soldiers were cowards and it took a hardened sort like himself to hold them in line. If only he had been given the time to whip these forces into shape, they would not have fled the battlefield. No, they would've stood and fought like men. Fortunately, he was there to do what they could not, and thus few would know of their cowardice.

He arrived at the weapon and found that only four soldiers remained. Well, at least there were four who chose to act as Azorians should. He marked their faces and mentally filed them, as they were the kind of soldiers he could use.

He was wrong on one point. Yes, there were four soldiers who remained, but one was doing all he could to not be seen, crouching underneath the weapon with his hands covering his head in terror.

Osirah shook his head in disgust. "You there! Coward," Osirah yelled. "You are completely pathetic! Get out from under there and help load this thing!"

Besides the four soldiers, another man was present. Eston Strongheart, the former Chief Knight of Ambrosia, was at the weapon, though most certainly not by choice. He had been nabbed by soldiers, after his ill-fated attempt to warn his daughter.

He was again a prisoner and treated accordingly, with one of the soldiers keeping his sword drawn on the elder man. He was also tethered to the ground, to prevent any attempt at escape. Osirah walked to the soldier and squeezed his shoulder, a small commendation for doing his duty well. It wouldn't do to have the inventor of the Dragon Killer running off when they might need him. Osirah may have loathed Eston but he needed him, and thus loathed him all the more.

Still, the Dragon Killer was not complicated. For all practical purposes it was simply a catapult, although Eston had perfected the firing mechanism to give it great accuracy. The real secret was the ammunition used in the weapon.

Many human lifetimes had been spent struggling with devising ways to kill a dragon, but all who tried wasted many hours before determining it was an impossible task, for they simply could not be killed through conventional means.

Dragons were covered in scales that could not be penetrated by human weapons. Finding a solution was a constant struggle, one that weighed heavy on the minds of Kings, Generals, and peasants alike. It mattered little that dragons had shown little aggressiveness to humans - what mattered was that if dragons so wanted, they could wipe out mankind, and humans would be powerless to do anything about it. So, they chose to seek preemptive measures.

It had remained an impossible dream until the mighty Osirah discovered the secret of killing a dragon. It was so simple, yet until he stumbled upon an infant dragon in the woods, it had never even crossed his mind.

It was a glorious day. Osirah was returning from a fruitful attack on a clan of Mulvarians and walking through the woods, enjoying a brief moment of peace. He was away from his troops, off the beaten path, when he came across something curious - a baby dragon, all alone. Osirah sat and watched it for some time, figuring the loathsome thing's mother would return, but after watching the creature sob and lament for some time, it was safe to say it was completely and utterly lost. How it got there Osirah never knew - it was simply a gift of the Fates. And Osirah would not turn back such a gift.

He attacked it, taking it unaware while the creature stared forlornly at its reflection in a lake. Most would have taken pity, but not Osirah. To refuse such a gift would be a sign of a deep madness.

Though the dragon was young, it was a vicious struggle - even a baby dragon is deadly - but soon the dragon succumbed, lying spent on the ground, scarcely clinging to life. Osirah looked at the lake and had a revelation - the answer he had searched for his entire life was revealed in the choppy waves. It was so simple.

He scraped the weakened creature from the forest floor, carried it to the water, and submerged it. The creature raged, blowing fire into the lake and bringing the water in its vicinity to a boil. The hot water bubbled to the surface and Osirah desperately hung on until it struggled no more, the last kick from its hind legs cutting his forearms deep. He had unlocked the secret of the ages - the way to kill a dragon was to extinguish its flame.

Of course, it was nearly impossible to drown a grown dragon - the entire army would be unable to hold one down. So they remained as far from a solution as ever until, much to Osirah's dismay, Eston realized the secret to taking down a grown dragon. When a dragon flies, it does so with its mouth wide open for reasons unknown, though some thought it was to cool its body. Eston theorized they could fire artillery shells filled with water down a dragon's gullet, snuffing out a dragon's fire from inside.

Soon Eston invented the weapon that would be known as the Dragon Killer, working alongside his brother-in-law Akari, and they proved their mastery in making it. With Akari gone, only Eston knew the secret of the artillery shells, and he was expert at working the controls that aimed the shot, so Maldazor insisted that he be used despite Osirah's protests. But as much as Osirah despised Eston, he despised dragons more, and thus would use Eston to serve his aims. For now.

Returning from death had done little to dull his hatred for the beasts, so Osirah had eagerly waited for this day. The King had sworn there was a dragon in their midst, insisting it would eventually reveal itself. For that reason, Osirah had worked the prisoners hard, even harder than he normally would, as he greatly desired to complete a fleet of Dragon Killers before any attack. Because of that, in the nick of time they were ready to face their ultimate test.

The anticipation was just about killing him.

"Prepare to fire," Osirah yelled, watching as the soldiers took their positions. Eston was set free from his tether and forced down into the cockpit of one of the weapons, where he would take aim at the dragon and bring it down to its death. "This is what we've been waiting for, men. On my command, fire away, *Strongheart*." He spat out the last word, making clear his disgust with such a label. Osirah's mind wandered at how such a man as Eston had earned that name but turned the thought aside. They would give Osirah a much more glorious name when the dragon threat was dealt with.

Eston nodded grimly in assent to Osirah's order, though he was very clearly humiliated, which pleased Osirah even more. As soon as Maldazor gave him permission he would relish destroying him. But it would have to wait - until Eston did something Osirah did not expect.

The soldier's sword was held tight to his throat, but Eston used his bare hands to push the blade away. It cut deep into his palms and he winced in excruciating pain, but he did not call out or lament. Eston rose from the cockpit. The soldier struggled to turn him back, and then the old man kicked at his knee, his boot clanging against the armor. It was a strong kick, hitting with such force that the soldier dropped the sword, and Eston promptly picked it up.

"I will not fire this weapon," Eston yelled, waving the sword. "My daughter is on that dragon! Kill me if you must, but I will not fire upon my own flesh and blood!"

Osirah's face snarled in anger but soon relaxed and revealed a malicious grin. "Fine by me, Eston *Strongheart*. I would rather have done it without you anyway, even if Maldazor had insisted otherwise."

He drew his sword and pointed at another soldier. "You, fire the weapon! The dragon is almost here!" Osirah yelled. The soldier ran into the cockpit to replace Eston, who had dropped to the ground below.

Eston scrambled to stop the soldier loading ammunition, but Osirah stepped in his way to block him. It was time for a duel that had been a long time coming. The roar of the dragon filled the air as both men swung their swords hard. Eston parried and slashed back, which was easily countered.

There was a flurry of activity while the swords clanged back and forth. The men made mighty strikes. The Dragon Killer fired away. From above, flames licked from the dragon's mouth, its roar deafening the soldiers, and the smell of burnt sulfur filled the air, causing many of the soldiers that remained to decide they too had seen enough. They fled to the castle for relative safety.

Dragons were known as unconscionable killers with little ability to reason or plan, but to the few who were not scrambling for cover, it was clear this dragon was far from mindless, despite what they had been led to believe. It was heading straight to the weapon, seemingly on a mission.

For those few who were brave enough to look, they were stunned to see a girl and what appeared to be a Sasquatch riding on the dragon. No one could make sense of it. Their minds reeled at such a sight. Some even thought that the riders were controlling the beast.

Eston's heart shivered each time the weapon went off, hoping the soldier would be a poor shot. Fighting Osirah was difficult enough, without the added distraction of worrying about Caroline. Osirah was strong and daring, a difficult match for Eston even when he was in the prime of his life let alone now, as he was approaching old age. But Eston took a deep breath, and fought with renewed urgency.

He slashed and parried aggressively to fend off Osirah's strikes. He never much cared for Osirah when he was alive, and cared even less for this resurrected version. But the odds were against Eston. Osirah was stronger, he was faster, and now he was younger. Eston fought off these negative thoughts and dug deep.

The dragon had flown off, relieving Eston's fear for his daughter – but now it circled back, renewing his concerns. Eston could no longer stand and fight Osirah; he had to stop the onslaught. Eston scooped up a handful of dirt and threw it in Osirah's face. It was a dirty trick, but the momentary distraction allowed him to slip away and run to the Dragon Killer.

He was old and slow but used that element of surprise to escape Osirah. Eston moved as fast as he could, knowing the dragon would again be in range. The soldier shot repeatedly, with each blow landing down its cavernous throat, forcing the dragon to recoil in pain. The dragon appeared to be on the cusp of death - even one more hit could bring an end to the dragon's life. But Eston was determined to end the assault.

He made it to the first soldier and threw more dirt in his face, then knocked the sword from his hands. He kicked him off the weapon, but left him alone from there. Eston didn't much feel like killing a soldier who was only following orders. After all, he had been a soldier himself once.

Another soldier charged at him, and Eston managed to duck the blow. The soldier had failed to wear a helmet and he soon regretted it as Eston hit him over the back of the head. He fell down unconscious.

All that remained was the soldier firing the weapon. Eston grimaced as he watched the man fire another series of shots in a matter of moments, wincing as the dragon writhed in pain and struggled to stay aloft. *How much more could it take,* Eston wondered. But the dragon still swooped down and headed toward the weapon.

Soon, the dragon was close enough to see the whites of its eyes and Eston was astonished, watching his daughter Caroline perched atop the dragon. For an instant, Eston thought the dragon was heading right toward *him* with its claws pulled down, but before he could know for certain another shell hit its target. The dragon loosed a vicious scream and retreated to the sky yet again.

Eston cursed himself. He alone had perfected the weapon's design, and it was a job he'd done too well. This soldier, who had never even used the weapon before, was firing with great accuracy. Eston had to stop him before it was too late, or his own daughter would go down with the dragon.

He desperately climbed up the weapon surface and came face to face with the soldier, who was intently focused on the task at hand, following the dragon as it circled around. Before he could even realize what was happening, Eston reached out and tried to tear him from the cockpit. But just as he did, something grabbed Eston's legs, nearly knocking him from the catapult. It was Osirah.

He had caught up.

Osirah gave another jerk and Eston fell from atop the weapon, a distance of some twenty feet. It was a sick feeling to fall so quickly, and though he tried to brace himself there was little he could do. He landed hard on the ground below, knowing at once he had broken a rib or two and was lucky it was not worse.

Osirah clambered down the side of the Dragon Killer and soon stood in front of Eston. With considerable pain, Eston managed to climb to his feet.

"It's all over, old man," Osirah taunted. "Give up now and we can find a place for you in the new Azorian-Ambrosian Army. We still have need for weapons and you'd make a fine slave in the armory, once we beat some of this pride from you!"

"Never," Eston snarled. "Not until you promise that my daughter will not be harmed."

Osirah laughed bitterly. "You mean this daughter that rides dragons," he said, a cruel sneer on his face. "You should be so very proud! But we will take excellent care of her, providing she can survive the torture we put her through first!"

That did it. A rage tore through Eston. There was no doing business with a man such as Osirah. Surrender was not an option and he knew it. He would fight.

Eston struck hard with his sword, though his ribs ached and he could barely stand. Osirah quickly went on the attack and it was all Eston could do to block each shot, each blow sending ripples of pain through his body and sending him backwards. Eston could not hold him back much longer. It was time to make his last stand.

He dug his feet into the ground while Osirah smirked, an evil, grotesque grin that chilled Eston's blood. Eston used what little power he had left and swung out recklessly with his blade, but it failed miserably. The blow landed woefully short as Osirah easily dodged it. Eston fell to his knees as the sword was planted helplessly in the earth, buried deep into the ground. He was beaten. Still on his knees, Eston prepared for the death blow, which Osirah was only too happy to deliver. He raised his sword high in the air, relishing every second. Soon his cursed enemy would be dead, and the dragon would follow.

Eston closed his eyes, hoping somehow that his daughter would survive. But the death blow never came.

Osirah screamed in anger and soon Eston felt a warm embrace around him as his feet left the earth and rose into the air. He opened his eyes to find Osirah far below on the ground, getting smaller with each passing second. Eston was dangling from the arms of the dragon, one that weakly flapped its wings, teetering back and forth in the air.

Eston looked ahead and yelled - they were heading directly into a thick forest. The dragon failed to pull up and Eston's legs crashed into treetops as both dragon and Eston struggled to stay in the air. The old warrior managed to hang on but the dragon was losing altitude fast. He was going to crash, it was just a matter of time.

"Caroline," Eston shouted. "Hang on! Hang on for all you can!"

If she yelled back he could not hear, and he could only hope she had heard him. The dragon flapped its wings, a mighty effort, and they rose a bit higher in the air to put more distance between them and Azoria. But it was the dragon's last gasp and it began to sink slowly, then suddenly it went limp and dropped from the sky. Eston braced for the terrible impact, never imagining his death would come from being crushed by a dragon. But there was no escape as the leviathan went unconscious in mid-air.

# Chapter Twenty-Six - Into the Abyss

Akari yanked on the reins of his horse, halting it at the crest of a small hill that offered a clear vantage point of the plains spread out in front of them. They had been traveling hard for a week with little rest, so his horse took the opportunity to snatch mouthfuls of grass while Akari waited for his nephews and Abigail to catch up. As they approached, Akari turned in the saddle and held a finger to his lips, requesting silence from his fellow travelers.

Jonas was the first to pull beside his uncle. "What's wrong?" he whispered while his horse also pulled big clumps of grass from the ground.

"You see that?" Akari said, climbing from his horse and kneeling in the dirt. He used his hands to shield the sun from his eyes as he peered into the distance. He was holding a mysterious device to his right eye, a long, cylindrical tube with a piece of glass at the end. It was crudely made — yet another invention by Akari, Jonas guessed. Soon they were joined by Mouse and Abigail. They all looked in the same direction, but they only saw endless plains that stretched to the horizon.

"What do you see?" Mouse asked. "Something important?"

"Well, that depends, Mouse," Akari replied. "In the big scheme, it means little. But in our little scheme, it's big. Very big."

"What are you talking about?" Jonas asked.

"You really can't see?" Akari pointed off in the distance, but still they saw nothing. "Most unusual. You don't see a mass of horses and soldiers clad in armor, loaded to the teeth with weapons? It appears we are heading directly into a gathering war party. Listen - I believe I can hear their hoofs stamping around."

"You must be mad," Jonas declared.

"That thing you're holding, Akari," Abigail said. "Let me see it."

"But of course," Akari said, handing it over. "How silly of me. *Now* you'll be able to see."

Abigail looked over the item and held it to her eye while Jonas and Mouse watched. Seconds later, she threw it to the ground and pulled out a sword given to her by Akari, slashing wildly. Jonas and Mouse followed her lead and drew their weapons, although they had no idea as to why.

Akari ran over to calm them down. "Hey, take it easy. The army is miles away. Abigail, that's a little invention of mine. It makes things far away seem closer."

The three of them let down their guard, put their swords away, and looked around sheepishly. "I saw an Army, just like you said Akari," Abigail said. "Azorians, I presume."

"Definitely," Akari replied, stooping over to pick up the instrument Abigail had dropped in her excitement. "If I had to guess, they are preparing for war against the wild men of Mulvaria. Wasting no time in getting their little plot going, I see. Maldazor has just taken control of Ambrosia, yet already he is moving against another country!"

"Maldazor is always on the move, in one way or another," Abigail said, then pointed to the item in Akari's hands. "What do you call that thing? They looked so close, yet I can't even see them now."

He furrowed his brow. "You know, I hadn't figured out a name yet." Akari shook his head, noticing the glass had been shattered into a thousand different pieces. "I suppose *spyglass* would be appropriate, for that is what I use it for - spying from great distances. But back to the drawing board with this one."

He flung the remains of his invention aside and became serious. "Well, this is how it is. If we wish to go to Azoria in search of Caroline and your father, we have two options. First, we could head right into the column of an army preparing to march. It would be foolish, but maybe they're all so distracted planning to kill people they've never met that we can simply slide right on by. Unlikely, but it's an option.

"Or we can travel through dark and hidden ways. I know a few places, long forgotten by most and feared by those who remember. That's where I'm going. All in favor, come along, and those that disagree are welcome to head south and hope you find a better way back into Ambrosia. Or you can head east, far away from these distractions."

Akari paused briefly, as if to allow others to speak up, but before anyone else could do so, he opened his mouth again. "So nobody wants to march into an army? Good! I figured as such and agree wholeheartedly."

"Wait, Akari," Abigail interjected, finally getting a word, refusing to take the warrior's bait. "My friends, I am afraid I cannot follow. I want to thank you for all you've done, but I must return to my people. It has been far too long since I've been home. But before I go, there is something I want to say." She paused to gather her thoughts.

"Akari, I want you to know this. I know how you feel about mankind and the way you favor the beasts of the earth. I don't blame you, most of the time. Yet, there is much good in us. We just need someone to show us the way.

"For too long we have obeyed the whims of Kings, and spent too much time following our Fate." She spit on the ground, adding emphasis to the word. "Fate. My *Fate* was to be snatched away from my family at the age of fourteen to work in the kitchen of the royals. Some life! Akari, I know you have often run from your talents, but I say to you this. The people want to be free. You may not know how most really feel about Kings, but I do. And many of them are the soldiers you once led. Freedom can be ours. There is a revolution to be had, if you will lead it. Find a way, Akari Dragonslayer, Akari Dragonkiller, whichever one you are. Overthrow Maldazor, and free us from the ways of these Kings!"

Akari looked at her with a far off look in his eyes. For once he found himself without words, with no comeback at the ready. "Well, I'll, umm, take that under advisement."

"Do more than that, Akari. You must, because only *you* can," she said.

The words found him. "Dear Abigail, there is naught that I can do. These are ill times. Never before in history has one person been able to do so little."

"Maybe so. But you are not just one man, or perhaps you forget. You have your nephews, for starters, and you will find that many will support you, but only if you show them the way. I have already told you that many in the armies would follow you. From there, Maldazor could not turn you back any more than he could the tide."

Akari looked grim, shaken even. "You seem to have thought this over."

"I have! Lead us, Akari, and I will bring word to my town, word that change is on the way. From there it will spread like wildfire. The great Akari, returned from the dead and ready to lead our people away from Kings and Queens, from wizards and Fate."

Her eyes raged with intensity, easing as she realized she had made her point and it was now in Akari's hands. "You're a stubborn man, Akari. It's rather unsettling. In fact, I'd say there is nothing more unsettling to me than someone so settled in their ways, except that sounds like something *you* would say." She chuckled at this, with Mouse joining her. Akari looked nonplussed and Jonas watched impassively.

Abigail then pulled Mouse to her and hugged him, thanking him for all he had done before kissing him on the forehead, lightly and sweetly.

She turned to Jonas, who had been pouting throughout the short time she had known him. "Hey Jonas," she said. "Chin up. Maybe things will change for the better. And maybe *you* can make them change."

"Yeah, sure," Jonas stammered. "Take care of yourself, Abigail."

"I'll try," she said, and turned again to the great warrior. "Akari, think about what I said. Until we meet again!" She climbed on to her horse and galloped away, the three of them watching as she did.

"I hope we see her again one day," Mouse said.

"Yeah, me too," Akari replied absent-mindedly, staring after her. It was some time before she disappeared over the horizon, at which point Akari shook his head, the words of Abigail weighing heavy in his mind.

## Chapter Twenty-Seven - The Catacombs

It didn't take Akari long to move on from Abigail's absence. He simply acted as if she had never been there and went back to business, though Jonas and Mouse knew her words lingered in his thoughts.

Still, Akari pretended otherwise. "Well, it's the three of us again. Good! So we are all in agreement that it is to dark and hidden places we go? Excellent! Come along then. To the catacombs!"

"What are the catacombs, Akari?" asked Mouse.

"Aw yes, the catacombs. Amazing things. Underground tunnels built by ancient Kings to bury their kin. They have been long hidden from the world, largely built over by Azoria City. Quite a history lesson I'm giving you on this journey, boys. We've gone from Cemetery Hill to the long-forgotten catacombs.

"But let me warn you. This is not for the faint of heart – good thing none of *that* ilk is with us. So are you ready?" Before they could respond, he answered for them. "Good, I figured as much.

"Now, the catacombs are long since deserted by humans, but they remain filled with all kinds of awful and dangerous things. But we can deal with that. Awful and dangerous things are our specialty. Right, Mouse?"

Mouse's face turned bright with embarrassment and Akari winked at him, then continued. "We are willing to go through these dangerous and awful things because the catacombs run directly into Maldazor's dungeons - *if* you know the way, and I do. Did a lot of exploring here years ago. Interesting times."

They rode across the plains for some time. Eventually, the plains began to disappear as groves of trees began to pop up, and before long they stood at the crest of a massive forest. Akari dismounted his horse and patted its neck. "Drat that Abigail. Where we're going we don't need horses, and if she hadn't been in such a hurry we could've sent these fine animals with her!"

He shook his head sadly. "I suppose we'll have to let them loose. But, horses take to the wild as quick as can be and they'll find plenty of grass to eat. Horses do much better in the wild than *we* do."

He stripped his horse of its saddle and reins, gesturing for his nephews to do the same. The horses took no notice, too busy eating to care. The travelers left them at it and departed.

They entered the woods, sticking to areas off the beaten path to avoid any stragglers from the Azorian Army. It was tough slogging until they finally came to a little stream that trickled through the jungle.

"Perfect. This is the right way," Akari said. "Follow me, we're getting close!"

They kept marching until they came to a grove of thick trees. There were large weeping willows and ancient cypress trees amidst waist-high weeds and vines that wrapped around and between the trees, filling in the spaces between branches and creating a canopy that blocked out the sun.

Unusual bird calls filled the air, while bats fluttered occasionally, from branch to branch. This jungle-like place was quite the contrast to the wind-swept plains they had just journeyed through. The thick undergrowth proved challenging to their progress.

Akari slashed through the undergrowth with his sword, sending bits of weeds and leaves flying through the air. It was hard work, and he was forced to step aside at times to let Jonas and Mouse take a turn. They were soaked with sweat and exhausted by the time they came to another small creek, where they each drank deeply. When they were done, they walked through the ankle-deep water before coming to an old moss-covered stone near the creek bank, barely visible among the thick plant cover.

Akari smiled broadly upon finding the marker, and left the creek to chop through more weeds. It was not long before his face again lit up as he found an ancient, crumbling staircase, which led underground. Akari descended to the bottom, turning as he did to stand in front of the lowest stairs. The stairwell was filled with dirt that had washed down throughout the years, and somewhere underneath all of that were stones laid there eons ago. It seemed there was nowhere else to go, as Akari was simply standing in a hole.

"A staircase that leads to nowhere. Well done, Akari," Jonas said as Mouse looked on with annoyance at his brother, too weary to respond.

"Patience, young Jonas," Akari said, examining the stairs until he found what he was looking for. He bent down to his knees, dug into the ground with his fingers, and somehow slid both of his hands entirely underneath the bottommost step. With a grunt, he attempted to lift the staircase, but it failed to budge.

"Say, what are you getting at, uncle?" Jonas quizzed.

"What do you think? I'm looking for the way in. As you can see, it's well hidden. After all, who would ever think to look *under* a staircase for an entrance? I'd almost forgotten myself! Climb on down and give me a hand, will you?"

"We'll be right down, Uncle," Mouse replied. Jonas looked cross, but soon he followed. They came down the crumbling stairs and lined up on each side of Akari, sliding their hands under the stairs. They lifted up, finding that it was immensely heavy. They strained under its weight, not budging it an inch.

"It's hopeless. Too heavy! Nothing we can do," Jonas said.

"That was a practice run. Let's give it another go," Akari said.

Jonas grumbled under his breath, considering further efforts futile, but he did as asked and after considerable strain they did manage to lift it up, only a few inches at first but soon the bottom five steps raised and swung like a door on a hinge. They were amazed to find the entrance to a large, black cavern, one that looked like it had not been entered for years, if the dust kicked up by the wind was any indication.

Mouse was stunned to see Akari produce another jar filled with fireflies. "You have more?"

"No, these are the same ones, Mouse. They caught up early this morning when you were off getting a drink. Not a single one was hurt, if you can believe it! I put in a good word for you and asked them not to hold your actions against you. They were rather upset, but I think they understand now."

Mouse's eyes looked as if they would pop from his skull. "I didn't mean to—" he said, but Akari cut him off.

"Course you didn't, but you ever try to make a firefly see sense? Flighty little things. But all is well." Akari unscrewed the lid and let them free. They wasted no time and flew into the cavern, casting their light over the filthy catacombs. Mouse and Jonas both had sinking feelings in their stomach as the light revealed an army of bugs creeping along the tunnel's floor. The hidden passage seemed to stretch on forever. It had an aura of ghosts and spirits, ancient curses and hexes, demons and witches from decades past. It felt somehow wrong to disturb the peace these spirits had enjoyed. Mouse hoped there would be no consequences.

Akari took no notice of the filth they were entering, feeling more inclined to boast about the fireflies. "Just wonderful, aren't they," he said to nobody in particular, his face glowing with pride. "Made acquaintance with them years ago, and they've been great friends to me."

"Is there anything besides bugs down here, Akari?" Mouse asked. "This place sets my hair on end."

"Well, there used to be a Cyclops, but surely he can't be alive," he replied, though not persuasively. "No, he must be long gone. Besides, he was sealed behind a closed door with no means of escape. No, there's nothing to worry about, just millions of bugs, a few spiders, probably rats, and maybe the odd snake or two. That's all!"

Akari led them down a sloped tunnel, while Jonas closed the staircase door behind them. It snapped shut with a sharp grinding sound, and Mouse couldn't help but wonder if they would ever see the surface again.

Jonas was on edge and couldn't shake the eerie feeling running down his spine. In closing the entrance, he felt he may have sealed their Fate. The catacombs smelled of death, a pungent, clammy smell. It carried through the space on cool air that chilled them to their bones. Jonas began to think a life spent creating weapons sounded good – or even one cleaning the King's dishes.

"Can we open that door again if we need to?" Jonas asked. "What if we need to escape?"

Akari stopped walking and thought it over. "You know, I don't recall ever having to go back, so I can't say. But there's not much we can do about it *now*. If we are trapped, I fail to see the purpose of knowing. We don't need negative thoughts swirling around our heads. Better not to know if we have no escape, I think."

"I think I'd rather know the truth, Akari. Our father always said honesty is the best policy," Mouse replied, rather meekly.

Akari turned and put his hand on Mouse's shoulder. "Mouse, if Eston told you honesty is always the best policy, he wasn't telling the truth. I've learned it's not wise to hold fast to iron-clad policies. Different situations require different responses. A lie could save the world one day, and bring down an entire kingdom the next. The inflexible and rigid tend to shrivel up and die because they are unable to adapt. The trick is in knowing when to lie and when to tell the truth. Right now I say there is no need to know the truth for we have no need to concern ourselves with escape. Upward and onward!

"So come along. The fireflies can't stay lit forever, and it's a long walk to the dungeons. But keep your eyes open and look sharp. Who knows what creatures still dwell in these catacombs? The dead are not the only ones who live here."

They came to the end of a long slope with the path flattening considerably. The tunnel ran straight ahead for some distance. Ancient torches unlit for a millennium lined the walls. Water dripped from the surface, leaving behind an algae-slicked stone surface. The ceiling sagged and stones occasionally dropped from above, adding to their collective unease. The tunnel did not seem like a safe place to travel, but Akari reminded them it was rather unlikely that a structure that stood for over 2000 years would choose this particular day to cave in. Still, that thought was hardly comforting when chunks fell from the ceiling, narrowly missing their heads.

"Relax," Akari offered. "That wouldn't have killed you! There's nothing to be scared of, yet. I'll tell you when to be scared."

They traveled for a good long while - it was impossible to tell precisely how long, without having the sun for a guide - when they reached a spot where they took a sharp right turn. As they rounded the bend, they saw a shocking sight. They were surrounded by walls packed tight with old bones. Skulls and leg bones piled high and bones were stacked on top of each other. The grotesque display was created by the remains of ancient peoples who lived well before Ambrosia's time. Mouse and Jonas looked on with an equal mix of horror and awe.

Only Akari maintained his composure. "Amazing. Simply amazing," he said. "I forgot how incredible these feats of architecture were."

"Incredible? It's morbid. Repulsive, I'd say," said Mouse. "Making walls from skulls and bones? That's too much."

"They're just bones, dear Mouse, and nothing more. Something we simply leave behind on our way to the next world, or to the nether-lands between the worlds, as the case may be. Shall we continue? I'd like to make it through these tunnels before the sun comes up tomorrow."

"Well, I guess we don't have a choice, Akari," Jonas replied.

"You always have a choice, Jonas, although in this case you must choose from a series of bad options. And this is the least bad, so come along."

They walked down the endless catacomb, happy to move beyond the skeleton walls. They took care to avoid puddles that filled in sunken areas of the stone floor, and every now and again they would step on something that would crunch, leaving them to shudder. Otherwise, there were no difficulties.

At times, they would come to a section that led into a new direction, but Akari moved straight ahead without deviating from his route. After passing a few such routes, curiosity took hold of Mouse.

"What happens if we go the wrong way, Akari?" he asked.

"We don't go the wrong way -- and then nothing happens. Straight ahead, Mouse, until we can't go straight any longer," Akari replied. "As I said, I know these ways well. Upward and onward!"

"Upward and onward, upward and onward," Jonas grumbled under his breath, low enough to escape notice.

They went on for what seemed to be hours, nobody daring to even speak, afraid of alerting anything to their presence. They pushed past tedium and exhaustion. Gradually, Mouse and Jonas grew accustomed to the pale light cast by the fireflies and became less anxious as they made their way through the dark recesses. Their courage was building with each step.

The journey went on for what Akari judged had been three full days, though, again, it was difficult to tell. It seemed even longer to him, as he waited in darkness while his nephews and the fireflies rested. Mouse and Jonas had no idea how Akari passed the time while he waited. But they suspected that he may have been thinking about Abigail's parting words to him.

*

Akari had promised today would be their last in the catacombs. They picked up the pace accordingly, making good time until coming to an old stone door embedded in the wall. They paid it little attention, but just as Mouse crossed its path, the door thumped as something banged against it loudly - *very* loudly. Mouse jumped backwards as whatever it was crashed again with a fury, sending both Mouse and Jonas scrambling to Akari's side.

"What is that?" Mouse spat out.

"You don't want to know," Akari replied, shaking his head sadly. "Poor fellow. That is the giant Cyclops I spoke of, trapped in a prison underneath a hidden door above the surface. I can't believe he is still alive! *Good for him.*"

Akari shuddered before continuing. "Needless to say, we won't be setting *him* free any time soon." He stopped, mumbling under his breath and shaking his head as if trying to convince himself that his idea was crazy. "No, that wouldn't work. Would it?"

He then spoke directly to Jonas and Mouse. "I don't know that he's ever been taught to say *thank you* so we might live to regret it if we did set him loose, but the option begins to appeal to me. He does deserve it. I rather pity him, trapped as he is. A terrible fate for anyone, or anything."

"How can he still be alive?" Jonas asked. "Does someone feed him?"

"Feed him? Of course not. He's been long forgotten by the Azorians. If I had to guess, I'd say he eats bugs, snakes, rats, and other things that slither down this way, though mostly by accident. I once slid him a piece of bread under the door, to change things up for him, but I didn't stick around to see if he ate it. I figured he'd be long gone by now. He is quite a survivor!"

Mouse and Jonas stared at the door as they passed, hoping it was sealed as tightly as it appeared. Letting him free did not seem prudent, though they could not imagine spending a life locked away in darkness. They were even more grateful for the fireflies that fluttered overhead, lighting the pathway nearly as well as any torch could. Their light gave an eerie glow to the tunnels, revealing even more of the ethereal world they were traversing.

Then, just ahead they saw a chilling sight. It was difficult to make out from this distance, but based on the glowing eyes, sharp teeth, and hairless long tails, it seemed likely they were about to encounter a pack of giant rats. A big pack – probably 50 – was swarming together in a snarling mess of fur, claws, and teeth. Even Akari recoiled at the hissing sounds they made as they writhed in the filth.

"I don't think we're going to get through that, Akari," Mouse offered.

Akari's only response was to wrinkle his brow while his eyes darted back and forth, deep in concentration. Jonas knew he was hatching another one of his plans but one he had serious doubts about. For once, Akari did not have the answers. Jonas hoped that some of the cockiness would leave his uncle for a change. He enjoyed Akari's uncertainty for a fleeting second before remembering that his future depended on the success of this plan. Seeing as he had no plan, it was a bit foolish to root for his uncle's failure.

The expression on Akari's face said it all: he looked back and forth, between his outstretched palms, clearly weighing the pros and cons of the plan he was conjuring. Then, he nodded his head and pursed his lips, signaling he had made up his mind.

"What's the plan?" Jonas asked.

Akari looked distracted. "Yes, um, the plan. Well, the chances of success are not the best, I admit. But if we're to make it into the dungeons of Azoria, the catacombs are the best way, we're all agreed?" Before anyone could reply he continued. "Yep, that's what I thought. We *must* make it through the tunnel ahead. No way around it. Now I don't know if any of you have had to kill fifty rats in tight quarters before - I worked in King Wilhelm's castle for years around *human* rats, and it's almost the same thing, but not quite. That said, killing rats is not something I would relish.

"Well, why kill rats when you have a known rat killer at your disposal? It would be foolish, right? When I heard that Cyclops banging on that old door, I thought to myself one thing - he sounds hungry. The poor thing must be famished. And you know what a Cyclops likes to eat? Well, like I said, you can bet the only things he's come across are the occasional rat, maybe some worms and centipedes, things like that. Now that doesn't sound real tasty to me but I bet *he* thinks they're just fine. Who wouldn't?

"I'm not one to let things starve if I can help it, so what we do is simple. We'll invite the Cyclops to supper for a rat smorgasbord! He'll love it." He waved his hands around as he said this, hoping to convince his nephews of the plan's utility, but then quietly added something not so reassuring. "Let's only hope that he doesn't decide *we* might taste better in the process."

"Let's hope? I think we need a little more than hope, Akari," Jonas retorted. "We need to be *certain* he eats the rats. What happens if he goes charging out the end of the catacombs all the way to the dungeons? Won't they figure out there's been a breach? And once they do, we'll *never* get into the dungeons."

"Jonas, you're not thinking this through. Here, come with me," Akari gestured for them to follow as he walked to the Cyclops' door. "You think he's going to bash his way through with fresh meat for the taking? That he'll just pass it over? No, he's going to fill his belly, and justifiably so. A Cyclops should rightfully have a big old gut, but I'm guessing this fellow has been wasted down to just about nothing.

"So this is what we're going to do. It's simple, but when it comes to plans, simple is usually better, and don't let anyone tell you differently. The devil is always in the details, so the less details to mess up, the better. So all we are going to do is sneak right on by as he's chomping on a pile of rats. Nice and simple."

"That's your plan?" Jonas exclaimed. "That's awful! I could come up with something better than that *in my sleep*, Akari."

"Oh good. I'm open to other ideas. Let's hear it!"

"Well, umm, let me think for a second," Jonas stammered back.

"Perhaps you should sleep first. When you wake up, can you let us all know what you've come up with? I suppose Mouse and I will wait patiently until you do."

Jonas tried in vain to think of something and failed. "Aw, what's the use? I guess that wizard knew what he was talking about after all. I'm no warrior." Jonas kicked at a centipede that happened to crawl by. Mouse tried to pat Jonas on the back for encouragement, but Jonas would have none of it. He brushed off Mouse, preferring to pout.

"Well Jonas, here's the thing. Plans are a lot easier to make than they are to keep. When I say I have a plan, I only hope that it works, but if not, we'll think of something on the fly. Now let's go. The fireflies will light the way. It seems that when a creature, and this goes for just about any kind, has a choice in the matter, they will almost always head the way that's lit, even a Cyclops that's been in the dark for decades or more.

"It's always been a mystery to me. Take a moth. A moth won't come out during the day, sleeping when the whole world is nice and bright, but what does he do first chance he gets at night? He heads right toward a flame. All the light he could possibly want from dusk to dawn and he sleeps right through it, then flies directly to a little itty-bitty piece of light and if he isn't careful, burns himself up.

"And here we are." They had arrived at their destination, where dust was still flying as the Cyclops continued to pound away.

"Are you just going to open the door and take our chances?" Mouse asked.

"Certainly not! Just watch." He reached into the pack on his back and removed a small cloth bag made from purple velvet. He undid the drawstring and sifted his fingers through a blue-ish powder. "Sleeping powder," he explained before Mouse could ask. Jonas was already quite familiar with it, sneering as he looked upon it again.

The Cyclops was thumping steadily on the door - it was the most excitement he had experienced in years. Mouse looked down the tunnel to watch the rats make their way down the hall, getting closer and closer. His hands shook; they needed to work fast.

"Don't look now, but here come the rats," Mouse warned.

"That's good. Better than good, it's perfect!" the warrior said. "Let their smell waft through the air. I'll bet he's licking his chops back there."

He knelt in front of the door and held his hand flat, with the powder lying on it. "Stand back. It won't work on me, but it'll put you boys down." Once they scrambled from range, he blew the powder under the crack at the bottom of the door.

At first, nothing happened. The Cyclops kept pounding away, and Mouse panicked with the rats getting ever closer. "Why isn't it working, Akari?" he squealed.

"Patience, patience," Akari replied. "Listen, he's tiring as we speak."

He was right. The thumps came slower and slower, and in short order they ceased entirely.

"See! All right, let's open this door. Give me a hand."

"But how?" Jonas quizzed.

"Always the doubter, Nephew. Mouse, what do you think? How do we open this door?"

Mouse looked the door over, wrinkling his brow as if trying to make sure Akari was not trying to trick him. "Umm, we use the handle?"

"Exactly! You are wise beyond your years, young Mouse. Simply, this door opens from the outside only, not the inside, so the Cyclops couldn't escape unless he could tear it down, and as you can see it is very stout. Now get behind me everyone - yes, right there.

"When I open the door, don't go rushing in case he's not quite asleep. This Cyclops prefers rats I'm certain, but there's no sense in tempting him with our flesh either. OK, ready?"

Together, the three of them stood behind the place the door would open, with Jonas pulling on the handle. The door squeaked loudly as it turned on its stone hinges, with dust and pieces of dirt shaking loose as it did.

Akari peaked around the door while a few fireflies flew into the chamber, revealing the Cyclops lying flat on its back, safely asleep. Even as it slumbered, it was a terrifying sight. The fireflies reflected dully on its pale gray skin, mostly exposed except for a tattered breech cloth that hung from its waist. It clutched a big wooden club in one hand while the other was empty.

There was a filed-down horn in the center of its head, capped with a piece of iron. It had been a mighty horn, but all that remained was a stump. His nose and ears were pierced with dull brass ring, and his right arm held three different handcuffs that had been broken away over the cruel years of this creature's life. His legs both bore the remains of leg shackles.

His left arm held the remains of only one handcuff, but he had long since outgrown it, and now, it dug painfully into his flesh. Scars ran up and down his body, striking evidence of years of neglect and battles that went bad. He - and it was safe to say he, though none could really tell you why - had a little patch of dark black hair sprouting from his head on an otherwise hairless body, and he smelled unspeakably bad. Still, his muscles bulged in spite of his emaciated state, and there was no question that this remained a formidable creature.

"Some life he has led," Akari said. "But his outlook will very shortly be improving."

"Akari, what good is he to us now? He's fast asleep!" Jonas complained.

"Yes, and he will soon be fast awake," Akari retorted. "Don't you think I would have thought of that? After I created a sleeping powder, I went to work on a waking powder. You can't have one without the other, really." He pulled out another little bag from his pack, the same as the other only it was crimson red, which matched the color of the contents therein.

"OK, go hide behind the door out in the tunnel. Here goes nothing!"

Akari sprinkled some of the red powder under the Cyclops' nose. "OK, big fellow, I'm going to need your help." The Cyclops lay in silence, but soon his nose twitched, followed by a loud and powerful sneeze, almost knocking Akari down. The Cyclops shot up from the floor, looking around crazily with his lone eyeball going around and around in circles. If Akari wasn't in such a tight spot he would've laughed uproariously at the sight, but as things were, he stayed close to the wall and hoped to remain unseen.

The Cyclops' nose twitched and snorted as it picked up the new smells that came through. Then he noticed that his door was wide open and he grunted in glee. After all of these years, finally he could be free.

Just like that he was on his feet, flying out the door and thumping his chest. It took a right turn and shot down the tunnel straight toward the rats, never noticing Akari in his room nor Jonas and Mouse hunched behind the open door.

Akari stepped from the room and watched the Cyclops sprint down the cavern. In an instant, the rats saw him coming and stopped in their tracks, their high pitched squeals sending shivers down Akari's back as they turned and fled.

"Follow me! Stick to the plan," Akari yelled while he raised his sword high over his head. The three adventurers took off after the Cyclops, who was incredibly fast and difficult to keep pace with. Soon his giant figure was reduced to a dim outline far off down the tunnel as he chased after the scurrying rats.

They made good time as they trotted after him and after a bit they found him with a pile of dead rats nearby. He was sitting on the floor with his legs crossed, digging into one of his victims, the remains of which were quickly added to a pile of rat bones from those he had already consumed. It was rather disgusting, and Mouse could not help but feel a few pangs of remorse for the victims. Rats weren't the most pleasant things in the world, this was true, but a rat couldn't help being a rat any more than he could help who he was. And maybe less so, when he thought about it. He could go to school, learn, and discover new things that could make him a better person, but a rat's lot in life was pretty well set at birth. A rat was a rat and that was that.

But this was no time for philosophy. Akari asked for silence and led the way, creeping quietly until he stood just steps from the monster. He took a deep breath and sneaked by, holding his breath as did, too scared to even exhale, then Jonas and Mouse did the same. It was terrifying, with the hot putrid breath of the Cyclops stopping them dead in their tracks a time or two. But the monster paid them no mind, stopping only to discard one carcass before moving to the next, taking from one pile to add to the other.

It was a tight squeeze and slow going, but they finally made it past. It took some time before they felt completely safe. When they did, Akari stopped tip-toeing and took off in a sprint without saying a word. He didn't need to, as the others were dying to do the same. They ran as quick as their legs would carry them for an indeterminate amount of time - it felt like five minutes and five hours all at once. They had lost all sense of time in the subterranean darkness. Then, when all seemed lost and they thought their journey would never end, they came huffing and puffing to a staircase. It was almost completely eroded away, likely from the years of a steady trickle of water dripping down the center, leaving the stairs covered in a thick green slime. Nasty as it was, they were thrilled to see it. Akari quickly confirmed what they had hoped.

"It is the end of the catacombs, my friends. That's the good news. The bad news is we are going to enter the dungeons of Azoria, home of evil King Maldazor."

"Finally," Jonas said. "Let's go rescue my father!"

They stepped on the worn away stairs and carefully made their way to the top, sliding on the ooze and hitting their heads on low overhanging rocks that had filled in the entrance many, many years before.

The fireflies flew to the top of the rubble and formed a line which led to a narrow tunnel they could pass through between the rocks. They were almost to their goal, and Jonas and Mouse could hardly breathe in anticipation of what lay ahead.

"I have to say, I miss the sun. Now, climb on up. You first Jonas," Akari said.

"For Father!" Jonas said, squirming through the tunnel. He was quickly followed by Mouse, with Akari bringing up the rear. The great warrior took one look back at the catacombs, biting down on his lower lip to steel his resolve. Things were not about to get easier, despite all they had already been through.

# Chapter Twenty-Eight - Well, Well, Well

As Jonas crawled through the rubble, grateful to leave the catacombs behind, a thought hit him. He could've kicked himself. Why hadn't he thought of this before? They had come all this way, just steps from Maldazor's dungeon, and they weren't even certain their father was there. And even if he had been at one point, it was entirely possible that Caroline had rescued him already.

"Akari," Jonas hissed. The anger in his voice was amplified by the quiet chamber. "How do we know our father is even here?"

"We don't know," Akari replied. "We only know that he *was* here."

"And how do we know that?"

"Simple. I have a source around the castle. Didn't I explain this already?"

"Not as I recall," Jonas replied.

"Me either, Akari," Mouse added He was trying to remain on Jonas's good side while showing Akari respect at the same time. It was a fine line, but so far, Mouse was walking it well.

Akari stopped a few steps from the end of the narrow passageway. "I see. Well, if you must know, we have a dragon near the castle."

"A dragon?!?"

Akari hushed them. "Don't say that too loud. You never know who could be listening. But yes, a dragon. Or more accurately, a dragon disguised as a bat. A good little dragon. At the Dragon Council they passed on tidings from him, and that is when I confirmed that your father was here." He stopped and laughed rather heartily, all things considered. "Fellows, you don't really think I'd come all this way just to take a little vacation, do you?"

Now it was Jonas's turn to look embarrassed, though that only momentarily slowed him. "Why didn't the Dragon Council call for him to return, the way they did with our three dragons?"

"Why bother? From what I know of Jomey, he wouldn't listen anyway. Kind of an odd dragon from what they say, though he seems normal enough to *me*. Besides, nobody knows he is there - our dragons were no longer hidden."

Of course, Akari was right, like he always seemed to be, so Jonas changed the topic. "OK, well, how do we make it out of here?" The tunnel had come to an end, with no exit visible.

Akari walked to the end and pointed up. "We go up. Take a look."

Directly overhead there was what appeared to be a drain. The circular and rather narrow hole was lined with stones. Conveniently, metal rungs led to its top. There was just one problem, though. A metal grate covered the bottom of the drain, and there was another at the top. The slats were so narrow that not even Mouse could squeeze through them.

"We'll have to dislodge the cover," Akari said. "It shouldn't take us long - you can see it is rusting away. Same with the one on top, it's nearly rusted all the way through. Come on, help me pull this one down."

As Akari predicted, the grate came off easily. It nearly broke in their hands. "I only hope the rungs aren't as rusted," Jonas said, cynically.

"Yes, let's hope," Akari replied. "Mouse, how do you feel about going up first? As the smallest, you're less likely to break any of the rungs, and we can follow from there."

Mouse stared up the drain. He could hardly make out the top of it, as it was quite high – and a long way down, if he happened to fall. But really he had no choice and he knew that.

"Of course I'll go," he said. And with that, he jumped to grab the first rung, kicking out his legs and pulling hard with his arms to lift himself up. He scrambled to the third rung, and then was able to rest his feet on the lowest one. It felt strong and easily supported his weight. It showed no signs of weakness from rust. He hoped that would hold true throughout his climb.

Everything was going along quite nicely – it was easy, in fact – until he approached the top. With only three rungs remaining, one broke off in his hand. He quickly moved up a rung, then reached for the last one. As he did, his foot kicked at a loose stone jutting out of the wall. Mouse didn't give it much thought, as he broke away the remaining rusted remnants of the grate covering the exit, and scrambled loose to the top. He took a deep breath upon exiting, feeling relieved. But then, more stones fell. Then more and more and more.

This was an ominous turn of events. He peered down into the drain and cringed - they were in big trouble. He yelled to warn his brother and uncle below, doubting they could hear over the noise, but there was nothing else that could have been done. The stones began to cascade, one after another, creating an avalanche that lasted until the entire drain caved in. Mouse could feel the ground shaking beneath his feet and feared it would collapse.

Would Akari and Jonas survive?

The rumbling came to an end. The entire drain was filled in. Any sign of the opening had vanished. Mouse peered at the rubble and panicked.

"Jonas! Akari! Can you hear me? Jonas! Akari!" He yelled frantically, but heard no reply. He could only hope they were alive, though it was hard to fathom how they could be.

Mouse was alone, utterly alone. He sat and cried. But those tears soon turned to anger. He reached into the pile of stones and began throwing them, one after another, down the dark halls. He didn't care where they landed. If an Azorian guard came to investigate, he could picture bashing him in the face in partial retaliation for the ordeal his father has suffered. If it wasn't for Azoria, and Maldazor, his father would've never been here and neither would he, so they'd deserve what they got.

After firing about twenty rocks down the hall and getting no relief, Mouse began to look around. In his rage he had failed to notice that a few of the fireflies had followed him. He was embarrassed by his outburst.

"Sorry, guys," he stammered, but the fireflies only continued to shine bright and hover in place. Whether or not they understood him, Mouse couldn't say. But they didn't seem to think less of him and that would do for now.

With his senses restored, Mouse realized he was in an area of the dungeon that seemed rarely used. It was not much different from the catacombs that they'd just left behind. The floor was slimy, with water pooling in places. It was coming apart in some places, with stones turned up. It was no wonder the drain had collapsed so easily, as the entire place seemed to be at the end of its days. This was hardly a dungeon that a king could take pride in. The palace might be magnificent above, but it was built on an ancient and crumbling foundation that might collapse at any moment.

Mouse knew he had few options. He decided that he had to see if he could dig through the rubble to find Akari and Jonas, and hope beyond hopes that they were still alive.

He began the impossible task of digging in search of his brother and uncle, but was distracted by a loud noise. The sound was becoming more intense and appeared to be closing in. Suddenly, the pile of stones he was standing on seemed to be taking on a life of their own. They bounced up and down, sending rocks rolling away from the pile. The rumbling grew louder.

Mouse nearly screamed as a rat squeezed through the pile, then another rat pushed out, and then another. Soon rats were swarming the hallway, running frantically.

Suddenly, nearly the entire pile of rubble flew into the air. Mouse had to cover up as a pile of rocks whizzed by, raining down on him as he fell to the floor and shielded his head. When the rock shower ended, Mouse pulled himself back to his feet and took off running, when he saw what had caused the commotion.

It was the Cyclops! He busted right through the rock pile and hadn't broken a sweat. In fact, if Mouse was not mistaken, the Cyclops was in his glory. He was smiling, laughing, and running wild with a large strand of drool dangling from his chin. The giant snorted and let rip a laugh. There was no doubt about it – he was having the time of his life.

Mouse found his joy infectious. The beast was scarred, mangled, slobbering, downright ugly, and missing teeth, but being free after years of captivity had transformed even this ugly creature into a picture of euphoria. The Cyclops was a living validation of freedom.

Still, Mouse did not wish to end up a snack, and was grateful when the Cyclops left to chase after the rats. Mouse's spirits were also lifted when he considered that the Cyclops was headed straight for the prison guards, who surely would not be happy to see him.

The dust soon cleared from the pile of stones and settled lightly along the dungeon floor. Mouse went off into a dark corner, hiding from dungeon guards who would come investigate, but soon the dungeons fell silent and Mouse remained alone.

Mouse left his corner to return to the landslide, fearing what he might find. But just as he stepped on to the rubble to climb down, he gasped! His worst fears were erased. Two shadowy figures stumbled up the wreckage. Akari and Jonas! They walked through the dissipating dust, looking a little banged up but overall no worse for the wear. With determined looks, they walked toward Mouse. Not caring how it looked, Mouse ran over to envelope them with hugs.

"I must admit, when I was scrambling to avoid rocks falling on my head, I found your plan wanting," Akari said. "But I want to formally apologize for doubting you! A rather ingenious plan, Nephew. With the ladder rotting away in your hands, it would have proved impossible for us to climb, so you cleverly brought the whole thing down, knowing the Cyclops would clear the way.

"I'm happy we weren't done with the old boy yet, and I daresay the prison guards will never notice us poking around while they're dealing with *him*." As if by design, they heard a loud crash as the Cyclops carried his destruction throughout the dungeon. Akari cringed in mock sympathy for the guards, laughed, and clapped Mouse across the back. "Well done!"

Jonas looked a little down, as seemed to be his normal, but he managed a weak smile. "Nice job, Mouse."

Mouse stood frozen, befuddled, but after an awkward silence he managed to stammer out a response. "But it was all an accident, Jonas. I thought I had *killed* you both. I never expected for you to come walking through the rubble behind the Cyclops! It was just dumb luck."

"No, Mouse," Jonas replied. "It wasn't luck. It was *Fate*. You really are a great warrior. If this isn't proof that there's something to Fate, than I don't know what is.

"As for me, I'll be a great helper for dad someday." He kicked at a loose stone from the rubble, hung his head, and took off down the hall.

Mouse followed him with his eyes. He didn't know what to say, so he decided to ignore it. "What now?" Mouse asked, turning to Akari.

"Do I have to spell everything out for you boys?" Akari asked, smiling. "We need to find your father. Come now, Mouse, really."

Mouse shrugged. "Well, I knew *that* Akari, I was just saying - how do we *go* about finding him?"

"Mouse, never say something just to say it. Better to keep quiet and wait until you have something important to contribute." He winked at Mouse, who smirked, then ran after Jonas, leaving Akari no choice but to join. He struggled to keep pace, as Mouse was going at a dead sprint, surprisingly fast. "What are you doing?" Akari yelled after him.

"Finding my father, just like you said," Mouse called back.

Mouse came around a corner and could feel cool air on his face. It was refreshing after the stifling air they'd been trapped in for days. He peered down a long, dark hall, littered with jagged stones that the Cyclops had left behind, with Jonas just ahead and Akari on his heels.

"Jonas, wait up," Mouse called after him, and was surprised when Jonas did, allowing Mouse to catch up.

"Go ahead, Mouse. I'm not any good anyway," he said.

"Jonas, come on. That's crazy talk and you know it. Let's go get Father."

Jonas didn't respond, but did start running again while Akari caught up. The three of them came around the corner and nearly ran straight into the Cyclops.

The creature's back was turned to them as he crouched on the floor. He had caught another rat and was munching away. The fireflies were just as surprised to find the Cyclops; they tried to fly away while the he playfully swatted at them. The beast snorted and emitted a rough, growling laugh, a strange noise from such a creature. He then shocked the three adventurers.

"Pwetty," the Cyclops said. "Heh heh heh!" It laughed loudly, and all they could do was stand back and watch. It never occurred to them that it could talk.

The fireflies seemed to be aware that they had his attention and formed a straight line. He stood up and followed as they led him further down the hall, hovering just out of his reach. He skipped away, jumping in the air, trying to grab at the bugs as he traipsed off.

Akari let out a deep breath. "Well, that was close. Don't think I'd like to chance running into *him*, though he does seem to be in a good mood!"

Jonas watched the Cyclops head off down the dark hallway. "I don't think the guards are going to like him too much."

"No, I suppose not, and therefore, I like him very much!" Akari exclaimed, wincing at the crashing noises echoing down the corridor. It was a metallic sound, clearly clangs from armor. The Cyclops had met his first Azorian guard.

"Well, there he goes! We better move fast. From what I can remember, the hall to the dungeons is just to our left," Akari said, leading them for a bit. "Aw yes, here it is. With our friend causing chaos elsewhere, we just may have the place to ourselves."

"Akari, I'd like to spend as little time as possible in Maldazor's castle," Mouse said, his face tense. "Let's find Father and get out of here."

"I agree. Follow me and look sharp for any prisoners. They may be able to tell us where Eston is."

After a short jog, they came to rooms covered by iron bars. Jail cells. Exactly what they hoped to find. The cells were clearly unoccupied, and had been for some time judging by the dust and cobwebs. It was a good sign, though, that they were on the right track.

They continued through the dungeon and rounded a corner to another row of cells, all unoccupied, save one - the very last in the row, a cell marked as BC-CC.

They found an old man sleeping in a dirty pile of blankets on the floor. There was a little tin plate, an empty cup, and nothing more. It was a sad sight.

Jonas drew his sword and poked the old man with it softly, just enough to wake him, but not nearly enough to hurt him. The old man shot up in an instant, freeing himself from the ragged blankets and climbing to his feet. He stared at Jonas with his eyes wild and black, buried in disheveled long greasy gray hair. His gaze was unbroken for some time before he finally spoke.

"Who are you? What do you want with me?" His voice was loud and clear, despite his woeful appearance.

Akari stood forward. "I'm—" But the words stuck in his throat as he gazed upon the prisoner. "I know you! Why, you're Claudius. Of all the people to find here! How can this be?" Akari reached through the bars and extended his hand, which Claudius grasped and held tight.

Claudius pulled himself closer to the bars, his eyes squinting. Then the old man smiled. "You don't say! Don't people stay dead anymore? First I saw that evil shell of a man, and now I see another of my old generals, the Dragon Lover himself, Akari. I don't believe it! Oh, happy day. But how ever did you come back?"

"Well, Claudius, it's a lot easier to come back from the dead if you never die in the first place. But it appears that Osirah has truly returned from the beyond."

"Yes, Osirah has. He's been stomping around here for a couple of weeks or so," Claudius explained.

Akari shuddered. "I was afraid of that. It's a long story, but we found his grave, empty and ransacked, on Cemetery Hill."

"Strange doings. Well, I can confirm that he really was dead, and not faking - unlike you, apparently. I was there when he was cut down. Took five arrows in the back, he did. Friendly fire they called it, but I don't think Osirah ever had a friend in his life. But if he did, a friend of his surely would have put an arrow in his back eventually, so I guess it's all the same.

"Some said I had something to do with it, but being happy something happened and causing it to happen are two different things." He was not ashamed in the least by what he was saying, even though it was a capital offense to talk in such a manner about one's superiors.

Akari wore a worried expression on his face. "So Maldazor finally, really did it. He finally beat me at something in magic and discovered how to bring someone back from the other side. Explains all that business up in the graveyard, just like I figured. Doesn't it, boys?"

Jonas and Mouse both nodded, although they looked confused. "I guess so. But how did he do it, and why?" Mouse asked.

"I haven't a clue or I would've likely done it first, but what Claudius says about Osirah is true. Pure evil, and a big reason for many of the wars we've had over the years. Thought everyone was out to attack Ambrosia whether he had evidence or not. A war monger of the worst kind. Just a despicable General, and a worse man. I wasn't sorry to see him go, either."

Claudius shook his head in agreement. "Truer words have never been spoken. He was the dirt worst, but he's back now, and general of the whole operation. Chief Knight of the Azorian Army! He's got us all working day and night making weapons for his army. Plucked us right out of our homes, and they've been sending up new young fellows as well, telling them it's their Fate. Bah! I finally had enough and tried to rebel. But it was no use. They threw me down in this basement, where I've rotted for a week. Least they could've done is put me upstairs with the other prisoners.

"It's a bad deal with this Osirah. No matter how hard we worked and how many weapons we made, it was always hurry, hurry, rush, rush, make more and more, whatever you're doing it's not enough. No concern at all for making a good sword or armor that was worth a darn. Shoddy stuff, all of it. Not worth a fig, and all for a war with the wild men who never did nothing to nobody. But the Mulvarians will eat them up with the kind of cheap stuff we're building."

Jonas finally stepped in, unable to maintain his patience. "Claudius, have you seen our father? Eston Strongheart?" His heart thumped loudly and his pulse drummed in his ears. It was all he could not to scream at the old warrior to hurry up and answer.

"Seen him? Course I've seen him. In fact, I was working in the armory with him a week ago, until a great dragon came through and plucked him right off the ground. That's when I tried to rebel.

"That dragon flew off and I don't know what came of him after that. It was pretty beat up as he was hit with blast after blast from the Dragon Killer weapon and was pretty wobbly, but it got away, and boy was Osirah mad! He sure took it out on me afterwards."

He held out his arms, both severely bruised. "Anyway, that dragon flew to the west with Eston in its claws looking like a wounded duck. From what I hear tell, they say it crashed and burned a few miles away, but nobody ever found anything far as I know. They gave up looking when they got too close to the border of Mulvaria."

The old soldier's eyes then filled with tears. "Boys, I hate to say this. I'm afraid your father may be dead. I don't see anyway he could've walked away after falling from the sky underneath a dragon - not even Eston Strongheart. And all at the hands of the weapon he designed, no less."

Jonas and Mouse gasped, and Mouse couldn't help but break into tears. Akari tried in vain to calm them, patting them on the back and offering soothing words.

"Don't count Eston out until you see it for yourself, boys. If anyone could survive such a situation, it's him. Well, and me, too, of course."

They were then startled to hear another crashing noise echo through the dungeon. This time it sounded as if there were all kinds of suits of armor being banged together. "Sounds like our Cyclops has made some more friends!"

"A Cyclops?!?" Claudius exclaimed.

"It's a long story, old friend," Akari replied. "Suffice to say we re-introduced him to the world from the catacombs deep below the dungeons. Now, was there anyone else riding on that dragon?"

"Funny you say that, Akari. How did you know? The darnedest thing of it all is there was a young girl and a *Sasquatch* of all things! Really gave us something to talk about. A *Sasquatch* riding on a dragon's back? Nobody had ever heard of such a thing!"

Akari looked pleased. "I knew some day the Sasquatches would have enough of Maldazor and his ways, and it appears that day is here. Good. One would be unwise indeed to turn down *their* help. Now you said it flew into Mulvaria?"

The old man nodded.

"And nobody has confirmed it was dead?"

"Well, those idiot soldiers said it was, and the Dragon Killer was a big success. But I don't know, they could've made it all up. The war machine is hard at work gearing up to conquer the wild lands of Mulvaria, by order of King Maldazor, and a little old dragon won't stand in the way of that."

"I see. One last thing, Claudius. You said Maldazor made Osirah the Chief Knight of Azoria?"

"That he did, and the men are none too happy about it, either."

Akari nodded, seeming quite pleased with this, though he offered no clues as to why. The only information Jonas and Mouse were able to glean came when he muttered quietly "once a general, always a general" to himself, though what that meant was unclear. Before they could ask, he turned to face them.

"Well Nephews, it looks like our journey is far from over. Bad luck that your father is no longer here, but I believe in him as well as Caroline. We're off to the Wild Lands in pursuit of a dragon, your father, a Sasquatch, and Caroline by my reckoning. And we need to stop a war."

He shook his head. "You know, I should probably make a list! That's an awful lot to remember."

"Akari, you really think it was Caroline riding on that dragon?" Mouse's voice was high in pitch with excitement and worry.

"Who else could it be? It explains a lot. You don't usually see a dragon just come along and pluck someone from the sky unless it had reason to." Akari read the expression on their faces and moved again to allay their fears.

"Don't worry. Call it a hunch, but I think it would take more than a dragon falling to the earth to finish off the great Eston Strongheart and his equally strong daughter Caroline. We will find them." He then turned to the old prisoner. "Now Claudius, what say we get you out of here?"

"Don't you do it," the prisoner warned. "I'm old and infirm, and I'd just slow you down. Besides, that would just raise the alarm. I can hold on for a while. And make no mistake, there will be plenty of time to get me out later, *if* you're going to do what I think you're going to do, Akari."

"And what's that?"

"*Once a general, always a general.* I know the ancient laws of which you speak." Claudius pointed to his forehead as if they shared a wordless secret. "You know, Maldazor is long gone, my friend. He went to Ambrosia some time ago to be inaugurated King, and has yet to return. As Chief Knight, Osirah is acting ruler until he returns, and the laws of our land state that if a commander overthrows the ruler of another nation, then the conqueror becomes the ruler. The door is wide open..."

Akari downplayed this. "Maybe so. There is much to ponder, Claudius. In the meantime, if you're sick of prison food take one of these." He passed him a pill, which the old man took in his hands and held between his fingers, staring at it with a confused look. "Trust me on this one. Well, maybe we'll be seeing you soon. You never can tell!"

"I certainly hope so," Claudius replied. "Boys, I hope to meet you again in better circumstances. To the Fates!"

"To the Wild Lands," Akari shouted, then stopped. "One more thing, old man. Waiting here might not be such a bad idea." He took out a small key that appeared to be carved from bone. "A skeleton key, my friend. When the time is right, perhaps the prisoners upstairs would help?"

A broad grin came across the old man's face. "Perhaps, Akari. Perhaps. Here's to you!" he said.

Akari turned and ran down the corridor, calling behind him to his nephews. "I know a good way out. No need to introduce ourselves to any of the guards. Besides, they may be about played out on meeting new folks by now."

Mouse and Jonas quickly said their good-byes to Claudius and followed their uncle. Their mission was clear - they were off to the Wild Lands of Mulvaria in pursuit of not only their father, but their sister as well.

They could only hope that somehow, both had survived, even if hope seemed futile. Maldazor was King of Ambrosia and Azoria, the evil Osirah had been resurrected, and they were venturing into lands that were the home of wild men and beasts that had lived in the nightmares of Ambrosian children for centuries.

Only one thing was certain - this journey was not getting any easier.

## Chapter Twenty-Nine - Through the Jungle

The humidity hung thick in the air on that sweltering spring day, choking anyone trying to breathe. The sweat ran off Jonas' face and the thick foliage of the jungle made him feel claustrophobic.

He felt helpless, knowing that around any tree, a Wild Man of Mulvaria could be waiting. Akari had claimed friendly relations with the Mulvarians, but Jonas was struggling to trust his uncle on such matters.

The climate of Ambrosia was strange, but Jonas had scarcely known it because he had spent most of his life anchored to Frogpond. But on this journey alone, they had come through the thick coniferous forests of western Ambrosia, then the gentle oceanic climate of Eastern Ambrosia. And then, after climbing up the coastline, they made their way across the rocky plains of Azoria. It was now quite a shock for them to find themselves in a rainforest. Jonas had never seen anything like it.

For the umpteenth time that day, he wiped his brow. It was annoying, but heat was something he could live with. Living with Akari, however, was becoming more intolerable by the minute. Jonas simply wanted some simple answers to some simple questions, but Akari seemed to be incapable of providing them. How many times had he asked if the Wild Men would take kindly to them entering their territory? In response, Akari mumbled assurances that all would be well. He would not elaborate. Jonas was doing all he could to get along with his uncle. At times, he even found him tolerable, but then he would grow frustrated with Akari's eccentricities.

Worse, they had not yet found any signs of his father and sister, who had last been seen riding on the back of a mortally wounded dragon in this general direction. So far, they had seen little evidence of this, and it was quite possible they were only following the ravings of a madman. Was there even a dragon? And how would Caroline come to be riding on it? Not only that, but he claimed she was joined by a Sasquatch.

Did any of this make sense? And yet Akari did not even bother to search for more evidence – he simply took the word of this Claudius. Jonas had seen enough, and it was time for a change. His feet hurt, he was tired, and they had been traveling for five days without finding any proof they should continue.

Jonas slowed, allowing Mouse to catch up. They were now splashing up a shallow creek -- a rare path through the jungle that was not overgrown with plants and a welcome respite after days spent hacking through the brush.

Still, this did little to improve his mood. He watched in scorn as Akari splashed in front of them, carrying on without a care in the world, until Mouse was by his side.

"Mouse, this is ridiculous! We have no idea where we are going, and Akari is only pretending that he does. We're wasting our time. That crazy Claudius sent us off on a wild goose chase while our father is still imprisoned at the dungeon."

"He didn't seem so crazy to me, Jonas," Mouse replied. "Besides, Akari trusts him. That's good enough for me."

Jonas sighed loudly. Even his own brother was against him. "Oh sure, he seemed perfectly fine. I'm starting to think that everyone else is sane, and I'm crazy." Jonas resisted the urge to throw an all-out temper tantrum, but it took a considerable amount of self-control.

"You're not crazy, Jonas, and neither are any of us," Mouse said, then smirked. "Well, Akari is a *little* crazy, I don't deny that, but he's brilliant, too. Sea horses, spider webs, fireflies - I can only imagine what he'll have next! He's crazy in a *good* way. How else would someone think of all that stuff?"

Jonas considered Mouse's point. Maybe there was something to it. Perhaps the heat was getting to him and he was being a bit unfair to his uncle. He took his eyes off the trail to look ahead to Akari.

But his uncle was completely out of sight. Now, Jonas felt certain - Akari is nuts.

"Where did he get to now?" Jonas said, trying to keep his voice at an even keel to avoid alarming Mouse.

Mouse stared into the jungle in search of his uncle, but all he could see were trees, vines, and other plants as the creek disappeared around a corner far ahead. It was one big green blur. "I don't know. He was just there!"

They stood quietly, hoping to hear a sound that would lead them to Akari's whereabouts. But there was nothing but birds calling and a gentle breeze rustling the branches of trees.

"What now?" Mouse asked, trying to hide the terror in his voice - and failing. His hands trembled and he bit into his lower lip while his eyes darted around.

Jonas drew his sword and Mouse followed. They feared the worst. "Something must have happened to him," Mouse said. He prepared to yell for his uncle when Jonas shushed him.

"*Quiet*. We don't want it to happen to us. We may have to fight, Mouse. Are you ready?"

"I don't think I have a choice," he replied. He felt far removed from being a great warrior with his sword shaking in his weakened arms.

"Then it is our *Fate*," Jonas replied, though the last word came out bitterly. He took off running with Mouse following closely behind. Any sore feelings he had for his uncle were set aside, as Jonas was determined to find him.

They came to an area on the edge of the creek where the plants grew thin and left the soil exposed. "Look," Jonas said, pointing to the ground with the tip of his sword. "Footprints."

He was right. One could clearly see where a person had walked out of the stream, leaving behind wet tracks from the damp soles of their boots. They were on the right track, though they wondered why he had not waited for them.

They followed his steps down the well-worn jungle trail until they dried up. They kicked up dust as they looked back and forth searching for their uncle, and quickly grew frustrated. Akari could be anywhere in this jungle, and Jonas and Mouse were just as lost as he was.

They came to the top of a small hill, giving them an overarching look at the jungle ahead. Jonas squinted, desperately searching for anything unusual, any movement or clue - a swaying branch, an odd color, anything out of the ordinary that could lead them to Akari. As hard as he tried, he came up empty.

Suddenly, Mouse yelled out. Of course *he* found Akari, thought Jonas. Mouse was the great warrior, after all.

"Over there! Someone is hanging from that tree, upside down, tied around the ankles." He spoke in hushed tones and pointed to a tree a good distance down the trail.

Jonas furrowed his brow and followed Mouse's instructions. It was as he said. "I don't understand. How did this happen? What should we do?"

But before Mouse could reply, they felt spear points stabbing them lightly in the back.

"We'd appreciate it very much if you'd come along with us," a gruff voice said from behind them.

"You say that as if we have a choice in the matter," said Jonas.

"You always have a choice in such matters. Do you not hold swords in your hands? Or are they just for costume?" The man stuck the point a little harder in Jonas' back. Jonas felt anger rising inside him.

"If poor choices can be considered choices, I suppose you are correct," Jonas retorted.

"Is life not but a series of poor decisions, one option weighed against the other to choose the least bad?" the man asked. "I've yet to vote in an election that wasn't that way."

"As much as I appreciate the philosophy lesson…" Jonas growled, but Mouse cut him off.

"Why are you doing this?" Mouse asked as they were led toward the man hanging upside down. It was definitely Akari. "We're only here to find our father and sister. We mean no harm to you or anyone else here."

"That may be. But you're traveling with someone masquerading as one of our former generals, though I know him to be long dead. Carried his limp body from the battlefield, I did," the Wild Man replied - stifling a sniffle, if Mouse wasn't mistaken. "So I don't feel qualified to assess who you may or may not mean harm to anyone at this time."

Jonas slowly and cautiously turned around, not wishing to agitate their captor. He found himself face to face with an older man with dark curly hair hanging limply from his head. He had a thick coarse beard that was out of sorts. Overall, he seemed to be a pleasant sort, and not particularly comfortable acting so gruffly toward two boys. Next to him stood a younger man similar in face, but with lighter hair, and straighter, with a scraggly beard that looked like it was fighting an uphill battle to grow in fully.

"Your general? You mean Akari, my uncle? How long ago did you say he died?"

"It's been about eight years now, give or take. He was a great general, but the invaders from the north were too much for him. And now to see this pretender! As you can imagine, it sickens me, though I doubt you boys knew anything about it. I don't blame *you*. Nonetheless, I must take measures to make sure I am correct in that!"

Jonas had to laugh at what he was hearing. "Incredible!" he exclaimed, then turned and yelled at Akari. "Faked your death twice, did you? Twice that *we* now know of, anyway. Any other times you want to tell us about?"

Akari looked rather ashamed hanging upside down from the tree, and the direction of this conversation was causing him even more embarrassment. He sighed before answering.

"Truth be told, there was another time. You see, I was captain of a pirate ship, the *Graveyard Filler*, and well, all we did was pillage and plunder, pillage and plunder. It got to be rather boring. I don't know how much time you've spent around pirates but they're a rather smelly lot, and all you can do is hope for a rainstorm to come along and wash some of the filth off of them, baths being hard to come by in the middle of the ocean.

"And if you want to be technical, there was a time that I faked my death when I was eight-years old, but that was just for a week. And I had a good reason for doing it!"

Mouse whispered to his brother as Akari rambled on. "Jonas, are we sure this is even Akari?"

Jonas shook his head. "It's him. Has to be. Don't ask me how, but I knew it from the start. Must be something to do with his oath to protect me."

Jonas then cleared his throat and spoke to the Wild Man. "Sir, he is who he says he is. We've been traveling with him for some time, and I daresay nobody else on this island would be capable of the things he's done."

Mouse spoke up. "Please sir, let him go. We need to find our father and our sister. Last we heard they flew in on the back of a nearly dead dragon. Well, my sister was on its back, with a Sasquatch, and the dragon, I guess it was holding our father in its arms..." His voice trailed off as he watched the so-called *Wild Man* staring with his mouth agape.

The man ran his fingers through his hair and seemed to mull the story over. "Call me crazy if you will boys, but I can't imagine anyone making up a story so ridiculous and expecting it to get them out of a tough situation. I hope you're not working me over, but here's what I'm going to do." He pulled a knife from his belt and walked over to the prisoner, cutting him free. Akari fell to the ground, landing clumsily with a thud, his legs and arms splayed out awkwardly.

Akari massaged his legs, which were rubbed raw from trying to escape the snare. "Now I remember you! And quite well, Morgan. It all comes clear from this angle, rather than upside down! You always were a good soldier, and I apologize for the, erm, misunderstanding, aw, about my death or, um, lack thereof. Quite the trap you set there, though I'm rather ashamed that I walked right into it!"

Akari then bowed, and the man known as Morgan surprised them all by saluting. "General," he said simply. "It is you, after all. Incredible. Never thought I would see this day! And we have a little surprise for you..."

Akari jumped as a young girl stepped out of the jungle from behind Morgan. Standing before him was a mirror image of his departed sister - his niece, Caroline.

"Caroline!" he exclaimed, running to embrace her with Jonas and Mouse quickly on his heels. "It's been too long, Niece."

"Uncle Akari, it really is you! I thought it was some kind of trick! I can't believe it," Caroline said, her eyes open wide. It was so strange to meet the flesh and blood version of her uncle, whom she had read so much about. Characters from books didn't just walk up and give you a hug, yet here she was. It was beyond surreal.

Words could not do justice to the reunion that took place between the three siblings, with smiles shared, tears shed, and hugs exchanged. Even Jonas was jubilant, leaving his worries aside for the moment.

It had been such a long time since they had said good-bye to each other back home in Birdsong. A very long time. It was a day Caroline had feared would never come yet here they all were, reunited in the land of the wild and free men.

"Caroline, so it's all true!" Mouse exclaimed. "You are here in Mulvaria! But where is Father? And the dragon, and the Sasquatch, and all of that?"

Caroline turned grim, her smile tightening as she revealed the news cautiously. "Father was hurt pretty bad - broken ribs, bruises all over, and considerable pain. But overall, he's fine. He's alive and free, that's the main thing. We rescued him, Brothers! There's so much to tell. But I think it will be better if you see him first. He's just ahead, tending to the dragon."

"So Jomey's alive!" Akari said. "That's good! But how bad off is he?"

"It's not good," Caroline said. "We've been taking care of him as best we can, though of course we don't know what we're doing. The Wild Men have been helping, as well. You've already met Morgan, and that's his son Ned."

The two of them nodded in greeting as Caroline continued. "I've never had to take care of a dragon before, although they're quite a bit like horses."

Akari smirked at that remark as Caroline continued. "And my friend Chupwah — he's the Sasquatch - has tried a few things that have helped, too."

"Wow," Mouse replied. "So it's all true. I can't wait to hear all about it, Caroline. You *are* some kind of warrior." Jonas couldn't help but recoil at that, bringing an end to his good mood.

"Just wait until Mouse and Jonas tell you the things *they* have been through - there's going to be a lot of catching up to do, all around," Akari said. "For starters, Mouse saved an innocent woman from the teeth of the Ambrosian Army, right out from under the nose of King Maldazor himself." Akari's face beamed with pride and Mouse looked down at the ground shyly, while Jonas said nothing.

"Looks like we all have a lot to tell," said Caroline. "But first, we better return to Father. He'll be so excited! I don't think that worrying about you has helped his recovery. Let me tell you, he was none too happy that I came after him." She smiled. "But he got over it."

After a short walk, they rose over a small hill, with the Wild Men trailing behind, and felt their hopes rise as they looked upon a weak cloud of smoke churning its way up the trees.

"Right ahead!" Caroline said. "Just follow the smoke."

"He seems to be feeling rather poorly," Akari said. "There's not much smoke to follow."

"That's true," Mouse offered. "Nothing like the three dragons we rode on."

Caroline turned to Mouse, her face lighting up. "You do have a lot to tell me! Jomey did mention that the three of you had ridden on dragons, and I can't wait to hear about it. But first, I hope Jomey hasn't taken a turn for the worse."

They all took off running. Jonas and Mouse were concerned for Jomey, but frankly, they were more eager to see their father and were elated to be so near to doing so. They had come so far and were nearly overcome with emotion to be so near the end.

Just footsteps from where the smoke rose into the sky, Akari raised his voice in alarm and stopped them all. He pointed to the trail of smoke, which had risen into the air and came to an end. The wind whipped through and blew the remains away, leaving the jungle as if it had never been there.

"It appears we might be too late," Akari said, then took off running again to where they had last seen the trail, with his nephews, niece, and the Wild Men right behind.

# Chapter Thirty - Reunited

Eston had just poured a cool cup of tea and kicked his feet up when he heard someone, or something, crashing through the woods toward him. In fact, it was several someones or somethings heading his way, and fast.

It figured. He was exhausted after a busy morning tending to Jomey and wanted to relax with a cold beverage. His ribs were throbbing and it had taken every ounce of his strength to get through his tasks. On top of that, there was the constant stress of worrying about Jonas and Mouse, which left him few restful moments. Whatever was heading his way was interfering with one of those rare opportunities.

He slowly rose from the chair and felt for his sword, for all the good it would do him. It hurt to even stand, let alone for him to swing that thing around. But if worse came to worst, he might be able to bluff his way through and send a foe scattering off. He turned to look back at Jomey who was bathed in sun and snoring loudly, without a care in the world. What good was a dragon if it slept through something like this?

Eston wished Chupwah was not off gathering more firewood, because he could sure use him now. Whatever was heading his way was not worried about being heard. What could it be? It could not have been Azorian soldiers, and there was no reason for any Wild Men to be running this direction that fast. Right?

Whatever it was, it was almost there. Eston could scarcely draw a breath, desperately trying to hear any sound that would indicate what was coming. Yes, it was *definitely* more than one thing. If he was not mistaken, there were *six* sets of feet heading his way. That definitively ruled out Caroline returning with Ned and Morgan.

Eston was never so happy to be wrong -- because not only did Caroline come whipping around the trees, she was with his sons Jonas and Mouse, as well as another man and the two Mulvarians. He could hardly believe his eyes. His ribs suddenly felt fine and his strength was restored, although as he hobbled over to meet them, each step sent shooting pains down his legs. But that was just a minor trifle at a time like this.

"Sons!" he yelled. "I don't believe it. I just don't believe it." They were reunited, the four of them, and Eston felt like the luckiest man in the world. He had wished his children had stayed home rather than taking the risks they had taken, but he would not trade this moment for anything.

"Dad!" his sons called out as they ran to meet him. They surrounded Eston in a giant embrace as tears streamed down his face.

When they let go, the boys took a good look at their father. He seemed to have aged greatly in the month or so since they'd last seen him. It was obvious that being captured and forced into slave labor had taken a toll on their father. And that's not even considering that he was nearly crushed by a dragon. Despite everything he'd been through, a twinkle in his eyes remained and Jonas and Mouse were overjoyed to be with him.

With all of the excitement, it was some time before Eston even noticed the other man among them. The rumors were true. He had long believed his brother-in-law was dead, yet here he was standing right in front of him. It was quite a thing to look upon his wife's brother, alive and well.

Akari had hung back, rather unsure of how Eston would accept him. The relationship between the two had its ups and downs over the years. Akari felt certain that Eston would not have approved of his fake death scheme, seeing as he rarely approved of *any* of his schemes. So rather than force the issue, he remained in the background, watching the happy reunion with a broad grin on his face. But when Eston finally noticed him, Akari was taken aback by his reaction.

"It can't be," Eston said, his voice choking. He was again overcome with emotion. He walked to Akari with his arms extended, and put his hands on Akari's shoulders. "Is this a trick? A mirage? Is my wife's brother standing before me or is this a nefarious trick of evil?"

"It is me, Eston," Akari replied, but before he could say more, Eston pulled the warrior to him, embracing him. Akari was shocked but hugged him back, the only response that seemed logical.

After some time Eston let him go. "How is this possible, Akari? Back from the dead, or never dead as it were?" As Akari started to respond, Eston shushed him. "Shh. You don't have to explain. What's important to me is that you are here now, and you were there for my boys when they needed you. Thank you, Akari."

Akari said nothing, as he was overcome with emotion at Eston's remarks.

"Strange times we live in, are they not? It seems that many Chief Knights are back from the dead in one way or another."

"So I have heard, Eston," replied Akari. "That's another reason I'm here. Number one, I'd like to see this resurrection experiment up close and personal, as I have keen personal interest in such matters. Number two, well, let me just say his return has opened up some doors."

"That it has, my boy," Eston replied, patting him on the back for emphasis. "Food for thought. Maldazor did not even deem to appoint a Chief Knight until now, fearing someone would know of old customs. A *Duel of Surrender* - will you take such a path? It could be fatal, and no faking it this time. There must be other options."

Akari shrugged. "Perhaps, Eston. Perhaps. It weighs heavy on my head, I admit."

"Don't get me wrong, I'd be tempted myself. But I wouldn't last two minutes in this condition, and besides, with events that have taken place, it seems that Azoria and Ambrosia are now one country and the old rules no longer apply. You, as a former *Mulvarian* General, could challenge Osirah—"

Akari cut him off. "Say no more. I know the old ways well. There is much to ponder."

"That there is," Eston replied. The rest of the group looked on, with confused expressions -- having no clue about what the two elder warriors were talking about. It did seem obvious, though, that they were devising ways to overcome the rule of Maldazor. In deference to Akari's difficult decision, Eston moved to another topic.

"I think I better sit down," Eston panted, tired from all the excitement. "And Akari, you better take a look at this dragon."

Akari shook his head to clear his mind. With all else going on, he had simply forgotten Jomey, who was lying prone on the jungle floor. He approached the dragon, noting that every now and again a meager puff of smoke would rise from its nostrils, the only indicator that any life remained in the dragon. "He's in dire straits. What have you been doing for him?"

"Well, Akari, I've never been a healer like you, and my knowledge is limited, to say the least. But we've been doing a few things."

Eston pointed to a roaring campfire, well fueled by large logs that kept it burning hot. "Caroline and I have been feeding him hot coals from there, which he said would help, at least as far as I could make out. I never was much good at understanding dragons, but it did seem to help. But he took a turn for the worse this afternoon. He's been asleep ever since."

"You've done well, Eston," Akari assured him. "You've bought him some time. Let me see if I can buy him some more. Boys, and Caroline, go gather up more wood. Good, dry stuff like this here, and as much as you can."

The group went into the woods as instructed. Akari took out his sword and asked to borrow Eston's, as well. He crossed the two blades into an "x" shape and wedged them under the entire campfire, logs and all, and pushed it forward until it was just in front of the dragon's mouth. "Open his mouth up, and wide, if you can, Eston."

Eston felt around the dragon's face and stuck his hand in his mouth, his hands brushing against razor sharp teeth. He tried in vain to lift the dragon's mouth, but he could not, and his ribs ached even more.

"I can't, Akari," he stammered, breathing hard. "I'm sorry."

Just then a large, hairy figure emerged from the jungle, silently appearing from the undergrowth. It was Chupwah.

Akari watched the creature with a wary eye until Eston introduced them. "Akari, I want you to meet my daughter's friend, which makes him *my* friend. This is Chupwah, and Chupwah, this is my brother-in-law - and Caroline's Uncle - Akari." They shook hands as Eston continued. "My friend, you are just in time. Akari needs someone to open up Jomey's mouth. I wasn't strong enough, but I don't think you'll have that problem!"

"I'd be glad to! So long as I don't have to *climb* in as well," Chupwah cracked, which made Eston chuckle. The Sasquatch dropped the firewood he had been carrying and lumbered over to the dragon's mouth, easily prying it open. Akari used the swords to lift the fire and shoved the entire thing into the dragon's mouth. Sparks and ashes swirled in the air as Chupwah let loose Jomey's mouth so that it snapped shut.

"We've got to heat him up," Akari explained. "The only way to make a dragon really feel better is to get his fire roaring inside. The hot coals were good, and they kept him going, but we need this dragon at full strength.

"Can't say I've ever had to shove it in before, though. They usually just gulp the whole thing down, but since this fellow shows no indications of waking up any time soon, we have to force feed him his medicine." He stepped back and watched as a black smoke began to pour from Jomey's ears and mouth, then through his nose and out from under his eyelids. His nose twitched and eyes fluttered, but otherwise he remained still.

"There we go!" Akari exclaimed. "That's exactly what he needed. But it will take some time to get him going. Give him some space and leave him be, for now." The warrior then turned toward Chupwah. With Jomey taken care of, he spoke further to the Sasquatch.

"Chupwah, the son of the mighty Sheena and her husband Worsi. It is good to meet you, as it is always good to meet one of your kind. I greatly respect the mighty Sasquatch."

Chupwah bowed. "Akari the Dragon Lover. I have heard much of you and your ways, and what an honor to find you in your element, tending to a dragon right before my eyes!"

Suddenly, Caroline and Mouse both returned, bearing large supplies of good, dry firewood.

"Well done," Akari complimented while Mouse dropped his firewood upon seeing Chupwah.

"So it was all true! Even the part about the Sasquatch!" Mouse exclaimed. "Caroline, we have a *lot* of catching up to do."

While Caroline introduced the two, Jonas returned with his arms filled with wood. He dropped it by the other piles and sunk his head. The wood was meager and wet, as if pulled from a creek, standing in contrast to the near perfect and dry logs that Mouse and Caroline had collected.

Akari noticed this but tried to deflect attention from his failure. "Thanks Jonas, that will do, um, nicely."

"Don't try to humor me," Jonas growled. "This was all I could find. Apparently, I can't even gather firewood right! It's going to be awfully hard to get the foundry good and warm if I can't even light a proper fire!" He kicked at his pile and stomped off into the forest with Mouse chasing after him. Caroline was baffled by his remarks but decided she better go along as well.

Eston was equally confused. "What's that all about, Akari?" he asked.

"Well Eston, perhaps it slipped your son's mind with everything going on," the warrior said. "I'm afraid that he paid a visit to that old wizard Wallary, and he didn't receive the best reading."

Eston's eyes boggled. "What was it?" he asked cautiously, fearing the answer.

Akari grimaced. "Now you know that I don't hold with this Fate business, Eston."

Eston cut him off sternly. "I am aware, but this is not the opportunity for you to sermonize."

"Yes. OK," Akari stammered, then took a deep breath. "He was branded as a servant for the King, to work in his foundry. Now does that not prove my point? The boy is a natural swordsman! As brave as they come! And now he's all screwed up, questioning his entire existence thanks to this backwards system!"

Just as Akari's passion was ready to boil over, Ned and Morgan emerged from the jungle, their arms also filled with wood for the fire.

"Akari and Eston," Morgan said. "We just ran into one of our countrymen. The guards are being called home to prepare for war. Instead of waiting for Azoria to attack us, we are bringing the fight to them."

Eston was incredulous. "You have got to be kidding me. This plays right into Maldazor's plot! By becoming the aggressors, it proves to the people of both Ambrosia and Azoria that he was right, that the so-called Wild Men were a threat all along. It gives him *exactly* what he wants! He'll crush you all and rule your lands in your stead. Morgan, Ned, you must warn the elders. This is folly!" His breathing again grew ragged as his energy was tapped. It had been a long day and it was wearing on him - and he still hadn't been able to enjoy his cup of tea.

"Peace, Eston," Akari said. "First off, these goodly men have no say in such matters. Secondly, you seem to have forgotten that I have been making plans to *counter* Maldazor's. This will force me to speed things up a bit, but no matter. Morgan and Ned, do you know of Maldazor's whereabouts?"

"We believe so," Ned replied. "Tidings brought to us indicate he has taken full residence in Ambrosian City after Wilhelm's daughter Natalia asked him to take the throne of Ambrosia, pleading with him to ensure their survival. So humble of him to accept!"

"I figured as much," Akari said. "It's been quite the successful turn of events for old Maldazor. I'm sure many in Eston's Watchtower group are cursing our failure right now. But to them I say *patience*, as he's made a fatal mistake."

"Has he now?" Eston asked. "Seems to me that things are unfolding exactly the way he wanted them to. He's King of two-thirds of his father's kingdom, and you can bet his sister will fall in line and let him rule Birdsong as well, if she knows what's good for her. No, I don't see any mistakes in his plan, fatal or otherwise."

"On the contrary - and with all due respect - but he has made a rather large, and yes, fatal one. He didn't account for any of *us*. I grant that it can be hard to account for the unaccountable, but it's the key to any good plan. Any plan worth its salt plans for when nothing goes according to plan! Always account for the unaccountable - and Maldazor did not.

"To be more specific, he didn't account for *me*. I suppose it's hard to account for the dead, or those believed to be, but you've got to do it all the same. I'll be more than happy to inform him personally, when the time is right."

Akari turned to the Mulvarians, who were itching to leave. "Gentleman, it has been an honor to be among you, and I anticipate that we shall meet again soon. Until then, I wish you all the best. And if you could bring word to your people that I have re-emerged, I would be most appreciative."

"We already have," Ned said as they turned and walked away. "Until we meet again, Dragon Lover!" With those words, they disappeared into the jungle, off to unite with their army and prepare for war.

"I hope you know what you're doing," Eston said grimly.

"I know *what* I'm doing. No need to worry about that," he replied. "I just don't know that what I'm doing is the right thing to do."

"We should do nothing, for there is nothing we can do! Never before in history has one person been able to do so little," Eston stated, his face grim. "Best we can do is find some corner of the island to inhabit and hope they never find us while we live out the rest of our days."

"Eston, it pains me to hear you speak this way, though I admit I recently said almost the exact same thing! But I was wrong. There is *much* that one man can do, so consider what a *group* of people can accomplish. There is much that we can do, therefore much that we *will* do. For too long, Kings and their ilk have ruled, some with an iron fist, some with a velvet glove, but nonetheless all have ruled and yet none have been accountable to the people. *We* can change all that."

Before Eston could reply, Jonas stomped back into camp with Caroline and Mouse fast on his heels. He grumpily rolled out a blanket and laid on it, then threw another over his head to mentally disappear from the world. Caroline and Mouse both looked at their father and shrugged. "We tried to talk some sense into him," Caroline offered. "But he wouldn't listen to a thing I said. I don't know what to do, Father."

Eston's eyes watered as old emotions long buried were dug up. "Your mother was always good at talking to me when such moods came my way. Always knew just the thing to say, even when I thought I didn't want to hear it. I feel for your brother. It's awfully hard finding one's lot in life even when the whole thing is mapped out for you, and to find out what he did, with his heart set on something else - well, it's rough. I'll go have a few words with him, but I sure wish your mother was here."

Before he could get out of his seat, Akari stopped him. "No, Eston, let me," Akari declared, then winked. "I'll try to make my sister proud." He drew in a deep breath, let it go, then spoke loudly so that all present could hear.

"Jonas, listen to me. All of you listen. We have come a long way and set out to accomplish what we came for. We have found your father, safe and sound, though a little worse for the wear. But safe nonetheless. For *now*. It will not last. Not so long as we tread under the feet of Kings, especially this King, Maldazor. Not worthy to rule a one-horse town and yet he stands on the threshold of ruling an entire island.

"Yes, we can hide. Yes, we can find some patch of ground where Maldazor has yet to raise his flag. But how long can it last? A year? Maybe five? That's all well and good I suppose - if you enjoy being a sniveling coward that the lowliest, hungriest mongrel dog would run from, even if you held steaks in both hands." With that Akari took his sword and cut through the air as if he was battling an imaginary army.

"But what can we do, Akari? I don't believe it is our Fate to take part in a battle we have no stake in," Mouse called out. He had been watching this discussion with eyes open wide, as was Caroline. Jonas simply lay motionless on his bed.

"Maybe it is not our Fate. So in that case, we will choose our own," Akari replied. "As Morgan and Ned have said, the Wild Men are marching to make war on the Azorians as we speak, and the Azorians will gladly meet them, swords in hand, spurred on by Maldazor through his crony Osirah. There is nothing we can do stop the war from starting - it's too far gone - but we *can* end it once started. All I need is for someone to disable the Dragon Killer weapons, and I will take care of the rest."

"And how will we do that?" Caroline shot back.

"I phrased it poorly," Akari replied. "*You* will disable them, Caroline, alongside Chupwah, Mouse, and Jonas. It will take the four of you."

"We will?" she replied back. "And what are you going to be doing, Akari?"

He looked back at Jomey, who was snoring away. "Well, you didn't think I wanted the Dragon Killers disabled just for fun, did you?"

He gestured toward Jomey and continued. "So long as this fellow gets to feeling better, then I will be flying to a little meet and greet with my old friend Osirah. To make that happen, it will be up to the four of you to take care of things on the ground."

Eston had heard enough. "They will not, Akari" he declared, his voice stern. "The more I think of it, there is too much risk and no reward. It's foolish. You think you can overthrow Azoria? Let's say you do. Then what?"

"Sometimes, the reward is in the risk, Eston," Akari replied casually. "As I said, you can find some far flung corner of this island, hide for a few years, and hope Maldazor never decides he needs that patch of country to complete his fiefdom. In the meantime, be careful to stick to dark and hidden paths with your cloak pulled tightly overhead and your eyes staring at the ground, clinging to the hope that someone or something doesn't recognize you for your true self and turns you in.

"Of course, by that point you'd be no more of a threat to Maldazor than a house cat, but you'd be dispensed with all the same. And for a split second, Eston, you might wish we had done something when we had a chance, albeit a small one - but a chance nonetheless.

"I can only speak for myself, but in so doing I say, *I am going*. My mind is made up. And all or none are welcome to join me."

"Well, *I* am going Eston, and your children can be of great help, of that I am certain," Chupwah declared. "If the boys are anything like Caroline, they might be able to take down the Dragon Killers on their own. Your daughter is as brave as anyone I've ever met."

Caroline looked down at her feet, uncomfortable at having such praise bestowed upon her. Mouse saw her reaction and winked, trying to get her to relax. He then gripped the hilt of his sword, which peeked out of the sheath fastened to his belt. He was ready to do what Akari asked, and Caroline did the same, moving to stand by her uncle.

Eston sat in his chair and said nothing, seeming to consider these remarks though he remained stoic. The silence hung thick in the air alongside the humidity. Akari was convincing, he'd give him that. Eston had to admit that Akari was largely right, and even in his dilapidated condition he found himself greatly desiring to ride alongside his children into the battle. They were indeed ready, as ready as they'd ever be.

Well, *two* of them were ready. Not Jonas. Jonas heard the speech, but he simply rolled over and pulled the blanket tighter over his head. He simply did not care anymore. There was no point. Akari was delusional, a madman, and Jonas would simply ignore him, as should all who hear the craven ramblings of a lunatic. If his siblings wanted to go with the fool, that was their business. Jonas would stay behind and he supposed that when they returned, he could clean up after and make sure their swords and shields were back in working order.

They watched the pile of blankets remain still for some time, hoping Jonas would emerge, but nothing happened. So Caroline broke the silence.

"Is this not what we were trained for, father?" Caroline asked. "I don't know if Akari is right about this or not. I guess I have some doubts. I don't know. But I can see with my eyes as well as you can, and Maldazor has certainly played many for fools. I certainly do not wish to be one of those fools, and this seems to be our best option to avoid that. Look at yourself, Father. You were kidnapped and dragged off to Azoria to build weapons? Had you taken away for basically no reason at all, did he not?"

Eston nodded. "This is indeed what I have trained you for, though in so doing I never relished the day when the need to use these skills would present itself. And even then it has come upon me much sooner than I thought possible. In fact, I'd say it has come upon me well before I even realized it came upon me at all!

"Was it not my own daughter that appeared from the sky on the back of a dragon to pluck me from my enslavement? Did my sons not stand before me after undertaking such an adventure? Against all odds, you have already done much, and it is folly to stop you from doing as you desire now. If you feel this is the right path to take, then I will not stand in your way." With that, Eston slumped back into his seat, again overcome by the strain of dealing with such matters in his condition.

Caroline and Mouse gathered around him, reassuring him that they were making the right decision. His face was worn with worry, but he embraced his children and tried to instill them with confidence. They would carry enough of their own fears; they certainly didn't need to bring his along with them. "I regret that I am unable to assist you, but I'd only make things worse."

"Father, don't bother with such thoughts. We understand. And we will return," Caroline said, before adding, "we will return victorious!" This did little to reassure the battered old warrior, but he nodded grimly and embraced her again before letting her go, though he loathed to do so. He then turned his thoughts to Jonas.

"Jonas, my boy," he yelled. "Get up, son." Jonas didn't move, so Eston groaned under the strain of rising from his seat to go over and speak more closely to him.

Akari watched Eston and felt a great responsibility lower on to his shoulders. Akari had come up with a plan that would require an awful lot of Eston's children. It was up to him to make sure they returned safe. It was a scary feeling, as never before had he put his own flesh and blood in harms way. He shuddered to think what his sister would say if she knew.

But they couldn't be protected forever. He looked over to Chupwah, standing by his side and looming large as he towered over them all. It certainly wouldn't hurt to have *him* along. He couldn't recall a time when a Sasquatch had been involved in a battle among humans. He had to admit that he wouldn't mind watching it happen, under different circumstances.

"Well Chupwah, my plan is either foolproof, or it will prove once and for all that I am indeed a fool."

"And there will be little doubt as to which one is which when it's all said and done, Akari," Chupwah replied. "Or perhaps the fool has found a foolproof plan! Regardless, it is a plan, and a plan is better than no plan. To our Fate!"

"Yes, to our Fate. May we be embarking on a good one."

## Chapter Thirty-One - Eyes Wide Open

The large creature filled his arms with palm leaves from the jungle floor, adding them to the handfuls of moss he had already scraped from the sides of trees. He gathered them together and scaled a wide sandalwood tree, testing various branches and finding them all unsatisfactory. Just then, Caroline happened to walk by under his feet.

"Caroline," he exclaimed. "Climb on up! I'm getting my bed ready for the night. This is the way to sleep, not lying on the ground cuddled up with bugs and snakes. There's plenty of room!"

"Hi, Chupwah," she replied, pleased to find him. They had gone their separate ways a few hours earlier, after a long day on the move following the Mulvarian Army. "I was wondering where you went. But I'm not sure about sleeping in a tree. What if I fell out?"

"Well, I suppose that would be a problem! Still, it's never happened to me, though maybe we are built a little bit better than your kind for such things."

"Maybe so, Chupwah. You know, I always thought Sasquatches lived in caves, like bears," Caroline said.

"Well, I much prefer a tree if it comes to that," he said before hopping to another branch, then bristling as he thought more about Caroline's remarks. "Did you say like a *bear*? We're nothing like bears, Caroline. You should know that by now!"

"I meant no offense, Chupwah."

"Oh, I know that, it's just one of those things that bother me! Any time a person says they've seen a Sasquatch, someone else tells them 'no, you must have imagined it, it was only a bear.' As if *anyone* couldn't tell the difference!"

Caroline chuckled, and Chupwah went back to his work. She watched as he hopped from branch to branch, feeling out each one before moving to another. He finally settled on a particularly stout branch, then spread out the leaves and moss, patting it down until he was satisfied.

"You sure you don't want one?" he called down.

"Not tonight, Chupwah," she called back. "Though I am rather sick of lying in the dirt!"

"Suit yourself, Caroline," he replied. "The only way to sleep is here in the treetops, if you ask me. Good night!"

"G'night, Chupwah."

She returned to her campsite and crawled into her chilly blankets, with Mouse already asleep nearby. It had been a difficult journey. The Mulvarian army moved swiftly with purpose, and each night had ended with Caroline sleeping like a log.

But not tonight. She was beyond exhausted, but no matter what she did, her mind would not stop racing. They were camped on the cusp of Azorian territory, which meant tomorrow would bring the battle, and filling her with dread.

Her whole body ached. She gingerly adjusted her position, trying to get comfortable on the hard ground. It had been a long four days and tomorrow did not figure to be any shorter. Of course, there was no guarantee she would live through the day. Caroline shuddered at the thought.

Caroline had read many books about war, and had gone through life or death situations on her way to rescuing her father, but this was something more. It was very sobering to know she would be in the thick of an actual battle, a battle that she knew was completely pointless, one that would only serve the aims of King Maldazor. It was up to Akari to spoil it all - with their assistance, of course.

Sleep was impossible under these circumstances. Caroline felt immense pressure to succeed. Even worse, Jonas had stayed behind, claiming he did not wish to burden the "great warriors." It had apparently never occurred to him that Caroline was Fated to become the *wife* of a great warrior, and she was not letting that stand in her way. No wizard was going to tell *her* what to do. If all went well, no wizard would tell *anyone* what they would do with their life. Tomorrow would be the first step to making that come true.

After wasting four or five hours tossing and turning, Caroline finally kicked off her blankets. If she was not going to sleep, there was no point in just laying there. Her nerves were stretched too thin and her mind filled with too much worry, so it was best to get up and try to be productive.

She crawled from bed and went looking for Akari, knowing she would find him awake. Maybe he could put her mind at ease.

With only the spotty light of the moon to guide her, Caroline took great care to avoid stepping on Mouse - at least *he* had no problem falling asleep. She kept her ears tuned for a telltale sign from her uncle. Mouse had said that Akari liked to work on various experiments throughout the night, so surely she would hear or see something that would reveal his location.

She started walking carefully through the jungle, but stopped in her tracks. Something was *growling*, fiercely. She froze, her ears straining to hear over the breeze that blew through the jungle. But there was nothing besides the gentle rustling of leaves and the distant babbling of a creek.

Just as she was ready to chalk it up to her imagination running wild, she heard it again - clearly coming from the trees directly overhead. Her fingers fumbled as she tried to grip the hilt of her sword. It slid from her hands, and she cursed herself for being clueless about the creatures that lived in these wild lands. She should have been better prepared; there was no excuse not to be.

She bent to retrieve the sword, but before she could, she nearly jumped out of her shoes. Something had fallen right behind her.

She grabbed the sword and swung around, ready to face down her foe. But she had to laugh. It was just a walnut, which rolled to a stop at her feet.

"Geez, Caroline," she said out loud. Her voice sounded strange in the darkness. She picked up the green-skinned nut, which was rather large. They had a grove of walnut trees in Frogpond, and she dimly recalled being hit in the head by one - not the greatest feeling in the world. She took the walnut and threw it into the jungle.

She then jumped back again. Whatever it was had roared again, and Caroline was so terrified she thought she would come out of her body.

She looked into the trees, searching for the source of this horrible noise. What could it be? Was it a lion? A wolf? Some other beast?

Or was it a Sasquatch? Of course! She had to laugh at herself when she saw a massive pair of feet dangling from a tree limb. She really was the only one having trouble sleeping tonight, for the growling belonged to Chupwah — in fact, he was snoring, which sounded like a vicious beast rather than the gentle and tame Sasquatch she considered a friend.

Caroline laughed harder now. She was losing it, she feared. But the laughter was good for her and the stress eased just a bit. Poor Chupwah must have been exceedingly tired, as she had never heard him snore like that. Caroline shook her head and chuckled one last time, leaving the Sasquatch alone to his deep sleep.

She was soon walking alongside a ravine, which was not particularly steep. Her eyelids sagged while she walked, and her concentration faded. Next thing she knew, her legs went out from under her! Before she could gather her bearings, she tumbled halfway down the ravine.

Twigs snapped, and she crashed through dead weeds that cracked as she rolled through, making enough noise to wake the dead. She came to a stop with only minor bruises to show for her fall, but she lay on her back while she regained her composure, feeling stupid and clumsy. After some time she dusted herself off and rose. What had taken her legs out from under her so fast? She climbed the slope to investigate.

At the top of the ridge, she shook her head. It was those walnuts again! She must have slipped on one, and then WHAM, down she went.

She picked a walnut up and fired it down the ravine, then turned to fire another down the path, but halfway through her throwing motion, she froze, stunned to find Akari standing in her way. The walnut slipped and careened sideways into the forest.

"Everything all right, Caroline? I heard such a racket, that I feared the Azorians were attacking!" He smirked, amused by his overstatement.

"Oh, I'm fine. I just tripped on these stupid walnuts and fell down the ravine," she said, then softened her tone. "Actually, I was looking for you. I can't sleep, and I know you don't sleep at all, so I thought I'd see what you were up to."

"Why can't you sleep, Caroline?"

She hesitated, not wishing to seem weak or "girlish," but decided there was no shame in how she felt. "I'm nervous, Uncle. How are we ever going to make it through two armies trying to kill each other?"

"Funny you should say that, Caroline. I've been trying to solve the same problem! It's good that you've come along. Perhaps the two of us, together, can think of something." Akari put his arm around her to comfort his niece and together they walked in the silence of the night.

"My feeling was that the soldiers would be too busy worrying about killing each other to even notice we were in their midst. But you're right, that's not good enough. Even still, there are no guarantees. All we can do is improve the odds." Akari then took another step and nearly fell over.

"See!" Caroline exclaimed. "It's not just me! Those walnuts are everywhere! It's almost as bad as walking on ice."

"Tell me about it," Akari replied. "I just about killed myself!"

Caroline stopped in her tracks and her face lit up. "I've got it! This is perfect, Akari." She stooped over and started gathering handfuls of the walnuts, pulling out her shirt to hold them. Akari looked on, puzzled.

"You're going to throw nuts at them? Hmm. Well, it's a start, but I think we can come up with something a bit better than that, don't you?"

Caroline cut him off. "No, we're not going to throw nuts *at* them. We're going to throw them *under* them. Think about it, Akari. We roll these along while the soldiers are in the middle of fighting and they'll be falling all over the place! With Chupwah picking off anyone else who gets in the way, we'll slice right through the battle all the way to the weapon!"

Akari said nothing as he held his hand to his chin and mulled over the plan. He looked to the sky as if looking for affirmation from the stars, then nodded, timidly at first and then strongly. He was convinced.

"You know, that just might work! Matter of fact, I am certain it will." He gathered some walnuts and rolled them in his hand. "Well, it's the best we've got. Let's go with it!"

Together, they collected as many walnuts as they could find, and there were plenty, as the trees were abundant. Akari produced a few bags and their seams were stretched to the limit as they were stuffed full. After gathering as many walnuts as possible, Caroline yawned. There were only a few hours left until daylight, but now she finally felt as if she could sleep.

"I'm going back to bed, Akari. Thanks for your help - I feel a lot better now."

Akari smiled. "Good night, Caroline. Tomorrow will be quite the day for us, if all goes well." He breathed in deeply and slowly let it exhale. "It must go well!"

"It will. I believe in you. Good night, Uncle."

Soon she was back in bed and drifted off the moment her head hit the ground - but not before wishing she still had her little cot to prevent her from laying on the same ground the centipedes, snakes, and other creatures called home.

## Chapter Thirty-Two - Running On Luck

Caroline was sleeping soundly when she snapped awake, and Mouse did the same. The sun had not yet risen, but they were hearing the first sounds of war – much sooner than they had expected.

Caroline heard the familiar sound of metal on metal as swords struck each other. Horses thundered across the field, machinery was being moved, and field generals shouted out orders. The worst sounds of all were the howls of agony, as soldiers met their ultimate Fate. She looked at Mouse, who was equally disturbed. He cringed with each calamity. The sounds were horrible and it took Caroline's breath away to know that they were heading straight into the arena.

Somehow, the Wild Men's plan to notify Akari before the war began had not happened. So now, time was of the essence. But Mouse and Caroline stood frozen, near their bedrolls, unsure of what to do next.

Chupwah jumped down from his tree and landed in front of them. "Time to take care of the Dragon Killers," he growled. "They'll never know what hit them."

The Sasquatch's appearance snapped Caroline into action. "I hope so, Chupwah," she replied. "And I've got a plan to help us along. Speaking of, here comes Akari!"

She ran to assist him. He was dragging along three bags, which were spilling over with walnuts. Chupwah followed and easily lifted the others.

Akari was grateful to be relieved of his burden. "Thanks! Those things are heavy!" He then whistled sharply, the sound echoing through the jungle. A bat soon flew down and landed on his shoulder. Caroline recognized it at once as her friend Jomey, though it had been some time since he had taken this form.

"Jomey! Are you feeling better?" she asked.

"Much better," he responded. "It's now or never for Osirah and Azoria! Are you ready?" The three of them nodded. "Good!" He flapped his wings and flew a short distance, making room as the transformation from bat to dragon took place.

"And now I feel even better!" he declared, stretching out his wings.

His skin was back to a shiny green and his eyes looked clear and strong. Having Jomey back to full strength warmed all of their hearts.

"Whenever you're ready!" Jomey declared. "Akari and I will distract them from above while you take care of the weapon." He winked. "And the faster, the better."

"We'll do our best, Jomey," Mouse said.

"Good," Jomey said. "Your best is all we can ask for! Hop on, Akari. I need to loosen up my wings a bit."

The warrior nodded. He looked grim, cracks showing in his normally confident visage – despite a concerted effort to conceal his concerns. He couldn't fool Mouse, though -- he saw through Akari's façade as the old soldier bid them farewell.

"Don't do anything stupid," Akari warned. "Remember, a good warrior knows when it's time to fight and when it's time to run. Do not mix up one for the other!" He climbed on to Jomey's back, and with a quick thrust of his wings the dragon lifted off. Akari held his hand out in a silent goodbye as the dragon rose from the trees and disappeared into the early dawn sky.

"It's up to us now," Mouse said, with what little confidence he had hanging by a thread.

"Yes, it is," Caroline replied. "And who better? We have Chupwah - in him we will find no equal. Mouse, you are now battle-tested and proven. Grab a bag of walnuts and I'll explain along the way how we're going to use them."

But Chupwah would have none of that. He slung his staff on to his back via a thin strap of leather, then lifted all three of the bags and effortlessly heaved them over his shoulder. "Don't worry. I'll get them."

"If you insist," Caroline replied, grinning. "Well, there's nothing left to do but to do it!"

*

In no time at all, they stood in the jungle only steps from the battle. Caroline and Mouse felt their legs turning to jelly beneath them. Mouse was so nervous it seemed that even his mouth was sweating.

The sounds of war were overwhelming - the crunch of broken bones, screams of agony, and sounds of weapons created a symphony of violence. Turning back, however, had never crossed their minds. They crawled forward and were soon at the edge of the tree line. The vicious battle was right in front of them. What they had only been able to hear before was now standing before them, in an awful, bloody scene.

The field in front of Maldazor's Castle was filled with soldiers slashing at each other with swords. Others rode on horseback, jousting at their enemies to disable them. Mouse shuddered and Caroline, wearing a horrified expression, could scarcely manage to watch. Chupwah looked on with his hairy face passive, although even he was taken aback by the ruthlessness of war. Men truly could be evil to one another.

The time for watching was over. They needed to move quickly to disable the Dragon Killer. Once they did that, Akari could bring this conflict to an end. Getting to the weapon was daunting and risky, but it had to be done to lessen the war's death toll.

That said, it would do no good to rush in without the proper opening, so they waited for the right time. The fighting had spread to the entire field and there was no clear path through. Of course, Caroline thought, nobody ever said it was going to be easy.

With no path revealing itself, Caroline turned her gaze to the castle. Seeing it from this angle was even more intimidating than when she had been on the castle grounds. When she stood next to the castle, it was difficult to appreciate how truly large and imposing it was. But from this distance, the castle loomed high over the landscape and blocked the morning sun, allowing the monolith to cast its shadow over the battlefield. She squinted and saw a man in sparkling gold-plated armor standing in a tower that jutted from the center of the courtyard.

"That must be Osirah," Caroline whistled through her teeth. "He doesn't have the guts to lead the charge on the battlefield, does he?"

"Akari knew *that* all along," Mouse said. "That's why he needed Jomey to bring him to the tower."

"He must not want to risk being shot in the back again," Chupwah growled. "Perhaps dying once was enough for a lifetime!" He chuckled at his joke and Mouse and Caroline joined him, though they quickly grew serious again.

"There it is," Mouse pointed, his finger aimed at the Dragon Killer. It stood in the center of the field, waiting patiently to be called into action. Three soldiers manned the weapon and another ten guarded it, some holding spears, and others, swords. One soldier stood on the weapon and looked skyward, his hand shielding his eyes as he searched for a dragon. Another sat in the cockpit ready to fire, upon command.

Caroline's face was grim. She clenched her fist and jaw, steeling her resolve. There was nothing left to do but charge forward and hope for the best.

"It's time! Act like we belong there until someone decides we don't," Caroline instructed. "Chupwah, you're not going to be able to crack heads holding all of those bags. Better pass one to Mouse and me. We can manage."

He nodded and handed over a bag to each, then removed his staff. "All right, then. Follow my lead," he growled. "I get first crack at them. Let me take out those I can, and you can pick off what's left. Let's take out that Dragon Killer!"

"Let's do it," Mouse replied.

"Enough talking," Caroline spat out. She dug her heels into the ground and sprinted off, taking them by surprise. Chupwah ran after her with his long-legged gait, his wood staff now swinging out in front of him. His heavy feet rumbled across the field like a galloping horse.

Most of the soldiers were so engaged in warfare that they took no notice of the interlopers. Even if they had, there was nothing they could do, as they were tied up in combat. The few that did notice were so struck by curiosity of the Sasquatch that they could only stop and stare with dropped jaws.

They dashed to the weapon with arrows soaring through the air, spears whizzing overhead, and bodies flying. The noise was loud and distracting, making it difficult to maintain their composure, but they ignored it the best they could and kept moving.

Mouse pushed his small legs as hard as he could, tough work with the walnuts weighing him down. He tried to keep pace with Chupwah, feeling safer when he was near.

They weaved through the fighting. They dodged countless calamities, but their luck ran out - the way ahead was flooded with soldiers fighting ferociously, swinging their swords around dangerously, and jabbing at their foes with spears. There was no safe path; they would have to create one.

"Chupwah!" Caroline screamed. "Time for the walnuts!"

"Go for it!" he yelled.

"You first, Mouse!" Caroline ordered. She helped Mouse remove the bag from his back, and Mouse was relieved to lay down his burden. They each held a side and pulled it to the soldiers fighting in front of them.

They swung the bag forward until the walnuts spilled to the ground, with Chupwah doing the same. The nuts rolled out and slid under the feet of the soldiers.

The soldiers never saw it coming! Next thing they knew, they were slipping and sliding everywhere, losing their balance and falling over. It was working perfectly!

Those left standing were soon cracked by the staff of Chupwah. He swung it this way and that, mighty blows of wood on metal. With each clout, he knocked pieces of armor loose and sent men flying.

Mouse and Caroline stepped over the wreckage to continue their journey to the Dragon Killer. They dodged countless dangers and used more walnuts and thunderous wallops from Chupwah to arrive mere feet from the weapon. It gave Caroline the chills to stand so close to their target.

Sadly, the element of surprise was long gone. The guards stood ready with their menacing blades.

But they hadn't counted on the Sasquatch. The guards could scarcely believe their eyes! Before they could even blink, they were being battered and bruised by Chupwah's staff. One by one he either knocked them out or hit them across the back of their legs, not preferring one method over another so long as they were out of the way when he was done.

Before long, enough guards were cleared away to create a straight path to the weapon, with a lone soldier waiting on the weapon. The nerves were gone, the fear of failure was history, and Caroline stood at the brink of success.

She waved her sword, readying to take him down one way or another, when suddenly there was a loud scream from high overhead. Caroline craned her neck to look behind her and saw a large shadow cast itself over the land. It was the shadow of a dragon, and not just any dragon but Jomey, with Akari riding along.

The effect on the soldiers was immediate, as all eyes turned to the dragon overhead. Some yelled in terror, running here and there, unable to keep their composure, and some simply fell over and covered their heads. Some simply stood where they were, open-mouthed.

It was not the reaction Caroline had expected. These were fighting men, Azorians and Wild Men alike, and yet they were all driven senseless by the dragon. Watching them scatter, she was reminded of a hive of honey bees that had been poked with a stick. Jomey circled overhead and turned back to the jungle as a round of shots suddenly were fired from the weapon.

As far as Caroline was concerned, that would be the last round the soldier would fire. She dropped her bag and climbed up the Dragon Killer with her sword drawn. She moved quickly and had the drop on the guard, who was busy watching the dragon circle back for another pass.

But before she could swing on him, the guard noticed her. He scampered to his feet and tried to rip his sword from his scabbard, but he was so shocked that he slipped and fell from atop the weapon some twenty feet to the ground, landing in a heap below. Caroline could not believe her luck. Just like that, the first part of their mission was all but accomplished! All that remained was to disable the weapon lest someone else try to use it.

"Come on, Mouse! Give me a hand here," she shouted. Soon Mouse clambered up the side of the weapon, and together they cut away the myriad ropes that held together the device.

The catapult's arm was set loose and tumbled to the ground, crashing with a thud just feet from Chupwah. They were fortunate that the arm did not fall on him while he eagerly beat back a second wave of Azorian soldiers that had rushed to stop them.

In fact, the arm landed right between him and the soldiers he had been keeping at bay. They were cut off, buying him time to regroup.

He climbed the weapon to join his friends, his great arms pulling him up easily while Caroline and Mouse raised theirs triumphantly.

Caroline looked into the sky for Jomey. After some time she found him, the dragon's long neck appearing over the tree tops as he headed to the castle. The three onlookers cheered as the dragon soared over their heads.

But then their blood ran cold as a booming voice rang out from inside the fortress. It was the voice of Osirah, the resurrected Knight, deep and terrifying, yelling through some kind of horn which amplified his voice and carried it far and wide throughout the kingdom. He stood on his tower with a wicked grin on his face.

"Did you think I'd be so foolish as to only have one Dragon Killer, Akari?" Osirah yelled in a taunting tone. "We're not as stupid as you may suppose. Soldiers, fire... NOW!"

Caroline kicked herself. She had forgotten about the other weapons. Where could they be? That question was soon answered. It was so obvious that Caroline again cursed herself.

As soon as Osirah gave the order, cannon ball after cannon ball arced from behind the fortress walls and headed directly toward the dragon, fired with almost perfect accuracy. They winced as *boom, boom, boom*, three shots landed directly down Jomey's mouth. He jerked in the air, recoiling from the shock. Desperate to escape, he again circled away. His flying was already shaky and unsteady.

Caroline was in disbelief. They had disabled one Dragon Killer only to learn that there were at least two more, and safely behind the castle walls. How could they ever get to them? It would be suicide for Jomey to make another pass.

Worse, the soldiers nearby had regrouped. They gathered around the remains of the weapon and called out, begging them to come down, yelling out things like "Come on down, little poppet" to Caroline, and "Not so tough now, are you, Sasquatch?"

They were trapped. There was nowhere to go. Their entire plan was reduced to hoping for a miracle. There were at least twenty soldiers waiting below, too many for even Chupwah to handle, and worse, she had foolishly left her bag of walnuts on the ground. There was simply no escape.

Caroline bit her lower lip and tried desperately to figure out a plan. But nothing was coming to mind. The odds were completely stacked against them, once and for all.

Their luck had finally run out.

# Chapter Thirty-Three - His Father's Son

*E*ston stood over his eldest son Jonas, who had been lying motionless for hours, and searched for something to say. But no words came to mind, so he turned around and shuffled back to his work. He had already said everything there was to say.

*After all, Jonas was well aware that somewhere in the world his sister, brother, and uncle were three days away from their campsite, putting their lives on the line for the greater good. Jonas knew this but apparently did not care as he remained in bed.*

*In a way, and he knew it was a very selfish way, Eston was happy to have his son around, even in his current condition. If things went wrong he would still have one child, such as he was. But for the lump in those frumpled blankets he was all alone, fraught with worry for his other children as well as Akari and Chupwah. He had lived his life as a man of action yet now he was a burden, unable to be of use when he was needed the most. Worse, Jonas, who would have been of great help - all the talent was there - was now convinced he could be nothing more than a sword maker and had mentally given up. Nothing Eston said convinced Jonas otherwise. And Eston had said everything.*

*So, Eston went back to work on his project. He was nearly finished. If nothing else, he would complete his little invention, and for once in his life he would create something that was not a weapon, something that would not be used to kill, to maim, to destroy. He had created enough of those in his life. While it did not feel quite right to work on such a trivial thing while two of his children were in danger and another in such a dark place, it was also keeping him sane, distracting him just enough from the world's harsh realities.*

*Then it hit him. Maybe his trivial little invention was not so trivial. Maybe, it could solve all of his problems in one fell swoop. Yes, it very well could. Why, it was brilliant! But first, he would work feverishly to complete his work, and then he would go back to Jonas.*

*This would get his son out of bed. Eston only had to hope that the invention worked, and in time.*

Akari had never been very comfortable around people. Given the choice, he preferred to be as far away from them as possible, though he seldom had such a choice. It was not anything personal, but when you were an elite member of the King's Army, you spent an unreasonable amount of time at social events, pretending to be interested in what some Duke had to say or listen to the blabber of a pampered rich kid there to mingle with the other elites. It had worn on him, souring him on any and all social functions.

In truth, Akari never felt lonelier than when he was surrounded by swarms of people. All things considered, he was happiest by himself, doing his experiments and trying to make the world a better place, despite his detachment from that very same world.

There was one exception, and that was when he was on the back of a dragon. *That* was when he was happiest. Nothing else compared to the force of the wind, the pure beauty of looking down on the world with the great power of the beast beneath him, a beautiful creature misunderstood and wrongly feared by the world that rushed by below.

Well, he normally was happy when riding on the back of a dragon. Usually. But at this moment, he was terrified. His dragon was barely clinging to life, and the chances of success were fading fast.

He was furious with himself. Why hadn't he figured that they would have Dragon Killers behind the fortress?

And what of his kin below? He knew the first weapon had somehow been disabled, but as he leaned over the side to take a look, he saw that they were surrounded by a host of Azorians. Panic rushed over him; his worst fears were coming to bear. From his perch atop a disabled dragon, there was nothing that could be done.

The only thing to do was to try again, to see if the dragon could withstand the barrage and bring him to Osirah, who stood on top of the tower impassively watching the death and destruction take place below. Even with the dragon bearing down on him, he remained calm and assured. Akari could not wait to see his face when it all came crashing down.

That said, there was good reason for the General to be so assured. They had destroyed one Dragon Killer weapon, but with the two others, he remained protected.

"How could I be so stupid?" Akari yelled in a panic, though it went unheard by Jomey, for the dragon had been hit, again, a direct shot that caused his whole body to convulse. Akari was nearly thrown from his seat and Jomey let loose a guttural growl, one that came from deep inside. The horrible cry echoed throughout Azoria.

Akari cursed. His lack of preparation threatened to endanger all they had set out to accomplish, not to mention the lives of those fighting for him down below. Maldazor and Osirah had outsmarted him, and rather easily.

Akari had to think of something, and fast. And he would, but first he had to remove Jomey from the line of fire.

The relationship between a dragon and the rider on his back could take various forms. In most cases, the dragon was completely in control, flying where it wanted to with no input from the rider, who would merely be grateful to ride on a dragon. But in the case of someone like Akari the rider had a bit more control. In some cases, Akari even took over, using the reins in the same way one would take control of a horse. Akari had been much celebrated for his ability to steer a dragon to safety, one of many reasons that he was revered by many dragons who had witnessed him getting others out of tough spots.

With that knowledge, Jomey allowed Akari to take the reins. Akari grabbed them tight and steered the dragon so that his back faced the onslaught of cannon fire while angling it toward the safety of the jungle. The cannonballs would still hurt as they crashed against his frame, but doing so would limit the damage.

With that first move complete, Akari looked backwards, grimacing as there was more cannon fire on their tail. It would be tough to dodge them all, but he expertly led the way, pulling the reins and causing the dragon to go left and right, up and down, a constant blur as it evaded the storm of fire. Adrenaline coursed through Akari's veins as he watched the shots go by, whizzing loudly through the air as they missed by mere inches.

Jomey and Akari were soon out of range and flying to the jungle, where they disappeared from sight. Akari could hear the faint murmur of cheering as the men at war celebrated their escape, happy to see the dragons leave.

Jomey dipped below the tree line, weakly flapping his wings and slowly dropping to the ground. But Jomey took a deep breath, recovered some strength and again flew skyward until they found a clearing to safely land.

Akari leaped from the dragon and paced back and forth, wracking his brain for a solution. "What are we going to do, Jomey? We need to get them beyond the castle wall," Akari shouted.

But Jomey said nothing, just sat on the ground panting, puffs of smoke soon clouding up the jungle floor like low-hanging fog.

This was not looking good, Akari thought. They needed a miracle.

*Eston set about being as loud as possible while working on his project, hoping to invoke his son's curiosity. He didn't have many tools to work with, just a few things the Wild Men had passed on, but he had enough. He clanged them together, banged on them, and threw branches around, hoping the noise would pique his son's interest. He was dubious, but nothing else had worked.*

*After some time carrying on, for the first time that Eston had seen in days, his son rolled out of bed. He was a mess, with his hair going in every direction and wearing a hangdog expression, but he was finally up and moving. It could only get better from here, Eston thought.*

*"What are you doing?" Jonas asked, not hiding his interest.*

*"Oh, nothing really," Eston responded coyly. "Just getting back to an old project of mine while I wait for the others to return." He turned his work over and revealed a dragon pattern drawn on the underside of a large sheet of canvas. It was crude, but from a great height it might fool even the least skittish soldier on the ground.*

*"OK, good. But what is it?" Jonas asked.*

*"Well, son, I always wanted to fly on the back of a dragon, but they never really wanted any part of me." He shrugged. "I suppose it's because I invented the Dragon Killer. I understand. And when I did finally get a ride, I was nearly crushed! So with no other options, I came up with this."*

*He pointed to a collection of wooden poles that had been lashed together with rope. They were light in weight, forming a kind of frame though Jonas knew not what it was. Eston then took the piece of canvas and attached it at the corners to the wood.*

*"I came up with the idea of painting it like that after Jomey carried me around"* he explained. *Eston then looked meaningfully at his son. "I'm afraid I'm going to need someone to test it out. It just won't do for me to get up there in this condition."*

Akari looked down through the jungle canopy, hoping inspiration would strike. Perhaps they could find some heavy stones and drop them on the wall to tear it down piece by piece. Then Chupwah, Caroline, and Mouse could walk through and destroy the Dragon Killers. But such stones would be massive. Akari doubted Jomey would be able to carry such a heavy burden fast enough to evade the oncoming artillery. And that assumed they would even find a stone large enough to do the job. No, he would have to think of something else.

But all he could see was trees. A jungle filled with trees, trees, and more trees. Well, what did he expect?

But then an idea hit him. Well, that's just too perfect. But of course! He yelled out to Jomey, straining to be heard in the bee's nest that had become the dragon's brain, scrambled from the punishment he had suffered. "Jomey, I want you to uproot the biggest tree you can find!"

Akari jumped on Jomey and pulled on the reins, causing the dragon to take flight. Akari quickly explained what he was looking for, and they searched the trees that bordered the area for a good candidate before settling on a large tree that stood tall over the others.

"Perfect," Akari said. The dragon sunk his large claws into the bark about halfway up the trunk and flew upwards, straining with effort. His claws dug deep, sinking far into the wood. The dragon flapped its wings and Akari watched the dirt loosen from the ground. It was a mighty struggle, but it was working, and soon the whole tree came up from the earth, roots and all. It was an impressive show of strength, especially from a dragon that had only been nursed to health a few days before, only to endure another torturous assault. With the tree safely in its grasp, they made way to the castle.

*"How do I test it?" Jonas asked. He was completely on board now. Eston was nearly overcome with joy, although he was careful not to show it and risk upsetting the high-strung boy.*

*"Well son, test may have been the wrong word. We don't actually have time for a test. Call it a hunch, call it a feeling, I don't know, but my gut tells me that your brother and sister, along with Chupwah and your uncle, need you," Eston replied.*

*"Don't you think it's too late, Dad? They left three days ago!"*

*"Too late? Not with this!" he said, pointing to the invention. He smiled. "Do you think you can climb a tree? You'll have to start high up."*

Caroline looked on in exasperation as Akari and Jomey flew into the jungle. What were they supposed to do now? A huge stone wall stood between them and their target and their leader was flying away, with furious soldiers waiting below. They were stuck.

The Azorians were not pleased that one of their weapons had been disabled, showing their displeasure by brandishing their swords. They waved them menacingly and shouted all kinds of awful things, their courage emboldened by the dragon's disappearance.

The Azorians started to climb what was left of the weapon. Chupwah growled furiously and threw a few to the ground, but someone tripped him with a rope around his legs. He fell hard to the surface. The soldiers then flooded the weapon, swarming like ants that had discovered a dropped piece of fruit, and before long they had tied up Caroline and Mouse. Chupwah continued to struggle, but fight as he might, he could not last long under such numbers.

Caroline struggled against her bonds, but there was no escape. Her lower lip trembled as the reality of their failure crystallized, and the bitter truth hit her like cold water in the face. They never had a chance anyway. Not really. Too many things had to go right for it to work.

The soldiers gruffly passed Caroline and Mouse to the ground, where the Azorians leered and taunted them. Caroline wished the Mulvarians would bring their fighting this way and distract their captors, although for all she knew, the Mulvarians had already lost.

Soon, using great strength, they brought Chupwah down to the ground. He lay with his face buried in the dirt, struggling while they kicked and stomped him, until he too was tied and bound. Akari could say what he wanted about most of these soldiers *just following orders*, but it seemed to Caroline that many of them were as rotten as Maldazor and Osirah.

All hope was lost. It would be impossible for Jomey to make another pass now without being killed. Caroline bit her lower lip, refusing to cry, but it took all she had.

She was looking into the sky, holding back those tears, when she saw it. Another dragon was flying toward them, one that was smaller than Jomey. It moved stiffly, and Caroline realized it was not even flapping its wings. Instead, it glided toward them, rather like a hawk circling the sky.

As it drew closer Caroline realized it was not a dragon at all, nor was it a hawk or even an eagle. In fact, Caroline was unsure as to exactly what it was. But whatever it was it was holding a man, heading their way with his arms spread out wide as if they had the power of flight.

"What is that?" Caroline yelled.

The Azorian soldiers saw it too and took off running. "Dragon!" they yelled, seemingly in unison. "Run! Run for your life!"

It glided downwards toward the ground, whizzing at a high speed. The man lowered his feet and dragged them along the ground, trying to come to a stop. Whatever it was that had flown down, it was clearly man made and not a dragon.

It finally came to a halt, flipping over itself and crashing in a heap, with the sounds of fabric ripping and poles snapping as it did.

Chupwah crawled to his feet slowly. He looked around – they were all alone. In their fear, the soldiers had left, believing this device to have been a dragon.

Chupwah had small cuts and scratches covering his body, but he was in good shape, overall. He promptly ripped the bonds from Caroline and Mouse's arms, and together they scrambled to the wreckage, where the man had not moved since the rough landing.

"What is that thing?" Mouse asked, to which no one had an answer.

"Let's find out," Caroline said. "Whatever it is, it saved us, for now." She looked around the battlefield searching for the soldiers, who did not yet realize they had been fooled.

They ran to the wreckage and dug through the ripped fabric, some of which was painted a dark green to imitate the scales of a dragon. They found the man's legs, which Chupwah grabbed to pull him free.

"Jonas!" Caroline and Mouse yelled, reaching down to hug him. His hair was littered with stray bits of grass, and dirt covered his face, but otherwise he looked fine. In fact, the smile on his face made him look better than he had in some time.

"How'd I do?" he said, his grin broad and wide. "Sorry I wasn't here sooner. But you can't argue with my timing, I guess." He pointed to the rubble he had left behind. "It was Dad's invention. He called it a glider."

He then grew somber. "Please forgive me, Sister," Jonas said, before turning to Mouse. "You too, Brother. I don't know what I was thinking, or if I was even thinking at all."

"Of course we forgive you, Jonas," Caroline said. "But right now we've got to find a way over that wall. Akari and Jomey need us!"

The group ran to the castle wall, although they knew not what action to take. The fighting had moved toward the jungle, which left them a clear path.

They were soon at the edge of the wall and looking up the massive stone structure, searching desperately for a foothold that would allow them to scale it. Reminded of his experience at the cliffs, Mouse dug his fingers into a small crack in the mortar that held the stones together and tried to pull his body up - and doing so, but he only made it ten feet or so before finding no further holds. He dropped down to the ground and kicked the wall in frustration, managing only to stub his toe, which left him even more frustrated.

"What do we do now?" Mouse asked, his face growing red with impatience. He was ready to take action. For once, he was the impatient one.

"Nothing," replied Jonas.

"Nothing? Are you crazy? We didn't come all this way to do nothing!" Mouse spat out, his frustration spilling over as nothing seemed to be going right.

"Easy Mouse, I think he means nothing yet," Chupwah offered calmly. "*Yet* being the key word." He then pointed up to the sky.

Mouse turned around and his eyes seemed to double in size as he realized what Chupwah was referencing. Jomey had returned with Akari on his back, clutching a massive tree in its claws.

"What's it going to do with that?" Mouse stammered. Nobody had an answer - all were equally mystified as to the dragon's intentions and waited eagerly to see what transpired.

The cannon fire resumed as soldiers yelled from all over and a warning bell was rung to let the Azorians know the dragon had returned. With such an onslaught, Akari again took the reins, and though the dragon moved slower from the tree in its grasp, Akari managed to avoid most of the heavy fire. But the shots that did hit their mark took their toll on Jomey.

But the dragon finally cast his shadow on to the wall. He had made it, although not without considerable cost. Every muscle strained under the stress and each blow weakened him that much more.

He let loose the branch, hoping he had estimated the angles correctly. It crashed from the sky, branches breaking and leaves scattering into the air as the top of the tree landed lengthwise across the wall while the trunk fell to the ground below.

"Yes!" Akari yelled. "Nice job, Jomey!" It was exactly what he wanted - a ramp had been created that would allow Caroline, Jonas, Mouse, and Chupwah to walk up the surface of the tree and into the fortress of Azoria.

Jonas quickly understood. "Akari's done it again," he declared. "Now let's take care of our part!" Jonas started to climb, but Chupwah stopped him.

"I'll go first, Jonas. Climbing trees is kind of my specialty."

Jonas stepped aside, but quickly followed behind as the large beast padded his way up. It was a steep climb and rather slippery, but for Chupwah it was easy, and he made sure to assist the others as needed. They slogged up and stepped onto the fortress wall just in time to meet a handful of Azorian guards, who seemed ready to defend their castle.

Well, they were ready to defend until they saw the large frame of a Sasquatch rise over the wall. Suddenly, they cared little about Maldazor's castle. In fact, where was Maldazor now? If this castle was so important, why wasn't he here to defend it?

Chupwah saw the guards and roared, intending to scare them into doing something stupid. They did not need much encouragement. The roar served its purpose as the six guards stood frozen with their eyes bugging out, unable to move as fear pulsed through their body.

Chupwah was quickly on them with his sharp teeth bared, ready to unload with his staff. The soldiers threw down their weapons and took off running without looking back. Despite the fierce reputation of their resurrected ruler Osirah, it seemed that these soldiers simply did not have their heart in fighting this battle.

With the opposition removed, they ran down the walkway and came to the end of the battlements, where they found a door that they knew led to a staircase. Mouse was the first to arrive; he took a deep breath before turning the door handle. *It was their time now.* The other Dragon Killers awaited them, and it was time to clear the way for Akari and Jomey.

They flew down the stairs to the courtyard below. Caroline looked up and noticed Osirah, who stared coldly at Caroline and her compatriots. He laughed, giving off the impression that he was completely unconcerned, though Chupwah noted that he stopped to order his guards to meet the invaders.

The Dragon Killer weapons themselves were each manned by large groups of soldiers. Caroline gulped - she saw no way that the four of them could overcome such a force.

Just then, as if in answer to her pleas, a great door sprung open. Though Caroline did not know it, an old friend had returned.

"Claudius!" Mouse yelled.

Jonas' eyes popped out - his brother was right! The ancient soldier Claudius was leading a ragtag group of prisoners from the dungeons. They spilled out of the door holding weapons taken from the guards they had overthrown only moments earlier. Jonas had forgotten all about the prisoner, who Akari had asked to wait to escape until the time was right.

The time was definitely right.

Azorian soldiers ran over to the prisoners, who took the fight to them. It was an extraordinary battle, but Maldazor's plan of imprisoning old Ambrosian soldiers was not going well for his army.

"We have backup!" Jonas called out. "Now let's take down the weapons!"

In all the confusion, the group, led by Caroline, made it to the first weapon without anyone stopping them. The soldiers manning the weapon were all sweating profusely, tense with worry as they waited for another attack from the sky. Little did they know their doom was already there on the ground.

Caroline yelled at one of the warriors, who barely managed to raise his sword in defense. She swung hard and knocked the blade free, then threw a kick that sent the guard flying.

A second soldier swung his sword at Jonas, who parried it deftly. They engaged in a brief duel, their swords clanging furiously until Jonas managed a powerful strike that sent his opponent's sword flying. Rather than risk further injury, the Azorian held his arms up high and surrendered.

Jonas and Caroline moved to assist Mouse with his opponent, and together they quickly dispatched another guard. Mouse shrugged his shoulders sheepishly at needing assistance, but Jonas clapped him on the back and told him he did well.

It was then that they noticed Chupwah was not with them. Finding matters well in hand at target number one, he had sneaked off to the other weapon. They watched in awe while he used his staff to rain down mighty blows upon the soldiers.

Chupwah then decided to simply rip the weapon apart piece by piece while the soldiers standing on it scrambled for safety. Everywhere they looked pieces of wood went flying, ropes went airborne, and cannonballs rolled across the fortress grounds and crashed into the walls. It was complete and total destruction. It took the army weeks to build these weapons, but the young, powerful Sasquatch destroyed them in minutes. When the soldiers climbed from the rubble, Chupwah roared and sent them on their heels.

Just like that, their mission was accomplished. The prisoners had dispatched Osirah's guards and the battle was won.

Now it was up to Akari to win the war. They could only hope that Jomey had enough left to make it happen.

As if they had read their minds, within seconds of having the weapons dismantled, the dragon reappeared. He was clearly in bad shape, making a last ditch effort to bring Akari to Osirah and willing to die to make it happen.

Akari stood on the dragon's back holding his great sword aloft. Caroline was nervous as she watched, impatient to see what shape Akari's great plan would take to end the war between the Azorians and the Mulvarians. Then a sudden realization hit her.

This was the moment for which they had all sacrificed, though only now did she know it. Not even Akari was aware of their greater mission until he too had reached the same conclusion days earlier. The entire time they had assumed they were simply on a journey to rescue their father, but in doing so, in challenging their Fates the ways that they had, they each had made their first stand in the battle for freedom from the rule of kings. Freedom was a road seldom traveled by those on this island, but today they had all taken the first steps.

Now they could only stand and watch, hoping that Akari could win the first battle in the war for freedom.

*Eston thought back to early that morning, as he watched Jonas hold his arms out and leap from the tree. "I'm sorry for the way I acted, Father," his son called out before the glider caught a draft of air and quickly floated skyward, and soon his son disappeared into the horizon. Eston's heart swelled. The glider had worked after all, and it had helped bring his boy back from the brink. Eston only hoped that he would see him again soon, with the rest of his family.*

# Chapter Thirty-Four - The Duel of Surrender

Jomey was in big trouble, and that was putting it mildly. In fact, he was very likely dying. Akari was not certain, but he did know that his best-laid plans were being shattered. There were still Dragon Killer weapons, his dragon was barely clinging to life, and his cohorts were surrounded by the Azorian Army. Not exactly the hallmarks of a successfully orchestrated plan.

Just then, something passed by that nearly caused Akari to fall off of the dragon. It was Jonas! He was flying past on, well, *something*. Akari tried to figure out exactly what it was, but all he could do was wonder at the sight. He didn't know if his nephew had seen him because Jonas was hanging on for dear life. Whatever was carrying Jonas was made from wood and canvas, and gliding rather than flying, though traveling much faster than the crippled Jomey. It was amazing. He had never seen anything like it, but he knew Eston had something to do with it.

Akari didn't think he was cut out to be a father, but Eston seemed to handle it well. He watched as his nephew glided by and was stunned by his apparent change in attitude. Maybe, just maybe, Jonas would be able to save Caroline, Mouse, and Chupwah, who were surrounded by Azorians the last he saw.

Jomey found another clearing in the jungle and landed roughly, unable to properly judge his speed. As soon as they touched ground Akari jumped from his seat and went around to speak with Jomey. But before he could say anything, Jomey cut him off.

"One more time, Akari. I can get you to Osirah," he whispered, his voice almost gone.

"That's suicide, Jomey," Akari retorted, but Jomey cut him off before he could say more.

"I know. But my mind is made up," he declared. Akari tried to talk again, but Jomey shushed him. A small lick of flame fired out as he did, which singed Akari's eyebrows. There was no arguing with that - Jomey had made his point.

Akari shrugged. "Well, your flame seems to be coming back a bit."

The dragon sighed. "I don't know where that came from. That's the most I've had since the fall," Jomey said. He painfully leaned to the side to allow Akari to mount. They waited for some time while Jomey gathered his strength.

Jomey flapped his wings to begin the journey to Maldazor's castle. Akari could feel Jomey struggle, giving it his all to push past his pain. It was all Akari could do to not force the dragon to turn back.

He had to laugh at the thought. Forcing a dragon to do what it doesn't want to do would be like forcing the tide to go back into the ocean, or taking control of weather patterns.

Akari took the reins because Jomey was simply too battered to remain in control. The warrior held back his tears, for he saw no chance that his friend would survive. It would take a miracle to even make it to Osirah's tower.

Akari held tight to the reins, fearing the dragon would nosedive at any second. But Jomey fought on, refusing to give in. And before they knew it, they were hovering over the battlefield, with Osirah back in eyesight in all his golden terror.

All eyes were fixed on Akari the Dragon-Slayer as they flew in. Afterwards, many claimed Akari had enchanted the warriors who had been fighting down below, or that the dragon did, or some combination of the two as only moments before, the soldiers of both sides had been locked in lethal combat.

But the dragon moved his eyes back and forth and seemed to stare into the very hearts of the men below, who stood rapt as Jomey soared overhead with his giant wings stretched to their limits, whooshing high above.

Akari viewed the scene below and shook his head sadly at the results of the bloody battle. If only they had been able to disable the weapons faster, many lives could have been saved. But time had not been on their side, as it almost never is, and he counted himself lucky that even now they had been able to bring pause to the fighting.

Then it dawned on him that they were no longer being fired upon by the Dragon Killers. His heart leaped, and he realized that his kin was nowhere to be seen on the battlefield below. They must have made it up the tree to the other side of the castle! Maybe there was hope yet.

Still, it would do no good if he failed to carry out the rest of his plan. Those lives would only be temporarily saved, as fighting would quickly resume the moment he was struck down.

Carrying these thoughts heavily in his heart, for the first time he fully embraced the weight of expectations that he had carried his entire life. Today, he could bring an end to hostilities, and if he failed, it would likely cost him his life. But there would be no more running, no faking his death, no excuses. Today was the day he would truly become a great warrior and live up to the Fate he had chosen for himself long ago - or he would die in the attempt.

The dragon glided toward the tower and a clamor arose among the Mulvarian soldiers. The strange tale brought back by Morgan and Ned was true. Their former general was alive and ready to fight for their freedom. All were stunned as they watched Akari fly overhead.

The dragon slowly made his way over the battlements atop the castle wall, narrowly clearing the height. His tail lashed out and knocked over one of the guard towers, where it crashed to the ground below. The dragon was barely hanging in the air, weakly flapping his wings while it soared above Jonas, Caroline, Mouse, and Chupwah. They watched desperately, feeling helpless, fearing that the poor creature could fall from the sky at any time.

From deep inside the castle, arrows and spears flew toward Akari and Jomey. For a dragon, these weapons were usually as harmless as a mosquito bite, but in his weakened state, each one stung sharply. His neck and head rolled in the throes of pain, and his legs flailed about wildly. But he fought through, stretching his wings out wide as they gave one last push to bring Akari to the edge of the tower, steps from Osirah.

With one last gasp, the dragon reached out, sinking his claws into the stones of the keep. He hung on for all he was worth, straining his arms with effort.

Akari raised his sword high in the air and jumped free of the dragon. He stepped out onto the keep wall, standing bravely above the Azorian General.

Caroline watched with her hand over her mouth and her heart in her throat. She gasped as the life seemed to leave Jomey. He lost his grip and slid down the wall with his claws scraping against stone. His claws ripped from the tower and he slowly fell from high above the earth, his massive body plunging limply to the ground. It would crush anything that stood below, including Caroline, who stood just under the beast.

But he had just enough energy to shrink in size one last time. He took the form of a bat, the form Caroline knew so well. It was a sad sight as his little wings went limp and he floated quietly to the ground, fluttering in the breeze like the last autumn leaf falling from a tree. Caroline held out her hands and waited. She caught the poor thing, cradling it in her arms, tears flowing freely as she held him close. It was an awful sight to witness.

Akari saw none of it. It was up to him to make Jomey's sacrifice worth it, and he vowed to see it through. This was more than revenge, more than a conquest. This was for freedom. He blocked out all other thoughts and gazed angrily upon Osirah, whose face was in a rage, his eyes blazing with anger.

"How dare you step on to my keep?" Osirah yelled. "You have no call to be here!"

Akari drew in his breath. He removed a small device of triangular shape, his latest invention, and held it to his mouth. It would amplify his voice the same way Osirah's horn did and carry it throughout the battlefields. It would enable both armies to hear him speak as it was of great import that he be heard.

"Dare to step on your keep? I dare to do more than that, Osirah," Akari said, his voice loud. The soldiers looked on in surprise, just another shock from a man who constantly amazed.

"Warriors of Azoria, for those who do not know me, my name is Akari. Some call me Akari Dragonkiller, others call me Dragonlover. It matters not. Furthermore, I am a former Chief Knight of Ambrosia, as is this uncouth ghoul who has returned from the dead to torture us all. This fool, who stands in his tower and sends others to fight and die.

"Unlike that fool, I was also a General in the Army of Mulvaria. And as they say, once a General of Mulvaria, always a General of Mulvaria." With that, he pointed his sword at many of the soldiers clad in Mulvarian armor, who responded by raising their fists and cheering, energized at seeing their former General alive and well. It was a reaction that heartened Akari, giving him strength that he so desperately needed.

"Today, old laws will be cast aside and torn apart. Soon. But not yet, and thus we remain under old law."

He paused. Soon, words of recognition went up among the Mulvarians, realizing the significance of a General of one country challenging another under the tradition of Ambrosian law, which still ruled the land of Azoria under King Maldazor.

The Azorians cheered just as loud, with many of the soldiers within the castle walls yelling loudly for Osirah to fight, egging him on with the hope he would fail, for they despised the resurrected General and were eager to leave his command. If Akari won the duel, the war would end and Mulvaria would be declared the winner, which gave them the upper hand in subsequent negotiations. In fact, since Osirah was ruling Azoria in Maldazor's absence, in effect Akari could take control of the entire nation if he was the victor. It was a staggering lapse by Maldazor.

Akari leaped from his position on the wall and approached Osirah, looking him squarely in the eye. He pointed his sword at the Azorian Chief Knight.

"Yes, Osirah. I, Akari, on behalf of the Army of Mulvaria, challenge you, the once Chief Knight of Ambrosia, now resurrected as Chief Knight of Azoria, to a Duel of Surrender."

Osirah stared back, hard, his face like stone. He said nothing.

This enraged Akari further. "Do you accept? Answer me! Or stand down and let this bloody waste end!"

Osirah moved little, but he began to laugh, a cold laugh that sent shivers down many spines, loud enough that many could hear though they stood far away. The crowd was driven to silence, and the Azorians shifted uncomfortably, knowing that they had perhaps been a bit too eager for their General to accept the Duel as they recognized, rightly, that Osirah was one of the fiercest warriors in the history of the island, and even the well regarded Akari might succumb to his force. It would be unwise to do anything that could cause problems if and when Osirah walked away the victor.

The laughing stopped and Osirah's face turned cold. "I accept this challenge." He cracked his knuckles, slowly and dramatically, playing up the theatricality of it all before continuing.

"And I shall enjoy it. For far too long did I reside in the Netherworld, drifting aimlessly, and now that I have returned I have eagerly awaited a challenge that would satisfy me. But to feel your hot blood spilling out upon the hilt of my sword shall refresh me like water to a man returning from a trek in the desert. A fitting present to welcome me fully back into this world, where cruelty and ruthlessness are rightly celebrated. Only when you are dead by my hand shall I feel truly alive." He ran his finger along the edge of his blade and drew blood from the thin cut left behind.

"Yes, you will soon feel fully alive," Akari said, his tone cool. "And soon, you will feel fully dead once again."

"Fool!" Osirah spat. "You cannot conquer me! Many times have you faked your death and succeeded, but I assure you, all will believe you are dead this time. For they shall bear witness."

Akari jumped back on to the wall in the blink of an eye and leaped down, desiring to utilize the high ground as the battle commenced. But when he swung his sword at Osirah, he missed.

Akari landed cleanly on his feet with his sword held in his right hand. His left hand served to steady himself from the fall, but Osirah was prepared and slammed Akari down to the ground with a shove. Before Akari could return to his feet, Osirah was on him, stabbing his sword down at Akari, who spun to avoid the strike.

Akari swung out his free hand to pull Osirah's ankle out from under him. Osirah fell and landed hard, face first, his teeth jarring on the stone surface of the tower. His wrist landed awkwardly, knocking the sword loose. Akari scrambled on his hands and knees to his opponent with sword in hand. But he was unable to use it effectively from this position. Instead, he struck Osirah in the face repeatedly with his free hand.

After absorbing these blows, Osirah broke free, sending Akari sprawling. He ran to his sword and quickly wiped away the blood that was flowing freely from his nose. Akari recovered quickly and dashed to the Azorian General, striking with his sword, which Osirah deflected. Over and over the warriors exchanged mighty blows, smiting each other until sparks flew. It was grueling combat at a level only these two were capable of.

Akari attempted a backhanded strike, which struck true against the chain mail worn by Osirah. It staggered him, but he shrugged it off and lashed back with a mighty strike, which Akari narrowly ducked. The blade smashed powerfully against the wall behind Akari, knocking a stone free from the masonry. Akari whistled softly, grateful to avoid such a clout.

He moved to take advantage of the missed strike, but Osirah quickly turned and parried Akari's effort, responding with one of his own. Again and again they struck at each other, each managing to graze the other with minor cuts, each having their share of near-misses, and each failing to land a decisive blow.

It was a fight for the future of the Northern part of the island of Ambrosia, and all looked on in a nervous, edgy, torturous silence.

# Chapter Thirty-Five - Out Of Reach

When it came to duels in Ambrosia, sword fighting was the usual method. In fact, none could remember a duel happening any other way, though some old-timers said a joust would be perfectly acceptable. But that did not mean other methods were forbidden - it just had never been done any other way. But Akari and Osirah would soon have no choice.

After exchanging powerful blows, Akari swung his blade so hard that it wrenched free from the hilt. It scattered across the stone surface of the keep. But in so doing he knocked Osirah's weapon free, which flew to the opposite edge of the tower. Just like that they were wrestling, each desperately trying to gain the edge as they engaged in raw and brutal hand-to-hand combat.

Down below, Caroline, Jonas, Mouse, and Chupwah watched in astonishment with considerable trepidation. Worse, it was difficult to see exactly what was happening from their vantage point, and even when they could, their view was skewed. It would seem that Akari was in control, but just when it appeared he was ready to end the fight they watched as Osirah turned the tide and took control.

They went back and forth, pummeling each other while trying to collect Osirah's loose sword. It was heart-wrenching to those who watched, who were powerless to do anything and desperate for Akari to win.

Akari again slipped free from Osirah's grasp and clambered on top of his foe. He hit him with all he had, but he could not seem to finish his opponent. He walloped Osirah's face, trying to knock the wicked man unconscious, but Osirah wouldn't give up.

Osirah was strong and vicious, doing all he could to kill Akari, but Akari merely wanted to subdue his opponent. The distinction was important, as Osirah had no rules or limitations while Akari had handicapped himself by trying to keep Osirah alive. Akari now realized he could no longer afford such a luxury. He would again have to deal with a conscience made guilty for taking a life, but he had no choice.

Akari grabbed Osirah's arm and tried to wrench it from the socket. It was a violent move, and frankly, it made him sick. Akari hated reaching into this dark place, deep inside himself, but it was a means to an end - a path to freedom, and the first strike against the rule of Maldazor, who was a brute of a King. Sometimes you had to fight fire with fire, but it was hard to live with.

He gripped Osirah's arm and held it tight, but before he could pull back even harder, Osirah kneed him in his groin, sending shocks of pain through Akari's body. Osirah was free.

Akari rolled backward, his legs going over his head, and he pivoted to his feet while Osirah crawled toward his sword. The pain was excruciating. Crawling was too much on Osirah's injured arm, and the joint of his injured elbow finally gave out on him. The warrior fell flat on his face, tantalizingly close to the blade. His fingers stretched to reach it, the pain agonizing, and his fingers finally managed to weakly grasp the hilt. If only he could use it to kill that accursed Akari.

But as Osirah scrambled to get back up with weapon in hand, Akari ran right by him and stepped on the blade. Try as Osirah might he could not lift it. Akari would not move. The strength left his body for good and he again toppled on to his face. It was almost pitiful to see him this way, if one did not know that Osirah himself would cackle with pleasure to find his foe in the same situation.

Akari watched him fall to the ground and felt no pity. All he felt was his own pain, which throbbed through his body. He could feel his lip swelling, blood was trickling down his forehead, and his groin ached something fierce. The adrenaline pumped violently through his veins and amplified his anger, which caused rash thoughts to race through his mind as he stood and watched the Chief Knight wallow in misery. He could take the beaten Osirah's life now and everyone would cheer. Songs would praise his name, books would detail his life, and poets would feverishly put ink to paper to honor his glory. All he had to do was lower his sword.

Osirah tried yet again to lift the sword, his fingers reaching for the hilt. Akari watched him come within a hair of it, his arm stretching, so close to wrapping his gnarled fingers around it as he pushed past the pain in his elbow. His fingers brushed the handle and he could imagine taking it and driving it through Akari's chest - and just like that Akari reached down, grabbed the sword, and flung it to the ground below. It flew from the tower and landed straight and true, sticking into the dirt with the hilt waving back and forth as it settled into the ground. The desperate look in Osirah's eyes gave Akari a certain amount of pleasure that turned his own stomach, revolting him while he reveled in it.

"No," Akari said, simply and sternly.

Osirah's eyes then turned to Akari's sword, which lie just behind Akari on the floor, separated from the hilt. Osirah's mind told him to try, but his body no longer had the will. No, he would never use that sword. It was only Akari's to use, and he knew it.

Akari looked at the blade. "No," he said again, simply and sternly.

"Then kill me, you gutless coward. Death doesn't scare me unless it comes without honor. And I've had an honor-less death once already."

He put his hand on Akari's boot, submitting to his will. "Kill me. Look into my eyes and kill me, not like that shameful swine that filled my back with arrows! Kill me like a man! Like a warrior!" His breathing was heavy and labored as it struggled to keep up with the intensity of the moment.

Akari looked down at Osirah, and lifted his sword from the ground. The steel felt cold in his hands, and he could feel its power. All he had to do was lower the blade and drive it home.

But again he said, "No."

He could hear the soldiers egging him on, Azorians and Mulvarians alike, all of them screaming "Kill him! Kill him!" He gripped the blade tighter, the anger still pulsing through his veins. His arms shook from the tension. Despite holding it as strongly as he could, it still felt weak in his arms as it wobbled back and forth.

And then it stopped. Suddenly the tension was released. He did not need to kill this man, for he had done what he set out to do. The Azorian Army would rebel against the rule of Maldazor - he knew it now - and the

Mulvarians would treaty with them. The Duel was won. Maldazor remained strong and a threat, but there was now a new force that would sweep the island. There would soon be no more kings, and of this Akari felt certain.

With that realization, the anger dissipated from Akari. He looked down upon the battered body of Osirah and felt only pity for what a human being with power left unchecked could become. A selfish shadow of a man, only concerned with his own power and lust, no compassion for anyone or anything. Here he was, a snarling, nasty mess, a beast, begging to be killed for a second time, reasoning that this time he could die right, with supposed honor, felled by another warrior. Even in death he wanted things done his way.

But Akari would not give Osirah what he desired. He could not.

Again, loudly, simply, sternly, the single word: "No!"

It was possible he would regret it later, but to kill a defenseless man was something Akari could not do. Thus he lowered the remains of his sword, held it by his side, and flung it from the tower, where it landed flat near Osirah's departed sword sticking from the ground.

The crowd gasped in unison, unsure of how to react. The Azorians and Mulvarians were equally confused, wondering why Akari refused to finish off his opponent. Only Chupwah seemed to understand as he nobly looked up in the sky at Akari, and in his demeanor the other three seemed to comprehend it as well.

Osirah saw what Akari did and smiled, a queer little grin that normally would have chilled Akari to the bone. But, he still felt only pity. Osirah pulled himself up on a wall, his teeth gritting from pain. He struggled to get back on his feet, just managing to do so. He rested with his back to the wall, watching Akari with his eyes nearly closed, glaring, huffing, and puffing with a puddle of bubbly drool resting on his chin.

He gave Akari a mocking salute, then gritted his teeth as he pulled himself to the top of the wall and plunged over the ledge.

He fell noisily, crashing against the sides of the keep before landing near the sword. Some said that even in death his fingers reached out desperately for his blade, where they would remain positioned until the end of time.

Akari cringed, unable to stop Osirah from his rash decision. There was nothing he could have done, and maybe he would not have chosen to stop him if he did have the chance. It would not linger in his thoughts, that much was certain. And now Akari had bigger things to do, so he moved to the front of the tower and faced the crowd gathered below.

As he looked down from his perch upon high, the red flag of Azoria flapping lightly in the breeze overhead, his face lit up in surprise. It was a sight that he did not expect. Down below, other than a few Maldazor loyalists who scattered when the fighting stopped, the Mulvarians and Azorians were all mixed together, huddled in a single mass of humanity. The members of each country were virtually indistinguishable from that height. They almost seemed to be one people and one country. He felt overwhelmed by the moment, realizing he needed to present a speech equal to the event. Where could one begin such a speech? But as the words failed him, he noticed something else was going on. There were sounds from the crowd, a rhythmic cheer that had taken root and spread far and wide.

Then it hit him. He did not have to speak to the people yet, because the people were speaking to him.

Akari listened. The cheer began with only a few scattered voices, but it gradually picked up amongst the entire group, and soon they were all on the same beat, their chant unified and loud. Over and over they chanted: "King, King, King." They repeated the refrain until the chanting overpowered Akari's ears. He looked below into the courtyard and searched for his family, finding that even his own relatives were chanting. "King, King, King." What little they knew, he thought, and with that the words he had been struggling to find came to him. Now, he could speak. But first he wanted Caroline, Jonas, Mouse, and Chupwah by his side.

He caught their eyes as he leaned over the tower wall and motioned for them to join him. They did so, climbing the now unguarded stairs that would take them to the top of the tower. He was pleased to see Claudius standing below, standing with the other escaped captives among the cheering throngs.

Akari held up his hand, waiting for both the chanting to cease and the others to arrive. When they finally made it up he hugged them all, so grateful that everything had miraculously worked out. He shook his head in relief while a great roar again arose from the crowd. When it gradually died out, Akari spoke.

"I hear you all," he shouted, again holding the device. He was interrupted once again by loud cheering, and another refrain of "King, King, King," to which he again held up his hand.

"I hear you," he repeated, but held up his hand to cut off any further cheering before it started. "So now hear me. I hear the chants, and I know your hearts are in the right place. But the time for Kings is at an end."

The crowd looked on, enraptured. There were pockets of confused grumbling. There also were many who disagreed vociferously. But Akari continued.

"I say again - the time for Kings is at an end! For a thousand years we have lived to support the Kings, and whatever scraps fell off the kitchen table would be left for us to pick over and fight for, so long as we didn't complain too much and then used those scraps to pay *tribute* to the King.

"For a thousand years this kingdom has stood, but never has it stood for the people or the beasts or anything else. It stood only for the Kings, and those that they chose.

"This kingdom was first formed on the backs of dragons, who were friends of the early Kings until those Kings wanted more and ever more, and still ever more until the dragons had enough.

"Then, it was set upon the backs of the other beasts of burden, the elephant and the donkey, the camel and the horse, until they too were nearly used up and left to roam the last few wild corners of the island.

"Finally, lastly, it was put on our backs. Our only true purpose in life was to tie our Fates to the King and serve his every whim." He paused, letting his words sink in. "But now, that time is at an end!"

To Akari's great surprise, the crowd was now with him, and they roared back with cheers. He soaked it all in, serving his own ego for a brief moment, basking in the glory before continuing.

"But one man's end is another man's beginning, and so shall it be for us. In fact, this is no ending. Far from it. There are no ends, only beginnings, and this will begin the era of the free man!"

Again the crowd roared, and Akari let it roar for some time before adding a little more. "I say, we shall have no more kings, but it's for far better minds than mine to determine what we will have instead."

He then stopped speaking as he gazed toward the horizon. His eyes grew large as he watched a dragon flying their way. In short order the crowd noticed it as well, gasping as the dragon sailed overhead. It circled the castle and made its way down to the fortress tower with, of all people, Eston on its back. It was a younger dragon, female, deep purple in color with fiery yellow eyes, quite unique, both beautiful and terrible like all dragons, and one that was unfamiliar to Akari.

Eston wore a grin on his face though he winced as he climbed down. But he looked much better than he had since they had found him in the jungle and it appeared the dragon ride had been rather enjoyable for him. He smiled as he was greeted merrily by his children.

"Well, I daresay I enjoyed that landing quite a bit more than my previous one. That was a dragon ride worth having!"

He turned to his brother-in-law. "Akari, it seems that the dragons have more than one source for tidings in this kingdom. Jomey was not alone! This fellow found me in the jungle and brought me glad tidings indeed, though I feel rather sick about Jomey. Aw, there he is."

Caroline was holding the creature in her arms, which Eston gently took from her grasp. He presented him in bat form to the purple dragon. She held him in her arms, roared in appreciation, and just as quickly as she appeared she was gone.

"We could've used her a few hours ago!" Jonas declared.

"True, son," Eston replied, a twinkle in his eyes. "Very true. Strange beings the dragons are. But I rather think they wanted to see how Akari would do on his own, with only Jomey and you all to assist. Put him to the test, as it were." He shook his head again. "Strange beings indeed. I wonder how much we will see of dragons now, seeing that this fine gentleman Akari has proven humans can be worthy indeed, in my humble estimation."

Akari listened to this, but said nothing. There was truth in Eston's words. He only hoped that if it was indeed a test, he had truly passed. The entire Alliance of Dragons would make a powerful ally in the war against Maldazor, but he wondered how they would feel after finding Jomey in such poor condition, and made so in large part by his failures. Only time would tell.

Akari was then struck by a sudden inspiration, and decided to speak again to the crowd gathered below.

"Mulvarians and Azorians, Azorians and Mulvarians. We are at a crossroads. In the near future there will be much to do, and much that will need to be done. Until we can find a way to make decisions as a unified people, I move that Eston Strongheart, former Chief Knight of Ambrosia, be made acting ruler and steward of this land. Many of you know him, and many more of you know *of* him. I can't think of a better or fairer man to lead us into this new beginning. If agreed, say aye!"

A thunderous aye was roared, to which Akari nodded, satisfied with the way things had unfolded. He did not know what the future would bring, but he had done his part to bring about a new, better country that would be prepared to deal with the scourge of Maldazor.

He motioned to his family and friends to follow him - Eston, Caroline, Jonas, Mouse, and Chupwah. Together, they stepped up to stand on the edge of the wall. In a moment that would stay etched in all of their minds forever, Akari raised Eston's hand to the cheers of his new and old countrymen, joined, for now, as one people. A new, better future was just out of reach. It was up to all of them to make it so.

# Epilogue – The Message

The steady clip-clop of a horse could be heard trotting down the pathway. The guards watched from the tower surrounding the Ambrosian castle, waiting for it to emerge from the shadows in the fading daylight. Soon, the horse, covered in trail dust, was revealed, carrying a smallish boy of about age twelve. He was holding an envelope aloft in his right hand and the reins in his left, signifying that he was unarmed, only a messenger. He brought the horse to a stop at the gate and waited patiently for permission to continue on his errand.

A guard opened a door, emerging from the lowest level of the tower. He carefully approached the young boy, gripping the hilt of his sword as he did. One could never be too cautious in these times.

"I've got a message for the King, sir," the boy said in a high-pitched voice, holding the envelope into the guard's site line. "For Maldazor."

The guard snatched the envelope and sneered. "I know the King's name, fool."

He glared at the boy and held the envelope out, reading it. The King's name was on it as indicated by the boy, and in the writing of Osirah - the guard recognized it as he was trained to do so. It also contained a marking used in such messages for authenticity. The writing included the rather curious notation that the message must be delivered by the boy squire himself, though this handwriting was a bit more suspect, perhaps added at a later date. Still, the guard saw no reason to doubt its veracity.

"So you're to deliver it personally, eh? Well, best of luck to you - hope you brought good tidings or Maldazor is likely to breathe fire!" He chuckled softly to himself, imagining what it would be like to see

Maldazor raging against a small boy. For a split second, he imagined himself in the midst of such a rage, which brought the laughter to an end.

The guard held the horse by the bridle and called up to have the castle gate raised. As it slowly rose, the guard was stunned to find Maldazor already waiting on the other side. He was accompanied by his royal counselors Cyril and Fritz, one on each side. He was clearly eager to receive word from his Chief Knight of Azoria, although he stood impassively and allowed the guard to bring the messenger to him.

"Who is this being led into my castle?" the King asked, referring to the young boy.

"Not sure, sir, but he has brought a message from Osirah - the writing on the envelope indicated the squire was to give it you directly. The code was there." He took the boy's forearm, which was attached to the hand that grasped the envelope, and pointed to the small symbol hastily scratched upon it.

"Very good," Maldazor replied. "You did well, Harvey. Now, back to your post." The guard shuffled off without waiting another second, stunned by the praise from the King for something so minor, and did not bother to wait for him to change his opinion. When he was gone, Maldazor turned to the boy.

"So, my young lad, it seems you were given a job of high import. How was it that you were chosen for such a duty?"

The boy cleared his throat and replied dryly. "My size, your majesty. Said I'd make good time on the horse."

"Very true - you are a small one. I've seen mice bigger." He grinned slightly as he reached out and took the envelope from the boy's shaky hand. "What do you have for me here? Good news, I presume?"

"It's an invitation, I believe, sir," the squire stated shakily, still residing on the back of his horse. He looked for all the world like he would put spurs to it at the slightest provocation.

"An invitation? An invitation for *what?*" The King's face betrayed a slight bit of agitation, his lip curling on the right side of his face, showing off a bit of his teeth. Otherwise, he revealed nothing.

"Well, sir, from what they told me, it's an invitation to vote, sir. I was told that in thirty days, they are holding the first election of Azoria. All who have claimed citizenry are welcome to join." He cleared his throat before hastily adding, "Your Majesty."

"To vote? Vote for *what?*"

The boy cleared his throat. "A new leader of Azoria, they said. The letter states: *'You are cordially invited to participate in the first election of Azoria to replace the deposed King Maldazor. You have been assigned to vote at the northern precinct headquarters, formerly known as Castle Maldazor.'* " He winked as he finished, then offered an answer to the King's unasked question. "Saw them write it, I did."

"Deposed? Me deposed? Lunacy." He ripped open the envelope and removed the paper inside, scanning the document. His eyes moved back and forth and his curled lip changed into a full-on snarl. When finished, the King turned to his advisors.

"It's worse than we feared possible. Seems they have the fool idea that they can simply take the whole kingdom from us through the casting of a few ballots! Preposterous!"

Fritz's eyes grew big and he looked on stupidly, saying nothing. But Cyril threw his arms up in disgust and yelled loudly. "The audacity! The gall!"

Maldazor took the letter and crumpled it up, throwing it to the ground. The boy pulled on the reins, forcing his horse to move backwards.

Maldazor saw this and moved to stop him. "Don't go anywhere, Boy. I'm not done with you. What happened up there? Who told you to send this?"

"My uncle did, sir."

Maldazor noticed that the boy was now speaking with a deeper voice. He was gaining confidence, and Maldazor didn't like it.

"Is that so? And just who is your uncle, *Boy?*" There was no attempt to hide his agitation now.

"His name is Akari. I believe you know him, but if it helps, some call him Akari Dragon Killer and others Dragon Lover, depending on whom you ask."

The King whistled through his teeth. "Is that so?" He pulled his sword from its sheath while the horse backed up a few more steps. "Well, you are going to come along with me. Then you can tell me everything! I think there's an awful lot you have to say that I'd like to hear. Now get off that horse!"

"Horse? Oh, I'm afraid that this isn't a horse, your *Majesty*." The boy shook his head. "No, it's not really a horse at all."

"Well, what is it then, you impish fool?"

"You really haven't figured it out yet? It's so simple. Why, Azoria is now *crawling* with the things. You'd probably think it was awful - there's Sasquatches, and In-Betweeners, and giant elephants - all sorts of things. Get this - there's even a Cyclops running around, a nice chap - and well, there's these too." He patted his ride on the neck. "Yeah, there are lots of these."

"Yes, yes, out with it! What is it, Boy?" Maldazor's voice was loud, powerfully loud, and he was beyond furious with anger.

"Well, like I said Azoria is crawling with the things - I've always called them dragons, though they prefer to be called another name by their friends." As he said this the horse began to shake underneath him. Soon, wings sprouted from behind the boy's legs, and large fangs appeared in its mouth as the transformation rapidly took place.

Maldazor was enraged and charged at them, but before he could do anything, the dragon's wings were completely revealed. They swung out and bulled Maldazor over. Fritz saw this and went running toward the castle, leaving Cyril to fall flat on his back while he kicked his legs, desperate to get back to his feet.

The dragon lifted from the ground, harmlessly shaking off the arrows that rained from the watchtowers. For good measure, he blew a puff of fire just over Maldazor's head.

The boy called down to Maldazor, who had ignored the flames to climb back to his feet and shout orders to various guards.

The young man's timid expression disappeared as he revealed his identity. "By the way, they call me Mouse, your Majesty, and this is Jomey. I have the strange feeling we will meet again sometime! I rather look forward to it!"

The dragon rose into the sky and soon its shadow shrouded the castle in darkness. Mouse pumped his fist and yelled with excitement at the successful completion of his mission. Standing in front of Maldazor while keeping his composure was quite an accomplishment, and he knew it. He had done well. A great warrior, indeed.

Maldazor ran out of the gate with his arms held high above his head, as if he could capture the dragon if only he could catch up to it. But he finally gave up and skidded to a halt to look around his kingdom. For once, there was nothing Maldazor could do except stand and watch.

Looking on, his eyes grew wide as from different areas around the landscape other dragons took flight, springing up from the countryside with riders on their backs—Caroline, Jonas, and Chupwah, along for the mission as backup in case something should befall Mouse.

The dragons flapped their wings and quickly rose above the treetops, joining together with Mouse and Jomey. They turned and flew away in a blur. Soon they disappeared over the horizon, the four of them riding jubilantly on the backs of dragons.

## Acknowledgements

You don't usually see lengthy acknowledgements in works of fiction for whatever reason, but that's not going to stop me. Too many people have helped me along the way! So, with that in mind, thanks to my wife Abby, I'm so lucky, I love you. To my daughter Madelyn, I love you so much. Thanks to my mom for everything. And thanks to my brother Jason, for reviewing what I wrote.

I want to thank those who specifically helped in the creation of this book: Shawn for his amazing art and encouragement along the way, and B.C. Manion and Erin McIntyre for their expert assistance in editing. I can't thank you enough!

Thank you to the Morong family, Karyn, the Behrens family, Dad, all of my uncles, aunts, cousins, in-laws, etc. etc.

Thanks to all of my family, friends, co-workers, teachers, neighbors, and classmates over the years. It would be impossible to thank everyone who has ever been kind to me, but it is appreciated all the same!